Kracker Flats

Kracker Flats is a work of fiction. Names, characters, places and incidents are either the product of the author's imagination or used fictitiously. Any resemblance to the persons, living or dead, events, or locales is entirely coincidental.

KrackerFlats@gmail.com

ISBN 978-0-9789187-1-2

1. Hurricane—Fiction. 2.Florida—Fiction

Cover Design and Art

Annelisa Ochoa

Dedication

To my beloved wife

Mary Ann Iezzoni

You bring authenticity to the selfless act of caring

One can make a day of any size.
~John Muir

Kracker Flats

Mario Iezzoni

A Novel

Chapter 1

Matador Room ♦ Hacienda Hotel
New Port Richey, Florida

The extended minute hand on the antique wall clock flicked to 3:45 am. The escapement gear cranked out the partial St. Michael's chime. Cledus Rosewood flitted his jittery bloodshot eyes toward the bothersome tavern clock. And for some reason, as the poker game drew toward closure, the lengthening, ever-complaining knell became annoyingly amplified.

When the Pasco County Commissioner glanced back to the card table, his opponent, Florence Carter, had fixed her beady brown eyes upon his ball-nosed pumpkin head.

"Well, Cledus," wiry Florence said, burning her stare a bit longer. "Looks like darn Hoinky won all our money tonight." She referred to a third player on her right sitting with neatly stacked piles of cash.

Cledus shoved back his chair. But he was too fat; the weight on the legs wouldn't allow the oak caquetoire to budge. He tried again. This time the shorter leg gave way and scratched along the warped plank-board that had stabilized the distracting rock, but it still sat at an uncomfortable tilt. Clasping the splayed seat, Cledus lurched and locked the short leg onto the warp again.

Florence dropped her eyes and needled her fingers, fixing an undone blouse button. "I guess it's that time," she said, purposely avoiding eye contact. "Anyone want to chicken out and call it a night?"

The Commissioner smiled. "Florence, I've waited the whole damn night for this hand to come into play. And can't wait to send your scheming, land-grabbing, scalawag Kracker ass back to the Virginia highlands where you belong."

Florence's wrinkled expression refused a response.

"Dale, wake up!" barked Cledus, projecting his voice across the weakly lit room toward the dark hotel lobby. "Get over here, muck rat!"

Sleeping on a wooden bench just outside the arched entryway was young Dale Carter, Florence's son. The dark-haired, deeply tanned Florida flats boy emerged from the blackness.

"Go wake Judge Grady," Cledus demanded, as if Dale was his servant.

Florence turned toward her drowsy son and nodded, sanctioning the unacceptable directive. "Go ahead, Dale." She winked her left eye so Cledus didn't see.

The fit boy vanished into the hollow blackness of the hotel and scurried up the grand staircase.

Rolling her narrow shoulders, Florence hunched her thin frame over the raised lip of the poker table and gathered the scattered playing cards. She'd lost all her money.

"It's always the same bet, hain't it, Hoink?" Florence said to the third player at the table, confirming what he'd wager as his final hand.

Hoinky nodded.

Bobby "Hoinky" Mack was the owner of a large track of isolated gulf coast property on the south side of the Fivay rail spur. Where, years ago, after drifting aimlessly in the Gulf of Mexico, Hoinky's houseboat had finally washed ashore. To survive, he bred a deformed pet sow named Elnora by tying her to a banyan root-drop in a nearby oak grove to lure local wild boars whenever she was in heat. Then roasted Elnora's mutant offspring over cedar woodchips and sold them as a tasty pork barbeque to migrating Florida-bound snowbirds.

To get them to stop at his shabby roadside food stand along a desolate stretch of Highway 19, Hoinky yodeled his trademark yelp, which sounded like a simultaneous car honk and pig oink. The curious noise slowed south bounders long enough for the smoky smell of sizzling sweet cedar pork to fill the cavity of their Michigan-made Oldsmobiles.

Sitting with stacks of fifties and hundreds neatly squared, frosty-haired Hoinky produced a ragged, folded document from the thigh pocket of his baggy fishing shorts and tossed it as his wager into the center of the octagon table. The black calligraphy read *Certificate of Marriage*. At the bottom were three signature lines with two names scrawled, his and Florence Carter's. The third line, the certification, awaited Judge Grady's official seal.

"Ya ain't winnin', Hoink," Florence said. "Ya ain't getting married this morning."

Cledus chuckled. "One day you're going to lose to ol' Hoinky. I hope it ain't tonight though. Cuz I want that piece of property you and your lad Dale are squatting."

A compulsive gambler, the commissioner never missed the concluding play of what Florence called The Barter Hand. But little did Cledus know, Florence had worked as a chambermaid at the

Hacienda for many years; and the Matador Room, where they regularly played poker, was her dominion. It was no accident Cledus was uncomfortable. There was a bothersome glare that deflected off an enormous glass-covered painting of a dominant bull munching the greenery of a palmetto pasture with its dangling testicles about to snag the briars. And as long as Cledus' chair sat just right, ironically positioned on the warped plank-board, the glare forced him to dodge the reflective distraction by hunching into the table to view his playing cards.

"What will it be this time?" said Florence, reaching beneath, verifying the presence of the wedged cards she'd pilfered from the poker deck.

Ducking the glare, Cledus saw her hand disappear and was about to call her out when it emerged with two cigars. His eyes grew large. Cubans were his weakness.

"Cigar?" Florence asked.

Snatching the skillfully hand-rolled tobacco, Cledus rotated it beneath his bulbous nose and inhaled the rich, aromatic freshness. His thick rubber lips, the distinctive trait that had elected him, lifted into a broad, pearly grin. Striking a match, he extended his fat arm and politely lit Florence's stogy. A sweet-smelling haze filled the simple, yet historic room, where it was rumored Gloria Swanson once practiced her acting.

Overhead, creaking bedsprings followed two hefty foot thumps. Yellowed particles flaked from the chipped ceiling paint and drifted as aged dandruff onto the velvet-covered table. Young Dale's lighter footsteps scuttled along the upstairs hallway. Judge Grady's heavy gait followed.

"As miserable as the judge gets for waking him," Cledus said, "he'd be more miserable if he missed watching this hand play out.

Besides, this is how we play the barter hand anymore. No waiting for the courthouse to open on Monday to finish the wager."

Sitting silent, arranging his winnings, Hoinky had nothing to risk but his cash this time.

"Hoink, what is it you want from me in case you win?" Commissioner Rosewood asked.

Opening his mouth as if he were about to yodel, Hoinky drew in a gasp of air. With two fingers he pressed against his vocal cords and expelled four rough, odd-sounding words from deep inside his throat. "*Building. . . Permit . . . Flea Market.*"

"That's fine and dandy with me," Cledus said. "If you win, Judge Grady will assign you the permit right here on the spot. But I'm warning ya, Hoink, don't put that pile of money you won into building your flea market. If I win Florence's swampy track with that nasty suffocating banyan growing in the center of the oak grove, I'll be asking the county to condemn your property next to it."

Blowing a thick cloud of smoke toward her opponent, Florence spoke. "Cledus, what the hell do you want with my piece of swampland and ol' Hoink's palmetto scrubs? They ain't worth nothing and flood all the time on the full moon tide. It's your elevated property upside ours that's the sweetest to own."

Florence stoked her cigar then finished what she needed to say. "Ain't no hurricane surge going to ever drown your property under, Cledus."

"Sheee—it, Florence, what da ya think, I'm stupid or sometin'?" he called her out. Cledus was well aware of sly Florence; she'd homesteaded her property by hoodwinking Judge Grady after befriending his gospel-worshiping wife.

"You know what I want—that property for Florence. It ain't no secret. Army Corps of Engineers agreed to finish dredging the channel that links with the rail spur. Pasco County wants snowbirds to settle here and pay taxes. With the rock from the limestone mine I own on the topside, your swampland, and Hoink's property, I'm going to build a development into the ocean and sell waterfront winter homes to Yankees who want to live on the Gulf of Mexico."

Cledus leaned back and folded his fat arms. "I know what you and your dead old man Buck did years back. You filled in patches of your swamp with limestone stolen from my mine and rented trailers you stashed in that mosquito-bitten marsh to those indigent transient Krackers that keep arriving from all over."

The cigar's nicotine had elevated the commissioner's heart rate and given him a burst of adrenaline. He couldn't resist running his mouth. "And listen here, Florence, Pasco County ain't ever issuing you a liquoring license for that barroom your lad and his dead poppa built to gin up my quarry workers."

As he flicked his cigar ash, Cledus' rosy lips dissolved into a confident, content smirk. "I'm going to call my development Tropical Harbors," he said with pride.

Judge Grady's heavy footsteps crunched down the complaining staircase. Dale had left the hotel as previously instructed by his mother to ready a quick getaway.

"Ya know, Cledus," Florence said, "don't bet all your dimes on that cockamamie idea you hatched. Someday, a badass hurricane will scrub your sorry-ass waterfront development from the face of the earth."

"Florence"—Cledus blew cigar smoke directly at her—"I'll take that chance. Everyone knows this part of Florida ain't never gotten struck that bad. You've been preaching about that big blow to keep anyone from buying coastal property, so you git it for free by homesteading like you always does. I ain't buying any of your hurricane bullcrap, you cantankerous dung beetle."

6

Cledus slammed his round fist onto the card table. "It's your deal, Florence."

Patiently, Florence Carter shuffled the deck. She wasn't ready yet. The annoying wall clock hadn't ticked off enough minutes.

Judge Grady arrived and hadn't bothered to wear pants, just a long-tail button-down white shirt which extended over his bulging stomach to cover his blue pinstripe boxers. As Grady moved past the poker table, his attention drew to the unusual painting behind Florence. He adjusted the waistband of his loose-fitting briefs before he sat.

"Making sure your oysters got some room to breathe, ain't ya, Judge."

Scratching his gray stubble, Grady didn't respond.

"Did you hear ol' legless Moog cut a deal with Cledus to open a strip joint over on Grand Boulevard?" Florence asked.

Halfway between drunk and a hangover, the judge grumbled, "I ain't heard nothing of Moog's plans to move one of his lap-dancing joints over the county line."

Florence's tactful query had suddenly put Cledus in a difficult spot. Grady's God-fearing wife opposed any construction of Pasco County strip clubs and would make the judge's life incredibly miserable should he allow it.

Beads of sweat started to drench Cledus' prickly jowls. He leaned forward, his large stomach shoving the table toward Florence. "No, Judge, that's a rumor Florence keeps spreading; like that doomsday hurricane bull crap she spouts off about all the time."

After snuffing her cigar, Florence slowly slid the shuffled card deck forward. "It's your cut, Hoink."

"Go ahead, place your wager, you flat-chested, dried-up skank," said an agitated Cledus.

Florence didn't react to the nasty insult. Instead, she produced a yellowed, trifold property deed.

Judge Grady spoke as if he were sitting in his courtroom. "This time I want you to sign it, Florence."

"Not until Cledus signs the deed to the limestone quarry," she snapped back.

Swiveling his bald head, the judge eyeballed the commissioner. It was Florence's comment about Moog's strip club that made him seek a signature from Cledus this time. Even though Cledus was his crony, Grady didn't trust him when it came to underhanded deals with Moog.

Scribbling his name, Cledus angrily tossed in the document as his wager.

Florence scrawled her signature and slid the deed far enough so it was within reach.

"Hoink?" said Cledus, bobbing his head trying to avoid the painting's reflective glare. "You got all the luck tonight. What ya going to do if you win? Take Florence back to your houseboat and boink her right away? I'm sure she ain't gotten laid since her old man died after fallin' into my quarry."

Again, Florence showed no reaction. He'd used this tactic before. If she showed no sign of hurt, it pissed him off even more.

"Your bet, Hoink," Cledus said, squinting.

Thumbing his money, Hoinky sliced the winnings into thirds then pushed one stack into the pot.

Florence spoke for Hoinky. "Is that enough for you, Cledus?"

Nodding, Cledus accepted the cash bet. He was more interested in winning Florence's property. She was a thorn and he wanted to send her packing for good.

"The game, as always, is five-card draw." Flicking her wrist, Florence skillfully spun cards toward each player. "And it's agreed Judge Grady will tender the winning document as legal."

She paused, laced her fingers, and looked directly at Grady. "Or one of us will tell his wife about the lap dances Moog's girls give him in the judge's chamber."

The judge scowled. Squealing was the guarantee that Grady would sign the wagered document the moment the hand was laid down. That's what made gambling with Florence so addictive. She had a way of managing everyone.

After studying her cards, Florence's facial expression suddenly showed emotion. For the first time that night she became flush. She set the cards against her chin and tried to settle her quivering hands. With a crack to her voice, red-faced Florence glanced over at the wall clock and asked, "Hoinky, who's watching Elnora? I heard she's in heat again."

Hoinky rasped his words. "Two cards."

There was a pause. Both Grady and Cledus drew sharp looks at Hoinky. It wasn't an acceptable response. The courthouse had received several complaints from angry constituent wild boar hunters, because they'd shot several retarded piglets on the north side of Cledus' limestone mine recently. And complained the mutants came from Elnora.

Hoinky took a deep breath then rounded his mouth. Out came that unfamiliar sound in the form of a sentence. "I tied Elnora in Florence's oak grove." He inhaled. "It's cool there. Don't like Elnora baking on the houseboat all day while I'm gambling."

Considering the ramifications of his reelection, Cledus rolled his plump lips inward to form a thin purple line. The boar hunters had banded with the orange grove owners and threatened to replace him next election if he'd not dealt with Hoinky's pig by then.

"Hoink, I'm telling ya!" yelled Cledus, frustrated.

Cledus' stomach shoved the table forward. Florence reacted by dropping her cards into her lap to block the table from crushing against her.

"The locals are gnawing my hind-side, Hoink. Elnora's contaminating the wild boar population with her mutant gene by dropping litters in the groves. Those retarded piglets are surviving on fallen fruit and living long enough to get knocked up again."

Cledus' eyes bulged. "And those half-pint wetbacks refuse to pick oranges, cuz they think those mutants are some Mayan voodoo monster. Spooks the hell out of them. And that osprey that built its nest in my disabled dragline shovel at the mine is snatching those damn piglets and dive-bombing them onto my workers when they walk to work in the morning."

Judge Grady felt he needed to end this before Cledus erupted and flipped over the table like he'd done in prior games.

"Hoink, I warned ya not to let that sow off your boat when she's fertile. I'm sending the sheriff over to shoot Elnora first thing Monday, when the courthouse opens."

Hoinky said nothing. Tactfully, he handed the politicians the rest of his cash, buying them off once more. His love, his sympathy, for Elnora bankrupted him, once again.

The timing of Florence's question had upset the game. The hefty good ol' boys were livid and sweating profusely. Little did they know the heat that absorbed during the day within the hollow ridges of the barrel tile roof had sunk into the room, replacing the escaping cooler air that exited through the darkened hotel lobby, because young Dale Carter had wedged an exit door wide open.

Holding two pairs, Cledus yanked one card from his hand and spun it on top of the signed documents.

"I'll take one," he said angrily.

Florence tossed him a card. She looked toward the wall clock. The longhand ticked to the hour.

Cledus got the card he wanted, a full house. His posture relaxed just as the annoying clock started to grind its gears, gonging a tune that ended with four prolonged bellows, disguising the sound of young Dale starting a motorboat docked behind the hotel on the Cottee River.

"What ya got?" Cledus growled, his ears ringing from the chimes, confident he'd finally own her land.

Stone-faced, Florence fanned her playing cards in front of her.

Mario Iezzoni

Chapter 2

Years Later

Florence Carter's Junkyard
Hudson, Florida

Dale Carter lifted the comb that rested beneath his reflection, buried the black prongs into his scalp, and dragged the plastic prickles through his chestnut hair mat. Strands gathered, greased and glued. He quick-flipped his wrist. The waxy follicles recoiled and heaved into a wave. A clean, respectable part aligned perfectly with the high cheek-knob that branded his seclusive demeanor.

Staring into the mirror, a face that hung his mood revealed nothing, no emotion, no ego, no sin, just a vacated lust—a stone coldness that glared a glacial expression so chilling it seared like dry ice.

The brilliant sunlight that set the bedroom's hardy contrast faded. Dale's pupils unclenched as the ornate maroon canvas of wallpaper darkened. A beveled mirror, crimped in hand-carved black walnut and bolted to the Pulaski dresser, showed a solid swath of overcast behind him. Turning, he stared across the bedroom out the drape-framed window. "Momma, why'd ya have to go and die? That there hurricane you been tellin' about is comin'."

He surveyed the flocked wall covering and the impeccable suite of quality hardwood furniture. "How did ya git all this shit in here, Momma? The doorway and window, they're too narraw. Ya hadda build this bedroom around the damn stuff, cuz it won't come close to fittin' through an opening.

"Momma," Dale said, talking to the dim emptiness, "it's stayin' here forever, ya know. I wonder if ya planned it that way, you wise old coot."

The warped screen door slapped shut. Dale moved at a measured pace beneath the roomy Key West overhang. "Hard to believe four days ago was your last, Momma."

Off the corner of the wraparound porch, a wind gust chattered a spiny sabal palm. A swirl of dusty sand engulfed Dale's white pickup truck. Twin Adirondack rocking chairs smacked the double-lap pine-shake siding as their oak rockers selectively crunched tumbling limestone nuggets. They'd talked most mornings, thought Dale, with Florence never allowing him to leave until the content of her conversation was conveyed. The thought those chats were finite was a heavy burden. He hadn't anticipated the instant emptiness and the loveless loneliness her sudden death brought.

From the prominent porch Dale inspected the stretch of coastal land trust he'd just inherited. They had that conversation too—what he must do with it. She'd left him a junkyard, stocked brim-full with a lifetime collection of odd, egg-shaped cars, broken-down RVs, used-up school buses, de-wheeled container trailers, and an assortment of surplus military hardware. All pointed southwest, the direction of the most consistent wind.

Stretching westward, the trust tapered nearly a mile along a steady, barely noticeable slope that ended at an extended, bushy hedge of black and red mangroves. On the other side sprawled lumpy tidal flats with its rocky outcrops and sea-soaked sprouts that prickled and sifted the changing tide. And standing as sentinel, overseeing it all atop a limestone quarry, was a rusted dragline shovel with its massive steel bucket disguised in an overgrowth of crab's eye and milkweed.

Florence Carter had won it all—the shovel, the quarry, its caustic blue lagoon, the highest piece of land in western Pasco County, in an underhanded poker game.

Dale leaned over the porch rail and looked inland; the sky remained clear and sunny. The squall line that brewed over the Gulf of Mexico hadn't arrived yet.

Passing the Adirondacks, he leaned against the south-facing banister and peered where the Fivay rail spur once ran. It dead-ended just short of the Gulf of Mexico. On the south side of the spur sprawled Hoinky's flea market. It was a large block of property, land Florence didn't own, unless she was willing to remarry. It too butted the Gulf, with a deed that sat in a questionable trust whose beneficiaries were the roaming offspring of a sow named Elnora.

Dale panned the flea market's rectangular, interconnected, H-shaped building with its silver, corrugated covering. "Why didn't you marry Hoinky, Momma, for just one day? Hoinky would've done it. I guess you were as stubborn as Hoinky, weren't ya?"

Unable to yet break from the morning ritual of conversing with his mother, Dale took his seat in the Adirondack, lifted his binoculars and pointed them at the old dragline. Woven firmly into the metal lattice of the towering boom was an osprey's nest. Dale squinted into the oculars. "Come on, you crazy gal, you may be senile but you ain't as old as Momma was."

And as if the majestic bird of prey heard, she hopped from her nest onto the spun cabling and readied for flight. The osprey cocked her head and looked down, as if she too, missed Florence. Stretching her six-foot wingspan, the osprey pressed forward. The firm onshore wind effortlessly lifted her vertically without a single flap into a climbing spiral, riding upwards and over the caustic blue water that flooded the quarry.

"Least you ain't left me yet, you crazy fowl." Dale leaned back and let the comfortable wicker catch his weight. "Momma, she's up on the hunt," he called out like she was sitting with her binoculars pointed in the same direction—pleased that her precious son was with her.

Tightening her black and white wingspan, the osprey banked eastward into the direct sunlight and disappeared. Blinded, Dale swung away and panned the junkyard. "Little lady, what ya looking for this time? You better not find one of those damn piglets again."

Her silhouette suddenly reappeared in the dry sand. It darted swiftly across the earth, becoming big and small, thin and wide, her shadow distorted with each junked vehicle it traversed. A fruit rat hunched on the chrome bumper of a '73 Volkswagen didn't dare twitch. A sunning pygmy rattler, slithering beneath a sun-bleached red Maverick, quickly disguised itself within a knot of roots that bound the axles and coil springs. And lurking within sparse grasses that grew beneath a row of aligned school buses, an overexposed gray rabbit became a frozen stone.

"She's heading for the mangroves, Momma."

Flying low, the osprey reattached her shadow, humped over the leafy mangrove barrier to the gulf side, and raced subsonic inches above the retreating tide. She whizzed past a nervous raft of laughing gulls, where all heads turned at once and squawked and complained until she banked toward shore again. The patrolling bird of prey broke from her swift, stealthy glide into a deliberate, lumbering, pelican flap, spooking a pointy fin red drum from its sea grass lair chasing it into the crystal clearness of the rocky shallows. But the too-large drum didn't interest her.

The osprey darted through an opening within the mangroves. The lumbering bird switched back into her speedy profile and jetted along the flooded swales that paralleled Dixie Highway. She lifted onto a rising thermal, spiraling, gaining altitude, soaring toward the dragline boom; flared, batted the onshore wind, then wrapped her talons onto the cabling.

"She ain't found anything she likes, Momma." Dale set the binoculars in his lap. "She's got more hunt left in her."

It was out of the corner of his eye, as he set down his coffee and lit a cigarette, that Dale saw her coming. "Holy shit!" He ducked. The osprey's wingtip brushed his head and flipped his greased hair-flap over his eyes.

Dale jumped to his feet and brushed back his hair.

"What the hell?"

Puzzled, he clenched his fist, lifted his tattoo laden forearm, and cursed. "Friggin' bird's gone rabid."

The osprey flew high and fast over the yard, heading straight for Hoinky's. "Momma, she's back on flight and sees something she likes."

Tracking, Dale watched her come off wind and descend. "She's heading for Hoink's grounded houseboat." Angling the binoculars, adjusting the focus, he searched the weedy area around the ruptured pontoon. "She's trying to spook up something."

Holding the field glasses close, fearful he'd miss the kill, Dale leaned over the banister and released the cigarette. It dropped into a palmetto bush. "Whatever she sees gotta be inside that busted pontoon."

From within the weeds poked a tiny head. It jutted forward and backwards, like a slinking snail pushing ahead—its body reluctant, uncooperative. The piglet bobbed and shoved until the tiny boar hobbled into clear view.

"It's one of Hoink's mutants!"

He cursed one of his longtime employees, nicknamed Critter. "That friggin' rat face swore all of Hoinky's mutants were disposed. That lying turd!"

Grinding his teeth and craving nicotine, Dale watched the osprey swoop with her claws at attack. She struck but failed to grab hold.

"You're getting old, you crazy buzzard. I ain't never seen ya miss like that before."

The tiny animal tumbled and scratched in a circle, trying to get to a safe place beneath the houseboat. But its deformed left legs had no hooves, just wiggling baby fingers. The appendages stuck straight out, perpendicular, spinning in swiveling circles.

"Dammit," Dale yelled. "That frig Critter is breeding them again, and running that damn freak show scam at the flea market without telling me!"

This time the osprey didn't miss. She came at the swine with such speed her sharp claws snatched the squiggling sow from the ground. Her momentum never slowed as the piglet squealed and contorted into frantic angles, lifting skyward.

"Momma, she got hold of one of Hoinky's pigs. I hope she drops the monster into the lagoon. Water's acidic enough to kill it right away."

Flapping hard, the osprey traversed the expanse of the junkyard until an ocean-born tailwind caught her from behind. She struggled to gain altitude, but failed and released the yammering swine.

"Holy crap!" Dale said, ducking behind the porch rail.

18

In it came like a lobbed torpedo. The screaming swine smacked the back of his mother's chair, flipping it onto its wicker back. The tumbling piglet slammed into the tin grate of an air-conditioner that stuck out the porch window. It let out a curdling squelch and lay with its tiny mutant body parts twitching.

"Momma," Dale said, looking westward at the approaching squall line. "Is that you who done that?"

Chapter 3

A half-mile away, carrying a silver Toyota Camry, a rollback tow truck veered off Dixie Highway and passed through a tubular swing-gate into Carter's junkyard. A chalky dust storm erupted and chased the flatbed up the grade toward the quarry. Dale Carter righted his mother's rocker and punted the dead piglet from the porch. It landed and tumbled beneath his pickup.

Eyeing the rollback Dale lit another cigarette and headed into the junkyard.

"Gotta oil that damn road," he muttered. "Critter is driving too damn fast. Son of a bitchin' lead foot scamming bastard don't wanna ever listen."

The rollback swung sharp left and bounced along a narrow, tightly packed row of scraped autos. Critter leaned his bearded head out the window, looking for a hand signal showing where to park.

Dale pointed. "Park it next to that ugly red Maverick with the windshield busted out."

Crunching the emergency break, Critter leapt out. Three inches shorter than Dale, he had been released from the Pasco county jail two weeks ago after getting caught for the fourth time planting a so-called pet alligator named Piggy on the Trinity Meadows golf course. The judge had warned him not to salt the golf course with his gator ever again, and he paid for it with thirty days in the slammer.

Walking along the flatbed, Dale inspected the vehicle.

"It's a repo," Critter said. "Lifted it last night from that there snooty Trinity neighborhood. Good pickin's over there these days, ya know."

"Chadda says finance companies are calling all the time to go over and repo vehicles. Those weenie husbands don't give much of a fight as long as we snatch it at night and the neighbors don't see so's they can claim it stolen."

Dale sucked hard on his cigarette. The Camry reminded him of the chested gal in tight-ass chinos shopping in one of his retail stalls at Hoinky's last week. She had a kid hoisted on each hip and a Coach purse hanging from her elbow. She'd bought a miniature bong from Chadda, a cousin who ran the head shop for him on Saturdays. The bong purchase was odd given how well-dressed she was.

Lately, he'd seen several *Trinityettes,* as Dale liked to call them, wandering Hoinky's dimly lit corridors. They displayed a distinct attitude of clever snobbery, with noses lifted so not to let Chadda's sweaty body odor rise into their trimmed nostrils. They flaunted a sparkly diamond that clued they married a man who obviously provided for them. Sometimes he caught them nervously rolling the diamond on their ring finger to hide it, fearing it'd get chopped off by one of the Flats folk. . . . For some reason, these shapely inlanders intrigued him. Their physical form was cut much tighter than Kracker gals'—their fresh perfume more noticeable, luring, lingering. Last week, a *Trinityette* pawned her husband's skinny-tire race bike at his pawnshop on Highway 19. Snot-ass woman must've maxed out her credit cards and needed cash, he thought. . . . Yes, he did notice. They were good-looking, desperate, wanting, in financial peril and dissatisfied. And secretively got stoned to escape the pitiable lives they pretended to live.

Nearly blind in his left eye, Critter turned and pointed inside the Camry. "Nice dual kiddy car seat in the back. The wench must've had twin rug rats. Betcha it'd fetch a good buck on Craigslist."

After pondering how much he'd ream out Critter, Dale finally unleashed his temper. "Critter, you ain't worth a rat's ass. You drive my truck too damn hard, you vagrant. Slow the hell down. That moccasin that spit and froze your left eye should've spit in both, so you don't drive no more. If it weren't for me you'd be begging sponge dock tourists in Tarpon Springs for smokes and beer money like a carnival monkey."

It was time to mention the piglets. "You scamming scumbag bastard, you're operating a freak show in the back of Hoinky's again, hain't you. Go throw that mutant underneath my pickup into the lagoon."

Critter was busted. He almost said he did it for the extra cash but knew better. Dale would give him more junkyard work, which wasn't as much fun as watching the facial expression of the kiddies he coaxed behind Hoinky's marooned houseboat for two bucks to peek at the wiggling creatures.

"You bred more, didn't ya?" Dale asked.

Critter didn't answer. He deserved the reaming. Dale had made it clear no more piglets were to be bred because they got loose all the time and sometimes copulated.

Avoiding eye contact, Critter kicked the sugary sand then lit a cigarette. The white paper burned brown, black, then light gray. The ember drew bright red. A flame leapt out. The ash dropped, sizzling a hole through his beard.

"Chadda sure could use that car seat. Monkey Wrench done knocked her up with twins this time," Critter said, changing the topic.

"I know that, dip shit," Dale said. "I got eyes."

Critter kicked at the sand again. "When Monk was home on leave from Iraq he was all the time stone drunk at Gator Tales. That's when Chadda got penetrated by Monk. Cuz she can't stand to be alone without a man, ya knows. She'd screw this here liftgate knob to get off . . . Shit, Dale, what's she going to do with all those kids? Already she got three boys and nobody knows who the daddies are. Might as well call them all Monk's, he's the only one beside you that got spare dollars."

"It's Momma's money, Critter," Dale corrected him. "She earned it and left it with the mine-hole. And watch your mouth about Chadda, it ain't no good sewering her reputation, especially for her boys."

"Don't unload the repo," Dale said. "Leave it on the wrecker. I need you to tear the seats out of those school buses I bought at the government auction last summer. Going to turn them into sleeping quarters."

"Any of them run?" Critter asked.

"Shit yes!" Dale said. "They got plenty big gas tanks for fuel storage for during the hurricane. They're dual tanks. Pasco School District had them made so's they don't waste time refueling."

"Man, you got a deal. There must be twenty of them. You want me to do them all?"

Critter's answer came back as a cold stare. Dale knew only a few would ever get prepped.

"Did you hear Monk's going to be on TV at noon?"

Dale didn't answer. He was studying the arriving squall line and measuring its distance from shore.

"Are you heading to Gator Tales to slump some beers and watch?"

"Later," Dale finally answered. "Gotta pull the air-conditioning units out of my windows and hang shutters. A hurricane is coming."

"Are you sure?"

Dale pointed to the low cloud layer over the Gulf of Mexico. "I'll need you to help me evacuate the Kracker folks in the trailer park and move them into these here junk cars and buses."

Critter tugged his beard. "Your momma was always dead-on about the weather," he said. "She's been predicting this hurricane for a good long time."

"It's all Momma talked about. Damn woman never relaxed about it. And now that she's somewhere else, I betcha she got something to do with bringing that hurricane this way," Dale said.

Chapter 4

The text message read, *at gate . . . there in a sec.* Marci Lindum set her cell phone on the glass-covered desktop, slipped her index finger into the fragile slat of the window blind, bent it, and peeked out. She waited. Seconds later, halogen headlights appeared, flashed briefly, panned the diagonally cut Floratam lawn, and beamed their way into the driveway. The motion detectors that lit the long side of Marci's stucco home activated.

"Crap!" Marci shook her head in disgust. "What a twerp," she whispered, carping about her husband. "Robbie must've reconnected the outside garage lights again. Better sneak out the pantry window so that nosy neighbor won't see."

Crossing the glossy hardwood floor of her great room, the tall woman snuck into the cramped kitchen pantry. She yanked open the cabinet door above the dryer and removed a two-liter green tea container. With her free hand Marci ran her fingertips along the nearby window sash and found a thin wire lead that attached to the security sensor. She tugged and disconnected it. Then she lifted the vinyl window, hoisted her big-boned frame, and crawled out onto the vibrating grate of the chattering air-conditioner. Her spongy flip-flops blew off and wedged in the surrounding viburnum hedge.

"Damn it! Where'd they go?"

Marci knelt doggie-style while hot exhaust blasted and flapped her cotton nightgown. She backed off, crunched barefooted along the pine bark mulch, and shimmied along the rough stucco past the viburnum hedge until she emerged in front of the garage door.

Waiting in a bright, purple-colored Cadillac and barely visible until the window rolled down was tiny Patti Washington. Sleeping in the back seat were her twin infants.

"Hi, Patti," whispered Marci, limping, rubbing her kneecaps, trying to flatten the linear red wrinkles that indented her skin.

Big-eyed Patti Washington looked up at her close friend. "Sorry to come in the middle of the night again, but it's Friday and I have to work all day. I'm all out of . . . well, you know, dried parsley. Clarence gets home from work before me and will jump my bones as soon as I walk in the door."

"Was Clarence home when you left?" Marci asked.

"No, he left for Ocala about an hour ago. Last week Feldon issued another one of their corporate energy conservation initiatives and demanded that all subcontract delivery trucks travel before dawn. They told him to pick up the pharmacy meds at their distribution hub when traffic on Interstate 75 was less to conserve fuel."

Marci handed Patti the container then examined the purple car and giggled. "What, a jalopy? Looks like someone painted it using a spray can. And why are you sitting so low?"

"I borrowed it from my Kracker neighbor, Cooterman Pat. The seat has a big hole in the cushion because his pit bull dug out the foam. The springs pinch my ass cheeks."

"Cooterman Pat?" Marci questioned.

"Yes, that's what he wants me to call him. The old goat is eighty-two and obsessed with those waitresses at that barroom on the Cottee River in Port Richey. Pat lets me use his car whenever he's not up there ogling the girls."

Marci rubbed her knees again.

"You know. . ." Patti's voice became serious. "Two days ago the leasing company repossessed our Camry. Clarence was big-time upset because the kids' car seats where in back. He had to replace them with used seats from that thrift store on Trouble Creek Road."

"Sorry to hear that, Patti."

Marci paused, looked at the sleeping children, and considered not charging Patti. Andrea, her college roommate, who taught her the trade, often said, *"Never give product away unless you get something of greater value in return. Every customer wants to be your friend."* Andrea had emphatically preached this to Marci. *"You'll go broke if you don't get comfortable charging close friends."*

But Marci caved; it was Patti who put her in this business anyway. She owed her, because her husband's income wasn't enough to allow them to continue to live in their beautiful Trinity Meadows community.

"Patti, don't give me money for the goodies."

"Thank you, Marci." A tear dragged down Patti's peachy cheek.

Marci squatted and peeped through the driver's side window.

"How's Clarence holding up?"

"He's having a tough time covering the delivery truck bills. Gas prices are killing us. And now with these predawn deliveries, Feldon refuses to pay any added fuel surcharges. I don't know how much longer he can continue to operate. Plus, Tahiti Villages won't allow us to park the delivery truck alongside our apartment anymore. Clarence is afraid it will get stolen with a full load of pharmacy medications if he parks somewhere else. You know how those Krackers are about scoring some free oxycodone."

Marci felt bad; Patti and Clarence didn't deserve such hard luck.

"Are the brownies helping any?"

"Shit, yes!" Patti said. "It's weaned me from that Zanaflex my gynecologist prescribed to prevent those spasms I often got. Your concoction loosens and zones me out. It's way better."

"Good, I'm glad to hear that." Marci reached for the car door and braced herself.

"Clarence wants sex at least three times a day. Before you turned me on to these brownies I had developed a tolerance to the Zanaflex. It didn't relax me much."

Patti winced and tried to adjust her position on the uncomfortable seat cushion. "It wasn't much fun having his big pool stick play billiards with my spleen each time we went at it. And on weekends—" Patti's brown eyes widened and became round. Her peachy cheeks lifted and grew flush. She clenched the steering wheel. "It's gotten worse. I got slammed by Clarence six times last Saturday. He's so anxious, you know, losing his job at Coastal Bank and everything. He needs that release. Your brownies help me give him the sex he always needs."

Imagining Clarence naked with his chocolate, stallion-like hunches humping away tormented Marci. She'd fantasized many times about Clarence when her shrimpy husband, Robbie, made love to her. Clarence, busily pounding away within her wrapped thighs; six, eight, ten slams a day would've been fine with her.

Suddenly both women turned their heads. There was a crisp, sharp clack followed by a prolonged bumblebee buzz. It came from the irrigation pump hidden within a shroud of coral-red firecracker plants. A gurgling, underground echo of PVC tubing filling with well water raced beneath the expanse of the deep green lawn. Zone-1 pressurized. The sprinkler heads popped, spitted, hissed, and jetted a watery arc, cutting a pie-shaped splatter across the driveway.

Patti spoke a bit louder. "Just to let you know, I saw a humongous snake cross the street before I pulled into your driveway."

"You did!"

"Yes, it was super fat, not like those wiry black snakes we saw when Clarence and I lived across the street from you. . . I flashed the high beams to scare it away."

"I'll keep an eye out." Marci stood, looked over the roof of the ancient Cadillac, and panned the yard.

"Last week's homeowner newsletter listed several reptile sightings in the neighborhood. The Yings found a nest of bark scorpions in their mulch pile and had to hire a company from Hudson to remove the nest."

Marci watched the sprinkler splatter behind Patti's car and rotate onto the lawn again. That sprinkler needs an adjustment, she thought.

"You know, Patti," Marci chuckled. "The Kracker worker who captured the scorpions mentioned it was odd to find that kind of species living in Florida. He speculated the scorpions were discarded pets and might've come from Hoinky's flea market, where those fly-by-nights sell all those reptiles."

"Maybe someone's planting them here," Patti said.

"That's what I say," Marci said. "I think someone's dumping them into Anclote River that runs along the back of our development. There's a storage lot on the other side full of abandoned boats and junk trailers. They say the owner's an unscrupulous character named Deuce. Just two days ago, the Association hired one of those Krackers to remove a fifteen-foot alligator from the retention pond behind our house."

"No kidding," Patti said, peeking behind the seat to make sure the kids were asleep.

"My son Bradley was with me," Marci said. "We watched the Kracker lure the gator from the pond and into a trailer. It was ugly looking. The tail was mangled and bent like it'd been run over. Its snout had this bulging, open sore the size of a grapefruit." Marci shivered. "And the Kracker who caught the gator had a fitting nickname. They called him Critter."

Patti laughed. "Those Krackers get creative when it comes to nicknames. I'm curious, though, how'd he coax the gator from the retention pond."

"He used the oddest contraption; some sort of wire-rope snare hooked to a truck battery," Marci said.

"A battery! How come?" Patti asked.

"To shock the alligator," Marci said. She paused and glanced over at the neighbor's house. She thought she heard something.

"That Critter guy slid a wire noose around the bent tail of the gator then attached the cord to his truck battery. When he revved the engine of his pickup all hell broke loose. The alligator ran from the pond, across our lawn, and into the Kracker's trailer, as if it knew right where to go.

"But that wasn't the end of it." Marci got excited. "On our lawn was something that popped out of the gator's mouth."

"What was it?"

"Oh, Patti, it was disgusting! It looked like a smooshed baby pig with missing legs." Marci quivered. "But before I got a good look that Kracker scooped it with a shovel and flipped it into his truck bed."

"You know, Patti, I swear I saw a pig like that when I was as a teenager visiting my aunt in Florida."

"Yuck, that's gross!" Patti said. "Why don't the men in the neighborhood get together and capture some of these wild creatures to save the Association money?"

"The Board said you need a permit, otherwise you'll piss off the PETA people—like that materialistic witch Jennifer Dink who lives next door to me."

"Why didn't she report the Kracker that caught the alligator? That wasn't a humane way to capture it."

"She's probably afraid they'd find out who filed the report and break into her house and steal something expensive." Marci adjusted the shoulder strap of her nightgown.

"That Critter guy charged fifty bucks a foot to remove that ugly alligator. Everyone's bitching because the Association had not budgeted for it."

"The men around here are such witless weenies," said Marci, while scratching her bare foot against the concrete to release a stuck pebble. "They'd rather play golf and ride skinny-tire bikes along the Suncoast Parkway."

"Well, I better get going before the twins wake," Patti said, slipping her hand out the window waving good-bye. The brilliant purple Cadillac backed down the triple-wide driveway and left the immaculate neighborhood. The red taillights passed the ornate black lampposts and melted into a layer of amber-infused fog.

Walking along the driveway, Marci paused and looked above the hip-shaped rooftops of the McMansions that lined the quiet street. The dead of night is so peaceful, she thought. The perfect landscaping, the massive mats of Floratam and tastefully planted palms that surrounded the custom-built homes offered comfort, suggesting Mother Nature was the decorator. The tranquility reminded Marci of her childhood home in West Virginia, when she'd sit at daybreak on her modest front porch peering into the fog that layered the rumbling river below. Of a time when life was simpler—not the hectic, vain lifestyle she pretended to live.

The sprinkler splashed her bare feet and interrupted the pleasant memory. It rotated away, drenched the grass, and pelted a newspaper wrapped in a plastic sleeve.

"Just my luck, I gotta run through the wet grass."

Stepping from the warm concrete, she trotted along the trough of the swale and snatched the newspaper.

"Shit!" She'd mistimed the sprinkler. It blocked her retreat and forced her to dash toward the pantry window. But as she took her next step, her foot landed on something round and rubbery. It squashed, became unstable, and rolled beneath. "Ouch!" Her ankle twisted and collapsed. The newspaper flung into the air and Marci's long legs flipped from under. In the brief moment before she landed she thought of her son, Bradley. *Little shit left his wiffle bat lying in the grass.*

Whooumph!

Landing hard in the slick grass, the wind knocked out of her.

"That hurt," she grumbled.

Suddenly, something meaty slithered over her right thigh and filled her lap.

Holy crap!

A monstrous water moccasin with its jaw unhitched, reeled and lunged. Protruding fangs sank into her nightgown and punched through the thin fabric. But there was nothing solid to bite. Venom squirted and spattered the exposed skin of her inseam. With its fangs snagged in the fabric, the thick snake panicked and wriggled wildly, spinning and whipping its reptilian head, trying to escape.

Marci couldn't scream. She didn't want to wake her husband or the nosy neighbor. The hissing jets from the rotating sprinkler arrived and pummeled her. Leaping to her feet, she ran through a barrier of misting sprays trying to shake off the serpent that dangled by its tangled fangs. The swirling brown tail of the cottonmouth wormed her ankle. The moccasin tried to strike several times, barely missing, again and again. In a violent panic Marci ripped open her pajama top and yanked until the garment tore to her navel. Topless, she shoved the gown downward, dropping the squirming bundle to the wet grass.

Naked, gasping, Marci heard a chuckle. It sounded like it came from Jennifer Dink's house.

The sprinkler made another rotation and chased her. Marci dashed behind the viburnums and crawled onto the air-conditioner. Bruised, brush-burned, she gathered herself and gingerly inched through the open window and into the pantry.

In the darkness of her upstairs study, sitting in front of a computer monitor, Jennifer Dink manipulated the mouse and directed the camera hidden inside the roof eave. She'd followed the purple Cadillac from the security gate and watched it pull into the Lindums' driveway. But there was no way to position the camera to see what was going on.

With the upstairs window cracked Jennifer tried to overhear the conversation that carried in the darkness. This was the third time this week someone visited after midnight—always women who never entered Marci's house. Jennifer suspected her neighbor was dealing drugs but couldn't gather any evidence from the hushed chitchat. All she overheard was that the late-night visitors had hectic lives with pissy, gropey husbands. And whatever she handed them eased their stress.

Listening, with nothing better to do, Jennifer Dink waited patiently. And when Marci ran into view, landed on her ass, got blasted by the sprinkler and danced like a crazy person tearing away her pajamas, darting naked across the lawn, Jennifer laughed hard.

Is Marci loony? she thought as rolling waves of laughter overcame her.

But her happiness quickly faded into a sad, sorrowful, jealous sob. Jennifer Dink, alone in her perfect home, surrounded by her treasures, had no one to share the comical moment with. On the desk, dribbled with teardrops, were divorce papers awaiting her signature.

Chapter 5

Lying in bed, her muscles aching from fright, Marci trembled. Etched to the backside of her eyelids was the nightmarish, recycling video of the moccasin's scratchy brown scales grating against the sensitivity of her inner thigh—its bulbous, reptilian head lunging, attacking. Clutching the pillow, she glared at the ceiling fan; the fan blades dangled still and hung silent. Something's wrong, she thought.

Slipping from bed, Marci tugged the nightie that gathered above her muffin-top hips. "The circuit breaker must've tripped. What the hell happened to cut off the electricity this time?"

Arff!!

"Charlie, you damn dog, I almost broke my friggin neck." She'd stepped on the family's chubby golden retriever and cursed loud enough to wake everyone in the household.

Charlie lumbered to the other side of the king-size bed, sighed, and curled into a ball.

"I can't believe that breaker tripped! It's the third time this week."

Her daughter, seventeen-year-old Kathleen Lindum, yelled from her bedroom. "Mom, why don't the lights go on? Why can't Daddy fix the electrical problem?"

"Just a moment, dear, I'll have it on in a second."

Footprints left in the thick nap of the bedroom's beige carpeting followed Marci into the great room. A Burmite glow leaking in from the streetlight lived as a horizontal light-ladder taped to the hardwood floor. Her gangly shadow carved through the light. Seconds later, the door to the garage squeaked. Marci scuffed along the grit of the concrete floor and stopped at the breaker panel.

Snap!

She reset the breaker.

Instantly, ceiling fan blades with outlining black paraffin dust coasted into a whirl. The answering machine, asleep in a den trimmed with white crown molding, bleeped. Hidden behind hollow bifold closet doors, an ancient inkjet printer clattered. The water softener, parked between garage stalls, hissed. And buried outside in a mulched ring of viburnum hedge, an irrigation pump sucked alive. But before each energy-eating apparatus came fully alive, there was a lull, a browning stall. For a split second the fan blades coasted. The refrigerator gargled. The arc of the spurting pee ejaculating from the sprinkler heads shrank to a dribble before bursting into a full, youthful, pissing stream. And the garage light, which had alerted when its sensor smooched Marci's figurine, dimmed then lusted at a full eighty-five watts.

It was 5:23 am, Friday.

Restless, still anxious from her terror just two hours ago, Marci stood pigeon-toed and looked toward the ceiling. "Hmm," she said. "What happened to throw the breaker? I'll crawl into the attic once Robbie leaves for work."

The rash on her inseam burned. She scratched it, soured, and glared at her wobbling thighs. Cellulite, a gift from her second childbirth, had never gone away. Her bratty daughter called them *thunder thighs*.

"Here, Charlie," Marci called. "Get outside and take your morning dump. And chase that snake away, you mindless mongrel." She cracked the front door, the security alerted. A fugitive breeze raced past her legs and toppled a top-heavy basket of silk plants positioned inside the doorway.

"Mom," Kathleen called from her bedroom. "There's going to be no hot water. Homecoming's tonight and there's a pep rally. I can't come home to wash my hair later."

"It'll be warm enough. Just be quick about it," Marci said.

"But Mom, I want it steaming hot. You know that!"

"Deal with it," Marci responded in a stronger, bolder tone to let her daughter know she wasn't going to tolerate another morning rant.

Digging the remote control from between the sofa cushions she pointed it at the television. . . . *Click* . . . The sixty-two-inch high-definition screen came alive.

. . . *Overnight, Hurricane Kate moved out into the Gulf of Mexico. But we don't expect it to make landfall on Florida's west coast. We expect it to move northward, across the Gulf,* reported the morning weatherwoman.

"That's just great!" Shaking her head, Marci plopped onto the sofa. "How high will the price of gas go this time?"

. . . *Stay tuned for* Good Morning America. *President Clinton is going to report on the progress of her universal healthcare initiative. Also, we will have a special report on the final withdrawal of our troops from Iraq.*

"Mom, tell Dad to get someone to fix the electricity. My cell phone didn't charge all the way." Kathleen swung open the bedroom door, whacking the wall, then stomped into the bathroom, slamming another door behind her.

The knot on Marci's brow thickened; her stomach ached because of the daylong struggle it would be to deal with her daughter's nasty demeanor. Sipping black coffee, she fought to relax. Last night Kathleen learned no one voted for her as homecoming queen, not even her gossipy friends, despite their lying affirmations. That evening when Marci scolded her about parking on the street and not in the driveway, Kathleen went ballistic. She yanked down the bedroom window treatments and threw them with her Beanie Baby collection into the pool.

. . . *Gasoline prices jumped another thirty-five cents overnight.*

"Christ! I remember when gas was cheap at five dollars a gallon." Marci cringed as the television blared.

. . . *President Clinton reminded us that we must all practice a kind of social tolerance. We must remain patient and support her initiative by enduring the temporary measures approved and imposed by our Congress.*

. . . *Yesterday, President Clinton said, "Congress' gas tax initiative was twofold and should stop our country's environmental decline and lessen our dependence on foreign oil. The 'Save Our Environment Tax Bill' will entice all to conserve energy and cut carbon emissions. It's a plan to make those who continue to drive SUVs and those who do not consciously conserve energy to start conserving today or foot the bill. Gas-guzzlers should get with the program and help us all save the earth. Also, with each gallon of gas sold, our government will earmark Initiative tax dollars to pay for Phase I of our country's new universal health care coverage plan."*

. . . *"President Clinton, when do you think your gas tax will go away?" asked the reporter.*

. . . *"First, let me correct you, Jim. It's not my tax. We're all in this together. I don't want to give any definitive answer just yet, but I do believe, once Middle East unrest stabilizes, fuel costs will normalize to where the tax will be more palatable."*

. . . *President Clinton went on to say that when we achieve a savings to cover every citizen's health care, the initiative will be reduced, but not until we see a drop in global warming temperatures.*

"Robbie and I voted for you, Hillary. I hope you're right." Marci's face contorted. "This is an expensive sacrifice. Perhaps we should lease a hybrid?"

Scrolling the program guide, she looked to see what Oprah was going to talk about today. She smirked. The TV guide read: Married women who fantasize about other men during sex.

"You know, Oprah," Marci said beneath her breath, "it's necessary, especially in my marriage."

Today's date suddenly flashed on the television screen. Marci butted her knees. "Oh crap, my birthday's this weekend! Robbie will feel obliged to give me birthday sex!"

"Yuck!" Her frustration fermented because her husband lacked that dominant, masculine aggression she often desired. He failed to satisfy her and she would leap at any chance to gratify the harlot that lived inside.

I gotta shift gears here, Marci thought. It's time to get everyone moving.

"Bradley, get ready for school," she called.

There was no answer from his bedroom.

Up most of the night, gaming on the Internet, twelve-year-old Bradley Lindum slept like a stone. A thin, platinum, politic kid,

Bradley was an adaptable adolescent. He wasn't unruly, showed strong signs of reason, and lived most days gaming on the Internet. For now, though, cyber-world was his reality—the physical earth was simply an institutional distraction to contend with, feed him, and on occasion, entertain him.

"Brad, get moving," Marci called.

Brad rarely responded to her verbal requests to prepare for school, which Marci considered ample warning to get physical. Setting her empty coffee mug into the sink she went into Brad's room, dug him out of bed, dragged him by his ankles into the hallway, and left him to lie in front of Kathleen's doorway.

"You'll move quick once you realize your sister is on the move."

She chuckled. "You little shit." He was toying with her. That's why she favored him and remained in her marriage. She didn't want to break his tender heart.

The bathroom door swung open. "Out of my way, nitwit." Kathleen jammed her sneaker into Bradley's ribs.

"Ouch! . . . Mom!"

Bradley crawled to his feet, rubbed his bony ribcage then dug the sleepers from his eyes. He shuffled to the sofa and cuddled into the arc of his mother's waist. Looking sweetly at her he smiled. "Mom, what's the Gore Prophecy? Mr. Pegerella, our science teacher, talked about it in class yesterday. It's kind of scary."

Lovingly, Marci combed her lengthy fingers through Brad's wispy hair. The texture was identical to hers. "The Gore Prophecy is a predication made by a politician who ran for president and lost. After that, Mr. Gore became an environmentalist and led a crusade to stop global warming."

"Mom, Mr. Pegerella said greenhouse gases are the reason the Gulf of Mexico temperature is so high this year. He told us it makes hurricanes much stronger."

"Yes, Brad, I heard that too. Everyone is concerned."

"Mom, why doesn't anyone do anything?"

"Some scientists argue the earth is in a warming cycle and claim there is no definite proof mankind caused global warming, or that we can do anything about it," Marci said. "But President Clinton is trying hard to do something. That's why our fuel costs are so high."

"What's an expatriate?"

"You're talking about Mr. Gore, aren't you? No one cared to listen to his warnings. He got frustrated and moved to New Zealand and now calls it his home. It's a trend with people disgusted with our country's inability to cut back energy consumption. They fear our government may soon collapse, and chose to emigrate. Mr. Gore was one of them."

Marci wrapped her arm around her son and comforted him. "Don't worry, we aren't going anywhere."

"New Zealand? Isn't that in the southern hemisphere?"

"Yes, Brad. You're so smart."

Again, he smiled sweetly. "Mr. Pegerella says the Coriolis Effect makes toilets flush in the opposite direction when you travel below the equator."

A confounded grimace arrived. "I suppose it could be true."

"I'd like to see that," Brad said. "That'd be cool."

"Let me watch the news." She had enough of his toying and shoved him away.

"Mom, if it's true, then there's got to be an exact spot where toilets flush straight down."

"Huh?" Marci got annoyed. "Why don't you ever ask your father these questions?"

Brad gave her a sly, boyish grin. "If a toilet below the equator flushes counterclockwise, and one above the equator flushes clockwise; think about it, Mom. If I set a toilet exactly over the equator, it will flush straight down. How cool would that be?"

"Get ready for school and brush your teeth." This time Marci pushed him off the couch.

. . . At noon we will have an interview with the last soldier to leave Iraq. Oddly enough, he goes by the name Monkey Wrench and lives in Hudson, Florida.

"Hudson! That's where the Krackers live," Brad said, returning to the sofa.

"Bradley!" Marci scolded. "Please don't call them Krackers. It's not good to say that."

"Sorry, it's just that all my friends mock the ones at our school. They say the Krackers are stupid, lazy, and live hand-to-mouth. What does hand-to-mouth mean?" Brad tried to crawl onto the couch and nuzzle. Marci rejected him.

"It means they live on very little. What they earn, they spend. If you think about it, they mustn't be stupid if they're able to survive as they do, on so little. It's called being resourceful, Brad."

"Huh?" Brad pondered her advice.

"Honey, think about it. The less-to-do that live in Hudson took Florida wasteland and turned it into a community. I don't think any of us in Trinity Meadows could do that and survive. And besides, they aren't real Florida Crackers. Real Crackers were cowboys who used a short whip to herd cattle, not the indigents your friends refer to. Now move your butt and get ready for school." Marci levered her knee and shoved him away.

The sound of the blaring hairdryer in Kathleen's bathroom muffled as the nozzle buried into the pile of her kinky black hair.

Marci upped the television volume.

. . . Monkey Wrench, what an odd name for the last soldier to leave Iraq.

When the hairdryer cut off, the furrows on Marci's brow bunched into tight wrinkles. Her shoulders tensed. The bathroom door burst open.

"Mom, I need twenty-five dollars to put gas in my car. Dad didn't fill it last weekend. It's nearly empty." Shrewdly, Kathleen split the difference between twenty and thirty, a tactic to coax an extra five dollars with no penalty.

"What happened to the fifty-five dollars I gave you two days ago?"

"I spent it on cheerleading sneakers. See!" Kathleen lifted her knee and kick out her foot. "Charlie chewed my other sneakers."

"You're not getting any money from me. Be responsible by keeping your shoes on a higher shelf."

Squaring her shoulders, Kathleen stiffened then knotted her nose. Several seconds elapsed, until finally, she twisted on the heels of her sneakers, leaving black smudges on the hardwood . . . then charged into the bedroom, slamming the door.

Chapter 6

Robbie Lindum closed one eye and tried to chase down the spinning vortex of the Hamilton Bay ceiling fan. He squinted then opened both eyes. As his eyeballs wobbled in oblong circles, a lipless grin arrived. He did it! Cherry wicker paddles spun clear and in focus. But suddenly, the smirk flattened. His thoughts shifted. The wickers blurred. It's Friday, my reimbursement check is late once again, thought Robbie, a bit perturbed. Those Feldon bastards are gaming me.

Too lazy to crawl from under the bedcovers, Robbie lay there and analyzed the spitted splats of Spanish Lace. The ceiling splatter pattern was perfect. He examined the multilayered crown molding that boxed out the master bedroom. The miters were precise, the design rich. Those were the only things the contractor got right with his new home, he thought. Why couldn't they get the electrical wiring right?

At the foot of the bed, balled on top of his slippers and twitching his nose, Charlie detected a familiar scent. Marci's silhouette arrived and crowded the doorframe. Robbie flitted her a glance. Her message was clear. *Get up!*

After stalling the appropriate amount of time Robbie slipped from bed. And with a short man's gait disappeared into the bathroom, turned on the shower then stepped in front of the mirror. There was no meat on his pale, wilted shoulders and ghostly ribcage which sat atop of his protruding stomach. His orthodox haircut, with its odd pewter color, hadn't changed since college. The only difference was his narrow face; it drooped, which allowed his chin to sag. And his bald spot had grown from saucer to a nearly plate-size.

He tested the shower water. *Too cold!*

Naked, he sat on the decorative travertine stool next to the stall and stewed over the delinquent reimbursement check, recalling the day he met with the campus employment recruiter from Feldon Pharmaceuticals. "What a great company," said the young interviewer who could easily be mistaken as Robbie's twin. "Feldon will hire you if you lift your GPA one more point to a 3.0."

So to boost his grade, he enrolled into a less strenuous physical education class, badminton. Where, on the first day of class, on the other side of the badminton net, he discovered Marci. She was stunning, and couldn't keep his eyes off the tall, legged, natural blond in tight black gym shorts.

Weedy, agile, and eager to show off, Robbie discovered he wasn't totally devoid of an athletic skill. He was good at diving for the shuttlecock and flicking it accurately over the net. And received enough of an ego boost each time Marci applauded, to ask her on a date.

Lacking a suitor, Marci accepted.

But Robbie had a problem; Marci's roommate, Andrea, was a bad influence. She was a partier, grew pot in the closet, and slept with any horny college boy that hung around for more than a day. He feared losing the only woman that took a liking, possibly sleeping with him. So he convinced Marci to spend time at his off-campus apartment, where they cuddled. And after several premature ejaculations, Robbie sealed the deal in April, one month before graduation. He recalled how hot, bothered, and wanting Marci got each time he rolled on top—like she'd done this before. And when Marci opened her gaping thighs and took him, it was like falling into a cavernous, fleece-lined marshmallow fold, with the greatest pleasure coming when she locked her commandeering Russian legs around him and refused to release him until she climaxed.

For Robbie Lindum it was *bliss*.

Fearful of losing the hedonism he'd discovered, Robbie quickly proposed marriage. Marci, absent a suitor, and under pressure from her mother and stepfather not to return from college without a definite direction to her life—translation, get married—accepted Robbie as her mate.

Sporting a tiny erection, Robbie tested the shower water then stepped into the stall and lathered. He let out a self-indulgent sigh. Marci's birthday was this weekend. She was obligated to let him give her birthday sex, because a Lindum birthday still held the marital requisite for a halfway decent night of intercourse.

It's been a long time, too long, he thought.

Tepid water spit onto his hairless chest. It turned cold and startled him. "What happened? Why isn't there enough hot water?"

Stepping from the shower, he resumed the brooding about his longtime employer. *Should I file a complaint? Perhaps not, I can't afford a layoff.* He'd mismanaged his self-directed 401k by following the stock advice of his small circle of Trinity Meadows friends. And his entire paycheck disappeared to household bills and vehicle lease payments. It wasn't a good time to piss off Feldon. Plus, his sales territory had been under considerable pressure lately. Gift-bearing competitors lured away his dwindling network of over-prescribing doctors by hiring sales reps using the "Six-B" strategy—

big-breasted, bleach-blond and beautiful in black. And Feldon wasn't about to change the way they did business to compete. The small midwestern drug distributor, owned by staunch certified public accountants, didn't subscribe to the industry's titillating tactics to peddle pain medications. There was too much turmoil with horny doctors who freely fondled the curvy Spanx-squeezed young women with their spray-tan cleavages and naughty hemlines.

Kathleen Lindum banged and rattled the bathroom door. "Dad," she called. "I need sixty-five dollars for new cheerleading sneakers, the homecoming game is tonight."

Robbie froze. Kathleen was taking this to a new level. She'd never disturbed him during shower time.

"Just a minute, I'll be out in a moment."

More door banging, this time harder.

"I don't have any money, Kathleen." He knew that answer wasn't good enough and imagined her standing there with demonic black eyes, quivering.

He waited for a tantrum to erupt.

"Did you ask your mother?"

"Yes, she said you had money."

Robbie wondered if Marci was watching this unfold from the sofa.

"Kathleen, I'm expecting my reimbursement check to arrive any day. I'll give you seventy-five if you'd wait."

"Eighty-five," called the voice from the other side.

"All right."

Robbie didn't like to give in. She outmaneuvered him many times. This was no different.

Robbie shook his head. "What next?" He cheated entirely too much on his expense report these days. If it wasn't for Feldon storing extra inventory at his house for stock shortages and reimbursing him for the space, he'd have no extra money. And the first thing he did with that cash was placate Kathleen by leasing a bright red Mustang instead of the Chevy Cobalt he'd rather get her. He figured the raised social status the Mustang provided would make her less miserable—and perhaps she'd warm up to him. But the warmth that did occur didn't last when Kathleen ran out of gas halfway through the Trinity Meadows main gate. Her stalled Mustang blocked an agitated landscaping crew that mocked her with a blistering blur of gender-specific Spanish curse words.

When she called to tell him what happened, Robbie imagined that Kathleen's cell phone was drenched in spit-bile after bitching him out for not including a full tank of gas with her gift.

"That check better arrive today," he said, drying himself.

Chapter 7

By 8:00 am, Bradley Lindum had drifted to the end of Leiram Avenue and waited for his school bus. Speeding by in her Mustang, Kathleen ignored Brad and turned left onto Perrine Ranch Road.

Robbie emerged dressed in a neatly pressed, apple-green dress shirt and glided past Marci without saying a word.

As she sipped black coffee, Marci's glare stalked him into the kitchen.

"Honey, did my reimbursement check arrive yesterday?"

"No, Rob, I told you that last night." Tapping her fingernails on the rim of the mug, she flipped a damp glance toward the television.

"When Feldon first hired me my check came every week, then once a month. Now it's six weeks late. It better arrive today, or I am filing a grievance again. It's Friday and I want to pick something up at the flea market after work."

"I heard you promise Kathleen money. You shouldn't give in, it's bad parenting."

"Honey," asked Robbie, ignoring the remark, "can you call me on the cell when the mail comes?"

"Will do, Rob." The honey comment irked Marci. She often protested that the expression was condescending. But Robbie didn't get it; he half-listened, half-noticed, and half-loved her. Robbie believed it was her responsibility, as long as he was the breadwinner, to fill their marriage cup the rest of the way.

Ah crap! I know why he's so cheery this morning, she thought. He's on the prowl for sex tonight!

There was this odd connection between buying a new gadget and Robbie's compulsion to want sex. Which meant another driveling, missionary position thumping so predictable, she'd medicate herself to conjure he was someone else—like Clarence Washington, Patti's husband.

Marci shook her head. Something must change, soon. "Rob, what are your thoughts on the hurricane?"

"I'll gas the cars early Saturday, before morning traffic picks up." Robbie answered her second question, the one alluded too but not asked.

"Looks like it's not coming our way," Robbie said from the kitchen. "I'm not concerned, honey."

He's being evasive. Time to unleash the honey-do list, thought Marci. "Gas grill's getting low. Can you take care of that, Rob?"

"Will do, honey," Robbie replied.

Marci thought about the clutter in the third garage stall. She'd nagged him for weeks to get rid of the junk he amassed from the hobbies he no longer had interest in. "The garage, Rob." Marci's tone was firmer. "You need to empty the third stall before you buy anything else at that degenerate flea market."

Again, Robbie pretended to ignore her.

In the kitchen he opened a small plastic file box with a cache of coupons cleanly clipped and arranged alphabetically. He selected a packet of 2-for-1 hot wings coupons from Scooter's Oceanside Wing

House. "Feldon will repay me thirty-four dollars for sponsoring today's in-service at the Bippinotti Clinic. With these beauties, it'll cost almost nothing."

"Rob, are you heading to Hudson today?" It was time for her to inquire about his agenda, so she could avoid crossing paths during her travels. Robbie was a cynic, and though he trusted her, his constitution told him to keep a wary eye. But Marci was keener. Occasionally, to quell suspicion, she'd stumble across him, presumably by accident, acting surprised—at least it looked that way to Robbie.

"Yes, I have three office visits. Doctor Patel in Port Richey, then Doctor Sing over on Fivays Road. And I'm giving a lunch in-service at the Bippinotti Clinic on pain medication management. The staff asked me to bring Scooter's hot wings."

He's using a visit to Scooter's as an excuse to get horned-up for a try at sex tonight, Marci thought. I bet they never asked.

"I guess you'll have lunch there, won't you?" She imagined him in the same booth with Patti Washington's elderly neighbor Cooterman Pat, both dribbling drool each time a young waitress pranced past in skintight shorts and bulging boobies.

"Marci, you know another shipment of sample pain medications arrives today, don't you?"

"Yes, Rob, got it on my calendar. Do you know there's not much room left in the garage? You better get rid of that golf cart you never use or we'll have to move the minivan out into the driveway. I'm afraid the deed restriction committee will cite us if we leave two vehicles outside."

"I know, I know," Robbie responded. "But those holy-roller homeschoolers across the street always leave that fifteen-passenger van outside." He pointed through the pantry window. "That's a commercial vehicle. It's not allowed to remain in the community overnight. The homeowner's association should cite them first. And did you see those animals in their garage? It's a zoo full of rabbits, hamsters, turtles, even a cage of dirty parrots. Something should be done about that too. It smells."

Tired of hearing Robbie's prudishness Marci didn't care to fuel his carping by feeding him a response. Too often, he grumbled about the homeschooling neighbor, believing it wasn't fitting to rear children that way. All four children displayed a latent maturity, a slowness, and clung endlessly to their mother's waist.

. . . *It's 4 pm in Baghdad and we are awaiting the last Humvee to load and fly out of Iraq. We have word there's been a delay. We'll have live coverage and an interview at noon Eastern standard time.*

. . . *In other news, it looks like Hurricane Kate is intensifying and will soon reach Category 4 status. Currently, it's fifty-four miles southwest of the Dry Tortugas and turning. We will not know how far from the Florida west coast it will pass until it completes its northwesterly turn. It looks like Kate is heading toward the oil fields off the Texas-Louisiana Coast. Expect another spike in gas prices, folks . . .*

. . . *The Gulf of Mexico has been baking all summer. Water temperatures are way above normal at ninety-five degrees. There's plenty of tropical water to fuel this hurricane, and no doubt fuel support for Hillary's greenhouse initiatives.*

. . . *President Hillary Clinton said that if necessary, she will suspend the gas tax should the oil patch experience another devastating hurricane.*

"That's a help," Marci said. "But it never lowers the price of gas."

Opening a cabinet drawer Robbie lifted his wallet, car keys, and cell phone. "See you later, honey buns."

"What time will you be home?" Marci asked, struggling to control her temperament. "Kathleen's got a homecoming game tonight and Brad has soccer practice."

"Four-thirty, sweetie. Call me if Feldon's check arrives."

Marci gnashed her back teeth. *Sweetie! Honey buns! Yuck!*

"Oh, I forgot." Robbie brought out his own honey-do list. "Did you hear that humming last night? I think we need to call a new electrician, something's still wrong in the attic. Ask him if he can adjust the water heater too, it's not making enough hot water. Also, dear, I wasn't happy with the lawn guy this time, he's gypping us on weed killer and fertilizer. The weeds are growing back and the grass is yellowing."

"I'll call the electrician today," Marci said. "And that's what you get when you hire a cheap lawn care service and jimmy him down on price."

"Oh!" Robbie's purplish lips drew into a thin smirk. A contorted Grinch-grin arrived. "Anything you want special for your birthday, sweetheart?"

Forcing a feigned, sweetened smile, Marci had prayed he'd forgotten her birthday.

"Rob, I'm fine. Save money, and don't get me anything."

"After the kids are asleep . . ." Robbie blew her a kiss and exited through the garage.

Shaking her head in disgust she punched the buttons on the television remote.

Chapter 8

Sitting with her gangly legs tucked beneath her buttocks, Marci flipped to the Weather Channel. Hurricane Kate had intensified and eclipsed the more prominent event, the end of the Iraq War. Although the tropical storm forecast center did not predict a Florida landfall, what she saw on the television screen made her nervous. *What if the forecasters are wrong?*

She muted the sound and headed for the garage to fix what went wrong in the attic before Robbie called the electrician. Though their home was two years old, it was under an extended warranty and Robbie sought every opportunity to call someone in to punch out free repairs. The last two times the breaker tripped she fabricated a story, saying the electrician came and changed a faulty breaker, because she did not want anyone besides herself in the attic.

Charlie followed Marci to the garage. "No, you mooch, I'm not feeding you." The garage door slammed behind her.

Working her way around Robbie's clutter, Marci recalled what a good decision it was to redesign the roof truss by adding open attic space directly over the great room. At first, Robbie balked and vetoed her idea, arguing the cost for truss alteration was not in the family budget. But Marci insisted, and won by refusing to screw him for several weeks.

Lucky for Marci, claustrophobic Robbie never cared to venture into the attic. He feared triggering a panic attack—something that hadn't occurred since he was fifteen. She suspected he faked such maladies to avoid extra housework, which seemed a trait of most of the men that lived in Trinity Meadows.

A yank on a nylon cord lowered the spring-loaded, ceiling-mounted ladder. Unfolding the steps, she made sure the ladder set firmly on the concrete then shimmied into the overhead crawlspace. Her beefy hips barely cleared the two-foot opening. Immediately, sweat poured from her pores. Her T-shirt clung to her tiny chest. A humming noise came from the other side of stacked boxes that deliberately blocked a concealed entry. "It's gotta be the exhaust fan."

Shoving boxes aside, she exposed a black canvas curtain. And when the curtain drew back, fluorescent light brightened the entire attic.

After allowing her eyes to adjust, Marci crawled along a pathway made of interlocking planks nailed to the bottom chord of the evenly spaced yellow pine trusses. On each side sat ten-gallon buckets potted with peat moss. Each contained a bushy cannabis plant. Chicken wire stapled across diagonal web members held the burgeoning plants upright. Overhead, a tangle of hunter-orange extension cords powered sunlamps clamped to the top chord of the trusses.

Marci worked her way to the gable, where a cardboard box blocked the exhaust fan vent. The fan motor hummed but didn't rotate. She removed the brown box and pressed a red reset button. "Ouch that's hot."

Licking her finger she watched the blades rotate. The hot attic air rushed past and exited through the spinning fan blades. "That's better."

Shoving the damaged cardboard box toward a cramped work area, Marci flipped open the flaps. Suspended from strips of notched quarter-round molding were leafy stems with seedy buds. "They're dry and thick with resin. Andrea would've been proud."

To her right, resting on wire shelves, were brown lunch bags with enough room between each to breathe properly. With care, she unfolded each bag and rotated the buds that lay in the bottom. . . . It took nearly an hour to harvest the burgeoning plants. She separated the buds from their stems, bundled the waste, and dragged everything to the attic ladder. She didn't mind the sweaty work; it was a way to lose weight.

As she lowered down the ladder, the cool air in the garage felt good. "Whew, glad that's over with." But when Marci pricked her T-shirt away from her sweaty body, she felt something crawl onto her neck. A cobweb, she thought, instinctively brushing it away. But it skittered and stopped below her right ear.

"Yikes, a spider!" She batted the hairy tarantula. It flew across the garage where the family ski boat was stowed.

"Oh my God," said Marci as her heart beat at a panicked rate. She ran into the kitchen and sat on the barstool. "What's going on?"

She set her face into her hands and tried to calm herself. "Where the hell did that snake and spider come from?"

For Marci it was futile to think she could ever change or motivate Robbie. He had this deep-rooted, conservative, Midwest persona, which came with a healthy dose of gullibility. He was a sucker, easily conned into worthless transactions. Like the fifty-dollar check he cut last Friday, the day he worked the Hudson sales territory, to the Save-A-Swine Foundation supposedly aligned with PETA. And he had nearly zero financial motivation beyond his thirty-five-hour workweek. The only incentive he had to earn extra cash came from a concocted coupon scheme that jacked his travel expenses and screwed Feldon for delaying his reimbursement checks.

As Marci struggled with her marriage, Andrea's collegiate, mind-numbing remedies made their way into her world; first, through steeped tea bags, then within a mix of chocolate cookie batter. She experimented, making a corn syrup resin mixture and letting it cool into hard candy, which she routinely sucked on. And when she was stoned, Marci found Robbie's stiffness laughable—almost palatable. On occasion, she mixed the marijuana into brownies with double-dark chocolate and espresso grounds to add kick, and let Robbie unknowingly ingest one. He was almost fun to be with, nearly normal. However, lacing the brownies ended when Kathleen scoffed half a pan and went into a terrible rage, tossing a hot iron through her bedroom window because Marci took away her cell phone as punishment.

Four months ago, to make money, Marci expanded her agrarian attic enterprise to include a select group of Trinity Meadows wives. Gas prices had skyrocketed, insurance premiums soared, her property taxes reached all-time highs, and Feldon had stopped all cost-of-living pay increases. Her Trinity Meadows lifestyle was no longer sustainable on one paycheck anymore. Needing cash, she realized there might be a pent-up demand for her herbal creations after reading a critically written editorial in the *Sun Coast Chronicle* accurately depicting the women in her neighborhood.

> *They're called Trinityettes. They birth one, two, and*
> *sometimes a mother in-law's guilt, third child. Always*
> *on the e-go, with twittering touch screen iPhones,*
> *these driven Gen-X's zigzag Pasco County strip malls*

in roomy SUVs. With burgeoning credit card debt and inside-out mortgages they slurp nonfat soy Frappaccinos heaped with luscious white whipped cream—always conspicuously careful their wedding bands, matched with sparkly multi-diamond engagement rings, are prominently displayed.

These narcissists, who'd lured a once handsome, educated Republican husband, boast in unsubtle fashion that only one W-2 is e-filed with their itemized tax return. They proclaim a stay-at-home-mom rank, which means real Trinity Meadows status.

Nourished by a steady diet of fast and faster fattening food, they order quick deliveries of preplanned, prepared meals. They idolize Oprah, Ellen and Doctor Oz, and mimic and bicker like The View, *while pathetically trying to decorate the Martha Stewart way. They never shop at Walmart or Ikea. And to be spied inside a Target is a misdemeanor. They breed soccer field runabouts and chase with frantic trips; to baseball, ballet, tap dance, music lessons, and tae kwon do, while making sure their housekeeper arrives in their driveway when the neighbors will surely notice.*

But behind closed doors, marital problems and personality fissures broaden while salivating, separating divorce lawyers lie in wait. Surrounded by cuckoldry temptations and the needy gnaw of apathetic sugar-laden, video-captured brats, Trinityettes crave therapists and graciously accept abundant supplies of more Paxil, Prozac, Wellbutrin, Zoloft and Ritalin. Prescriptively unbalanced, emotionally destabilized and avoiding the Big 4-0, Gucci handbags stow ample amber bottles of sedatives to scrub off the anxious edge, to Novocain and scuttle all frustration, and soften the all too surreal Meadows lifestyle—covetous, empty, and deceptively inferior.

Chapter 9

. . . And now we return to the hurricane forecasting center and Doctor Paola Estrada with an update.

. . . Good afternoon, I am Doctor Estrada from the National Hurricane Center.

. . . It's been a long, hot summer, and there's plenty of energy locked in the Gulf of Mexico water. An hour ago, at two o'clock we upgraded Kate to a Category 5 with sustained winds over 180 miles an hour. It's a serious hurricane, folks; everyone must pay attention to this monster storm.

Napping and half-listening Marci felt her heart rate spike.

. . . All shipping and oil activity off the Texas and Louisiana coast is halted. As we speak, oil rigs are being shut down and evacuated. Expect gas prices to soar.

Marci sat straight, brushed back her hair, cleared her throat, and took a deep breath. "Damn it, I told Robbie not to wait for the weekend to gas the minivan. I can't leave now because Clarence is delivering Feldon's shipment!"

. . . Kate is a monster and could possibly top the hundred year tropical cyclone list . . . Please stay tuned.

Reaching for her iPhone on the coffee table, Marci texted Patti Washington. *When is Clarence arriving?*

Moments later Patti responded. *Any minute, and has something important to tell you.*

Clarence Washington, a Tampa native and former mortgage broker, had fallen on hard times. After graduating as a Florida Gators linebacker, Clarence tried out for the Tampa Bay Buccaneers but failed to make the squad. The following year he played minor league professional baseball for the Yankees, where he met his wife Patti at Legends Field. But his visual reflex was too poor and he couldn't follow the baseball across home plate. So Clarence abandoned his sports career and took a job at Coastal Bank as a loan officer, leveraging his short-lived sports notoriety to draw new customers.

Personable, with a genuine manner and good diction, Clarence was well liked. Involved in community athletics, he coached Pee-Wee football, soccer, and Little League. He was a muscular, charcoal African-American who deeply loved his wife, Patti. Their communication was fluent, respectful, and effortless.

As a banker, kindhearted Clarence often went on a limb for customers, writing mortgages destined to go bust. And at the height of the building boom, he flipped real estate like everyone else. On the day Hillary Clinton took her oath of office Coastal fired him and foreclosed his portfolio of bad mortgages. The last home auctioned was Clarence's, on Leiram Avenue, across the street from the Lindums'.

Nearly on welfare, Clarence moved his family into a two-bedroom apartment west of Trinity Meadows. The rundown rental complex built in the 1970s sat on low coastal ground. The change in school districts meant their children would go to a 'D' rated school as opposed to the Class 'A' schools further inland. To survive, Patti got a job at the Trinity Meadows day care center.

Trinity friends quickly abandoned the Washingtons, not wanting to be seen with them now that their status had lowered—fearing their misfortune was contagious. However, good friend Marci didn't. She visited Patti regularly, slipping her cash and helping with her twin boys.

One day, the Feldon driver who stocked the pharmacies in Robbie's sales territory quit. Marci asked Robbie to put Clarence in contact with Feldon and recommend him for the delivery job. Immediately, Feldon hired trustworthy Clarence, but said he must work as a subcontract driver. Desperate, he agreed on a fixed rate to deliver pharmaceuticals throughout Robbie's district. But gas prices soared after the implementation of Hillary's healthcare and gas tax initiatives, forcing Clarence to renegotiate the contract. But Feldon refused.

Barely able to put food on the table, Clarence clung to his dignity and continued to work for the few dollars that remained.

Sitting in the den, Marci scrolled through her text messages. A text sent by Patti over the weekend read, *Seven times today. God help me.* She pondered if she could last seven rounds in the sack with Clarence. And considered what she'd do if he made an illicit advance toward her. Would she cross that line?

Hunkered in the den's cushioned window nook, Marci opened the blinds. Across the street an oak tree wrestled with the buffeting wind. A black crow attempted to land within the crooked branches, but abruptly veered and wisped into a stand of cypress behind the Peltzes' home.

Marci thought back to the night she learned of Patti Washington's problem, during a neighborhood bunco party, which was more of an excuse to chitchat and gossip. After several Jell-O shots, the conversation digressed into the topic they all loved, sex. And Patti, being the only woman married to a black man, fielded many questions once the alcohol removed their inhibitions. "What's it like to sleep with a black man?" the girls queried. "Is it true their skin is smooth and cool to the touch?"

Wishing she lived in Trinity Meadows once again, Patti exploited the one thing she had over them—a superior-looking, loving, devoted, masculine husband. And she taunted them with it, answering, "Yes, nice and cool . . . smooth too."

"Are black men hung like a horse? Does it fit? Does he like top or bottom?" the frenzied women would ask.

"Yes," Patti said. "Too hung and it won't fit all the way."

Jaws dropped.

To the bunco gals Clarence was a fit specimen. Unknowingly, he flaunted his superior physique. Rarely did he dress in anything more than close-fitting knit shirts and skintight gym shorts. His well-defined muscles were enormous and proportioned. Any women that stood close ached for the challenge to please this massive man. They all drooled. And Patti, jealous of the smug lifestyles her friends enjoyed, didn't help matters with her exaggerated details of titillating bedroom revelations. And on occasion, Marci was no different. She too lived for the enticing, X-rated conversation. Doing Clarence seven times would be Utopian.

One night, when the cranberry cosmopolitans flowed too liberally, the topic turned to penis size. Patti confessed screwing wasn't enjoyable because of his size. "Even worse," she said, "without his banking job, he's home more often and wants it several times a day. He's a terrific husband," Patti went on. "But getting humped by him is like having an oversize, lumpy, granite dildo shoved inside and pinning you to the mattress. It hurts most times because I can't relax." Patti paused as tears flowed. "I must confess. I've never experienced the orgasms you girls boast about."

"Never?" queried aghast friends with expressions that implied orgasms were common within their marriages—falsely pretending their husbands were considerate enough to allow them the pleasure of finishing first.

When Patti left the room, the bunco group wagered they could gratify Clarence if given the chance. And yakked endlessly about the mind-blowing, long-lasting, multiples they'd easily achieve.

A true friend, Marci pulled Patti aside and asked if her gynecologist could help.

"Yes, I did ask," Patti answered. "Doctor Narrish, my GYN, practices holistic medicine. He said India woman, particularly reticent virgin brides forced into arranged marriages, were often uptight. The brides are taught from childhood they mustn't fail in bed on the first night of their marriage because Indian men are proud and will become temperamental if not proven virile. Doctor said Indian brides regularly ingest hashish to relax before sex. It's an ancient, unspoken practice."

To Marci, it seemed Patti seriously considered Doctor Narrish's suggestion.

"Have you ever gotten high?" Patti asked.

"Yes, I have," Marci confessed.

That's when Marci told Patti about her college roommate Andrea, a promiscuous, free-spirited Kentuckian who financed her entire education and extensive partying with two pot plants grown in a dorm room trashcan hidden in their closet. Andrea had taught Marci the subtleties of marketing her pot. "Selling requires careful use of language," Andrea would say. "Never mention your product when negotiating a transaction. Don't convict yourself. Use phrases like, 'Wal-Mart has fresh parsley on sale today. It's exceptional and reasonably priced. Do you want me to select a dime bag for you?'"

"And I should tell you something, Patti."

"What is it?" she asked.

"You know Robbie is . . . uh . . . you know, kind of a dutz. There's not much of a marriage between us anymore, though he thinks, or at least pretends, there is. Oh, Patti, I'm so ashamed to tell you this because you have such a terrific husband."

Patti didn't respond. She allowed Marci her moment.

"To cope with Robbie and my bratty teenage daughter, I get . . . well . . . you know, stoned on pot." A bit embarrassed, Marci produced a guilt-ridden smile.

"Where do you get the stuff?" Patti quickly asked.

"I grow it in my attic."

"Does it help you cope?"

"Yes, very much so," Marci said.

"Do you take it for sex?"

"All the time, especially for sex," Marci answered. "Robbie typically broadcasts his need for a release first thing in the morning. He likes to think about it all day, and goes to that Scooter's Wing House for lunch to eyeball those attractive waitresses. It's some sort of ritual that gets him even more horned."

"Guys are predictable, aren't they?" Patti said.

"Yes!" Marci answered. "Especially Robbie, who sometimes comes home early afternoons before the kids arrive from school to get into my shorts. I cut him off by giving him a list of things to get done since he's home early. And said sex must wait 'til the kids are asleep."

"Did it work?" Patti asked.

"It did, he stopped coming home early. However, he started hanging at that flea market—Hoinky's on Highway 19. He's gullible, you know. The Krackers are always selling him useless shit we don't need."

"How can you enjoy sex with a husband who isn't particularly attentive and who you perhaps don't love anymore?" Patti asked.

"That's easy! By pretending he's someone else."

"Really!" Patti said.

"Hell, yes!" Marci said. "Usually some soap opera hunk. I get so high the experience becomes real."

Patti was amazed.

"Do you want to try some pot?" Marci asked.

"I got to do something," Patti replied. "I'd rather get high to relax than take expensive medications I can't afford."

That evening Marci gave Patti a batch of laced chocolate espresso brownies, her specialty. Two days later Patti called saying the brownies worked. She was more relaxed, and for a few hours didn't worry about their hardship. And when it came time to please Clarence, his oversize manhood slid deep and she took him entirely.

Charlie lifted his head and sniffed. His ears spun, searching. They narrowed, pressed forward, and detected a familiar vibration. There was an air blast from the hydraulic brakes of a tractor trailer lurching to a stop. Then intermittent chirps as Clarence's rig backed into the Lindums' triple-wide driveway.

Dashing into the bedroom, Marci rummaged through her dresser. Perhaps something silky and tight, suggestive, she thought.

Tugging up a snug pair of jogging shorts, Marci skipped on one leg from the bedroom and dashed toward the kitchen, nearly tripping over Charlie. She hit the garage door opener.

Dressed in an embroidered, short-sleeve shirt with the Feldon logo over his right pectoral muscle, Clarence Washington climbed from his rig.

Walking from the garage, Marci eyeballed his tight-fitting denim jeans. *They're about to split open.*

"Hi, Clarence," said Marci in a solicitous, welcoming octave. "How's Patti?"

"She's doing remarkably well considering the tough time we are having." But his expression quickly flattened. "Marci, I have bad news. I have to stop my deliveries."

"Ah, Clarence! . . . Why?" Laying out sad eyes, she pouted.

"Feldon hasn't paid me. They're two months late . . . It's gas prices. I can't afford to operate this truck anymore."

"I am so sorry, Clarence, and I feel for you. Things will improve after hurricane season." Marci offered encouragement. Fondly, she set her hand on his shoulder and held it there longer than she should have. *Boy, he's a solid man.*

Clarence spoke, "With two children to feed I can't drive another mile. I must drop the Fledon contract, today. But I've got a problem. I picked up a full load of pain medication last night at the distribution hub in Ocala only because Feldon said the check was in the mail. So I waited until the mail arrived before I came over. There was no Feldon check. It's time to end this job."

Marci stepped back. She watched his big brown eyes scan her entire frame then quickly flip away.

"Marci, I have nobody to oversee this truckload of meds. I've got nearly all of Pasco County's antidepressants and painkillers in here. I don't want to be responsible for it. Can I offload the entire truck into your garage in case it's repossessed?"

Marci wasn't about to say no.

"Sure, Clarence. I'll do anything for you." She hugged Clarence and squashed into his chest. It took everything not to thrust her hips against him.

Clarence took several steps back. "What do you think about the hurricane, Marci?"

"I'm nervous, to tell you the truth. Robbie isn't prepared. He thinks it's not coming."

"Didn't you guys buy a generator during the sales tax holiday?"

"No," Marci said. "Robbie claims the prices are jacked up."

"I regret not getting one."

Clarence lifted the lever that unlocked the trailer and crawled into the trailer. He removed the bungee cords that secured the hand truck and brought forward a stack of symmetrical boxes. He handed them down.

Beaming, Marci leaned forward to allow the neckline of her blouse to fall open. She wondered if he thought about her, perhaps spying her chest hoping to see more. She couldn't get it out of her head that this guy sometimes boinked Patti six times a day. If Clarence would cross that line she'd strip his tight-fitting clothes, escort him into the shower, and coax him to grow to that unbelievable size she imagined.

It took an hour to unload the trailer. Marci had worked herself into a nearly uncontrollable frenzy, dropping boxes several times, nearly fainting each time Clarence bent over to lift another box from the hand truck. His jeans were incredibly tight.

Finally, he jumped from the emptied truck, politely apologized like he always did, and mentioned the landlord asked if he could install hurricane shutters on his apartment building in exchange for next month's rent.

"Nice thing about renting," said Clarence, wiping his forehead. "If the hurricane takes our apartment away, it's not my problem."

As she escorted her large friend down the driveway Marci's ankle rolled off the edge of the concrete. She stumbled. Clarence quickly caught her. Her heart raced. And suddenly, she found herself unable to restrain herself. She lifted to her toes, wrapped her arms around his broad shoulders and pressed her hips against his groin. A shiver ran along her spine. With his massive hands Clarence clutched the narrowness of her waist and held her close. Panting, she humped him for several seconds until abruptly, Clarence shoved her away.

He jumped into his rig and failed to gesture good-bye.

Marci couldn't believe what she'd done. Clarence's solid grip drew and held her close. Lust and desire had taken over. She prayed he wouldn't tell her close friend Patti about the encounter.

Jennifer Dink, sitting at her computer monitor, panned the neighbor with the camera hidden in the upstairs eave. She'd seen the Feldon delivery truck before; however, it came on the wrong day and remained way beyond the time it took to make a normal delivery. Finally, when Clarence and Marci came into view, Jennifer zoomed and witnessed Marci's sexual advance. She couldn't believe it. She was in heat, humping him until he peeled her away.

"The spouse is always the last to know," Jennifer whispered, allowing another teardrop to splash onto the black cherry desktop.

Chapter 10

Hurricane Kate circulated in a box on the lower right-hand side of the television screen.

. . . Before we take you to Baghdad let's get the latest on the Hurricane.

. . . Kate is now a dangerous Category 5. Winds exceed 185 miles an hour and forward progress has slowed. All eyes are on the oil patch.

"Screwball Rob should have gassed the cars last night," Marci mocked. "It's not part of his routine, that's why. Damn it! It's going to cost at least a dollar more per gallon. That's if we can find any gas."

She tried to call Robbie on his cell phone. There was no answer.

. . . Expect intensification. Kate is a hundred-year hurricane; bigger than Camille. It's going to be a sad day for whoever is in her path.

. . . Now let's go to our Baghdad correspondent for the latest on our troops.

. . . I'm standing here with staff sergeant Mickey Spinneki . . . Staff sergeant, you are the last soldier to leave Iraq soil?

Ma'am, you can call me Monkey Wrench or just Monk. That's what the fellers in my squad call me. Hum . . . what's I thainks? Just kinda glad to be outta here and headin' to my woman back in the States, ma'am.

The soldier leaned his narrow face into the camera.

Chadda, I'm comin home.

Is your wife looking forward to you returning?

She ain't my wife just yet. But when I get home, I'm goinna marry her, cuz she's gestating my twins. And she got a set of milkers that'd put dairy cow to shame.

The reporter laughed.

Goes to show you what a great country we live in. Young men, soldiers like staff sergeant Monkey Wrench come all the way from the back country not knowing where Iraq is and risk their lives to prevent terrorism. Our nation thanks you, sergeant.

The reporter shoved the microphone into the soldier's face.

I've got to ask. Why do they call you Monkey Wrench?

Grasping the microphone he leaned into the camera lens again.

Cuz I fix damn near anythang. The Iraqis are sad to see me goes too, ya know. I've been stationed at the Baghdad hospital. And when there was no electricity, it was my job to get the generators running.

Iraq loves staff sergeant Monkey Wrench. He's heading home to marry his woman . . . Better get those milkers ready, Chadda of Hudson, Florida.

Marci cracked a half-smile. "Cute story, glad we're finally out of Iraq, thank goodness."

Chapter 11

Adrenching shower converted the dusty potholes of Gator Tales parking lot into milky pods of limestone putty. Dale Carter parked far from the cluster of well-worn vehicles that ringed the barroom. Stepping from the running board he slipped and jammed his left shin against a cedar post that jutted from the ground. It tore an angular hole in the denim of his pants leg.

With his rough hands he yanked the post from its hole. But before he tossed it into the swamp Dale noticed the carved notches. He laughed. His father had driven the spike nearly thirty years ago.

Flicking away the gray muck that filled the notches, Dale recalled his father's instructions. "Cut notches exactly one foot apart, evenly spaced, with neither a quarter-inch difference, son." It triggered a fond and sad fatherly memory of Joe "Buck" Carter.

Buck Carter had worked at Cledus Rosewood's limestone mine. He operated the conveyor that ran from the mine hole to the railcars on the Fivays spur. When Dale was barely old enough to push a loaded wheelbarrow Buck brought him to this exact spot and handed him a hatchet. "Dale," he said, "it's time you learn what hard work and persistence brings. Take this spike and cut five notches exactly one foot apart."

Dale recalled his father's reaction when he asked for a measure. "No, son, it'll slow you. Learn to use your eye."

A rugged but gentle man, Buck Carter was few with words. Whenever Dale completed an assigned task, if he did it incorrectly there was never a scolding. Buck would peer down, set a firm face, and say, "Not quite right, son, keep on it."

The day Dale cut the spike Buck had led him into an oak grove where a banyan dropped several thick feeder roots from a horizontal, limb-like trunk. "Practice on these here root-drops, Dale. I want notches set exactly one foot without you using a measure." Working vigorously, it took Dale an entire day to accurately strike the ten, crisp, sequenced hatchet chops needed to carve the notches, a task that destroyed many of the banyan's vertical roots.

Finally, toward evening Dale sharpened his hatchet, called for his father, and cut the cedar post exactly as instructed.

Examining the spike, Buck offered an approving nod.

"Follow me," Buck said, pacing a straight line into the marsh. He rammed the spike into the spongy soil, driving it to the first notch. "Son, I want you to fetch a wheelbarrow and spade from the shanty and wheel it to where the conveyor loads limestone into the railcars. Fill the barrow with the spilled stone and bring it here and dump it."

The next morning, after arriving with the wheelbarrow, Dale removed the shovel and buried the spade into the crushed, cement-like overspill. He broke into a heavy sweat. Mosquitoes gathered and swarmed.

"Son, when you're ready, take your load down the rail tracks and fill me in a one acre lot up to the second marker."

"But Dad, it will take forever!"

"Exactly, that's what the notches are for; one for each year it will take to elevate that swampland." Buck walked away.

Lugging his first load along the crunchy ballast took nearly an hour. A voice called from behind. "Son, push into the marsh and dump it around the cedar post. And when you are done meet me on the train tracks."

Grunting, groaning, Dale struggled. The wheelbarrow toppled several times. His father's commanding voice floated above the head-high palmettos and through the shading cedars. "Not there!"

When young Dale emerged he was gasping. It was sticky and humid and thick with mosquitoes and no-see-ums. As he scrambled back to the train tracks, Buck handed him a stick of 6-12 repellent. His low tone bellowed. "The swamp will toughen you like a soldier . . . For the next five years you got a job. And while you're elevating the marsh, be thinking about framing a building three feet off the ground."

"Where will the stone come from?" Dale asked, flicking a struck mosquito.

"From the railcar overspill," Buck said. "At the end of my shift, after everyone's left the quarry, I'll see that there's plenty of stone for you to wheel off."

As he greased his neck with the 6-12, Dale's eyes traced the train tracks toward the two-story hopper and a chute that filled the railcars. It was quite a distance.

"Every day after dinner you'll start," Buck said. "And I ain't helping you, son. But I won't be leaving you alone. On the other side of that oak grove I've started another project, making lots to set trailers to rent to the new guys at the quarry."

While working with his father those many years, Dale learned of his parents' plan to homestead the land they lived on. And after many months, as he toughened, the task got easier and almost routine. Each night they hauled stone—Dale leaving the grade where the shade from the live oaks began, and his father continuing a half-mile further, making a road and filling in spots for a planned trailer park.

Five years later, Dale had lifted the marsh several feet and built a barroom named Gator Tales. Buck had completed his trailer park project aptly naming it Cabbage Palms.

The stinging rain pellets that arrived with a sudden downpour disrupted Dale's fond memory. He tossed away the cedar spike and trotted for cover.

From inside Gator Tales came the clack and roll of a racking pool table and the thump of darts striking a corkboard. A television rebroadcasted a NASCAR race. Dale didn't go inside. Instead, he sat on the porch railing with a vacant stare. This time his memory wasn't so warm.

When Buck Carter applied to homestead the swampland, he was denied. Twice he tried, but died suddenly while relocating the conveyor. Buck was standing at the top of the quarry disassembling the hopper when somehow, the loaded conveyor switched on and the belt rolled in reverse, feeding stone uphill and knocking Buck into the flooded quarry. The entire belt emptied into the pit, entombing Buck.

At a young age Dale abruptly became a man. His mother was bitter because her husband's untimely death seemed no accident. She set out to acquire the mine where her husband was buried and the land of the man responsible for his death, Cledus Rosewood. And to survive as a widow, she worked as a chambermaid at the Hacienda Hotel in New Port Richey.

With the strong wind blowing Dale allowed the lonely sadness he carried since his mother's death to overtake him. Setting his thick hands to his face he wept.

Chapter 12

Cabbage Palms trailer park bordered the east side of Hoinky's flea market. It was within staggering distance of Gator Tales Bar & Grill. The Kracker community had nicknamed the trailer park *Cabbage Ears* because the moss-covered low ground that surrounded the ragged mobile homes was a perpetual cabbage-green color.

On tropical summer evenings when a firm onshore gulf breeze parked a drenching rain-line too close to the coast, Cabbage Ears made for dramatic, often entertaining news video. As a shallow lake formed beneath the trailers, camera crews arrived, lifted satellite masts, and fetched the first tenant trudging along. Usually it was some gourd-shaped character wearing baggy shorts and a black biker T-shirt with an inked-over tattoo of an ex-wife's name. The tanned reporter wearing hip waders would shove a microphone in front of the person and record that this flood was somehow "the dang government's fault." The reporter followed with a closed-end question. "Isn't it true FEMA should have fixed this by now?" It didn't matter what the answer was. The oblong slob, the backdrop of squalor, made for great visuals on a slow news night.

Dale Carter tended not to interact with the Cabbage Ears tenants. His instructions to the Kracker community came through the people closest to him—Critter, Flatch the bartender, and Fifty-Cal Gal, who likened herself as Dale's personal security guard.

Fifty-Cal Gal was his most valuable Kracker. She operated the pawnshop Dale owned on Highway 19 just north of the Dixie Highway intersection. A tough, angry dyke, she had the perfect temperament for churning pawned inventory into boatloads of cash. And like many Krackers, Fifty-Cal lived a checkered life. Raised by her grandfather, a former marine obsessed with collecting machine guns, she learned from him how to shoot each weapon in his arsenal, accurately. There was one particular weapon, a M2 Browning fifty-caliber machine gun, that engrossed her. And when her grandfather died from liver disease, Fifty-Cal laid claim to the Browning.

Firing the lethal gun was how Fifty-Cal vented the anger she carried from a childhood of molestation, which led to a lifetime of failed relationships with men and women. When in need of companionship, Fifty-Cal visited Gators, where she'd lure to her Cabbage Ears trailer whatever reasonably attractive woman that got stupid drunk with her. An entire night of capitulating lesbian love often ensued until each woman achieved ultimate satisfaction.

On Sunday the pawnshop remained closed—a longstanding order of Florence Carter. That's when Fifty-Cal practiced her version of religion. She'd hitch the M2 to her three-wheel Harley Davidson and haul it inland to Itchy Fingers shooting range on County Line Road next to the Pasco County transfer station. Her church attire consisted of skintight leather slacks, a leather vest with frayed tassels, a silver-spike dog collar with matching spike wristbands, and many dangling silver chains and braided necklaces.

Buried beneath the leather was an assortment of body piercings that titillated, tugged, and pinched. There was a massive array of tattoo body art. Her braided, fire engine red hair split into dual ponytails which she shoved behind the collar of her sleeveless vest. The Amazonian constantly sucked on a wad of chewing tobacco. And when the corner of her mouth dribbled a stream of molasses, she'd sip the seepage and gather the glug swishing it several times, allowing the juice to build. Then she'd eject a tarred jet of sputum that shot ten feet before it peppered whatever was in the way.

On Sundays a rough Budweisered crowd gathered at Itchy Fingers and waited for Fifty-Cal to arrive. After unhitching the Browning, Fifty-Cal would lock down the tripod stand and spin the turret toward the target. Ignoring bystanders, she'd drop to her left knee, set the crosshairs, and load the magazine with a disintegrating link-belt of massive 800-grain copper-encased lead bullets. A yank on the bolt-latch lobbed a shell into the chamber. Flaunting an evil smile she'd exhale and squeeze off three rounds. The mighty Browning would chuckle a deep, deadly laugh and spew sour puffs of bitter white smoke. Dust flew from behind a shredded school bus target one-hundred and fifty yards away. A full second later an intimidating, resonating thump arrived, followed by a sonic ricochet that shattered in a stand of low trees behind everyone.

Fifty-Cal never said a word. She entertained solely herself.

No one noticed Dale Carter arrive and sit in a dark corner at Gator Tales. Across from him and the herringbone dance floor, leaning against the bar rail sucking a cigarette, was Critter, jabbering about Hoinky's ugly pigs. Dale grimaced; he suspected Critter had secretly bred those mutant pigs again. And if they escaped during the hurricane, they'd get bred into the local wild boar population. It'd been a project to rid Hoinky's pigs the last time it happened. And

Dale didn't believe Critter when he assured him the last of Hoinky's mutants were decaying at the bottom of the quarry.

Dale watched Critter nervously fidget and look away. He's agitated, thought Dale. He's got a guilty look. How many pigs did he breed this time?

Fifty-Cal often covered for Critter, he thought. She'd know. So he slipped out the back and headed to the trailer park, the most logical place to search for those pigs.

Dale drove his pickup slowly along Dixie Highway, panning beyond the rippling waters of the roadside swales that flooded during high tide. He scanned the sandy patches of the palmettos scrub looking for circular sand furrows, a telltale sign there was a mutant nearby. He veered into Cabbage Ears, drove through large puddles, and arrived at Lot 23, where Fifty-Cal Gal lived.

The screen door on her trailer hung from one hinge. Dale grabbed the swinging door, eased it open, and entered. Fifty-Cal sat at her kitchen table reloading shell casings.

"You ought to fix that door hinge," Dale said.

Fifty-Cal was in the middle of loading a round and didn't answer.

Setting the die into the ammo press, she yanked and punched a slug into its brass casing. *Oomph, crunch!* She turned and locked her black eyes onto Dale. "I guess you come to talk a bit about the hurricane?"

"No need to discuss that," Dale said. "Momma told you what your job is. I come to ask what ya know about Critter breeding more of Hoinky's pigs."

Fifty-Cal was slow to react because she was funny about tattle-taling, being labeled as a Kracker turncoat.

Dale waited patiently. If she had a hankering Fifty-Cal wouldn't hesitate to speak her mind if it was important, eventually revealing the truth.

"Them's baby-arm sure is ugly, ain't they?" Fifty-Cal responded.

Avoiding eye contact she poured gunpowder into another casing using a tiny funnel.

"Guess you ain't tellin, are you?" Dale said after reading her body language.

Fifty-Cal always answered the affirmative with some sort of abrupt, physical jester. This time she rammed the slug into its casing ... *Umph!* "Gotta keep your powder dry, ya know."

Though Fifty-Cal wasn't very direct, her lack of an answer was enough not to alarm him. If she felt Critter's pig population was out of control she'd let him onto it right away. Also, she knew Dale would make her hunt down every single pig, just like Florence made her do that last time the mutant population got out of control.

"Ya goin to Gator's to see Monkey Wrench on the TV?" Dale asked, lifting the broken screen door. He stepped outside and squared the door in the frame to shut it.

Fifty-Cal came to the doorway. She'd removed much of her silver body décor. "Nah, I only go to Gator's when I'm good and horny. If the big one ya ma's been preachin' us is coming, I gotta git these empty shells reloaded to use up my leftover gunpowder. Ya never know what bad will come out of these Krackers once the storm is gone."

Through the crinkled screen Dale matched his chestnut eyes with hers, and stared at Fifty-Cal as if he were etching his concern directly into her memory.

Chapter 13

When word got out Monkey Wrench would be on television, nearly everyone left Cabbage Ears and headed for Gator Tales. Friends and supposed friends of Monkey Wrench, as well as those looking for an excuse not to work the rest of the day, arrived. Critter had snuck from the junkyard and claimed his usual barstool. Chadda Renfro, Monkey Wrench's pregnant girlfriend, occupied two barstools—one for each ass cheek. Overhead, a ceiling fan tossed her stringy black hair and kept her cool. And when Monkey Wrench's mug appeared on the television mounted behind the bar, a bottle-rattling cheer erupted. Chadda, with her freshly applied burgundy lipstick, squeegeed a gummy grin with her only good tooth protruding, pinching her lower lip.

Dale returned from his brief visit with Fifty-Cal and sat in a dark corner, opposite the dartboard. He nursed a beer.

Figuring it might be safe that Dale wouldn't bitch him out for leaving the junkyard early or lying about his clandestine piglet breeding enterprise, Critter pushed from the bar, crossed the dance floor, and pulled up a chair.

"Where's Fifty-Cal?" Critter asked, sitting across from Dale.

"She's reloading shells, Crits," Dale said. "And she didn't give you up, you fleabag swine propagator. You're running freak show tours inside Hoinky's houseboat again, ain't you? Scaring those Trinity snoots that are curious enough to let you soak them for a few bucks."

Critter pleaded his case. "Since the judge took my gator license, times have been kinda tough, Dale. Frigging Governor Simon raised the tax on my smokes by a buck. If I run low on cash, I'll be buying those foul-tasting generics at the convenience store."

Dale decided to change the conversation; he had more important things on his mind. "I need you to lug those water buffalos from the weeds near the black mangroves and haul them to the Bippinotti Clinic. So when Monk's arrives, he can fill them with fuel to keep the generators running."

"Ya think Monk will make it here after the hurricane passes?"

"There's no doubt," Dale said.

"I'd love to see Monk again," Critter said. "He never minds when I bum smokes. Plus, he's the only guy who will go into the Anclote River and drag Piggy out with me."

Dale didn't answer. Whenever Critter mentioned Piggy, he started spinning his yarn and wouldn't shut his yap. Dale didn't care to hear the piggy story one more time.

". . . Monk's not afraid of that canker-nose gator like the rest of thems are." Critter smacked a pack of Marlboros against his knuckles.

Dale looked at him with a frosted expression that made Critter uncomfortable.

"What we going to do if the 'cane hits?" Critter asked, deciding not to continue about Piggy. "It'll wipe out the Patch."

"The junkyard is high enough, the surge will not reach there," Dale answered. "Tell those freeloading cabbage heads to do as

Momma planned. Move into the buses and cars on the hillside nearest the quarry pit."

Gators Tales suddenly grew quiet. Flatch, the bartender, raised his vein-laden forearm over his head, pointed the remote control and upped the television volume.

. . . At 12:15 pm a hurricane hunter aircraft from Clearwater reported that it recorded the lowest pressure ever from inside a hurricane, 802 millibars. Winds now exceeded 225 miles an hour. The eye wall is tightly wrapped with a massive exhaust vent. Seas are more than 65 feet. Underwater gas pipelines to the Port of Tampa are shut down. Lines at gas stations are building throughout the Tampa Bay area.

"It's coming this way," said Dale over the blare of the television.

No one turned to look at Dale. They knew the voice and what it meant.

Chapter 14

Licking Spicy-Beaches barbeque sauce from his fingertips, Robbie Lindum finished a dozen of Scooter's famous Caribbean habanera wings. And each time a waitress passed, his eyes rolled right to left, at ass level. Two deep-cleavage waitresses slid into the pine booth directly in front and into the lap of a decrepit old man. They threw their arms around his hairy neck, warmly calling him Cooterman Pat. The old man smiled and slipped a five-spot into the waistband of each girl's silky purple shorts.

While waiting for his takeout order, Robbie listened to the giggly conversation between the old man and lap-dancing waitress. "If the hurricane comes, Cooterman, will you rescue us?"

A prickly grin arrived on Pat's scabby face. "I know of a nudist colony in Hudson were we can ride out the hurricane," he said.

The girls giggled, flashed their bronze, cleavage and accepted another five-spot.

Why don't those waitresses treat me like that? thought Robbie. That old bag is all crinkly and knotted.

Finally, several foil bags of habanera wings arrived. The waitress gave Robbie a generous glance until he handed her the coupons. Her unblemished face went flat after recognizing him as the guy who shorted her tip last time. The gorgeous girl snatched the coupons, danced to the next booth, dropped into Cooterman Pat's lap, and wiggled.

Disgusted, Robbie left. He had one more medical practice to visit before he headed to Hoinky's.

Watching the news, Marci thought of calling Robbie and egging him about cutting his work day short in case Hurricane Kate's direction changed. Then she decided not to frustrate herself. "He won't move any faster anyway."

But suddenly, her iPhone vibrated. A text message from Kathleen asked if Dad could come to school and gas her car. She ran out.

Marci called Kathleen, got a voice mail, and left a message to call Triple-A.

Moments later a text message arrived saying Dad should have gassed it last weekend. She was embarrassed and had to leave the homecoming rally to meet the Triple-A guy.

. . . We have an important alert. Hurricane Kate has stalled 250 miles southwest of Tampa Bay. It's a Category 5. There will be another hurricane hunter aircraft report at 3:00 pm. We are now going to take you to New Zealand for an interview with environmentalist Al Gore, Nobel prize winner.

. . . Mr. Gore, what do you make of this hurricane?

Well, just as our largely ignored global warming reports warned, hurricanes, particularly those in the Gulf of Mexico where the water is shallower and much warmer, are going to pack a greater punch. Our research suggests that this Gulf of Mexico hurricane might attain wind speeds that exceed 300 miles an hour.

Chapter 15

In Khuzestan, Iran, in the lowland desert outside the city of Ahvaz, President Mahmud Ahmadinejad stepped from his bulletproof car and walked toward a well-traveled white pickup truck. Two men perched in back branded RPG launchers. A tall, narrow, bearded man stepped out. Mahmud greeted the gaunt man. They exchanged traditional greetings.

"Good friend, your time has come," Mahmud said. "You have been patient. Our kind Iranian citizens have given you safe passage through our great country, Akmah. Soon, you will be my neighbor and ally. By tonight Al Qaeda will resurrect from the watery grave of our martyr leader Osama Bin Laden and secure a country of its own. We'll destroy the infidels that invaded our homeland and killed your great leader."

"May good fortune travel with you, Mahmud. Our plan is in place. In a few hours there will be a coup in southern Iraq. Soon, we will control all Mideast oil."

The men kissed cheek-to-cheek then parted.

The pickup pulled away and headed west into the open desert. Crossing the Tigris River by ferry, it sped through a date palm orchard and exited into the streets of Basrah. No one took notice when it stopped in front of Maqam Al Ameer Mosque. A small army emerged from inside. More vehicles arrived, joined the convoy, and continued. The caravan halted outside a government building. Akmah El Nasid stepped from the lead vehicle and boldly ascended the ancient steps. An Al Jazeera camera crew accompanied him.

He spoke in Arabic. "I am Akmah El Nasid. Southern Iraq is now under our rule. All of Iraq will soon become Al Qaeda's homeland."

The coup was quick and nonviolent, because Akmah had worked underground for many patient years. And when time came he acted swiftly, without bloodshed. The turncoat provincial leaders had quietly stepped aside to allow an Al Qaeda sleeper cell arrive and plant its flag.

"All oil is to stop flowing from this region," Akmah said in clear English.

The cameraman went back to his truck and transmitted the recording to Al Jazeera.

Chapter 16

By midafternoon nearly everyone at Gators had a load on. Tossing his last dart Critter missed the corkboard and pierced the screen door, leaving a perfect hole in the wire mesh.

". . . Piggy found me, I didn't find her," blurted Critter, telling his alligator story to a circle of inebriated companions that'd gathered. "I got one of them there reptile control licenses from the Game Commission to fetch cottonmouths and nuisance gators off public properties."

Critter opened his wallet and flashed the expired permit.

"Where'd you dump the ones you caught, Crits, in Dale's quarry?" a bar patron asked.

"No, brain fart," answered Critter, pulling his bar stool closer to the group. "Dale would have Fifty-Cal nip off my nut-sack if I brought any reptiles on his property and dropped them in the pit to let them dissolve in the lagoon. So I dumped them somewhere else."

"Where?"

"You know that son-of-a-bitchin' badass Deuce that Florence Carter didn't like much?" Critter said.

"Everyone knows of Deuce," someone answered. "Him and old lady Florence been feuding a long time over who owns the swampy part of the Flats."

"Deuce's rum-runnin' granddaddy had left him another plot of land on the Anclote River by that there Trinity Meadows development," Critter said. "Ol' Deuce rents the dry part for boat and RV storage. The chain-link fence in the back is busted and opens a big hole to the river. It's a nice spot to empty my reptile traps. And Deuce don't care as long as I slip him a few bucks."

Last week, I dumped a fat grandpa cottonmouth I snagged on the seventh hole of the Pecan Woods golf course with some hairy tarantulas into the Anclote. Fuzzy bastard spiders didn't sink, though, they skittered right across to the other side of the crik."

There was laughter.

"Sometimes when thangs is slow and I don't need to scrounge a few bucks to last the weekend, I light a doobee, grab a pack of smokes and a twelve pack, and fish for snoooks."

Nursing a glass of Diet Coke at the bar, Chadda Renfro swiveled her barstool. "Catch anything?"

"Chadda, you wench," Critter said. "Not a damn thang. Never caught any fishes there." Critter lifted his beer glass and chugged.

Someone else spoke. "I heard the Pasco game warden says it's because of all the fertilizer, insecticide, and sediment that runs off those Trinity Meadows lots that killed all the damn fishes."

"Perhaps, but I still love to fish there though," Critter said. "Who'd said you had to catch something anyways?"

Chadda struggled to twist all the way around to face the group listening to Critter's story. With both hands she supported her pregnant stomach and set one foot on the wood floor. "Monk says there's plenty of fish in the Anclote. You gotta know how to catch them." Chadda mashed a rubbery one-tooth smirk.

Stroking his beard, Critter stiffened. "Shut your yap, witch. Ya's interruptin' my story."

Chadda's chin disappeared into her neck.

"Don't be giving me that stank eye, woman! You look like a Gibsonton carny. Like that fat freak show woman who had the Siamese twins with three legs between two of them."

Drifting into Critter's field of vision, Flatch, the bartender, eyeballed him from behind the tap. He was born in Gibsonton and traveled with the carnies and didn't put up with carnival insults flying around his barroom.

Chadda called over to the patrons listening to Critter spin his yarn. "Deuce and Monkey noodled the Anclote plenty. Said it's full of big channel cats that hide under the bank stumps. Monk usta caught plenty snoooks too." She shoved her beefy forearm forward and chopped at her wobbly bicep with the other hand to show the length of fish he caught.

"Stop interruptin' me, you prego cow," Critter said.

Chadda winged an empty peanut bowl at Critter. "Chewbaccian asshole!"

Before the insults flew any further Flatch interrupted with a question to defuse the wrangle and return Critter to recounting his gator story.

"Hey, Critter," Flatch called. "How the hell did Piggy get her name?" The bartender grinned, displaying his twisted teeth.

"I named her Piggy cuz she's got a sloppy ol' gator nose that looks like a Carolina hog with a bad case of nasal syphilis. Piggy's a woman gator with an attitude like Chadda." Critter slid one leg off his stool and turned toward the listeners who had nothing better to do. After lighting another cigarette he leaned forward for effect and whispered, "That gator got no teeth on the left side of her ugly serpent noggin. It's all gums, ya know. And makes her look like she's got a happy-face half-smile on the toothless side, like she's glad to see ya."

Critter ran his hand along his shin and winced. "I knows, cuz she got hold of me right here and tried to death roll me." Smiling, his tobacco teeth gleamed.

"But I escaped, cuz she snagged me with her toothless side. When she death rolled, my foot slipped right out of the ornery reptile's rubber gator mouth."

"I betcha ya wet your pants," Chadda said.

Critter sent her an annoyed look.

"And when Piggy was creeping around Cabbage Ears ya hadda keep an eye on the youngins. Hadda yell at the little Cabbage Ears boogers that got too close, cuz of Piggy's half-happy smile. The Cabbage kids thought she was friendly, like Barney the television dinosaur. The brats don't know'd no better and run right to her." Pitching forward, Critter paused, tightened his knuckle around his cigarette, sucked hard, and glared at the attentive faces. "And . . . chomp!" Startled, everyone jumped back. "Piggy might snatch the little bugger and swallow the wiggly kid whole."

Laughter broke out. Flatch brought several bottles of beer, collected money, and emptied overflowing ashtrays.

"How'd Piggy end up here at the Flats?" asked a leather-skinned patron with deep-socket eyes and bulging Adam's apple.

Leaning forward, as if he were going to let them in on a secret, Critter whispered, "Piggy is from up nears Crystal River. She was born in a gator nest below the outflow tubes at that there nuclear plant."

Blasting him from her barstool, Chadda challenged Critter whenever his story didn't add up. "What the hell makes you think that?"

"It's cuz the way Piggy looks . . . Like you, Chadda . . . All deformed and prickle face."

The barb had landed and penetrated. Chadda hoisted her stomach and turned away.

"Remember when the mullet turned up dead on the leeward side of Crawl Key with all those lesions? The government snuck in with a pond scum skimmer and sucked them all up. Rumor was a radioactive spill at the nuclear plant killed 'em. Government kept it secret. Didn't want no one touching or collecting the mullet and using them for tomato plant fertilizer likes we do."

Eyes grew big as if they were privy to a conspiracy.

"Piggy was hatched the day of the spill. That's why she grew all lopsided. Halfway down her ass-tail it bends ninety degrees left. Her hind legs are cock-ass cattywompass—not all four gator claws touch the ground at the same time."

Critter slugged his beer, belched, then knuckled his cigarette.

The crowd that gathered had added more listeners. The jukebox went silent.

"Her nose has an open canker sore on top," Critter described. "It's all lumpy and bloody and somethin'. You should see how pissed she gets when a herd of fire ants crawl into it."

A burst of laughter broke out.

"There's only one answer for the way Piggy's nose looks. She must've snorted plutonium reactor water," Critter said.

Heads nodded. They liked the story. It wasn't boring.

"Does she glow in the dark?" The remark came from Flatch.

Critter smiled. "Nah, I wished she did though. I wouldn't want a big old grandma gator like Piggy sneaking up on me at night."

More laughter.

"When did Piggy come to the Flats, Crits?"

"Dale Carter saw Piggy first," Critter said. "He'd been walking the junkyard like he does all the time and found tires chewed off the cars buried nearest the mangrove section . . . Guess Piggy chewed them to kill the pain from being born lopsided and crooked. Kinda like in those Civil War movies where the soldier bites on a bullet as the doctor saws off his shot-up leg."

"Must've been those damned steel-belted radials that wore away all the damn teeth on her left chopper." Critter rubbed his calf. "Nothin' but gums."

"Dale said he found Piggy swimming in the quarry in that phosphate shit-water."

"Ain't that aqua water no good and killing anythang that swum in it?" Flatch asked while wiping a nearby table.

"According to Dale, Piggy loved it. Said there's somethin' in the lagoon acid water. Probably killed the bugs and leaches and diseases that lived on her pointy gator skin," Critter said.

There were several chuckles.

"Knowings I got a Pasco animal control license, Dale asked me to trap the tire-chewing dinosaur. Said he trade me a trailer if I'd get rid of Piggy."

"How'd ya get Piggy out of the lagoon?" someone asked.

"Ya know about Hoinky's mutants pigs showin' up all over the place, don't ya?"

"Yes," someone said. "Ain't Dale making you catch them all, cuz he caught you breedin and selling them to the carnies?"

Critter lit another cigarette and took several swigs, finishing his beer.

Burrrp!

"I told Dale them mutants started to disappear when Piggy showed up. If he left that gator alone, Hoinky's mutants would be all gobbled—every last one of them."

"He didn't listen, did he?" a voice said.

"Nay," Critter responded. "Dale said the kids from Cabbage Ears slingshot stones at the pig gator." One of them's might slip on the lime bank into the lagoon. Plus, Dale didn't like losing those damn tires Piggy chewed. Many could be resold at his used tire stall at the entrance of Hoinky's."

"How'd you snag that gator from the lagoon without getting your hands burned?" someone asked.

"I caught some of Hoinky's mutants, put them in the covered mower trailer Dale traded me, and parked it with the tailgate down near where Piggy swum in the quarry.

"Next morning, ugliest reptile I'd ever seen with a big ol' pomegranate nose lay in the trailer munching her choppers. That woman gator looked like she was happy to see me with that Barney smile on her left side. So I closed the tailgate and hightailed to Deuce's lot over on the Anclote. And when it got dark, I crawled onto the trailer ruff, unlatched the tailgate, let it drop, and ran like hell."

"Is that where you dumped all the creatures you caught, including that monster water moccasin that showed at Cabbage Ears when it flooded last week?"

"Yeppereee! Didn't cost me a damn red cent cuz Deuce was in the pokey," Critter said. "That fat moccasin slithered through the fence hole into the Anclote. And I tossed some of Hoinky's mutants there for kicks, to see if they could swim."

Critter laughed. "And ya know what's on the other side of the river, don't ya?" He didn't wait for a response. "That Trinity Meadows development with all those snub-nose, fake blond booby MILFs. Most of my repeat business comes from there. Especially when the cottonmouths and tiny gators scare the crap out of the mommies when they see 'em creeping in their shrubs. Makes their nipples stiffen like pencil erasers. They pay me anything to snatch them from their pretty lawns."

Someone blurted, "You should've traded for a titty squeeze to see if they feel real or not."

Another Kracker interjected, "My old lady got implants when she usta dance at Moog's strip joint over on Grand Boulevard. I swear I can feel the jelly sack inside."

"That's cuz she got them at that sleaze-ball plastic surgery clinic next to the Bippinotti. Heard them Trinity docs know how to slip them in and make them feel real. So when you feel up your wench, you ain't know'd the difference."

Critter couldn't stand the odor the ceiling fan blew his way. "Phew, Chadda, you reek. You done ate too many garlic wings."

Fortunately, Chadda didn't hear him.

He continued the piggy tale. "In the morning when I went to Deuces to close the trailer. That's when Piggy nabbed me, as soon as I walked around the tailgate . . . Chomp! . . . I thought I was a goner."

I fell to the ground like they teach in Joe Jitsu . . . Ya know, roll with your enemy. And when Piggy tried to death roll me, my leg slopped out of her mouth like a chow mein noodle."

The audience expressed disbelief. "Good thang you wasn't caught on the toothed side."

"Phew, you got that right," said Critter, gesturing with an animated nod.

"What'd you do next?"

"Piggy crawled back into the trailer and nested there," Critter said. "There was nothing I could do to coax her out. Back then Monkey Wrench was around and said we's can make some good money with a gator that size. Said going rate to rid a gator is fifty bucks a foot. Piggy paid . . . uh . . . umm . . . seven-fifty. Only thing was, she liked Dale's trailer and gave a nasty fight when Monk and I tried to drag her out and slip her onto golf courses at night."

"Why didn't you drag her out by her tail?"

"Stupid shit!" Critter said. "You try, Piggy's tail was bent which made it too easy to snap at you with her flapping choppers. But Monk is pretty handy, ya know. He made a rubber handle wire lasso and slipped it around her cockeyed ass claws. That crazy bastard Monk hooked a truck battery to the lasso. And when he hit the tricity, Piggy ran like a Pasco whore with a load of fire ants snipping inside her money hole."

Everyone laughed. Someone slapped Critter on the back and said he had to take a piss.

"When me and Monk planted Piggy on a golf course, no sooner than the morning fog lift we'd get a call from the groundskeeper to come git that ugly gator."

"How'd you catch her?" someone said.

"Easy," Critter answered. "I'd drive my trailer onto the golf course near Piggy and she'd crawl right in. Something about it she liked, a scent or sometin'. At night I'd park with the tailgate down at Deuce's lot. But sure enough, Piggy still'd be there in the mornin'."

Flatch announced last call then turned off the ceiling fans as a way to chase the Krackers out.

"The easy money ended when Monkey shipped to Iraq," Critter said, chugging the last of his beer. "He was the only one that could handle that electric lasso. . . . I tried it once. Got it around Piggy's ass but I almost shocked my own balls when the lasso whipped back and got hung up in my crotch."

Everyone laughed.

"What happened to the Pig Gator?"

"Left her in the darn trailer," Critter said, setting down the empty bottle and outing his cigarette. "Me and Monk made some good money back then. So I paid Deuce two months' rent in advance. Since then, I ain't returned to check on Piggy. For all I knows she still there eatin' all the damn fishes in the Anclote." He loosened the tightness of his belt buckle and headed for the bathroom.

Chapter 17

Charlie licked Marci's arm and woke her from a nap. It was time to let him out.

Crawling from her comfortable sofa Marci went outside with Charlie. The wind had picked up considerably. The humidity dissipated slightly. Marci gazed southward at an ominous charcoal cloud on the horizon. Not since her West Virginia childhood had she seen such an intimidating skyline.

Following the sidewalk to the street, she opened the black mailbox. Inside was a thick envelope from Feldon.

"Great," Marci said. "Robbie's check arrived. He'll stop being a pain."

Next door Jennifer Dink's garage door buckled and rumbled upwards. A shiny black Cadillac Escalade backed out. It was Jennifer with her neck twisted at an uncomfortable angle, struggling to negotiate the oversize SUV through the narrow width of the garage entry.

Here she comes. She's going to stop and show off her jewelry again, thought Marci.

To Marci, Jennifer Dink was a pesky snob who claimed to be a real estate agent, a fitness trainer, and a stockbroker—all at different times, not realizing what profession she told Marci the last time. Randy, her husband, was a handsome Tampa construction attorney who often traveled. Marci mentioned the last time they talked that she hadn't seen Randy in over a month. But Jennifer claimed Randy came in late last week and left early again on another business trip.

The Escalade rolled along the driveway. The window lowered halfway. "Hi, Marci," said Jennifer with her Android plunked to her ear acting as if she'd interrupted an important call to talk to her.

Jennifer's nose looks waxy, thought Marci, tight and papery. Her pulled forehead seemed pinned near the temples. *She must've gotten more plastic surgery, a new procedure. How odd it looks!*

"Hi, Jen, how are you?" Marci said, holding the mail.

"I'm going to the bank in case the electricity goes out," Jennifer replied, straightening, allowing her implants to tighten the cotton blouse she wore. "Randy gassed my Escalade and his Corvette yesterday before he left on his business trip. Thank God our gas tanks are full. You can never be too careful when a hurricane is coming, can you?"

Jennifer's platinum-dyed hair blew across her face. She snapped her head, but the strong breeze blew it back. This time she pinned it using her phone.

"Did your husband gas your cars yet?" Jennifer asked.

"No, unfortunately he didn't. I left him a message to do it before he comes home from work," said Marci, frustrated.

"Marci, I was looking on the Internet before I left. Racetrack on Trouble Creek Road is already closed. Your husband will have trouble finding an open station. Remember the last hurricane."

Marci frowned. Robbie had ignored Marci's warnings the last time, too. They were lucky the hurricane missed them.

Jennifer Dink twisted her hand in a manner that showed the fiery, four-carat engagement diamond and accompanying white-gold wedding band.

Hypnotized, Marci couldn't avoid looking at the enormous stone.

Jennifer followed Marci's glaze toward the princess-cut gem. She cocked her head and opened her neck to expose a glittering diamond necklace. "I need to go, Marci. Tell Robbie good luck finding a gas station."

Marci wanted to throw a brick at the SUV. "Duck-ass snob!" She pointed her toes outward mimicking a waddling penguin. Jennifer asked such annoying questions. Fuming, Marci went inside and tossed the mail onto the desk.

Her iPhone rang a tone that said it was Robbie. "What incredible timing." She lifted the phone. "Yes, Rob, your check came."

"That's great. I finished my in-service at the Bippinotti and heading to Hoinky's to buy something that will cut our air-conditioning costs."

"Rob, I hate to tell you this but you need to gas the cars. I'm getting nervous. The hurricane stalled."

"No, it's moving again, to the west, away from us. I just heard a report. We'll be fine, honey, it's not coming our way," Robbie lied. He didn't want to feel guilty about making one last stop before he went home.

"Are there lines at the gas station?" Marci asked.

"Yes, several have closed." Robbie didn't like her tone. "I'll go to Racetrack once I get . . . uh, I mean . . . in the middle of the night and wait for the fuel truck to arrive."

Marci caught the pause. He almost said *when I get home*. If he offered, she'd agree, ruining his plan for birthday sex.

"But I'd rather you go when you get home," Marci said, agitated.

"Bye, honeybunch." Robbie ended the call.

"Crap, he's buying a new gizmo to tinker with. What am I going to do with this guy?"

Wanting to relax in the pool, Marci climbed into a one-piece suit which fit a bit snug.

Splash!

She dove headfirst. The ninety-degree water offered no relief.

Dangling on the edge of the fiberglass, she looked across the backyard. The neighbor, George Ying, plodded in deliberate straight lines tending his garden of food-bearing plants. Olivia Ying was inside the garage preparing the fruit. They seemed an unlikely couple, Marci thought. Olivia was an outgoing Carib and George a quiet Cambodian. The only thing in common was their similar height and skin color. They were their nicest neighbors. Both were easygoing and obsessed with gardening, practicing a Caribbean form of permaculture.

A blast of wind rolled the lanai screening like ocean swells. The ornate clock that hung on the stucco wall near the sliding doors to the great room fell from its hook, only to be saved by the seat cushion of the chair below. Marci realized the afternoon newscast was about to begin. She grabbed a beach towel and went inside.

At the bottom of the television screen flashed blood-orange text: *Breaking News!*

. . . We interrupt our coverage of Kate and take you to our news center in Bari, Saudi Arabia.

There is a rumor spreading throughout the Middle East that one of Osama Bin Laden's sleeper cells in Basra claimed the southern part of Iraq. Al Jazeera says they've secretly brokered a deal with local clerics. There's rumor all oil shipments were halted. But we have no confirmation and believe it may be a hoax.

"What's that about?" Marci said. "Some sort of viral Internet hoax, I hope."

Chapter 18

The Cool-n-Save, a gadget that sprayed a halo of mist around the air-conditioning unit, sat in a carton on the car seat next to Robbie. He'd read online that it would save 30 percent in air-conditioning costs. He'd been charged one hundred fifty dollars on his credit card, plus another hundred for the water filters needed so the misting jets wouldn't clog. He was proud, because the Kracker that sold it said he'd make back his money in two months.

Approaching Trinity Meadow's main gate, Robbie stopped behind Bradley's unloading school bus. He rolled down the car window as Bradley came off. "How was school, son?"

"Okay, I guess." Bradley slung his backpack.

"Get in, I'll give you a ride."

Disheveled, Bradley crawled into the car. He wanted to sleep.

"Something weird happened today." Brad told his father about Iraq. "I thought because we killed Bin Laden nothing bad would happen."

"Huh!" It shocked Robbie to hear this from his son. Brad wasn't one to listen to news. *Perhaps he's maturing and not thinking about just gaming online.*

"It's a rumor, Brad," Robbie said, trying to put him at ease.

"No, Dad, it sounded kind of serious. Many of the moms came to school and got my friends. There weren't many kids on my bus."

"Brad, people overreact. They can get weird and panic, spreading rumors anytime a hurricane is nearby. It has to do with the lowering air pressure. Son"—Robbie deepened his voice to sound more authoritarian—"people should suck it up."

Weary, Brad offered no reaction to his father's counsel and almost fell asleep during the short ride along Leiram Avenue.

When the garage door lifted, a wall of boxed medications confronted Robbie. There was no room to park. Marci hadn't told him about Clarence emptying his truck into the garage stall.

Now what's Feldon up to? thought Robbie. That's entirely too much stuff.

Brad went to his room and logged online. Marci prepared dinner.

Entering the kitchen Robbie placed his wallet and keys neatly in a drawer.

"What's with the boxes, Marci?"

Marci told Robbie about Clarence closing his delivery business and why he didn't want to be held accountable for the load of medication.

"Poor guy, what a hard luck story," Robbie said. "Did my check come?"

"Looks like it. I put the envelope on the desk."

"Thanks, honey." Robbie disappeared into the bedroom. Moments later he reappeared dressed in pressed khaki shorts, a pale yellow T-shirt, and tennis sneakers.

Marci waited for him to change before confronting him. "Rob, I'm worried. Hurricane Kate is a Category 5. You need to go to Home Depot right away and get plywood to cover the windows."

Purposely, Robbie ignored her. He didn't think it was necessary just yet. And wanted to unpack the Cool-n-Save and read the instructions so he could install it in the morning.

Noticing he wasn't listening, Marci finally lost it. "Dammit, Rob! You should have bought those hurricane shutters the homebuilder offered. And a generator during the July sales tax holiday."

Robbie saw her anger and knew he wasn't going to get out of this. If he didn't go to Home Depot it might slam the door on sex tonight, perhaps the entire weekend.

"I'll go," said Robbie reluctantly.

"Don't you think you should buy a generator, too?" Marci asked.

Rob balked. "We can't afford eight hundred dollars. Plus, I'm not going to pay a hurricane premium on that generator. I can get the same generator for three hundred less after hurricane season ends," he explained.

"You should have gassed the cars." Marci kept at him. "When you get back I want you to head to the first gas station that has a line, and I don't care if you wait until dawn."

She must be nearing that time of the month, he thought. It was going to be a miserable evening. "Might as well get out of here until she settles," he mumbled beneath his breath.

Charlie greeted Robbie and begged to be scratched.

"By the way," Marci said, standing in the kitchen preparing dinner. "I heard an odd piece of news about an hour ago. One of Osama Bin Laden's sleeper cells surfaced in Iraq and claims to have taken over."

"Probably another Internet prank related to the troops leaving, no doubt," Robbie said.

"Robbie, I think we need to attend the next homeowners meeting."

"Why's that? Didn't we agree those meeting were a waste because of the bickering and endless debating?"

"There's something wrong with this development," Marci said. "I think it's infested with more than its share of snakes and big spiders."

"What!" Robbie said. "Have you seen any snakes?"

"No," Marci lied. "But the Yings did."

"The Yings' fruit trees attract rats, which draw the rat snakes. Perhaps we should file a complaint." Wanting to get back on Marci's good side, Robbie consented to attending the next homeowner's meeting.

. . . Hurricane Kate stalled in the Gulf of Mexico. It's just sitting there, intensifying. Warnings are issued for Florida's west coast from New Port Richey to Pensacola.

Setting her hands on her hips, Marci threw Rob a mean look.

Robbie became sheepish. A lump came to his throat. "I better go to Home Depot, gas the cars, and get supplies. What about this Iraq rumor, have you heard anything more?" Robbie asked.

Her stomach was in knots. Her new home, how much damage would occur? Who could she find that was reliable to fix it, because Robbie was too much of a klutz to do repairs?

. . . We have breaking news from Iraq. The rumor an Al Qaeda sleeper cell took over Basra seems accurate. There was no opposition. They came into the country and took it over.

The reporter seemed puzzled.

. . . The comment from the White House is that they are looking at this matter. President Hillary Clinton will make an announcement at 7:00 pm tonight.

The reporter looked dumbfounded.

. . . Can a coup be that easy?

. . . *Given the gravity of the hurricane and the news from Iraq we've cancelled all regularly scheduled programs.*

Pasted in the lower right corner of the TV screen was Hurricane Kate, churning in the Gulf of Mexico east of the Dry Tortugas. Broadcasts came from the streets of Tampa, Clearwater, Anna Maria Island, and Cedar Key. The citizens interviewed were nervous. Many were packing and heading inland.

"Robbie?" Marci asked. "Do you think we should evacuate?"

"Perhaps, but before we go I must get plywood and board at least the dining room window . . . There goes my entire reimbursement check. Where's Kathleen?" he asked.

"At school, it is homecoming," Marci said. "For sure, it's already canceled."

Chapter 19

When Robbie arrived at Home Depot with the family minivan, the parking lot was full. Fortunately, a Honda Civic with two sheets of plywood dangerously tied to its roof pulled from a parking space.

"Sweet," Robbie said. "If I get out of here fast enough with the items Marci wants, she'll owe me."

A puttering forklift emerged from inside the contractor's entrance and dropped another pallet of plywood. Two employees worked portable cashier stations as an assembly line of employees loaded cars and pickups.

"Looks like they're prepared," said Robbie, noticing a police cruiser parked nearby.

He went to the front of the line and approached a busy salesclerk. "I need to get some plywood," Robbie said. "Can you help?"

"Go to the end of the line, jerk off!" Standing in line a heavyset man with fat arms pointed across the highway.

Robbie twisted his head trying to see where the insult came.

"Go across Highway 19 and wait three hours like I did, dipshit. Bug out or I'll punch in your face." The angry man pointed to a line of cars on the other side of the busy highway. It stretched around the bend out of sight.

"Ah, shucks!" Robbie said. "I guess I have no choice."

"You're goddamn right!" the fat-armed man said. "Now scram."

With wilted shoulders Robbie headed to his minivan. But suddenly there was a commotion and gunshots. Robbie snapped his head to see what was happening. A brawl had erupted over a parking space. Someone pulled a gun and shot the person who stole the spot. A balding police officer with an overhanging stomach climbed from his cruiser, fumbled with his taser, and struggled to run. Abruptly he slowed, clutched his chest, and collapsed between two cars. No one tried to help the cop.

More gunshots rang as Robbie sprinted for his car. He tripped on a curb and tumbled. His cell phone flipped from his belt into an oncoming stampede of people and smashed. Someone kicked him; another stomped him. Struggling, Robbie crawled toward a small tree and clung to it. Several people tripped on the wire that held the tree straight and were immediately trampled.

The employees retreated into the store as the plywood pallets were looted, and the cash register robbed.

Stunned and bleeding, Robbie didn't dare budge.

Six miles away at Steak 'n Shake Kathleen Lindum was waiting for her cheerleading friends when her cell phone rang. The high school principal had canceled homecoming.

Enraged, she cursed her teachers and blamed anyone over the age of thirty who worked at Trinity Meadows High School. Gnashing her teeth she smashed her fist onto her French fries then tossed them at the plate glass window and stormed off. Kathleen jumped into her

Mustang and headed to find the person responsible for canceling the game.

Turning into the high school parking lot, the Mustang puttered and ran out of gas. Pounding the steering wheel Kathleen screamed and cursed. "Damn it, Dad, you wimpy turd! You didn't gas my car!"

She cursed her mother. "Mom, you're a cheapskate and should've given me gas money."

Gripping the key, Kathleen turned the ignition until the battery ran dead. Fuming, she punched the quick-dial on her cell phone to call her father. No one answered. After leaving an angry message she called her mother.

"Mom," Kathleen said. "Dad didn't gas my car. I ran out and now it won't start."

"What happened to the Triple-A guy? Didn't he come and give you two gallons of gas earlier today?" Marci asked.

"He didn't come," Kathleen lied. The serviceman arrived a half-hour late and apologized. She called him a lazy Kracker, accusing him of taking his good old time. But what she didn't know was that he shorted her gasoline because of her attitude.

Marci punched the iPhone, ending the call. "Walk home. It's only three miles. Maybe the walk will knock some sense into the little witch." Her thoughts ran rampant. Why was Kathleen so miserable? What would happen if the hurricane was a direct hit? Should she prepare to evacuate? Her attic plants wouldn't survive in the darkness.

After several tries to call Robbie, Marci left a voicemail demanding he buy a generator, any generator.

"Why doesn't he answer?" Marci grumbled.

The television blared. Breaking news speculated Hillary secretly sold large portions of the Strategic Oil Reserve to fund her Health

Care Initiative. There was talk President Clinton would invade Iraq. Academics answering closed-ended questions talked about classifying Kate as the first Category 6 hurricane.

Plastered on the colorful, high-definition television screen was Kate, spinning in the Gulf of Mexico like a giant exploding cyclone, going nowhere, rotating in ninety-three degree water and getting meaner.

Outside it grew dark. A heavy rain arrived and flooded the lawns, filled the swales, and raced in sheets across the macadam thoroughfares.

Chapter 20

. . . We interrupt our programming to bring from the Oval Office, President Hillary Clinton.

. . . My fellow Americans, today, at 3:00 pm Eastern Standard Time we received word from Iraq an Al Qaeda sleeper cell surfaced and claimed a coup. We believe this information to be accurate and credible.

Marci's eyes grew big.

"Huh?"

. . . For now we must take a wait-and-see attitude. Based on the lessons learned in the past, Americans do not want to return to Iraq. However, given the gravity of this situation we must prepare to respond militarily should this coup spread.

Jumping from the kitchen counter, Marci snatched the remote and upped the volume.

. . . Our biggest concern is that this crisis could spill into Saudi Arabia, Kuwait, and the rest of the Middle East. I've told the Joint Chiefs that our entire military should be placed on alert. All Reservists must begin reporting immediately for active duty.

. . . Because eighty-five percent of our energy depends on foreign oil, the United States must be prepared to act.

. . . I urge all Americans to be strong and stay calm. Keep a cool head. Now more than ever, we must come together as all great nations do.

. . . And finally, a hurricane of unfathomable size and intensity is poised to strike Gulf of Mexico residents. They need your prayers.

. . . My fellow Americans, I must tell you about our plan to curb energy consumption. Starting tonight at nine o'clock, all oil-fired and natural gas utilities must cut power. Each day, for twelve hours, electrical power will be restored. I know it's a hardship but we must act without hesitation, or we will not be able to respond to any homeland threat, leaving our great country vulnerable and without energy.

Let us all pray we find a quick and peaceful solution to this crisis. May God bless America.

Trembling, Marci became chilled.

What does this mean?

Where is Kathleen?

Where the hell are you, Robbie?

Chapter 21

At Gator Tales a pickup backed to the barroom steps and turned its radio full blast. "Gotta hear Hillary," the driver yelled. "Bin Laden's buddies are up to no good." The tavern hushed. Pie-eyed patrons listened to the President's speech.

"So what if the lights go out?" said a chicken-neck guy with shoulders that slumped. "Ain't like we's never lived without electricity before."

Nursing a beer, Chadda blurted, "Half the trailers in Cabbage Ears don't have electricity when the bills don't get paid. We are on a first-name basis with the collection folks at the electric company."

"Hell," shouted a soused Kracker swaying atop his barstool. "What a bummer for those Trinity Meadows folks. They won't know what the hell to do with no electricity and overflowing lift stations that float turds down their streets. We'll make a bag full of money off of them when it comes time."

"That's if money's worth anything," Flatch said. "Barter might be more valuable."

"Wonder what a window air-conditioner or generator will fetch in a barter," Chadda said. "Fifty-Cal says Dale's got an attic full in the pawnshop."

"Chadda, who's watchin your boys, especially Samson?" Flatch asked.

Like most Krackers they looked after each other when things got bad. Asking a question was Flatch's way of telling her it was time to leave and tend her kids.

"Flatch, they's carin' on their own. They're at an age where they can do that. Besides, if they get out of line, I'm sure Critter will drag them here by their cabbage ears for a straightening out."

Pregnant with twins, Chadda struggled from her barstools. She didn't want to leave, but it was time to go.

Chapter 22

A black curtain of rain dropped from the thick cloud cover and trampled the choppy waters of the Gulf. Stinging, buckshot pellets pitted the gooey muck flats. The rain-wall marched in, swallowing the expanse of black mangroves, licking the backside salt that oozed from their pear-shaped leaves. Canary palms that rested stealthy rat snakes swayed more east than west and resisted barely enough. At Gator Tales, a muffled country tune deadened, snuffed by the smothering rhythm of the drumming downpour.

Traveling along the rim of the limestone pit in his pickup, Dale Carter passed rows of anchored storage containers and stopped beneath the towering boom of the dragline shovel. Instead of swinging open the door, he squeezed his torso through the window, balanced on the doorframe, and stretched across onto the metal tread of the aged dredger. He crouched so the wind wouldn't knock him off. Bracing against the dragline's cab he unscrewed the fuel cap. The tank was full.

"A least Critter wasn't too damn lazy make sure this got done."

As water droplets rolled along the comb tracks that waxed his slick hair, Dale inspected the electrical cabling connections that snaked toward a junction box set six feet above the ground. At the base were prepared coils, to be strung to a pair of lashed-down RVs.

Satisfied, he nodded with approval. Everything was ready to go.

"Cane's going to be shit darn nasty," Dale said.

Now he understood the intent of all those morning conversations with his mother. It was a preparation, a scripting and continuation in case she wasn't alive when the hurricane came. She should have told him about the immeasurable loneliness and why no Kracker woman was ever good enough. He toiled, because there was no one to comfort him, to supplant her unconditional love, now that his mother was gone forever.

The rain-wall arrived and pounded the abandoned vehicles and peppered buses and RVs and muddied their dry-rot tires. A dirt road cutting down the center of the junkyard quickly flooded and became a river.

"It's arriving." Dale crawled into the pickup, turned on the wipers, and headed for his house, a place he referred to as the Icehouse.

The battering resonance of heavy rain traveled the narrow, lifeless, dog run hallway as the ghostly memory of his mother haunted him—her thin, scrappy frame darting room to room, always busy, endlessly productive. A sharp, echoing voice preached her tiring message. "Use my money to care for them, Dale. For they've known a hard life. Fix the clinic after the storm passes." That's all Florence had asked, a dying wish born from her own hardship.

Entering the simple kitchen, Dale poured a cup of coffee and sat at the chrome rim table. Sliding his forearms across the slick cream-colored Formica, he stared blankly into the blackness of the coffee, inhaled its steamy aroma, and remembered the story Florence told just once.

Why only once? he often wondered. Perhaps so he wouldn't forget. It was Florence's story—a tale of love, hardship, prejudice, and sorrow. And it explained why she worked so darn hard. "So there'd be no more hard times," as she often said.

Florence and Buck Carter grew up in a saw mill town close to Virginia's southern border, where the rolling Piedmont folded into the ankles of the breaching Appalachians. Childhood sweethearts, they married at age sixteen and eighteen and struggled like the rest of their hill country kin. After hearing the Army sent fifty dollars a month back home if a young man went to fight in the Korean War— more money than he earned in a month—Buck enlisted.

It was while shivering in a foxhole on a Korean mountaintop, listening to a Greek soldier from Tarpon Springs, that Buck Carter hatched his quick-rich scheme. The Greek infantryman said he wished he could bring this coldness back home to ice down the summertime shrimp catch. "If you figure out how transport ice to Florida, you'll be a millionaire," the Greek told Buck.

Buck shared with his foxhole buddy his life back in Virginia. When he sawed ice blocks from frozen lakes in the wintertime and hauled those solid slabs by mule-drawn sleigh to an icehouse his father built in the backyard. And when the warmth of spring arrived and transitioned into summer, the ice was sold to Carolina taverns where the tobacco grew.

Returning from Korea, Buck cut ice all winter. And in late spring, he leased a boxcar, insulated it with sawdust from the lumber mill, and stuffed it with ice slabs. He disassembled the icehouse his father built and crammed it into the railcar. Florence, pregnant, packed everything they owned and traveled south with their entire savings on ice.

But before their journey to Tarpon Springs was complete, the father of Cledus Rosewood, owner of the Five-A's rail line, had gotten wind of Buck's plan after reviewing a bill of lading of a railcar loaded with ice. Jealous a scalawag stole his idea, Mr. Rosewood halted the train short of Tarpon Springs. He ordered Buck's boxcar unhitched and parked along the isolated, unfinished spur. The railroad police padlocked it and posted a sentry. A message was sent telling Buck to pay a Pasco county transport tariff in order to complete his journey.

Penniless, Buck watched the railcar sit in the sweltering ninety-degree heat for two weeks. And once the dripping stopped from the porous underbelly of the steel sauna, the sentry unlocked the rolling doorway and told Buck to remove what remained.

Removing the dismantled icehouse, Buck reassembled it near a stand of oaks that offered substantial shade.

Stressed, Florence delivered prematurely and lost the child. The town's doctor, a Rosewood relative, had refused to travel from New Port Richey to tend the sickly infant. And to survive, Florence worked as a chambermaid at the Hacienda Hotel. Buck picked oranges alongside the migrants. And when the limestone mine opened, Buck got a job there and soon after Dale was born.

Years later, when Dale was a teenager, Buck died after falling into the mine's lagoon.

A widow chambermaid, Florence stole from witless hotel patrons, secretly building an empire, deal by deal, cheat by cheat, poker hand by poker hand, until she was self-reliant. Never did she move from the Icehouse to the more comfortable homes along the Cottee River. She remained in Hudson, relocating the Icehouse to higher ground after she'd won the deed to the quarry.

Florence had only one wish, a dream for a hospital. A place Krackers could go to care for their aches and pains. To deliver illegitimate babies, and die in comfort and with dignity.

If I do anything after the 'cane hits, Dale thought, I must make sure a hospital is up and running. "Sure wish Monkey Wrench was here," he said to himself. "Come on, Monk, git your ass back to Hudson. I need you."

Chapter 23

As a driving rain pounded her disabled Mustang, an impatient Kathleen Lindum nervously banged her knee against the door panel. She couldn't see through the windshield. No one is coming, she thought, then said out loud, "Across the high school soccer field is the YMCA. Maybe I can bum a ride from someone at the gym."

Kathleen swung open the car door and stepped into the whipping wind and made her way through a maze of chain-link fencing. She crossed the soccer field, angrily kicking apart soggy fire ant mounds that got in her way. The glue that held together her shoes dissolved, the cheap Brahma leather separated from the stitching. Barefooted, she continued alongside a flooded swale, smacking cattails to release her frustration.

Undeterred, she bashed through the thick reeds and into the thigh-deep water. "Dammit, friggin' trench. Ouch, damn sandspurs!" Kathleen growled, trudging.

Suddenly, her face contorted. Something was big-time awry inside her shorts. There was an odd, invading sensation, similar to what a necking football player tried with his hand behind the school bleachers. It goosed and wrapped her leg and pushed further into her shorts.

"It's a snake!"

Feeling the pinching scales, she froze. Its scissoring tongue nudged upwards and slinked into the crevice of her ass-crack. Goose bumps dimpled her skin as she watched the bulbous, reptilian head stretch the elastic waistband, emerging, flicking its tongue. The prickly tail unfurled and caboosed until the entire length pooped out, flopped into the swale, and slithered away.

Dumbfounded, Kathleen lugged herself from the water to the other side and found the YMCA closed.

The daylight had faded. The amber streetlights that lined the faultless Trinity Meadows thoroughfares ignited. Marci set out candles and prepared the best she could for the scheduled blackout. Venturing into the garage she searched for a portable radio, but the batteries were missing.

"How am I going to follow the hurricane when the electricity goes out?"

The lack of batteries made her realize there were other issues. Everything in the refrigerator would go bad. What will we eat, she thought? The pantry eatables consist of food no one liked. Stuff like sardines, packages of Mandarin noodles, chicken soup, and half-used packs of dried lentils and kidney beans.

If we get desperate it'll have to do, she thought.

Pacing, Marci couldn't stop staring at the rotating cloud mass in the lower right-hand side of the television screen. Hurricane Kate wasn't moving north anymore. It stalled. The last frame showed a slight jog eastward.

"Oh my God!" She turned pale and threw her hands into the air, screaming. "It's coming and going to hit us! What am I going to do?"

Grabbing the car keys, she headed for the garage. "I got to get Kathleen and find batteries." And just as she backed down the driveway in Robbie's company car, Kathleen arrived, limping. Her hair hung straight, mud smudged her clothing. She had no shoes. An angry, scowling sourpuss was welded to her face.

Kathleen marched into the garage and slammed the door to the kitchen behind her. Marci chased after.

"Kathleen," she said, standing at the bathroom entry. "In a few minutes there will be no electricity."

"Why?" Kathleen grabbed a towel to dry her hair.

Marci wasn't sure what to say. She'd made Kathleen walk home. And by her looks, it wasn't a pleasant experience. A wrong choice of words might be disastrous.

"You got candles, don't you?"

Kathleen stood in the hallway and stomped the hardwood floor. "They canceled homecoming. I'm calling the school board director at her home and demand to have homecoming tomorrow night."

"What I just told you, Kathleen, didn't it sink in? It's unrealistic to think the school board will accommodate you. More likely, Trinity Meadows High School will become a hurricane shelter."

Kathleen began to quiver and turn beet-red. But suddenly her mood abruptly changed. The redness in her face dissolved. She flipped her head, tossed the towel, and casually started to brush out the knots. "My cell phone doesn't work. It got wet. I need to go to the Verizon store and get a new phone. Tonight! When's Daddy coming home?"

"Dad went to get plywood." Then it dawned on Marci, perhaps Robbie's cell phone got wet. That's why she couldn't reach him.

"When Dad gets back, I don't care what time it is, he needs to run me to buy a cell phone. My car is stuck at the high school. It's his fault, you know. He forgot to gas it last weekend."

Marci wanted to choke Kathleen for how unreasonable her demands were. It was clear she didn't grasp that in a few minutes the lights would go out. Kathleen had a horrible day. She'd soon go into her room and hopefully fall asleep.

With her two children safely at home, Marci opted not to venture for supplies. Let's pray Hurricane Kate doesn't come this way, she thought.

At exactly 9 pm the electricity went out. Trinity Meadows went dark. The big screen TV sizzled silent. The counterclockwise spin of the ceiling fans slowed and coasted still.

"Shit!" Marci cursed. "I didn't anticipate this. No air-conditioning for the entire night. It's going to get uncomfortable."

After lighting several candles shortly after the lights went out, Marci went outside with Charlie. An uneasy eeriness had settled over the neighborhood. In the distance there was a puttering noise; a generator had started at the end of the cul-de-sac. A light flickered inside one of the homes. Soon, several generators came alive and more homes illuminated.

Next door, the Dinks' propane generator, smartly positioned in the garage attic and vented through the roof, purred. Their air-conditioning unit kicked on.

Marci glanced toward Jennifer Dink's dining room window just as the slats in the blinds separated. "Caught ya, you twit. I see your silhouette."

"Snoop!" She tried to say it loud enough for Jennifer to hear.

The window blinds snapped shut.

"She must do that all the time. It explains why I see her every time I'm outside. She's got nothing else to do but live inside her fortress, all alone waiting for something to happen."

A rumble came from inside the Peltzes' garage. Their generator had started and brightened the entire home. The children cheered.

Upset that she had no electricity, Marci called for Charlie and went inside.

Chapter 24

When the rain-wall rolled in from the Gulf of Mexico and engulfed the Home Depot, Robbie Lindum took refuge beneath the thin tree he'd clung to. The tiny leaves provided no protection. Oversized droplets blasted his bald spot.

Still in pain, using the tree as a crutch, he struggled to his feet. He'd lost his car keys.

Left with no choice but to walk home, he tried to cross Highway 19. A steady stream of cars passed. They must be evacuating, he thought. After finally crossing, he'd walked nearly two miles along Grand Boulevard when the streetlights went dark. He stopped his short strides and waited for his eyes to adjust. A rancid layer of creeping fog smelled like rotting leaves.

Robbie limped along, the roadside gravel crunching as he set one soggy size-seven sneaker in front of the other. He was worried. "Marci's going to freak. I'll never hear the end of this. I didn't get the plywood or the generator. And now we're short one car. It's not going to be pretty when I get home," he mumbled.

The stoplight at the Perrine Ranch and Grand Boulevard intersection wasn't working. "That's odd, it usually it flashes when the power is out."

Turning east, passing an RV and boat storage lot, he arrived at the concrete bridge that crossed the Anclote River. The bridge marked the unofficial dividing line between the newer, inland deed-restricted communities, and the rundown coastal neighborhoods built in the 1960s.

The reflectors marking the center of the roadway flickered. An SUV rounded the bend, flipped its high beams on, and lit the tangle of vines that draped the tall trees on both sides of the roadway. The headlights traced a galvanized guardrail that ran the length of the bridge. Robbie stuck out his thumb, hitching a ride. The brake lights turned bright red. "They're stopping." Then a tire screech came, followed by a thump, then the sound of a rodent squelching. "What was that?"

The taillights stopped glowing. The SUV continued.

"It must've hit something."

When the darkness returned it grew eerily quiet. Robbie had forgotten what total silence was like, because at home, the television was always on. He couldn't remember walking such a long distance, or being outside, away from the comfort of air-conditioning for a prolonged period.

His bruised legs ached and needed to rest. Stepping from the macadam onto the gravel berm, Robbie felt in the dark for the guardrail and sat.

He heard a squelch in the middle of the bridge. "What is that? Something's scratching the concrete." Robbie squinted. "It's a small animal and spinning in circles. That SUV must've hit a rabbit." He leaned forward.

"Yuck! It's a squashed pig. Poor fella, his guts are hanging out."

Suddenly, there was a loud snap behind him, within the vines. They swayed and pulled taut.

"What can that be?"

The mother pig, he thought.

Shuffling his sneakers on the gravel, he hoped to scare it away, but bumped against something solid. Just then, another car crossed the bridge and Robbie caught a glimpse of the object between his feet.

"Looks like the fruit I saw at the flea market with bloodred berries and white seeds."

"Hmm, some old Italian man told me what that was."

"A persimmon?

"No.

"An Indian apple?

"Uh, a pomegranate?

"That's it!"

Robbie reached to inspect it. "It's gooey and squishy." He tugged to get a closer look. It didn't budge.

"Huh?"

But before he let go, a massive alligator lunged from beneath the guardrail and clamped onto his ankle.

"Holy shit!" cried Robbie, lurching, lunging for the roadway. He slammed facedown onto the gravel and screamed and twisted, trying to yank free. But his leg didn't budge.

Panicked, he urinated in his pants.

"Ouch . . . Ouch, it got me!" Robbie scratched and pawed the ground. "Help me! . . . Someone, help me!"

Several strong tugs on his leg nearly dislocated his hip. The yanks and jerks continued. His belt buckle dug into the loose stones. His shirt lifted as his stomach grated against the gravel. The guardrail passed overhead. "It's dragging me into the swamp!"

He dug in his fingertips as his body angled down the embankment. The pull was steady—his torso flattening a pathway through the weeds. Robbie felt sharp, piercing pains traverse his stomach. "Ouch, briars!" The grasses grew taller and the curtain of vines engulfed him. Several cars passed and lit the treetops. Robbie screamed. "Help . . . Help!" But no one heard.

Oh my God, in few moments I'm going to be in the river. Robbie recalled the Nature Channel—feeding crocs tearing apart mangled carcasses, gulping them down. His ankle felt as if it were in a press. Several more erratic jerks drew him over grass clumps. He snatched at them but the clumps pulled from the soggy soil.

He lunged for a small tree and clung. But the big gator, with its momentum, its leverage, overwhelmed his weakling grip as his fingers slipped from the bark.

The ground leveled and became spongy and wet.

"The river!" Robbie cried. "Marci . . . my children . . . they'll never know! There will be no body."

Piggy's jaws clenched and held firm, and lurched hard several times.

"Ouch, my hip!"

Reaching the water's edge, Piggy snaked her deformed tail, pressed her claws into the mushy mud, and shoved and slithered into the murky pitch of the Anclote.

Robbie swung his free leg wildly, digging his heel to stall the gator. His sneakers plowed the muck. His fingers dug deep, linear grooves. I wonder if this is going to hurt, he thought. Any moment the gator will rip off my leg.

Spread-eagle, frantically he flailed, slipping further into the shallows. His waist, then stomach, and finally his entire torso submerged in the black water. He took a deep breath, but something jabbed his stomach and forced him to cough. It'd snagged his shirt and pulled it tight around his ribcage.

It's a tree root! Instinctively, he grabbed hold and laced his finger into the base of the woody knob. Turning his head, he looked into the nearly submerged alligator's evil eyes. And thought he'd soon die, as his memory slipped into the past, when as a child, he ventured into a gully, finding himself surrounded in sticker bushes. How he cried for his mother but no one came. And he recalled the singular, brave moment where he decided to burst through the gnarly briars, tearing his clothes and scratching his skin. How tough he was. He could be tough again.

Holding tightly onto the root-knob, his arms stretched like rubber bands as the fifteen-foot alligator begin her death roll, Robbie felt his leg twist. He closed his eyes and waited for the intense pain to arrive. But suddenly, his captured calf slipped. The pressure released. Piggy had opened her mouth to adjust her toothless grip and Robbie's foot slipped free.

"My leg!" He pulled hard on the root to gain some distance. Digging his fingers into the muck he clawed forward toward shore. Quickly, he wiggled like a tadpole and scurried like a clumsy opossum up the embankment and over the guardrail.

Chapter 25

On occasion a twenty-passenger minibus sat in the driveway across the street from the Lindums' home. Edward and Cindy Peltz lived there in a pale pink clapboard residence with four young daughters. The family was part of a tight-knit, well-organized, deeply religious co-op.

To Marci, it seemed the Peltz daughters lagged in many ways. They appeared socially illiterate and physically smaller in stature; sheepish, and at times clingy. Cindy Peltz, their homeschooling mother, never got a break from the children. Her kinky brunette hair had an overabundance of split ends. Permanent wrinkles had formed inside the tight furrows of her permanently stressed brow.

Most afternoons Marci saw Cindy Peltz leave in the small bus with other co-op mothers, usually to Howard Park or Green Key Beach to walk the nature trails as a form of learning. And as with homeschoolers, it seemed their education included a healthy dose of religious indoctrination.

If there was anything positive about the Peltzes it was their self-reliance, largely because they believed the Second Coming of Christ was about to happen. They stockpiled supplies and strengthened their membership with like-minded, fanatical families, each charged with a duty, a responsibility to contribute, so the co-op could adequately prepare for the Coming.

"Armageddon will soon arrive," Edward Peltz drilled into his children. "Do your fair share for the good of our church and the heavenly winds shall whisk you away to eternity to be with our loving Holy Father."

Like most of her close-by neighbors, Marci's effort to associate with the Petlzes was minimal. On occasion, she did manage a smile to Cindy Peltz, waving when the family came and went. Once, when Cindy was in a bind, Marci agreed to watch their pets while they went on retreat. But when she entered the home, it shocked her. She found several parrots, large lizards, free-roaming ferrets, mice, and a barely alive box turtle inside a cage with a pair of rabbits. An overweight, adopted stray dog lived in the garage.

Twice a day Marci fed the dog and cleaned poop piles and animal pellets kicked from smelly cages.

So when Marci found herself unprepared, she hoped Cindy would return a favor and lend her batteries for a portable radio she never used.

Removing her shoes, Marci tiptoed through the ankle-deep water that overflowed from the cypress head behind the Peltzes' house. She peeped into the garage. A chugging generator vented through a window sat on raised wooden platform. A heavy gauge power cord strung through the rafters plugged into the breaker panel.

As she pressed the doorbell she heard the children praying in the dining room. No one answered. She knocked and waited.

Cindy Peltz, with her youngest daughter hoisted on her hip, finally answered.

"Can I help you?" Cindy asked. "Oh, Marci, I didn't recognize you. It's so dark out. Are you okay?"

Marci tried to peek into the family room. There was some sort of shrine set up in the middle.

Leaning, Cindy tried to obscure Marci's line of sight.

"I'm fine, Cindy," said Marci, craning. "Well, so far. The news from Iraq and the hurricane is disconcerting, isn't it, Cindy?"

Cindy nodded and rehoisted her thumb-sucking kid onto her cocked hip.

"I need batteries. Do you have any?"

"I'm sorry, Marci, but we don't have any to spare." Cindy was unsympathetic. Her feigned expression said it all. *Why should I share anything with you? You had plenty warning and ignored it. You get what you deserve.*

"What's happening is all God's will," Cindy added.

What a stingy whack job, Marci thought. Now I know why we never bothered with them.

Again Marci stretched to see around Cindy.

"Our father thou are in heaven . . ."

"They're reciting the rosary," Cindy said. "Ed says the hurricane is the beginning of the Second Coming."

God help me, thought Marci. They've gone bananas.

Marci left by darting across the squishy lawn.

As long as I'm humiliating myself, might as well double-down and ask Jennifer Dink.

Randy and Jennifer Dink built their home on the lot next to the Lindums. Randy had poured an obnoxious amount of money into it. He installed automatic roll-down hurricane shutters and a modern security system with hidden cameras. Computerized temperature controls monitored and managed the residence. There was a high-speed satellite transceiver which was a more reliable form of Internet access.

Inside the home eloquently crafted window treatments smartly accented each room. Expensive paintings lined the walls. Prominently displayed, pricey Swarovski crystal figurines sat on polished black cherry shelves. Each piece of furniture conveyed the attitude of status, gluttony and, snobbery, exactly as Jennifer planned it.

It was on Thursdays that Jennifer cleaned the five-bedroom, five-bath McMansion, regardless if it needed cleaning. Though Jennifer could afford housekeepers, she refused to hire one, doing the cleaning herself. In fact that's all Jenny did, all day, every day; distrustful no one should touch her treasures. And rarely did Jennifer let anyone enter her home, fearful guests would track fresh dirt, or discover her extreme loneliness and deep insecurity.

Jennifer viewed Marci as a confident, beautiful, brave woman who had experienced the horrors of childbirth—twice. Though she desperately wanted children, Jennifer feared it would permanently reshape her beautiful figure. A child would set her in competition with well-to-do in-laws, with the attention going to the only grandchild. If her body gave out, Randy Dink would move onto to someone younger. He made plenty of money and easily attracted money-grubbing, legged, barely age twenty girls.

Sitting in her upstairs den Jennifer Dink watched Marci approach the front door using the hidden video camera that broadcast to her computer monitor. She'd made the house dark as if she wasn't home and watched as Marci knocked several times.

In her bathrobe Jennifer went down the grand staircase and stood silent on the Persian rug on the other side of the ornately carved front doors. She was envious of Marci—she had children, a family to stay the loneliness. And more importantly, a husband who came home on time and occupied her bed.

With tears streaming down her soft, well-tended complexion, Jennifer Dink, twisting the oversize diamond ring on her finger, refused to answer the door.

Chapter 26

Hobbling with a bull-legged limp, Robbie picked at his soiled inseam. He passed the security gate and made his way down Leiram Avenue. It seemed many of the neighbors had left. And for the few that remained, humming generators lit the comfortable homes.

Black kernels had dropped from the Brazilian palms that lined the walkway leading to the front door. Palm tree fronds lay scattered across the yard. What a mess, thought Robbie. More work!

Candles flickered through the dining room window. Opening the front door he wasn't looking forward to facing Marci.

"Marci . . . Marci, are you here?"

Charlie barked.

"Charlie, be quiet," Robbie whispered.

A sharp squeak came from inside the den.

"Marci?"

Behind the cherry-stained desk, reclining in the swivel chair and holding an empty wineglass, Marci was slow to react. Stoned, she'd been watching the candle flames dance. Her mind had stalled. She coughed to clear her cotton throat. "Did you get the plywood and gas the car?"

Startled, Robbie flinched. And though he couldn't see her expression among the flickering shadows, his mind painted an angry face.

"Nuh . . . no," said Robbie, waiting, expecting her to unleash.

Chuckling sarcastically Marci pushed from the desk. "Ha, ha, I should have guessed."

Robbie checked her feet. *If they're twitching, she's about to explode.*

"What the hell happened, honeybun?" Marci cleared her throat, again.

She didn't allow him to explain. "Rob, there's a gargantuan hurricane in the Gulf of Mexico. Fucking snakes and fucking spiders have infested the neighborhood. We got no gas to evacuate and nothing to protect my brand new home. And guess what? . . . No electricity because you're too damn cheap to buy a generator. No birthday sex for you tonight, dude!"

Slouching, Robbie accepted the criticism. With his ego bruised, he spoke softly. "What happened to the electricity? Did the rainstorm knock it out?"

Uninhibited, Marci seized the opportunity to be a smartass and unleash, "No, honeybuns, Osama Bin Laden's buddies took over Iraq today and shut off all the oil. And Gas Tax Hillary, to save our melting glaciers and healthcare system, outed the lights tonight."

Charlie sniffed Robbie's sneakers.

"Funny, real funny, Marci, I'm not in the mood for humor tonight. Our minivan is stuck at Home Depot where a riot broke out. I was trampled and almost eaten by an alligator."

He headed to the shower.

Marci laughed. "Too bad you don't believe my story. I sure as hell don't believe yours either."

After the shower turned on, Marci went into the bedroom and noted the soiled clothing stuffed in the hamper. "Phew!"

She peeked into the shower and saw the scratches, brush burns, and his severely bruised calf.

"Huh," Marci laughed. "You weren't lying."

Stoned, she sprawled on the sofa and passed out cold.

In the middle of the night Bradley Lindum woke, booted his laptop, and accessed Jennifer Dink's wireless connection. He chatted with cyber friends from other parts of the country. One asked about the hurricane.

"What hurricane?" Brad typed.

A friend sent a link to the NOAA Hurricane Center that told a Category 5 hurricane was coming his way.

Brad loaded the link his friend suggested. Bold fonts showed the lowest pressure reading ever recorded with wind speeds approaching 300 miles an hour. Bradley thought the spinning clouds looked cool.

Spins like a toilet. Do hurricanes spin in the opposite direction below the equator?

A bright red warning banner flashed on the screen calling for an immediate evacuation of Tampa Bay. It never dawned on him to wake his parents because they lived in New Port Richey. That wasn't Tampa Bay.

When morning came Marci's head felt like a chunk of lead anchored to the sofa cushion. Overhead the ceiling fan spun. The air-conditioning had kicked on but hadn't cooled the house yet. Outside, a blustery, rain-laden southwest wind pounded the home at intermittent intervals.

For a split second she thought yesterday was a bad dream.

Kathleen Lindum called. "Moo . . . aawm, I'm sweating."

Marci's head throbbed. "Do I need this?"

Kathleen groaned. "It's hot. I can't sleep. Did Daddy come home last night?"

"He did," Marci said. She waited for the next question.

"Why didn't you wake me? I need a cell phone to call my friends. I need to call the school district and tell them we need our homecoming tonight."

Marci ignored her daughter. There was no good answer.

In the bedroom Robbie snored. Marci shook him. "Rob . . . Robbie, get up."

He opened eyes. "Is the electricity on?"

"Yes, but it can go out at any time."

"Just great," Robbie said.

"Rob, what are we going to do?"

"What do you mean, Marci?"

"You don't know yet, do you?"

"About what?"

"I wasn't kidding when I said there's a blackout. The government is rationing electricity."

Robbie bolted upright.

"Should we evacuate?" she asked.

"I don't know," he answered.

Still frazzled about the alligator incident, Robbie didn't feel right.

"Rob, we need to prepare—like the Peltzes and Dinks. The President said we will only have power for a few hours."

"Let me take a shower first," said Robbie. He went into the bathroom, tended his cuts and scratches, and examined his discolored calf. *Why aren't there puncture marks?*

Anxious, Marci went back to the television.

. . . Hurricane Kate is 150 miles south southwest of Bradenton. Last night Kate's direction shifted, folks. It looks like this monster storm is heading right into the mouth of Tampa Bay.

. . . An evacuation has been ordered. However, we doubt very seriously anyone will be able to leave by now. There are many reports of intersections riddled with debris from accidents caused by the prolonged power outage.

. . . We are in crisis. A devastating hurricane is bearing down on us. Let's pray it veers away. Forecasters say the likelihood is nil.

Listening, Robbie sat there in shock. "No, this can't be! Why weren't we warned?" He tried to reason. "We are five miles inland. I don't think a surge will reach us. The wind is a greater concern."

Robbie pointed at the evacuation information at the bottom of the screen. "Do you think we should evacuate?"

"We can't," Marci said. "Look at the reports scrolling on the bottom. The interstates are jammed and shut down. "Perhaps we should head to a shelter."

He shook his head. "This is too much stress, I can't handle this."

. . . President Clinton.

. . . First, I want to apologize to all you brave Americans who endured the blackout last night. Thank you, and rest assured our country and Congress are reacting swiftly to the crisis in Iraq.

. . . Our Secretary of Defense is working on a plan to restore the flow of oil. For now, I must mandate every drop of oil be preserved. We do not see a solution on the foreseeable horizon. We must remain diligent, tempered, and strong. I assure you we are doing everything possible.

. . . Now, I want to mention Florida, where Hurricane Kate will make landfall sometime tomorrow. This is the biggest, most devastating hurricane ever seen in modern times. Right now, we are stationing the National Guard in Jacksonville. FEMA is right now

preparing. We don't want to go into the hurricane's path until we know where it will make landfall. I don't want to put anyone in harm's way.

. . . And finally, anyone with military orders should be on their way to their respective units and staging areas.

Marci flipped the channel. "What about the strategic oil reserves? Can't Hillary use those to help us?"

Ironically, Marci's question was answered.

. . . In other news, there's talk coming from Mississippi the sudden blackout is because President Clinton had ordered the strategic oil reserves drawn down months ago.

. . . Sources say President Clinton demanded that a large portion of the reserves be sold to fund her healthcare and greenhouse initiatives.

Chapter 27

Dale Carter shoved his forearm into the sleeve of his dark green army parka. He didn't need a television to tell him the hurricane was approaching. Each wind gust told him the direction and intensity. His home, the Icehouse, was secure. He wasn't afraid.

"Now that Momma's with the Lord, she'll keep the Flats folk safe," he said as the wind tormented his parka. He loved the fury, the commotion—the closeness of the low-hanging cloud layer. And somehow, the blackening of the daylight gathered his deep sorrow and stuffed it somewhere else.

Walking slowly, considering the hurricane's aftermath, Dale came to a stand of ancient live oaks. It was his favorite place. The sprawling banyan tree his father made him practice on before he notched the cedar spike had healed and grown thick.

Dale maneuvered the tight maze of the suffocating banyan that laced its tentacles amongst the oaks. He ducked under a massive horizontal limp and came to an opening where a buckled root snaked like a gargantuan anaconda toward the base of the oldest oak. Like a playful child he stepped onto the heaving bulge, balanced, and neatly walked along the feeder root.

All around, leis of Spanish moss silently swayed. Dale batted the soft moss, remembering as a child how he'd shimmy the limps and snip the stringy gray lace letting them drop. He'd bunch them into a spongy natural mattress then lie for hours waiting for the sea breeze to deliver the cranes and elegant herons to roost the craggy limbs. Within the canopy a chatter of red squirrels would give chase, leaping fearlessly, running headfirst straight-down the trunks. They'd mate and tend their young. And when it rained, it was the best of all. A mighty variety of tropical wildlife took refuge in great numbers all around him—the leafy umbrella of the great oaks wielding respite, keeping the ground cover dry.

Sitting like a king with his arm on the root that crawled across the earth, Dale traced his finger along an inscription cut into the bark many years ago. He closed his eyes and drifted into his pleasantly sad memory.

He only knew her first name. It was Jodi. Young Dale Carter had discovered her comfortably resting at the base of the live oak he loved to sit within to watch the wildlife arrive for the night.

Barely sixteen and smothered in rusty freckles, Jodi had offered him a welcoming smile. "You know there's plenty of room," she said, patting the flattened moss mattress.

Instantly, Dale was taken by her lively grin and quick invite. Though Flats girls behaved that way, his mother never allowed him near them. But with Jodi, there was this urge that arrived within, and a natural curiosity to engage.

Lifting her brilliant blue eyes, she asked his name.

"It's Buck," Dale responded.

"Is that your real name?"

"No, but it will do."

Quickly they became friends, and for a short time occupied each other's life. Each morning they'd meet at the oak then head to explore the Gulf. To Dale, it seemed the ocean intrigued Jodi, with its intricate maze of tidal flows, reedy grasses, squiggling mullet clouds, and lumbering sea turtles. They made a raft from truck tire tubes stolen from his mother's junkyard and pretended to be conquering pirates by paddling to Stony Lonesome Key, where they captured imaginary pirates with a make-believe army of stone crabs, dive-bombing herons, and scouting dolphins. They played, shucked scallops, cracked crabs, and swam with migrating manatees in chilly freshwater springs. And blossomed that summer into young adults.

It was within the oak's root enclave on a mattress of Spanish moss that Jodi offed her swimsuit. Mesmerized by her beauty and outgoing disposition, and drawn by a manifested urge he'd never known, Dale made clumsy love, and became a young man.

But the next morning and several more, Jodi failed to meet him. He was heartbroken.

Staring at the name cut into the bark, he sighed. It'd been a while since he'd been with a woman. Hudson gals were tough, rough, a lot like Chadda and Fifty-Cal—unfinished and not to his liking. The desperate women of Trinity Meadows that secretively pawned in his shop, how soft and desirable they were, like Jodi. With full lips and shimmering hair they seemed so supple, intellectual, deprived, and yearning.

He traced the apertures of the letters and remembered Jodi's womanly warmth. Sadly, he wiped away the length of a lonely tear.

Chapter 28

A molting raccoon rummaged the trash that spilled from a Dumpster behind Gator Tales. The masked bandit alerted and darted through a hole in the lattice that skirted the porch. Walking the length Dale entered through a screen door, crossed the herringbone dance floor, and sat at the bar directly in front of his closest friend, Flatch.

Andrew "Flatch" Hachem, the bartender, had an ostrich neck that jutted forward, like it had broken at the base of his skull and rehealed that way. Two large buck teeth punched out like a finch's beak. Borne from Gibsonton carnies, the nomadic man was the legitimate child of freak show actors.

Flatch was Dale's confidant. Both were homeschooled and well-read, something their parents made sure. Flatch never discussed their private conversations or personal business with anyone else. That's why Dale trusted him. And when Dale felt low, Flatch sensed it.

Gator Tales was the focal point for most Cabbage Ears tenants. It was the place where Dale passed along his orders to the Flats folks. And it was from behind the speed-rack and rinse-sink that Flatch tactfully relayed those orders.

"Andy?" asked Dale, accepting a beer. "We need to get word out lickity split. Can you help?"

"Always, Dale," said Flatch, dunking a soapy glass while scanning the bar to make sure no one was nursing a drink.

"Cabbage Ears tenants, tell them to move out before tomorrow's nightfall. Tell them to move into the cars and buses near the top of the strippin' hole. The surge won't reach there."

With busy hands Flatch listened.

"They should store their stuff in the junk cars and prepare to stay awhile. And once the hurricane passes, we must get Hoinky's flea market up and runnin', ASAP."

"Why the flea market?" Flatch asked.

"It's no good if we give away the food and supplies Momma got stored in the junkyard," Dale said. "Gotta make the Krackers work for it through barter."

Wringing his washcloth, Flatch flopped the dishrag onto the bar top and wiped in a circular motion.

Dale sipped his beer. "If they're willing to work and not be lazy like they are, they'll eat and bargain whatever they scrounge."

Nodding, Flatch had to agree. Krackers were difficult to motivate, even on their best days.

"Makes sense," Flatch said. "Was that your mother's idea?"

"Yes, that's why she started the junkyard. All those vehicles are stuck in the dirt with the axles rooted down. It's the best place to ride out the hurricane. Anything Momma collected had a purpose . . . Ya know, to survive the big one."

She's got shit stored in just about every piece of junk out there. Plus, she's been preaching for the longest time how it should be done."

"Guess this is a bad one, hain't it, Dale?"

Dale looked at Andy and nodded.

Andy saw something else on Dale's mind. And could tell when he'd been to the banyan. He was reeling from his mother's death. She was his closest friend.

"Sorry, Dale," Flatch said. "You miss her, don't ya?"

"Life ain't fair to take away the most important person and leave you all alone," Dale said.

Flatch reached into the cooler and set another beer in front of Dale. The amber bottle quickly gathered moisture.

He bent over the bar and whispered, "Are you going to be okay?"

"My shell's as tough as an armadillo," Dale said. "Ain't no ghostly buzzard going to poke a hole in me. I know it was Momma's time. But Jodi, where'd she go? She was to be mine for a good long time. I don't know if I can replace that feeling, ever."

Flatch listened patiently. Dale often lamented about Jodi, her sudden disappearance, and where he might search to find her.

"Now that Momma's gone, it's gotten worse," Dale confessed.

Staring blankly, he picked at the soggy label. "Andy, make things happen in the morning so people are safe. Circulate word, living won't be the same after Sunday for a good while."

"Sure wish Monkey Wrench was here," Dale said. "I'm going to need those mechanical smarts of his." Dale had been working for some time on the bigger picture. "The hospital must be up and running. We need Monk, Andy. He's crafty and can figure the tough problems. Momma wanted a hospital opened after the 'cane smacks us. She said the Bippinotti Clinic is the perfect spot, cuz it's close by."

"Monk's on his way. And sure as shittin' will get here." Walking the bar, Flatch emptied ashtrays, tossed glasses into the wash sink, and hand mopped the gloss surface again.

"He sure will," Dale said. "I'm not too worried, just wished I had it off my mind. Taking care of the docs concerns me. I'm gotta bribe them foreigners with food, supplies, gas, and electricity to keep them around."

Tilting the beer bottle, Dale pointed the nozzle toward the upright cooler. "Another beer, Andy."

When dawn came Dale went to Cabbage Ears and let himself into Critter's grungy trailer. Dozer, Critter's vicious dog, lay there. Only Dale was permitted to approach.

"Come on, Crits, I need you."

Groggy, Critter rolled from bed.

"What's up, Dale? Why so early?"

"Hurricane will be here tomorrow morning. We need to prepare. It's going to be a long day."

The Chewbacca-looking character crawled from his disheveled bed and lit a cigarette. Dale dug out Critter's raincoat and tossed it. "Put on your rubber boots and let's go."

The intensity of the ocean-borne wind had strengthened. The high tide that flooded Cabbage Ears had arrived and never left.

"I want you to park the fuel trucks on top of the hill but not too close to the quarry hole. I don't want them getting blowed in. Set the water buffalos there too, so the fresh water don't get contaminated by the surge. Put them so the water pipes run downhill," Dale instructed.

The windshield wipers of Critter's pickup smeared like grease. Struggling to see, Critter set his chin over the steering wheel. "Dale, you got this all figured out, hain't ya?"

"All in my head."

"The cabbage heads are lucky to have you." Critter negotiated a large puddle and arrived at the top of the quarry.

"Here are the keys to the vehicles I want you to move. When you are done head to the pawnshop. In the attic are generators. Bring them down so Fifty-Cal can load them onto the flatbed."

"Why can't Fifty-Cal get the generators herself? That Amazonian is strong enough to hoist two at one time."

"You lazy bastard," Dale said. "Go back to the Patch and ask Fifty-Cal yourself?"

"I don't think so," Critter said. "Last night she brought home a snookered stripper and ain't left the trailer yet. If I interrupt Fifty-Cal, she's liable to blow my head off."

"If not your grizzly noggin, it'll be your ball-sack and connected pecker." Both Dale and Critter laughed.

"You know damn well Fifty-Cal don't like to be bothered when she's pokin' with a woman," said Dale. "If we let her be, she won't be so shit-ass miserable later on. I need Fifty-Cal on her toes during the hurricane to keep an eye out for that bastard Deuce and uninvited stragglers."

"Fifty-Cal don't like jarhead Deuce, does she?" Critter asked.

"No, she don't. That's why it's Fifty-Cal's job to make sure Deuce don't make trouble by selling his clear whiskey and passing any Oxycodone he got his grubby paws on."

It took Critter most of the morning to reposition the buses and remove the backseats to make sleeping quarters for trailer park tenants. He hitched the water buffalos and hauled them uphill into position. He unlocked and inspected several shipping containers stuffed with military rations that somehow arrived from Mac Dill Air Force Base—a present Monkey Wrench had something to do with before he shipped off to Iraq.

Dale inspected the undercarriages of each car and spray-painted fluorescent orange circles on the ones he thought wouldn't blow away.

"They's ain't going nowhere," Dale said, unjamming a car door.

"What if we got to take a dump?" Critter asked. "Can't crap any old place. Who knows where them turds end up if they get caught in a surge?"

"Everyone shits in the quarry pit. That's why I bought a load of surplus sewer pipes months back." Dale gave Critter a serious look.

"Can't we use port-o-potties, Dale?"

"Go ahead and try, you stupid Fig Newton. Wind will blow the damn potties around like a manure spreader. You need to build shit sluices."

"Shit what?" Critter seemed puzzled.

"You know, sluices . . . pissin' aqueducts," Dale said. "Take the sewer piping and dig a trench with that Kubota we got. Angle the pipes into the strippin' hole so it hangs over the lagoon enough. Make sure the trench is deep, Critter, so the wind don't blow the piping loose. Cut the tops to forty-five degrees and sand the burrs. It'll work as a toilet just fine. And tell the cabbage heads that when they're done shittin' to dump a bucket of water to wash the turds all the way through."

Dale and Critter looked into the caustic blue water of the limestone pit.

"Make several trenches," Dale said.

"Gonna need an extra big pipe for Chadda." Critter couldn't resist the sarcasm.

"Tell everyone if they don't listen and follow the rules, Fifty-Cal will chuck them from the junkyard." Dale was serious. It was common knowledge no one defied his orders. There were no second chances. Double-cross Dale and you were banished like he'd done to Deuce.

By noon Flatch started banging on the trailers, telling tenants that before dark they must move into Dale's junkyard and find themselves a comfortable spot to ride out the hurricane. And assured Dale would care for them all.

Within an hour everyone living in Cabbage Ears knew what to do. Krackers abandoned their scrappy units. Families with noisy children packed essentials, went to the junkyard, and picked a vehicle to hunker in. If they had several children Dale or Critter assigned them to a station wagon or minivan—mother and father or whatever in the front seat, kids in the middle, and clothing in the rear. Guns, pets, reptiles, and pit bulls stayed in pickups; that way everyone knew where the danger was. The lawfully disabled, wheelchair diabetics, and "prego ones" like Chadda were housed in RVs or sturdy kaki military buses.

"Make sure there are no snakes living in them buses," Dale warned. "You don't want to suck venom during the storm."

Chapter 29

The relationship between Critter and Chadda was an odd one. Often, they fought like alley cats. At other times Critter looked after her like a big brother. Always, he kept a watchful eye on her boys, Samson, Buddy, and Artie, portraying a grizzly bear behavior to set some fear in them to minimize the trouble the lads typically got into. And it didn't take long for them to make trouble. He'd caught them rolling M-80s through the shitter pipes and watching them plop into the lagoon and explode like miniature depth charges.

Critter arrived at Chadda's trailer. "Come on, Chadda, Dale assigned ya the best Airstream in the yard." Critter frowned; her trailer smelled like moldy rugs.

Sitting in her La-Z-Boy, Chadda ate from a cereal bowl set onto her bulging stomach. "Don't make any smart-ass remarks Critter, I'm pregnant. It's the only way I can eat these days."

Playing a card game in the back bedroom were her sons.

"Boys, help your mother get packed," Critter ordered.

They didn't listen.

Stepping further into the dingy trailer Critter set his hands on his hips and blocked the hallway.

The cooped lads had destroyed the place and weren't buying Critter's nasty snarl.

Growing impatient and knowing the boys wouldn't listen, Critter scooped and bear-hugged all three lads. They wiggled and squirmed and cursed him profusely. But Critter was too strong and carried them from inside the trailer to the dock behind Fifty-Cal's trailer.

"Who wants to take a swim? Or are you boys going to help your mother?"

Samson, the oldest and boldest, laughed. "You ain't got the balls, sissy."

Dropping Buddy and Artie, Critter walked to the end of the dock and without hesitation tossed the brazen brut into the canal.

"Ah shit," yelled Samson, smacking at the saltwater to stay afloat.

Artie and Buddy raced to the trailer and started helping their mother pack.

"Samson," Critter said. "You ain't getting on dry land until you agree to help your momma."

Samson disappeared beneath the surface.

Wonder who this lad's father is, thought Critter. He's mean and looks like that pervert Deuce. Betcha the little shit is his.

Suddenly, Samson's shaved head emerged at the base of the dock. He flung a scallop, barely missing Critter's head.

Ducking, Critter quickly grabbed an oar and shoved Samson further away.

"Learn your lesson yet, Sammy girl?"

Samson snatched the oar blade and jerked it. Critter lost his balance, tripped on a lifted plank, and tumbled into a mat of red mangroves.

"Damn you, Samson."

Turtled-up with his ass soaking in the seawater, Critter struggled. And when he crawled from the prickly bush, Samson was long gone.

Chapter 30

Hurricane Kate Arrives

Hurricane forecast expert Doctor Paola Estrada gnawed on the plastic shaft of her pen. The petite, over-caffeinated Hispanic had barely slept in the last three days. She clicked the pen several times and when it jammed, threw it at the wall. For the first time in her thirteen-year career predicting the track of hurricanes for the Miami Tropical Prediction Center she found herself dead wrong. And now needed to explain the mistake to gulf coast governors and a host of city mayors and emergency officials.

"I thought that weak cold front would drop further south and swing westward toward Louisiana and suck Kate through the center of the Gulf of Mexico," said Estrada, speaking into a camera.

She shook her head in disbelief. "Often weather behaves like the fog in a witch's brew. We know lots about the jet stream and can predict atmospheric changes with reasonable accuracy. But sometimes air currents get knotted and don't behave as predicted. That's what happened to the hurricane you are looking at on your monitors.

"The Prediction Center has always held that hurricanes are unpredictable, no matter how sure we are. The public got too comfortable with our accuracy to assess where it will strike, thanks to sophisticated models we use these days.

"For me, this is a first. I missed it a whole bunch," Estrada said. "Unfortunately, with the most destructive hurricane ever recorded."

Paola paused, straightened her tight blouse, lifted another pen, and nervously tapped the keyboard. "Hurricane Kate will veer east and score a direct hit on Tampa Bay."

The bug-eyed officials taking part in the net-meeting didn't blame the saucy, smartly dressed meteorologist. They too, knew how difficult it was to judge a hurricane's path and agreed the public had gotten too comfortable.

Mesmerized by the burning multicolored picture of the massive, rotating cyclone two hundred miles off the Florida coast, the group listened. All eyes were locked on the satellite images taken an hour ago, at sunset. Kate made a turn eastward and threatened Tampa Bay.

"We can't wish it away," said the tough Florida governor, Albert Simon. "You folks in Tampa are caught with your britches down. And that shit happening in the Middle East ain't helping either," his voice bellowed.

Doctor Estrada interrupted him. "Clearwater. . . Kate will strike Clearwater, Florida, early Sunday morning. Winds will exceed three hundred miles an hour."

Gasps came from the computer speakers. "Is that wind speed possible?"

Paola slipped from her chair and made short, deliberate strides across the operation center to a large map. Using the mouse pointer she described the revised hurricane track. "Yes, it is possible. In less than thirty-six hours the eye-wall will breach and disintegrate the barrier island of Belleair Shores."

She allowed her words to settle then continued. "The cyclone's core, the part that does the most damage spans one-hundred twenty-five miles. And if you recall, Hurricane Katrina's core was half that size. Expect total devastation as far north as Horse Island near Hudson, and as far south as Bradenton."

"Are you sure about landfall?" Governor Simon asked.

"Yes," Estrada answered. "Five minutes before this meeting we received an update from the hurricane hunter aircraft flying out of the Clearwater Coast Guard station. The pilot reported they were halfway through the second grid of their run and aborted the mission. It was too violent; they almost lost the aircraft. But we did manage to receive some critical data."

Tampa Mayor Pamela Tollhouse interrupted. "Any chance their readings were incorrect?"

"No chance, Mayor, several gusts clocked over three hundred miles an hour quite a distance from the eye-wall. And the barometric pressure dipped below 800 milibars."

"Shhyiit!" In his prolonged southern drawl the governor cursed into his microphone.

Everyone was nervous, except for the New Orleans mayor and Louisiana governor. They looked relieved now that their states were no longer in the bull's eye.

"Tinky, what's going on across the bay in Saint Petersburg?" Governor Simon asked.

Leroy "Tinky" Tinkerton, Saint Petersburg's mayor, spoke in his slow orator's voice. "Y'all know Washington screwed us. The blackouts gotta stop so we can get the traffic signals working to evacuate people." The stubble-faced, very obese politician grimaced then shook his head. "The Pinellas County Emergency Center issued evacuation orders for Zone-A residence, which turned into pure chaos when the stoplights suddenly went dead. Our bridges and intersections are gridlocked. No way can we fix that mess before Kate slams us."

"People will drown—lots of them."

"I guess you won't evacuate Zone-B and some of Zone-C, will you?" the governor asked Tinky.

Paola Estrada's confident voice interrupted them. "Evacuate all zones! That means C and D too."

"That's the entire Bay Area, more than three million people!" someone said.

"Impossible!" Mayor Tinkerton responded.

Paola stared at the computer camera. Her face was serious. "Tampa Bay will get sandblasted and shredded, Governor, particularly north of the city. Mayors, your communities will get leveled. A surge will breach and undermine barrier islands and swallow your coastal municipalities. What's left will get backwashed and sucked into the Gulf of Mexico. And once Kate pushes through nothing will be left."

There was a deadening, nuclear silence.

Patrick Johnson, director of the Levy County EOC, studied the people sitting in the room with Doctor Estrada. It was like a scene in the movie he saw as a child, *The China Syndrome*—the reactor control room, the tension thick, visions of Hiroshima on their faces. He'd thought this stuff only happened in movies. It didn't.

The governor addressed the Levy director, who was the most experienced natural disaster person in the group. "Patrick, you're the expert, what's the plan?"

"The one you don't want to hear about is Plan Black, Governor— a strategic response to a catastrophic hurricane event," Patrick said.

"Or perhaps we should call it Black Sabbath, since Kate will strike on Sunday."

Patrick Johnson continued. "If you recall the governor's Hurricane Conference in Fort Lauderdale last May, keynote speaker Al Gore said, with the advent of global warming it was likely we'd see a storm this size within the next decade."

As a strategic response we developed a COOP called Plan Black, don't you remember? Y'all pooh-poohed the idea, saying it was wasted money to plan for such an improbable event. Fortunately, FEMA took Gore's observation seriously and developed one."

"We can't undo the past," said Tinkerton. "Now, what the hell is this Doomsday Plan?"

"All government, including fire, police, paramedic, must pull back to a predetermined location, out of harm's way. Once the storm passes, we'll work our rescue inward, mile by mile. And don't bother contracting someone to deliver body bags. Any corpses we cross must be burned, like they did in medieval times during the plague," said a confident Patrick Johnson.

"You thought this out, didn't you?" Governor Simon said.

"Unfortunately, I did, sir."

"That's why you're onboard, Patrick. Are there any more questions?"

They all looked at the live picture of Hurricane Kate and its eastward movement. In the short time it took to conduct the meeting, a definite direction took shape. The last three frames of satellite photos showed the hurricane heading for Tampa.

"Are you serious about Plan Black, is that all we have?" the Pasco County Commissioner asked.

Patrick responded. "I assure you, commissioner, we considered every possible alternative, including using cruise ships to house stranded residents. In fact, that's the plan we have for Miami but it won't work in Tampa. The mouth of Tampa Bay will clog with sand. Oceans channels as far as ten miles out won't be navigable because of the uncertain depth. You'll have grounded ships all over the place if you attempt it."

"Let's move on with this conversation." The Florida governor didn't want to waste any more time.

"Doctor Estrada, is there any glimmer of hope? Can you give us your best guess where this hurricane will go once it strikes?"

"Yes, Albert. And it's not a guess." Paola and the governor were more than good friends. She'd gotten her job years ago after sleeping with the married governor during an economic summit in Panama.

"My new forecast says there's a ninety-five percent chance that Kate will make landfall near Clearwater, head inland, then bear north. The steering currents are weak, though. Kate will move slow, taking at least two more days to move on. The damage in Pasco County will be catastrophic," she said.

"Doctor Estrada"—The mayor professionalized Paola's name on purpose—"Don't tease us with this five-percent uncertainty."

"Governor, Kate will curve north at some point. What we don't know is how far inland she will push, perhaps to Orlando before it turns. What we do know is this monster cyclone will suck along its own path like a vacuum cleaner, not necessarily following the steering winds."

"Can you be clearer, Doctor? We should end this meeting."

"Sure. Kate will loop around and exit back into the Gulf Mexico, somewhere north of Tampa, probably near Cedar Key. The five percent is the chance it turns before it hits land." Doctor Estrada batted her large Latino eyes. "Frankly, folks, I don't see that happening."

Florida's governor, Albert Simon, gave his order. "Patrick, you're in charge. Activate Plan Black Sabbath—Pronto!"

Chapter 31

The lanai screening chattered like a thick thumb flicking through a stiff deck of playing cards. Peering out the kitchen window, Robbie Lindum watched the bald cypresses oscillate in peduncular wags. His backyard neighbor, George Ying, spun wing nuts to fasten his hurricane shutters. Swinging a mallet he pounded plastic green stakes into the Floratam to anchor his delicate papaya and mango trees. His wife, Olivia, plucked unripe fruit, gathered vegetables, and loaded box after box, stockpiling their harvest inside the garage.

"Boy," Robbie said. "George and Olivia sure are busy bees. They certainly look prepared."

Disgusted, Marci flung her head side to side. Her slug of a husband reacted with such faint urgency and neglected to consider the hurricane may come this way.

How will I care for my attic crop if everyone is around all the time? she thought. The plants will need a good trimming to last several days without constant attention.

Everyone must leave for a few hours, she decided.

"Robbie, why don't you try to get Kathleen another cell phone? I know it's a crazy idea, but maybe that'll muzzle her. Besides, you need to get the minivan that's stuck at Home Depot and retrieve Kathleen's car from the high school."

"Good idea," Robbie said. "Perhaps I can use that bullheaded attitude of hers to get some supplies too."

"I sure hope so, Robbie. We are totally unprepared."

"I know, Marci," Robbie said. "If we need to, we'll head to the hurricane shelter tonight. After all, isn't that why we pay property taxes? About time we get some benefit."

"If we need to!" Marci leaped from the sofa ran to the kitchen counter and glared at her husband. "You don't get it, do you?"

Kathleen Lindum burst from the bathroom and jerked her father's arm. "Come on, Dad, let's get my cell phone. Then take me to my car and gas it up."

Robbie stared at his daughter. She was big-boned like her mother but thicker. Where'd she get that bullheaded attitude? Certainly not from his family tree.

"Kathleen, get Brad, he's going with you," Marci said. "Get him away from that computer for a while."

When Brad heard Kathleen coming, he jumped from the bed.

The door burst open. "Get dressed, pee brain, you're coming with Dad and I." Kathleen snickered. She'd caught him shirtless with one leg stuffed in his khaki shorts.

Brad knew what the snicker meant because Kathleen busted on him all the time. Her scoff suggested he hadn't gone through puberty yet—the underlying message was, guys she knew had body hair. "Bradley, you're scrawny, like Dad."

Ten minutes later Robbie exited Trinity Meadows and turned onto Perrine Ranch Road. Debris littered the roadway.

Fidgeting, kicking the door panel, and flipping the locks, Kathleen blurted, "Homecoming should have happened last night. I need my phone, Dad. Can we go to the Verizon store first?"

No cell phone. She's not a happy camper, thought Robbie.

"We'll go," answered Robbie, even though he felt an urgency to rescue the minivan and board the windows somehow. There wasn't much time to solve those problems. But if he didn't try to placate Kathleen, she'd make life miserable. His seventeen-year-old didn't understand their predicament—no amount of explaining would help.

Robbie wondered where Marci went wrong with his daughter. How could she have mismanaged Kathleen's upbringing? His son, Brad, was the complete opposite, more like him, quiet, well-mannered, poised.

Traffic on Highway 19 had thinned. It seemed the coastal residents had evacuated already. Robbie believed Hurricane Kate might come close, but would ultimately miss. They always veered and headed somewhere else at the last minute, he surmised.

The Publix on Marine Parkway was open, which affirmed his suspicion the hurricane may not be coming. "Good old reliable Publix." He made a mental note to backtrack and get whatever supplies he could after he solved Kathleen's problem.

"The Port Richey Verizon store across from Gulf View Mall should be open," Robbie said, afraid to suggest it might be closed. He'd deal with that when he pulled into the parking lot. The store wasn't that far, and should only use about twenty minutes of his time. Well worth it.

Moments later they arrived.

"Shit, it's closed!" blasted Kathleen after seeing the posted sign.

Robbie squirmed. He heard her teeth grinding.

Kathleen slammed her fist into the dash. . . *Wump!* . . . "Damn it, I want to text my friends to find out what's going on with homecoming."

Robbie shook his head in despair. Was she that clueless?

Slouching, Brad wanted to be invisible.

"Dad, there's a cell phone place at Hoinky's Flea Market. Take me!"

"No, Kathleen, I won't. I can't spare the gas, nor the time."

Kathleen whipped her head toward her father. With stiff arms she casted a convulsing, Medusa snarl. Holding her breath she cramped her face into a wrinkly knot. White-knuckled, she turned bloodred and looked about to explode.

Scrunching in the backseat, Bradley squinted. He'd never seen her so enraged. She couldn't release her frustration.

"If I try to find you a cell phone, Kathleen, I won't be able to get your car from the high school," said Robbie with a grim, defeated look. Shaking his head, he said. "No—I'm not taking you to the flea market."

Suddenly, Kathleen eyes diverted. Movement behind the store's plate-glass window drew her attention. "Someone's inside." Immediately she exited the car, darted through the rain, and pounded on the glass. "Open up, I'm desperate!"

The ghostly figure inside ignored her. Kathleen scowled at the shadow, thinking if the image saw her determination it would come and unlock the front door. Then she realized the shadow was a looting intruder.

Drenched, she dashed back to the car and pounded on Robbie's window. "Dad, get the police. Someone broke into the Verizon store. They'll call the owner to come back to the store."

"I don't have time for this. Besides, the police are doing more important stuff." He didn't want to get involved. "I'll flag down the first policeman we see," he told her.

Standing outside, Kathleen folded her arms and let the rain beat on her.

Robbie lowered the window. "Let's go and get your car."

Kathleen thought for a second. *If I have my car I can do as I please. I'll go to the flea market myself.*

Minutes later they arrived at Trinity Meadows High School. The rain let up. Robbie had brought a plastic gas can used to fill the riding mower he rarely used and emptied it into Kathleen's tank. He told her to go directly home.

Gathering her purse, she jumped into her Mustang. Fortunately, the battery had recharged enough to turn over the engine. She drove off, turning left onto Little Road instead of taking a right, like she was supposed to do.

Robbie shook his head. "Why does this have to happen? Damn hurricane."

Driving back toward the open Publix he stopped at an intersection where a policeman directed traffic.

"Dad, look at all those fire trucks, ambulances, and police cars coming this way."

An endless line of yellow, red, blue, and white flickering lights came toward them, turned, and headed east, inland.

"Why so many?" Brad asked.

"Not sure," Robbie said. "They're heading for where the hurricane will hit. That's a good sign. It must not be coming here."

It took nearly twenty minutes for the convoy to clear.

"Dad," Brad said. "I counted over a hundred vehicles."

After trimming her thriving pot plants Marci tactfully sprinkled the leftover leaves and stems around the backyard to disguise them within the brush that blew in from the cypress head behind the Peltzes' house.

By midafternoon Robbie had returned. The weather had gotten worse.

"Where's Kathleen?" Marci asked.

"I don't know. I told her to go straight home."

Marci couldn't blame Robbie for not exerting enough authority. No one could, not even her.

Suddenly, a robust wind gust shook the house for several seconds. The ceiling fans swayed. The miters on the crown molding separated then resealed. Something solid whacked the front door.

"Guess, we better head to the shelter," Robbie said.

"Rob, shouldn't we wait as long as possible for Kathleen?"

"The shelter is near the high school," he said. "Her life revolves around that place. No doubt we'll find her there if she doesn't come soon."

Outside the wind howled.

"Bradley," Marci said. "Go pack what you want to take with you to keep occupied at the hurricane shelter. Make sure you pack nice clothes, not just shorts and T-shirts."

"For how long?" Brad asked.

"Not sure, perhaps overnight. Robbie, do we have enough money?"

Suddenly, Robbie remembered that his reimbursement check had arrived.

"Oh, I should deposit my check in the ATM on the way to the shelter."

He went into the den and picked up the Feldon envelope. "Hmm, there's more than a check inside."

Charlie padded over and begged for attention.

"Holy crap!" screamed Robbie, realizing something.

"What's wrong?" said Marci, wheeling a suitcase from the bedroom.

"Charlie! What are we going to do about Charlie? Hurricanes shelters don't allow pets." Perplexed, Robbie thought for a moment.

"I guess we'll put some food in a bowl and lock him in the laundry room."

"Oh, no, you're not!" Marci said firmly. "I don't want that mutt inside my home alone. He squats on his ass and spins in circles and leaves brown spots on the rug. Charlie can stay in the pool area."

"But what if the lanai blows away?" Robbie said.

"He'll stay in the garage, then," said Marci rolling the suitcase near the garage entry.

"Poor Charlie." Robbie bent down and patted his head.

With a letter opener he sliced the Feldon envelope and looked inside for the check. Fumbling, he removed a folded document.

"Where's the check?"

Packing another suitcase Marci stopped, walked from the bedroom, and tapped her fingernails on the door jamb. "No check?"

"There's a form to complete," said Robbie, unfolding papers. "Something to do with filing a claim on Feldon's . . . bank . . . bankruptcy!"

"What?" He quickly scanned the cover letter.

Dear Employee:
    Feldon Pharmaceuticals has been in business for thirty-four years. However, because of spiraling energy costs, a costly government mandate to provide you with healthcare benefits, and competition from prescription mail-order houses, our company was adversely impacted. Feldon cannot compete and is no longer a going concern.

    Effective immediately your employment is terminated.

    The management at Feldon would like to thank you for your many years of dedicated service, and wish you the best with future endeavors.

"Huh?" Robbie was dumbfounded.

"What is it, Rob?" Marci demanded.

"Fe . . . Feldon went bankrupt and closed its doors. I have no job." He was numb and couldn't move from the desk chair. It was too much to absorb.

Shaking her head Marci walked away. "Now what?" There wasn't enough money in her checking account to cover the next mortgage payment. However, she had stashed several thousand dollars in the attic and figured they could last three months at best.

It didn't take Marci long to deal with the disappointment. The day to consider a divorce arrived. What an odd way for it to happen, she thought. Her comfortable lifestyle was now frail, possibly extinct. As devastating as this was, a change might forge a new direction toward true happiness.

In the background the television blared.

. . . Doctor Paola Estrada at the hurricane center said that Hurricane Kate will make landfall near Clearwater sometime early Sunday morning. Kate is moving slow, at five miles an hour. The Center says once inland, Kate will loop north and exit back into the Gulf of Mexico.

"My goodness, it's a direct hit!" Marci said.

With his head buried in his hands, Robbie moaned and shook his head. "What next? Are we destined to live like Clarence?"

Marci wasn't eager to console him. It'd been a while since she felt capable of mustering a warm emotion toward him. How'd she get like this? she asked herself. There was no compassion for the man she'd married. He'd lost his job. The putz did not deserve it.

"Rob, it's not your fault. You'll find another job. I'm sure of it." She struggled to offer a degree of sympathy.

Defeated, Robbie lifted his head. "Sorry Marci, I'm truly sorry. I've let you down."

"We must go to the shelter. A Category 5 is heading this way," Marci said.

Sniffling, Robbie rubbed his weary eyes.

"Kathleen," Robbie said. "Let's wait a bit longer for her."

. . . We interrupt our continuous coverage of Hurricane Kate with breaking news from our field reporter in Pasco County.

The television screen flickered to the reporter standing on the I-75 overpass. The camera panned a solid swathe of stalled traffic in both directions.

. . . About a half hour ago we saw hundreds of emergency vehicles heading east, away from Kate.

The screen abruptly jumped back to the television anchor. Searching for words, the anchorwoman seemed concerned. Finally, she asked the field reporter if he heard anything else.

I tried to contact the Emergency Center and asked why there was no one to direct traffic. No one answered. I think the emergency crews we saw were evacuating instead of aiding the public . . . They have abandoned us.

Gathering herself, the anchorwoman interjected.

I must caution viewers that our on-the-scene reporter editorialized. Please remain calm. There's been no confirmation regarding emergency officials evacuating.

Standing on the overpass the reporter became angry.

Denise, I report what I see. The interstate is gridlocked. It's too late to evacuate. One would think with a Category 5 hurricane bearing down, firemen and policemen would direct traffic and not retreat.

The screen went black.

Chapter 32

Behind Hoinky's flea market, miniature, wind-driven waves rolled through sifting mangroves. The expansive parking lot on the other side of the leafy hedge had turned into a shallow, choppy lagoon. Parallel wakes trailed behind Kathleen Lindum's Mustang as she circled the flea market searching for a retail stall that sold cell phones.

Abruptly, she jammed the brake pedal. "There it is." The trailing wakes rolled forward, washed into the tailpipe, and stalled the engine.

"Crap!" Kathleen pounded the steering wheel.

As the howling wind rocked her car the tenacious seventeen-year-old twisted the ignition key. It wouldn't start.

"Damn—it's raining and the door's leaking!"

She panned the lot. No one was around. "I'll go inside and borrow a phone and call Dad to come get me."

As she cracked the car door the wind ripped the handle from her grasp and jerked her out. Tumbling, she face-planted into the water.

The rain beat down.

"Shit!" Kathleen spit, coughed, and rolled onto her stomach. As she struggled to stand, another wind gust knocked her onto her rump.

Splash!

"Dammit!"

On her hands and knees Kathleen crawled around the Mustang to the passenger side to block the wind. She snatched her purse from the car seat, leaned into the oncoming wind, and trudged through the shin-deep lake heading for the cluster of interconnected pole buildings . . . Once inside, she bent over and gathered her hair into a ponytail.

Overhead, the corrugated steel roof rattled, buckled, and heaved. Daylight seeped through the Lexan skylights. Seawater filled along the floor cracks, forming rapidly expanding puddles.

In squishy sneakers she walked the maze of corridors searching for a mobile phone stall.

"There it is," Kathleen said. But her face went blank. "Darn, it's locked."

Yanking on the wire gate she tried to squeeze her thick frame through the narrow separation. But there wasn't enough of a gap. She wedged her arm and reached for the display case. *Not even close!* She looked overhead at the barbed wire. It prohibited climbing over. . . After several tries to force the fencing wider, Kathleen conceded. The effort was futile.

"What do I do?" she said, searching for a pay phone—the howling wind echoing along the abandoned corridors.

Tearing a cardboard flap from a carton to cover her head, Kathleen exited the building. She passed a series of rundown garages with stacks of used tires, truck hitches, and rows of used washing machines and refrigerators marked for resale. A lone car passed heading north on Highway 19. A sign with large black lettering— *Carter's Pawn and Gun Shop*—tore from its hinges, took flight and, wrapped a nearby streetlight.

Kathleen ran behind a Dumpster and waited for the battering wind to subside.

After several minutes she crept from the protection and dashed toward the pawnshop. Around the corner of the building was a camouflaged military truck with its engine knocking. Kathleen heard thumps and sliding boxes.

"Someone's here," she said, making her way toward the truck. "It's a pawnshop. They gotta have a pay phone."

A woman wearing a black skull-and-crossbones muscle shirt stretched over broad tattooed shoulders hoisted crated generators onto the truck bed.

"Can you help me?" asked Kathleen, approaching with her wet clothes clinging to her frame. "I need to find a phone."

When Fifty-Cal heard Kathleen's soft voice she stopped and walked to the tailgate. Below stood a pale, black-haired girl soaked head to toe.

"What are you doing here?" Fifty-Cal asked, staring and thinking. *She looks mighty good, soft and tender, and don't have that narrow, angry lady Kracker face. She's spongy, well-fed, and looks like that young Trinity meat that sometime come into the pawnshop.*

"Pay phone?" Fifty-Cal thought for a moment. *No reason to be a toughie. I had a lonely Trinity MILF once, but nothing young like this, yet.*

"Honey, you look lost." Fifty-Cal walked her eyes along the young girl's chunky curves and considered an approach. . . *Maybe?*

"No, I'm not lost. I am looking for a place to buy a cell phone," Kathleen said. "My car's stuck at the flea market. Is there any way you can help me? Doesn't your store have phones?"

"Nah, too much of a hassle, cutie pie. Krackers think because they buy a pawned phone that I gotta service them, too," Fifty-Cal said. "Hain't no money in it."

Shoving her boots into the wood slats that caged the truck bed, Fifty-Cal climbed the gate onto the shingled roof and made her way to the peak. "That your red pony parked over at Hoinky's?"

A jet of tobacco juice arced over the eave and traveled a long way, splattering on the wet sidewalk.

Kathleen lurched back. Her face soured.

"Pony?"

With deliberate downhill stomps Fifty-Cal walked the slant of the roof to edge and peered down at Kathleen. "Mustang. . . ya know. . . your ride."

"Oh yes," Kathleen said. "Can you tow me out?"

"Sweetie, it ain't going nowhere. Wind blowed in from the Gulf and swallowed the entire lot. Lucky you left. Ocean's at the car windows and buried nearly half of Hoinky's. It's a goner, honey. Your pony done drowned."

Kathleen felt befuddled. She couldn't fathom that she was carless. "Can I use your phone?" she asked.

Leaping, she slammed her black army boots onto the wooden truck bed, then onto the concrete. Fifty-Cal eyed Kathleen. *She sure is a thick gal. Nice melons.*

"You ain't a hard-looking gal like the ones here in Hudson," Fifty-Cal remarked. "Yins a Trinity woman, ain't ya?"

"Huh?" Kathleen didn't quite get the question.

This time Fifty-Cal spoke slower. "Where are's you from?"

"I live in Trinity Meadows," Kathleen answered.

"Ah-ha, I knew it!" Fifty-Cal swung her arm into the air and fist-pumped.

"Sweetie, you need to get out of those wet clothes. I'd take you to my trailer to get ya dry and give ya a shot of tequila to warms you, but it's flooded too. This here deuce-and-a-half is my home now, sweet thing. If you get in I'll turn on the heater so you can dry out."

Suddenly, it dawned on Fifty-Cal to ask how old she was.

"Seventeen," Kathleen answered.

Jailbait, thought Fifty-Cal. She's too young to feed alcohol. The women she seduced needed lots of alcohol before they'd loosen and have fun with her. I'm still on probation. This girl could land me in jail again.

Fifty-Cal directed Kathleen to the pay phones on the far side of the building. "On the side of the shop, go call your mommy."

Digging into her purse Kathleen found two quarters and slid them into the coin slot. Hmm, she thought. What's my home phone number? It was programmed into her cell. She was clueless to what it may be.

Kathleen let the phone hang, came back around, and interrupted Fifty-Cal.

"Do you have a phonebook?"

"Hah!" Fifty-Cal laughed. "The Krackers that run telemarketing scams on the old goat snowbirds stole them a long time ago. Phonebooks last fifty seconds round here, honey."

Kathleen paused. She didn't know her friend's phone numbers either—all were preprogrammed into her contact list and identified with a Facebook picture or typed names, not numerals. She hadn't a clue.

"What's wrong, tender teats?"

"I don't know how to get a hold of my friends, or my parents."

"You got a problem, gal. Storm's comin' quick. Don't they teach you memorization at yins uppity school?"

Kathleen looked perplexed.

Fifty-Cal's mood soured. This girl was a typical Trinityette, like the gals that snuck over and pawned their shit at Dale's shop all the time. Clearheaded, they accepted any rotten deal. The cash she got from those idiot women more than covered the cost of the ammunition she shot at Itchy Fingers.

But Fifty-Cal wasn't in the mood to be mean to the shaggitty doll face. She was brazenly cute and looked a lot like herself at age seventeen, but without tattoos.

"Hop in. I'll take you to someone who can help." The gal got no wheels; she'll never make it home, thought Fifty-Cal.

"What do you say, little lady?" Fifty-Cal asked. "If you're from Trinity you ain't goinna make it home before the hurricane hits."

Kathleen looked around. The buildings were boarded and there was no traffic. "I guess I have no choice."

She climbed onto the passenger side running board and tugged the heavy metal door. It was stuck and wouldn't open.

After stuffing a wad of chew behind her cheek Fifty-Cal grabbed hold of the truck mirror and launched her entire body through the driver-side window. Watching Kathleen struggle, she reached across and shoved open the door.

"Woman, you gots to use some muscle. Yank that son-of-a-bitchin' handle like you're trying to rip off your boyfriend's cock, cuz you caught the bastard dipping his dicky doodle into your best friend's cooter."

Dicky Doodle . . . Cooter? It tempted Kathleen to say something, but the oddball dyke was beyond her. This Amazonian wouldn't tolerate her like her parents did.

"Cigarette?" Fifty-Cal offered.

"No, thank you, I don't smoke."

"Have it your way, sister. I like my smokes. Settles me nips when they got a rise." Fifty-Cal looked at Kathleen's sopping wet blouse and blasted a huge smile. "Hey, hey, hey, nice minimarshmallows, they're plumper than mine, ya know."

Sucking her cigarette Fifty-Cal continued to stare. *Better get moving before I do something bad.*

The diesel engine of the deuce-and-a-half rumbled, carbon black exhaust billowed from the stack. The dyke shoved the clutch and forced the truck into first gear. The sturdy cab lurched. The generators slid in their crates until they slammed against the tailgate. Fifty-Cal flicked her cigarette out the window as the deuce-and-a-half rolled across the muddy parking lot. Kathleen clung to the door handle.

"Goin' to take ya to Chadda's trailer," said Fifty-Cal, raising her voice above the growl of the engine.

"Chadda?" questioned Kathleen, bracing.

"Don't worry, Miss Trinity, Chadda won't bite. Least not until she delivers her twins."

Kathleen hadn't a clue what she was saying.

The hard-rubber truck tires bounced upwards over a curb then rolled onto Dixie Highway. The dashboard lifted, the entire windshield filled with the low cloud cover. The generators jumped then slammed down. Fifty-Cal let out a yell. "Yee-haw, I love this shit!

"How yin's doing at Trinity?" asked Fifty-Cal, revving the engine, double-clutching then shifting gears. "Damn big hurricane is coming and going to fuck with you's big time."

"Yeah, it sucks big time," Kathleen said. "Fucking hurricane ruined homecoming."

"Homecoming? . . . Are you nuts, woman! You are a real nincompoop, ain't you? You're going to see dead people for the first time in your life, little lady."

Kathleen snapped her head toward Fifty-Cal. "Dead people?"

"If you ain't gone from Pasco by now, you better have damn good shelter, like we's do at Dale Carter's junkyard. Fucking cars are glued to the ground. Ain't nothin blowin them away."

"Mom and Dad said we might go to the hurricane shelter."

"Goodie for you, this is a motherfucker storm and comin' real soon . . . in the mornin'."

Rolling down her window Fifty-Cal snarled at the fury outside and spit a jet of tobacco juice directly into the crosswind. The maple syrup reversed and came right at Kathleen, barely missing, splattering the window next to her head.

"Yuck!" Kathleen said.

Fifty-Cal smiled. "Shoulda told ya to roll down the friggin' window."

The truck didn't travel far before it left Dixie Highway and made its way, easily managing the windswept terrain to Carter's junkyard.

"We Krackers are survivors," said Fifty-Cal, pointing at the occupied vehicles that suddenly appeared on both sides of the dirt road. "Look at everyone hunkered in them cars. They're holin' up pretty good and will come through this fine, thanks to Dale Carter and his wise old weasel momma, bless her soul. Buried the old goat a few days ago. It's like she brought this hurricane on us for plopping her brittle bones into a grave hole. Going to miss that crotchety lady."

With her muscles flexing Fifty-Cal worked the wheel. "Poor Dale, she was the only gal he had in his life."

As they rode along, the junkyard children played in the rain and splashed in puddles. Beneath suspended tarps, scary-looking adults lounged in removed car seats set downwind against the back bumper. Cigarettes hung from nearly everyone's lip. People trudged alongside the sandy road wearing army-green parkas that flapped in the wind. It's like the tent city in Saint Petersburg, where they house the homeless, thought Kathleen.

"Who's Chadda?" she asked.

"Chadda? . . . She's a big ol' cow with a fat wide ass. Nice gal when she doesn't smell like penguin dung."

Kathleen struggled to understand the dyke's rhetoric. She spoke as if Kathleen knew all these people already.

"Chadda's prego and has the best place in the yard. Squirts rug rats out like Brazilian pepper beans. Dale Carter is her cousin and sees to it she's taken care of."

The deuce-and-a-half passed alongside the Icehouse. Fifty-Cal beeped the horn then hastened to the top of the quarry, where the horizon abruptly disappeared. Kathleen cringed. "Look out, there's a cliff."

Fifty-Cal's biceps quivered and strained. The massive piece of wartime machinery yawed, nearly leaning onto its side. Stones kicked from under the tires. The cargo shifted. "Yee—haw." Fifty-Cal displayed an ear-wide grin. Brown juice dribbled down her chin. The vehicle slid around the sharp curve and bounced down onto all four tires.

"Fuck!" Kathleen fanned her face. "That scared the shit out of me."

"Trinity nips, don't you tell anyone you learned that fowl language from me."

Fifty-Cal smiled and winked. "Bet you hadn't had a rush like that before. Not even when you got your cherry popped."

Dumbfounded, Kathleen shook her head. This woman was rough and crazy, and spoke in a manner she couldn't gather her mind around.

Again, Fifty-Cal ran through the gears and drove passed a series of storage containers, finally stopping in front of Chadda's Airstream.

She blasted the horn.

"Chadda," Fifty-Cal called. "Got something for ya."

Struggly, Chadda lifted from the La-Z-Boy and waddled to the screen door. Her ballooning stomach pressed against the mesh enough to pop the door from the latch.

"Got someone to help watch your troublemaking lads," Fifty-Cal said. "A melon-titted teenie bopper. Get out, Trinity, this here is your new home."

Frazzled from nearly launching into the quarry, Kathleen fought the urge to insult Fifty-Cal. Then she saw Chadda holding the door open with her stomach. *She's huge!*

"Fifty-Cal dumpin' your ass here, ain't she?" Chadda asked.

Tightly gripping her purse Kathleen rammed her shoulder against the truck door to open it, leapt to the soggy ground, and followed Chadda into the egg-shaped, silver trailer.

Chapter 33

The weather worsened. Twisted strips of aluminum flashing, roofing shingles, and leafy vegetation gathered on the streets and faultless lawns of Trinity Meadows. Still, there was no word from Kathleen. It was getting late. Marci tried to call the police but no one answered. She dialed 911. The line was dead.

"I hope she's already at the shelter," Marci said, worried.

Since opening the Feldon letter Robbie hadn't said much. Jobless, he fumbled his words and didn't seem to understand the danger they were in.

"It's time, Robbie. Let's go to the shelter," she said.

"Uh . . . we ought to leave," Robbie repeated.

Bradley suggested they flip the main breaker.

"No, there's no reason to," Marci said sternly. "You don't look decent enough, Brad." She ordered him to change his shirt. "Put on one with a collar."

Marci needed the electricity for as long as possible to mitigate any rot, should the attic be dark for a prolonged period. Now that Robbie was jobless, she couldn't afford to lose the crop. She'd need the money more than ever.

"Do you think we should get the minivan at Home Depot?" Robbie asked.

"No," answered Marci sharply. "We must get to a safe place. And once we're settled, work on finding Kathleen."

After saying good-bye and locking Charlie in the garage, the Lindum family headed for the hurricane shelter. But as they turned left onto Perrine Ranch Road a small twister touched down ahead of them and toppled several trees. A head-high picket fence from the development across the street tore from the ground and lay in the way.

Robbie quickly U-turned.

"We'll head up Grand Boulevard," he mumbled.

The rain pelted the windshield at a nearly horizontal angle. The rapidly flipping wipers failed to clear the glass. Leaning and squinting over the steering wheel, Robbie followed the reflectors that lined the roadway.

"Mr. Pegerella says the reason those reflectors are red is to let us know we are traveling in the wrong direction."

"Brad, I don't need your wisecracks right now," Robbie said.

"Please Brad, it's not the time," Marci added.

"All right, Mom, but is Dad okay? He's acting kinda weird."

Reaching over the car seat she smiled then stroked his soft hair. "Dad's fine. Just a bit frazzled."

Robbie's stomach was in knots. He considered what might happen if he ran out of money—imagining living in Clarence's rundown tenement next to that Cooterman guy. His golf buddies would abandon him. Marci would make life miserable. Kathleen wouldn't have a clue and would ruthlessly blame him. And he'd need to explain to Brad why he had to change schools.

Fumbling with the car radio Marci found a news station.

. . . It is expected Hurricane Kate will make landfall before dawn. A Category 5 with wind speeds of 295 an hour, Kate will be a slow mover and take its time departing. The double eye-wall extends one hundred fifty miles from the center.

"Rob, I'm scared," Marci said. "We may lose our home."

He didn't answer. He was panning the guardrail that led over the Anclote River Bridge and saw the spot where the alligator had dragged him beneath. If he hadn't escaped, he'd be in that gator's stomach floating beneath the bridge . . . The thought rattled him.

"Robbie, watch out!" Marci grabbed the steering wheel and jerked it. "You nearly drove off the road."

. . . Kate will make landfall . . . Crash . . . Crack . . . Crunch. . .

Tires squealed. There was the sound of bending metal, snapping plastic, and crackling safety glass. The air bags exploded. Everyone lurched forward then bounced back, smacking the headrests. The front tires lifted off the ground. The tachometer redlined. There was a rush of wet air and the sudden smell of turpentine and the rustling of pine needles.

A massive pine tree had smashed onto the trunk, pinning the car solidly to the roadway. The pine slowly twisted and rolled. More sounds of bending metal as a large limb punctured the roof and sliced between the front and backseat.

"My God!" Marci screamed. Rain came into the car at all angles. The smell of freshly stripped pine bark mixed with the engine exhaust. Deflated air bags surrounded her.

Bradley called for his mother. "Mommy, Mommy, help me! I . . . uh . . . am squashed!"

Marci grabbed Robbie's shoulder and shook him violently. "Do something! Brad needs help."

Robbie was despondent. His hands were glued to the steering wheel.

Forcing the car door open, Marci crawled through the thick limbs that surrounded the vehicle toward Brad. Inside, a large limb pinned him against the seat cushion.

"I'm squashed."

"Are you hurt?"

"It's hard to breathe," he said, gasping.

"Robbie," Marci called. "Get out here and help me."

With his knuckles wrapped tightly to the steering wheel, Robbie looked like he had seen a ghost.

Marci yanked the door handle. It wouldn't budge. "Brad, are you hurt anywhere?"

"I . . . I don't think so." Bradley paused then caught his breath. "But I'm really smushed."

"Robbie, get your ass out of the car!"

Robbie's gaze was fixed. He couldn't hear.

Did he lose his hearing, she thought?

She yelled again. "Robbie!"

Finally, he spoke with garbled words. "I have no job. What am I'm going to do? I'm a failure." His foot punched the gas pedal. The engine raced. The front tires spun and spewed white smoke. In seconds the car became engulfed.

"Robbie!" Marci screamed. "What the hell are you doing?"

Bang!

Both tires exploded and sparks flew as the aluminum rims augured the black asphalt.

"You're going kill us! There's leaking gas! Brad, don't move." Coughing, Marci opened the driver's side door, reached in, and turned off the ignition.

The tire rims stopped spinning.

"Bradley, can you hear me?" asked his mother.

"Yes, Mom, I think I'm okay. Just stuck."

"How much can you wiggle?"

"Uh . . . a little bit." He coughed. "The smoke is burning my eyes."

Sticking her head through the smashed window Marci lifted the air bag and brushed away the glass shards that surrounded her son. If she could flip the front seat lever she might make room to free him.

Kathleen's lucky she wasn't with them, thought Marci. Or perhaps both her children may have died.

"Brad, I want you to wriggle . . . like you're stuck inside a sewer pipe."

"I'll try, Mom." Brad pointed the tips of his sneakers and jammed them under the front seat in a way that allowed him to lean onto his right side and maneuver underneath the limb.

Marci watched him struggle. "Can you twist or roll somehow?"

Brad groaned and contorted his torso. "I can breathe a lot better."

"That's good. Try to crawl under the limb."

"Ah . . . oomph, I think I can make it." Brad slithered and came free.

Carefully, Marci guided him through the window. She flicked away the safety glass that stuck in his skin.

In the pouring rain they hugged.

"Thank goodness you're okay."

"What's wrong with Dad?" Brad asked, shielding his face from the driving rain.

"He's in shock."

Marci wanted to punch Robbie in the face for nearly killing them. He deserved it. But Marci knew Brad was sensitive, often clamming up anytime she expressed discord toward his father. She must be careful not to hurt Brad's feelings by stressing him any further.

"Come, Rob, let's go back to the house." Using both hands Marci loosened Robbie's locked grip on the steering wheel and guided him from the car.

Hunched over and staggering, Robbie stumbled toward the guardrails, then jerked upright and pointed. "Look, the weeds are moving. It's that alligator!"

"Robbie, you're hallucinating." She gripped his arm, but he jerked free and sprinted down Perrine Ranch Road.

They gave chase.

"What's with Dad?"

"He's scared," Marci said. "Your dad thinks an alligator is after him."

Slowing to a jog, then a walk, Marci let Rob run off. "He's going to the house. Let him go. We have no choice but to go home."

When Robbie reached Trinity Meadows' entry gate the rain had subsided. He trotted down Leiram Avenue, stopped at the front door, and sat in a flowerpot. Minutes later Brad and Marci arrived, unlocked the entry, and sat Robbie at the dining room table. He didn't say a word.

There was no electricity.

Barking, Charlie wanted out of the garage.

After lighting candles Marci confronted Robbie. "You've lost it, bubs." Disgusted, she went into the bedroom and changed into dry clothes.

Darkness approached. Listening to the wind howl Marci flinched each time something smacked the house. An hour passed and Robbie hadn't budged from the dining room chair. She approached. "Robbie, we must prepare to ride this out. Put your job loss behind you for now."

Robbie tried to sit straight. He lifted his chin and spoke clearly for the first time since the incident. "Where do you think Kathleen is?" With a defeated chuckled he continued. His eyes wiggled and rolled. "Sh . . . she's probably still looking for that damn cell phone."

Then Robbie said something Marci hadn't heard in a long while. "Kathleen's a tough girl, a survivor. I have faith in my daughter. She'll come through this fine."

Was he hit on the head? He cared for his daughter? He's incapable of internalizing an emotion like that, thought Marci.

"Mom?" Brad stood near the refrigerator. "I'm hungry."

"Have Cheerios," Marci suggested. "Before the milk goes bad."

As she poured Cheerios into a large bowl her vision suddenly blurred. The house seemed to sway. There was an overhead snap as an eight-foot section of crown molding separated and swung from the ceiling but didn't drop to the floor.

Her heart raced. "Oh no!"

"Mom, can we walk to the hurricane shelter?"

"It's too dangerous. And your dad isn't stable enough to take with us."

Brad brought his cereal over to the kitchen window and ate while watching outside. "Look, there's Mr. Ying in the backyard!"

Trudging in his parka George Ying hammered in wooden stakes and tied a rope to one of his shredded papaya trees.

"It's reassuring the Yings didn't evacuate," Marci said. "I wonder if the Peltzes stayed." She hurried to the pantry window, looked across the street, and spied the Peltzes' dining room window. Their blinds were drawn open, and a ring of flickering candles with the statue of the Blessed Mother in the center of the dining room table.

"They've built some sort of shrine," Marci said. "The children are praying to it."

She diverted her gaze.

"They've painted a white cross on their front entry! Have they lost it?"

With the hurricane shutters lowered and the house darkened, Jennifer Dink used the many security cameras hidden within the eaves to look outside. An entire section of vinyl fencing flipped several times, splintered into sections, and laid flat at the edge of her front yard. Nearby, a stray cat meandered among fallen limbs. Then the camera caught someone running. It was Robbie Lindum.

Sitting in a silk robe, Jennifer uncrossed her shapely legs and sat straight. "What happened? They left not long ago."

Moments later Marci and Bradley arrived. "Huh? They have no car. Where's Kathleen?"

She became worried. What if they want something? No way, she thought. They'll track mud into my house, sit on the wrong furniture, and beg to take showers. They'll use my electricity and eat my food.

Leaving the upstairs den she went to the darkened bathroom, opened the medicine cabinet, and reached for a bottle of Ambien.

Chapter 34

Broadleaf shrubbery and plastic ornaments swirled across the littered and deserted thoroughfares of Trinity Meadows. Tattered sheets of lanai screening attached to twisted aluminum struts took flight and joined with peeled terra-cotta roof tiles and slabs of stucco. Rotted trees released their weakling and diseased limbs. A lone sabal palm swung in a confused and endless swing dance.

Inside her home Marci watched shadows dance in rhythm with the flickering candles. Out the corner of her eye she saw Robbie grab a candle and head into the garage. Brad was in his bedroom. He'd had quite a scare and she went to comfort him.

Lying with his laptop on his chest, Brad plunked on the keyboard. The light from the computer screen illuminated his young face. Marci sat on the mattress.

"What are you doing?"

"I'm watching the hurricane."

"What?" said Marci, puzzled. "There isn't any Internet."

"Yes, there is. That Dink lady next door has Wi-Fi. I know her password."

Marci moved behind him and watched.

"Where's the hurricane?" she asked.

"Thirty-two miles from Clearwater." He pointed at the screen. "See?"

With the projected path shaded in translucent yellow, big red warning fonts flashed: Category 5 Hurricane. Landfall expected at 3:10 a.m. during high tide.

"Looks like it will come real close, Mom."

An instant message popped on the screen.

"Who's that, Brad?"

"Oh, it's my friend Niko from school. He's at a hurricane shelter; says it's full and they're turning people away."

Brad typed a response.

A string of misspelled words appeared. Brad's eyes moved back and forth, reading. "Niko says people are trapped on the highways because the police aren't around. No one knows why. It's like they've abandoned us, he said."

Her stomach knotted. Marci glared at the warning on the computer screen and failed to ask if Niko saw Kathleen at the shelter.

"You know Dad and I saw a convoy of police and fire trucks heading east on Ridge Road today."

Marci eyes were locked onto the hurricane's wind speed, almost 300 miles an hour. "Oh my God!"

Brad patted Marci's knee. "It's okay, Mom."

"Can you save your battery so we can check the hurricane later tonight?" Marci asked.

"Sure!"

"Thanks. Why don't you read a book?"

"Book?" Bradley acted like he didn't know what one was.

Marci pulled Michael Crichton's *Jurassic Park* from a bookshelf. "Here, read this." I'll go and get a candle.

"That's okay. I have a reading lamp."

Just then the entire home shook; pelting rain pinged the windows.

Spinning her head in several directions, Marci listened as the walls creaked. There was a thump in the attic.

"What's that?" Brad asked.

"Must've been a limb hitting the roof." What she thought was one of her plants fell over.

After kissing her son on the forehead Marci went to find Robbie.

In the garage Robbie inventoried the boxes of medication stacked in the center stall. It was an Oxycodone shipment scheduled for delivery to the pharmacies near the Bippinotti Pain Clinic.

"Do you think you can cook something on the outside grill?" Marci asked.

"This is an entire shipment of painkillers," Robbie said. "Look at the address labels." He passed the dancing candle over a box. "It's the shipment that stocks Hudson pharmacies."

"So?" said Marci disinterested. "How about doing something important like taping the dining room window so it won't shatter?"

"I'm hungry." Putting down his notepad Robbie went into the kitchen, opened the freezer, and considered what he was in the mood to eat.

Chasing after him, Marci slammed shut the freezer door. "Try not to open the fridge until you know what you want. Keep the food cold as long as possible." She nudged him aside and pulled a stack of frozen hamburgers from the freezer.

"Here, grill these. Brad and Kathleen like burgers." A lump came to her throat. Kathleen wasn't there. *Where could she be?*

Carrying the hamburgers, Robbie rolled open the sliding glass doors to the pool area. "The wind is coming from the other direction. It's not so bad out here." He turned on the grill then pushed the igniter. Robbie tossed the frozen hamburgers onto the greasy grates and went back inside.

Without the continual chatter of the television an eerie, uneasy silence had settled into the household. Every outside noise was distinct and noticeable. In the kitchen Marci refolded dishtowels and reorganized drawers. Waiting for the burgers to cook, Robbie leafed through golf magazine he'd never read. And each time there was a crash or thump, they paused and looked at each other, not knowing what to say. A chasm existed between them.

It was time to check the burgers. But when Robbie lifted the grill lid, he realized the burners were out—the burgers still frozen.

"It's out of gas. Marci's will be pissed. She told me to refill it and I didn't."

With a glum expression he plodded inside. "Someone left the grill on and all the propane leaked out."

Marci grew flush. "You're lying." Angered, she threw a silk plant and hit him.

Sitting nearby, Brad gave his mother a concerned look. He didn't like the anger she displayed.

"Sorry you saw that, Brad," said a red-faced Marci. "We have nothing to cook with. We're eating peanut butter sandwiches and celery sticks tonight."

Chapter 35

Inside the tight quarters of the Airstream trailer, Samson, Chadda's oldest son, dealt from a double deck of playing cards. Chadda lounged in her Lay-Z-Boy with the back lodged against the imitation paneling so it didn't tip backwards.

"What are their names?" asked Kathleen Lindum, sitting on a heavily soiled couch.

"The one with the shaved head tossing cards is Samson. He's my oldest, and an ornery son of a bitch. See that truck tattoo on his left forearm? He did it all by his lonesome with a Dremel and printer ink.

"The wiry lad with no meat on his bones, that's Buster. But call him Buddy, he hates Buster and will flatten your car tires if you call him by his real name. Buster is eleven months younger than Samson and born in the same year.

"The runt of the litter is Artie. He's a goof cuz he loves to flush toilets. Whenever I take him to Gulf View Mall, Artie heads straight for the john and flushes the toilets. Then stands and stares until the security guard chases him off."

Raising her black eyebrows, Kathleen rolled her eyes toward Samson and inspected his partial tattoo. Samson flicked his middle finger then winked at her.

"It's best not to bother the boogers when they play canasta," Chadda said. "Their Aunt Katherine taught them. It's the most behaved you'll ever see them. And believe me"—Chadda itched her flabby bicep—"you want that to last as long as possible. Those boys cause lots of trouble when their hands ain't kept busy. The Patch folks help corral them when they're snooping where they're not supposed to."

"Patch?" Kathleen queried.

"The folks holed up in the junkyard come from a trailer park down the line. You'll hear 'em sometimes call it Cabbage Ears or Cabbage Patch, depends what words leak through their rotted teeth."

"Nice trailer. Who owns it?" she asked.

"It's Dale's," Chadda said. "He owns everything round here except Hoinky's flea market. Dale lived in this here trailer until Florence passed." Rubbing her stomach Chadda traced the bulging lump from one of the gestating twins.

"Active little sucker. Little bugger wants to get the hell out. He's a bit older than me, ya know."

"Who?" Kathleen asked.

"Dale, he's like my big brother but really not. Sees to it I'm okay all the time."

Kathleen panned her surroundings. The quarters were tight.

"Comfy, hain't it, Trinity?" Chadda gestured by pointing and directing with her toes. "Over there I got hot water and a fully stocked fridge, thanks to Dale and Critter. Lots of mac and cheese for my troublemaking noodle heads." She flicked her big toe and pointed at her kids.

"They like that military shit . . . those watch-ya-ma-call-them?" Chadda snapped her fingers. "Ah . . . MREs. My fiancé Monkey Wrench is in Iraq, ya know. He's in the Military and was on TV and told everyone he's comin home. Should be any day.

"The hurricane won't stop him neither." Her chinless expression brightened. Her ruby lips parted, revealing a protruding tooth that pinched her lower lip, burrowing like a sunken pillow. Reaching behind, she gathered her stringy hair and laid it across her chest.

"My hair gets so long sometimes. It's a pain."

"Why don't you cut it?" asked Kathleen, setting her hands between her knees.

"Love to, but can't. I grow it long enough to sell it to the wig lady."

"Wig lady?" It puzzled her.

"Hain't you ever seen her at Hoinky's."

"My dad's the one that goes to flea markets," Kathleen said. "Mom bitches at him for coming home with stuff we don't need."

"People need wigs," Chadda said. "Especially the cancer ladies. Ya know, Miss Trinity, you got quite a mop sprouting from your noggin and can make some bucks selling it."

Kathleen brushed her fingers through her hair and loosed several knots.

"When are you due?" Kathleen asked.

"Any day, I guess . . . Lost track."

Kathleen eyes grew wide. "How will you get to the hospital?"

"Honey, I ain't going. I'm dropping the litter right here," Chadda said. "That's why Dale gave me the nicest trailer."

Yikes! Delivering babies outside a hospital wasn't conceivable to Kathleen.

"Only Samson was born in stirrups. That brute's big ol' onion head stretched my coowanger so damn wide the next two plopped out during a poop. Artie landed right in the toilet bowl with my floater turds when he was born. Probably splains why he likes visiting shitter rooms all the time and running his hands on the porcelain like he likes.

"Hey, boys, teach Miss Trinity how to play canasta."

All three shaved heads turned and eyeballed Kathleen. Sporting angry sourpusses they glared at their mother. Chadda flattened her face like a monkey and mimicked the boys. "Don't you give me those gorilla faces!" She snapped her pudgy middle finger at them.

Buddy signaled for Kathleen to come join them.

When Dale Carter stopped by Gator's to ask Flatch how the Cabbage Ears tenants were progressing, Flatch relayed that Fifty-Cal brought back "one of them's Trinity Meadows gals from Hoinky's and dropped her with Chadda."

"What the hell am I supposed to do?" Dale questioned Fifty-Cal's decision.

"Fifty-Cal said she was too damn cute to let her drown when the surge comes. And when she learned she was jailbait material, dumped her ass the first place she could."

"Where the hell's Fifty-Cal?" Dale asked. "She can take the kid to the Port Richey police station on this side of the Cottee River. It's not far. She's got my big truck. It will go anywhere, for sure."

"Ain't you heard, Dale?" Flatch said. "Police is all gone. So's the firemen and anyone else in the know. They hightailed to the Atlantic coast."

Leaning on the bar rail Dale scratched his chin. He hadn't shaved yet.

"Them cops skedaddling don't matter anyways," Dale said. "It's not like they were planning to help the Flats folks. We're expendable to them because Krackers don't pay taxes and don't vote much. The Flats will be the last place the government comes after the storm."

"They're probably hoping we get sucked into the ocean, hain't it, Dale?"

"That's what Momma thought."

"Ya know, Dale," Flatch said. "Fifty-Cal is in a bitchy mood cuz she's been stag a good while and ain't found a permanent woman to ride out the storm with just yet. She hadda dump that tender white meat real fast, cuz it ain't a good idea being anywhere near Fifty-Cal when that horny dyke is liquored."

Dale agreed. "I don't need another episode to put Fifty-Cal back in jail after the storm leaves. I need her for when Deuce's jail time is up. He's going to head right for the Flats and cause big-time trouble by running drugs and selling his moonshine."

"Shit, Dale!" Flatch said. "I forgot to tell ya. The county jail freed Deuce along with the short-timers."

"Where'd you hear that?" Dale asked.

"From Critter," Flatch said. "He said Deuce is hanging at Moog's strip club over on Grand Boulevard."

"That's Critter's favorite titty bar, ain't it?" Dale asked.

"Yes, also Deuce's. It's where the cops go to find Deuce anytime they need to fill a line-up when some gal gets raped."

"Dale pounded his fist on the bar. "Pass word to let me know when Deuce is nearby. Only one person can keep him under control. It's Fifty-Cal."

Dale's thoughts jumped back to the young gal stuck at Chadda's trailer. "Does that Trinity Meadows chick have any value?"

"She can help Chadda with the boys," Flatch said.

"Okay, let her stay for now if she is some use. I'll check on her and make sure Chadda's boys are behavin'."

For Kathleen, understanding the canasta card game was difficult. It involved two card decks and some concentration. The boys kept cheating and changing the rules. She couldn't believe how adept and calmly they played because they looked more like indignant midget devils than card-tossing saints.

Kathleen found that her edginess had softened. And she felt a fearlessness and certain warmth among these odd, hard people who spoke in butchered sentences. And the tall, stone-faced man who had entered the Airstream and stood before her exuded a confidence, a presence that communicated everything was fine.

Gumming a chummy one-toothed grin, Chadda didn't budge from her reclined position when Dale arrived. "Meet the new baby-sitter."

Dale stepped further into the cramped quarters. There wasn't much room between the ceiling and Dale's waxed hair. At the kitchen table the boys stopped their card game and waited for him to acknowledge them.

"Boys, ya doin all right and behaving for your mother?"

Six pairs of eyes were locked onto Dale. They blinked then nodded.

"None of yin's cheatin' the young woman?" Dale cracked smile.

"The boys cheatin' her blind in canasta," Chadda said. "The gal got some learning to do. They don't mind her though. Must be the sister they ain't had yet."

"Fifty-Cal says you came from Trinity Meadows."

"I live there, yes." Kathleen responded.

"Lookit," Dale said. "I can't take you home until the storm passes—too much to do. Flooding shut down most roads. You gotta ride out the hurricane here."

Kathleen was disappointed. "Can I use someone's cell to call my parents?"

Dale flipped open his cell phone and checked his signal. Oddly enough the cell tower was still active. "Might as well tell them you're okay."

"What's the number?"

"Uh-oh, I don't know." Kathleen struggled to explain. "Everyone's phone numbers are names in my cell phone. I have no idea what the numbers are. I just scroll and push a button. Do you have a phonebook?" she asked.

"Nope," Dale answered. "Local folks scrounge them and sell them to the recycler. You mean you don't know a single phone number?" Baffled, Dale sent her a hard look. "Don't you know math?"

This guy is insinuating I'm stupid, thought Kathleen. I go to the best high school in Pasco County. His kind are the dumb ones.

Chapter 36

Hurricane Kate loomed on several large LCD monitors that ringed the Cape Kennedy operation center. No one was present except for Doctor Paola Estrada, who was hunched over with her laptop reviewing a set of satellite photos taken twenty-four hours ago.

Lifting her head she cricked her neck and studied the overhead screens.

Kate bore down on Clearwater. The monitor displayed: **Barometric pressure 802 millibars . . . Wind speed 318 miles an hour . . . northeast heading five miles an hour.**

Doctor Estrada squinted. To her right a smaller monitor displayed the jet stream wind patterns over the Florida panhandle. She was looking for a sign, anything that could influence Kate's path at the last minute.

Carrying black coffees, Governor Simon strolled into the cavernous room. Standing behind her, he reached over Paola's shoulder and set the Styrofoam cups on the console. His firm hands pressed into her neck muscles and squeezed out the tension.

Doctor Estrada rolled her shoulders.

"Hmm, that feels good, Albert. I've missed your backrubs." She grew flush, warmly reflecting on her affair with him.

"What's new with Kate?" His fingers kneaded her shoulder muscles. Bending his knees he gently slid his arms around her waist and lifted her blouse from the waistband of her black cotton skirt.

She struggled to concentrate. "Landfall will be an hour from now. We're seeing lots of wind damage in South Tampa already. Davis Island is submerged. People are stranded on roadways and bridges."

She allowed his advance, permitting his solid hands to go beneath her blouse and caress her olive skin.

"The surge is going to kill," she said. "Uh . . ." Albert's cologne was intoxicating. His warm hands clasped her waist. If she had a weakness it was acquiescing to the governor.

Not good, thought Paola, fighting to concentrate.

"Kill who?" Albert asked.

"People stranded on the causeways, barrier islands, or anyone that remains at an elevation less than forty feet above sea level," Paola said.

Attempting to kiss her neck he whispered, "It's not your fault. No one's blaming you."

"You're wrong, it's my fault," she said, leaning away slightly, refusing him. "If I'd gotten the prediction correct a lot more people might survive." Teardrops released from each of her large Latino eyes. "I will never free myself from this guilt."

"Look!" she said sharply, yanking the governor's hands from under her blouse and moving to the console. "See these satellite photos!" Using the laptop mouse she rotated the sequence of images forwards and backwards several times. "See the time these images were taken, Albert?"

"I can't see. I need my glasses."

"I never saw them, Albert!" Paola blurted.

The governor squinted.

"Never!" she yelled.

Turning to face him she pounded her fists on his chest. "Of the hundreds of satellite photos I've studied to get the projected path right, I did not see these until now."

"Look at the timestamps."

Paola became stiff. "I was with you."

"What?" the governor said.

"I thought I set my eyes on every satellite photo since Kate rounded the Dry Tortugas. I didn't know these existed until now. They clearly show Hurricane Kate wasn't going to continue in the same direction. The images were transmitted at 3 am." There was a long pause. Paola Estrada, with her beautiful Columbian features, looked straight at Albert. "When we were making love!"

Shaking her head, she didn't know what to say next. *What's with men and natural disasters that they need sex, believing they're entitled?* She had to decide if she should blame herself for the deaths that would soon happen.

Governor Simon came close and whispered into her ear. "This sucks, you know. Politically, my decision to abandon Tampa Bay and send critical government and emergency services packing across the state, out of harm's way, will end my career."

He kissed behind her earlobe.

She slapped him hard, twice. "Sucks doesn't do it," she said angrily. "People will die because you were screwing me. Sucks even more for those poor children in Tampa, Saint Petersburg, and Gulfport who can't evacuate and are destined to drown."

Fuming, Doctor Estrada struggled for control. She felt guilty because she couldn't resist his advances. To release her own stress she fed on his sexual appetite.

"You be the scapegoat," Doctor Estrada said. "I don't deserve it."

Governor Simon remained composed.

Opening the distance between them, Paola studied the overhead monitor. "Look at the buoy reading at the mouth of Tampa Bay."

Maneuvering the mouse she clicked on the buoy icon. A box appeared with current readings. *Wave height thirty-five feet—ocean water temperature ninety-three degrees—pressure 802 millibars.*

"Kate's much bigger than Katrina. The surge into Tampa Bay is going to behave like a tidal wave," she said.

"Yes, lots of death and destructions," affirmed Albert, removing his handkerchief and dabbing the sweat from Paola's forehead.

"Can you predict exact landfall yet?" he asked.

"Yes! This is the prediction." She read from a sheet of paper. "Kate's eye will pass over the barrier island of Clearwater Beach and score a direct hit on the city of Clearwater."

Setting down the report she ran the mouse pointer along the projected path.

"Those Scientologists won't be happy about losing all that capital investment they poured into downtown Clearwater. Kate will destroy their world headquarters," the governer noted.

"Funny you say that," Paola said. "The most predictable path goes right through the center of the building."

"Talk about experiencing some pain." The governor found it ironic that a natural disaster would scrub the cult off the face of the earth.

"Where will it go from there?" he asked.

"Dunedin . . . Safety Harbor . . . Oldsmar . . . West Chase . . . Citrus Park . . . then Trinity Meadows," she said.

"The surge will pack into Tampa Bay and drown Ybor City and Gibsonton. Even if it goes no further inland the geology and the head pressure of the surge will upwell and overflow many of the inland lakes."

"I don't understand," the governor said.

"Think of it as a reversing underground river, with the water heading back where it came from. The whole area will become a gigantic marsh, particularly Polk County."

"No more strawberries," Albert added to her assessment. "Farm soil will become contaminated with chemicals that leak from the Port Authority shipyards."

"That's a tiny example," said Estrada, carefully gauging and holding the distance between them.

"Patrick Johnson estimates over two hundred thousand people will drown," the governor said. "Could that be right?"

"Could be more," she surmised. "This surge will be huge, possibly twice as many deaths because of the evacuation screw-up. Kate arrives at high tide on the full moon. There will be no outgoing tide to release the surge."

"Any sign Kate turns?" he asked.

"Not until it comes ashore."

She showed a map with community names highlighted along the projected path. "Looks like it will run northward along I-75. Geologists say the limestone ballast beneath the interstate roadbed will soften and slump anywhere there's a swamp nearby. Don't forget, much of I-75 and I-4 were built through swamps. The roadways will dissolve if saturated enough."

Doctor Estrada straightened her loose blouse then darted Albert a sultry glance—a look she couldn't hold back.

"Your rescue personnel are not going to reach anyone in Tampa for quite some time," she said.

Governor Simon closed the gap between them. "Yes, I am aware, Paola. Places north of the city like New Port Richey and Hudson will wait even longer. Many could starve if they can't fend for themselves."

"Not much tax base there anyway," the governor said. "In fact, the area around Hudson is a Medicaid drain."

"Albert, you shouldn't think that way."

"Did you hear what Patrick Johnson said about those debris ridges that will form?" the governor asked, redirecting the conversation. "I have a hard time believing such a phenomenon can exist."

"Yes, I heard his reasoning," she said.

"What do you think, Paola?"

"It makes sense. And may be good for some people," she said.

"How?" Albert asked.

"The residences upwind of these debris fields will be protected once the pile is high enough to block the extreme hurricane force winds."

"Huh?" said the governor, trying to imagine what they may look like.

"Patrick says those debris piles will be like concrete walls and will take some time to tunnel through just one of them. He says I-4, because the way the storm is tracking, will look like a miniature Appalachian mountain range with rolling debris ridges blocking access to Tampa and areas north. You must get food to the survivors," Paola said.

"I know, but we have a big problem with air transport. That size of an airlift requires military aircraft equipped to parachute food into those areas. The aircraft isn't available with the problem in Iraq. Washington's in a panic and recalled the National Guard and the military equipment in their armories.

"Sucks big time," continued the governor, looking grim. "Florida is on its own with no help from the military to address the storm's aftermath."

Paola approached Albert and hung her arms around the governor's neck. She nuzzled against him and began to sob. Her confused tears released a flood of guilt and emotion.

Chapter 37

Sitting within the den's window nook Robbie Lindum watched a cluster of swaying oak trees near the retention pond. The surrounding soil heaved and became a hump, then settled flat.

"Boy, those old oaks across the street are getting hammered."

A tree branch smacked the glass. "Ooh! What was that?"

Another heavy gust came, and again, the sod surrounding the giant live oak lifted, except this time the hump failed to flatten.

"It's falling over!"

The Floratam rug tore and exposed a crawling root mass. The tree trunk angled sharply. The canopy crashed to the ground. Then another oak lost its footing, smashing across its fallen brother.

Mesmerized, Robbie watched as an upright lawn chair slid down Leiram Avenue, as if a ghost sat in it, until it tripped and tumbled into the downed oaks. Lengths of yellow vinyl siding whizzed into the cluster of felled trees, wrapping the thicker limbs and pointing the wind direction. Then a fifth and sixth oak toppled, its horizontal reaching limbs collecting more wind-borne debris.

"What a mess," Robbie said. "The homeowners association will have to plant new trees."

Marci sprawled on the sofa. It bothered her that Robbie had acted so strangely when the pine tree fell on the car, almost killing Brad. He'd perked up, like his adrenaline had kicked in.

"Those oaks," Robbie said. "They're in a giant pile that's growing by the minute."

Marci didn't care to listen. Her mind went elsewhere.

Nighttime arrived. The streetlights had failed to brighten. It seemed the wind was pushing through the walls. The front doors rattled; then something smashed against it.

"That scared me," said Robbie as he passed. "The door's leaking. I better get towels."

Still sprawled on the sofa, Marci rolled her head and stared at the double doors. The curtains that surrounded the dining room window swayed. Another section of crown molding had popped free and swung out over the great room.

"Damn builder didn't glue the molding properly," Robbie said. "I told the carpenters to use a premium brand of glue. I'll call Monday and demand they get their asses over here and reglue all this crown molding.

"Robbie, are you crazy?" Frustrated, Marci started hyperventilating. She finally had it. "We may not have a home on Monday, you blithering idiot."

"Marci," Robbie said, "the hurricane is heading toward Clearwater. We're twenty miles away. It's going to miss."

"Rob you're an ass . . ." But before she continued her sentence the dining room window shattered. A section of rainspout flew like a javelin through the great room and penetrated the sliding door that opened to the pool area. The spout pierced the lanai screening, traversed the backyard, and sliced through the bottom of George

Ying's papaya tree. The hurricane raged into the home. Magazines on the coffee table flipped to the back covers then rolled off. A glass shard sliced Robbie's right cheek and blood poured from the open wound.

Every candle blew out.

"What was that?" Robbie said. "I can't see."

Marci jumped from the sofa. "My dining room furniture, it's soaked! My window treatments, they're ruined!"

Too dark to see anything, Robbie thought the wetness on his face and forearm was from the rain that shot through the hole.

Leaping from his chair Bradley ran into his bedroom, found his battery-powered reading lamp, and turned it on.

"Dad . . . Mom!" Bradley said, directing the weak light beam.

"Bradley, stay away from the window. There's glass all over the floor. Keep your head low," said Marci, crawling.

The dining room window blinds ripped from their hooks and flew into the kitchen. "My Levolors! Rob, do something, you imbecile!"

Bradley hated to hear his mother yell at his father. It upset him.

Quickly, he crawled toward the window and yanked down the flapping curtain. Approaching from the side he climbed onto the marble sill and jammed the curtain into the hole.

The fury inside ceased. The rain that swirled had drenched everything.

Directing the tiny reading lamp Brad raced to the garage and retrieved a roll of duct tape. Returning, he climbed the sill, dried the area around the hole, and taped over the curtain. Charlie hid in the laundry room.

"There you go, Dad, no more wind." Brad pointed the light at the window, then at Robbie. "Dad, you're bleeding!"

Bright red blood streamed down Robbie's neck and soaked his entire right side. A red puddle surrounded his feet.

"Where?"

Lighting a candle, Marci brought it toward Robbie. "On your face!"

Blood dribbled along his thin forearm.

Marci grabbed a dishcloth. "Come into the kitchen and sit at the table, Rob."

"Brad," Marci said. "Come over here and shine that light at your father's face."

"How's that, Mom?" Brad held the light steady.

Marci inspected the cut. The incised wound was deep. She squeezed the cut closed and set the dishcloth over it.

"Grab hold and press hard, Rob."

"Wrap duct tape around his head," Bradley said. "That way the pressure will stay on it."

Circling his head in gray tape, Marci secured the dishcloth. "That should work. But it's going to hurt when we take the tape out of your hair. But if this is all that happens we'll be blessed," she said, nearly out of breath.

Chapter 38

The Airstream rocked and swayed like a traveling boxcar, its slick, aerodynamic egg shape deflecting the two-hundred-mile-an-hour gusts. Dry-rot tires sucked at the mud, while spiraling weedy vines clutched the undercarriage and held Chadda's trailer firmly in place.

There weren't many trees in the junkyard, just random palmetto scrubs and cabbage palms, nothing large enough to uproot and launch as projectiles at the cars, buses, and trailers the Cabbage Ears residents resided in. Many slept. Most consumed alcohol. Others cracked a downwind window to vent cigarette and pot smoke.

Dale Carter had ordered small generators shut down during the storm. He didn't want anyone doing a lamebrain act by running a generator inside their shelter and killing the occupants with carbon monoxide poisoning.

Chadda had slipped Benadryl into her boys' macaroni and cheese. Samson, Buddy, and Artie slept soundly. Awake in her La-Z-Boy, Chadda felt her contractions begin. It wasn't until they were two minutes apart that she said something.

Curled and sleeping on the musty couch, Kathleen Lindum's clothes had finally dried.

"Trinity, wake up."

There was no response from Kathleen.

Chadda tossed a pillow and hit her square in the head.

Kathleen opened her eyes. Chadda's stomach protruded like an overinflated beach ball.

"You got to help me push out the twins."

At first it didn't register. Then the horror flashed through Kathleen thoughts.

"Deliver your twins!"

"Ain't no one else around to do it, sweet pea."

Chadda's plump face grew stressed. Beads of sweat rolled along her thick neck as another contraction began.

She grunted. "Man, this one hurts."

In awe, Kathleen watched the contraction intensify then finish.

"Trinity, help me off this chair onto the floor."

Sitting straight, Kathleen said. "I don't have a choice, do I?"

Chadda shook her head no, then sat upright after yanking the recliner lever.

"Get towels from the closet. Also scissors, blankets, and pillows from my bedroom. And don't wake the boys. I don't want them to see the disgusting mess. Help me out of this chair."

Grabbing both arms, Kathleen pulled Chadda to her feet.

"Can you remove my trousers?"

At first Kathleen hesitated. "Must I?"

Chadda bounced her head. "Yes, hurry."

Kathleen pulled Chadda's sweatpants to her ankles.

"Get me something to lie on."

She grunted as another contraction came. "Shit, this hurts more than I remember."

Unfolding a bedspread, Kathleen laid it out and helped Chadda to the floor.

"See those couch pillows," Chadda said. "Prop them under my knees."

Tense, Kathleen moved quickly.

"Thanks, now squat and look between my legs, Trinity."

"Look between what?"

"See if you can see the head crowning. Oooh . . . ah . . . ouch!" Chadda screamed. "Here comes a contraction."

Contorting her face she groaned and pushed and turned beat red, then purple. Chadda shrieked. "Ouch!" Panting, she pounded her fist on the hollow floor. "I need you to help me. Something's wrong."

Chadda spread her legs wider. "What do you see?"

Kneeling, Kathleen became panicked.

"I am loose as a sow but nothin's coming."

Chadda grunted. "O . . . oomph, it hurts. What do you see?"

The contraction finally slowed and Chadda relaxed. "When the babies plop out, suck the smegma from their noses and mouths and make them cry."

More grunts and groans then a curdling scream. But nothing happened.

"Trinity, I need you to look in there and tell me what you see."

Hesitant, Kathleen moved between her legs.

"Spread my bumpers and look inside!"

"Here goes nothing." Kathleen poked with both hands and separated the bulging, hairy flesh. There was a putrid birthing odor. She gagged.

"See anything?" Chadda asked.

"Nuh, there's no head."

"Shit! . . . Shit!" Chadda cursed. "What body part do you see? Hurry, another contraction's coming!"

"Uh . . . looks like an elbow," Kathleen said.

"Trinity, I need you to do something, quick! Or I will die. So will my babies! My boys, they won't have a mother. And their fathers are no good. They'll be orphaned if you don't get these twins out of me!"

"What do I do?"

The contraction arrived and Chadda let out a bloodcurdling cry.

"Shove your hand in. Push on the shoulder and turn the baby so the head can plop down. Do it now!"

Kathleen wanted to run for help. But when Chadda let out that scream, Kathleen reacted and slid her whole fist inside. She imagined what the baby must look like stuck in the birth canal. She felt for the shoulder and pushed, trying to manipulate the infant.

The baby wiggled and suddenly the head dropped and butted against her wrist. "I think I feel the head." A jet of amniotic fluid squirted her in the face. She jerked out her arm. The infant crowned and slopped out like jiggling Jell-O.

Catching the newborn, Kathleen juggled the wiggling baby. It was blue.

"Grrr . . . ahh!" Chadda groaned and cried out. "Clear the mouth. Hang the bastard upside down."

Kathleen looked at the cyanotic infant. "It's dead."

"Not unless you clear its mouth."

Hesitant, she opened the child's rubber lips. "Yuk, there's lots of goop!"

With her pinky finger Kathleen scooped the cheesy mush. The infant took its first breath. A whimper became a cry. The blueness disappeared and the baby turned pink.

Kathleen set the newborn on a close-by beach towel and wiped with a cloth diaper.

A cord of veins ran into Chadda. A second head crowned. The identical twin flew into Kathleen's hands.

Chadda sighed.

Outside the wind howled. Proud tears rolled down Kathleen's face. "My goodness, I delivered twins."

Chadda told Kathleen how to cut and tie the umbilical cords; that her body would naturally deliver the placenta.

"Tug the cord." A bloody mass of vein-laden tissue arrived.

"I think we are safe now," Kathleen said.

A flush of warmth overcame Kathleen. She felt like a mother. It was an emotion she'd never known.

"Thank you," Chadda said. "Their names will be Kate and Kathleen."

Kathleen Lindum beamed with pride.

Chapter 39

Lounging in pajamas and sipping vintage Chianti from a crystal goblet, Jennifer Dink dimmed the living room chandelier. The sparkling prisms that dotted the solid maroon wallpaper faded. She feared the neighbors would discover she had electricity and beg to come inside.

She booted her laptop to check the hurricane's progress. Kate had slammed into the city of Clearwater with wind speeds clocked at 307 miles an hour. At Tarpon Springs a gust measured 214 miles an hour. Jennifer looked around her spotless home. It didn't even shake.

Down the street the Peltz children had gathered into a prayer circle in their dining room. With rosaries draped from their tiny fingers they prayed as they knelt on the Pergo flooring. Their narrow backs ached. The skin on their bony knees burned. Edward Peltz demanded they continue to pray. "Don't stop or God will banish us all to hell."

Painful tears ran down the girls' sad faces while their spindly legs wobbled and shook. None of them dared move, fearful they would be held responsible for them all going to hell.

Shingles peeled from the Lindums' roof and spun like Frisbees along the steep pitch. The garage door rumbled. Robbie was inattentive—the blood loss had set him in a mild state of shock.

"Brad, stay away from the windows," Marci warned.

"Mom!" Bradley called. "I remember reading about hurricanes once. It said find a spot in the house nearest the direction of the wind. It's the safest place."

Marci thought for a second. "That makes sense, perhaps we should do that. The den is the best place."

"Mom, let's drag in mattresses and build a hut in case something bad happens."

"All right, Brad." Marci felt that her home was taking a pounding. The wind's velocity was incredibly strong. Chunks of debris whacked the windows and outer walls. It made sense to gather in one place.

Dragging several mattresses into the den, they built a lean-to fortress in the southwest corner, next to the cherry bookcase. They sat Robbie within the mattresses and called Charlie to lie next to them.

"Mom, stack the mattresses so they will collapse in case a tornado hits." Brad tied a cord to the mattress handles. "In case they don't fall we can pull them down."

They stored food and water beneath the desk. Again, a suggestion of Brad's.

"Thanks for the help, Brad." Marci patted her son on the back and hugged him. "It doesn't sound good out there."

They huddled.

Holding his bandage, Robbie remained quiet.

"You'll be okay, Dad."

Marci saw the sympathy her son had for his father and wondered why she hated Robbie so much. It bothered her that if she divorced

Robbie, Brad would be heartbroken. She wasn't sure if she could hurt him in that way by dissolving the family.

"Bradley, can you boot your laptop so I can see what's happening with the hurricane?"

"Sure, Mom!" Bradley accessed Jennifer Dink's wireless network. Marci looked over his shoulder as the screen lit up and Bradley typed the hijacked password. The browser loaded the NOAA site that tracked Hurricane Kate. The cyclone was heading right at them.

"Dunedin," Brad said. "The eye is over the town . . . How cool!"

"What?" Marci asked.

"This website lets you fly right into the eye. It's right over the Dunedin Chamber of Commerce building."

Outside, a furious wind pummeled and shook the home violently. The roof crackled and popped. "It's coming apart," Marci said. "I think the shingles are blowing off. Turn off the computer, Brad."

Suddenly, a twelve-foot section of drywall released from the ceiling and smashed onto the coffee table in the great room. A corner piece of the drywall lacerated the television screen. White insulation swirled like a raging blizzard and stuck to anything wet. Another twelve-foot sheet dropped, this time in the den, smashing onto the mattress hut. Marci peeked out. The roof trusses were exposed and rows of potted buckets teetered. A labyrinth of bright orange extension cords and lamplights swung freely.

"Oh, no! Quick, Brad, secure the mattresses."

Brad yanked the nylon cord. The bedding flopped over and lay on top of them.

Outside, the neighbor's plastic picket fence that laid at the outer edge of Jennifer Dink's lawn became airborne and whacked the Lindums' front entry. White pickets impaled the decorative foam columns that provided the falsely rich design. The large oval of stained-glass that accented the Lindums' front door shattered, opening a big hole. Swirling rain shot through, drenching the interior walls. The rapid change in air pressure rearranged furniture. The cherry bookcase in the den levitated briefly, then flipped and pinned against the mattress hut.

Marci cried. "My beautiful home, it's ransacked."

Dishes, pots, plates, utensils, and knives sucked from flung-open cabinets and drawn drawers. Glasses smashed. Stainless steel mixing bowls pinged, plinked, and twanged. Silk plants in wicker baskets marched from distant corners. Freezer bags loaded with marijuana pulled from a concealed spot within the pantry cabinet, opened and sprinkled seedy parsley until the bags were empty. Absorbent towels that hung from brushed-nickel bathroom towel racks took flight like Halloween witches. Ceiling fan blades rotated at full throttle. Windows shattered. The sliding glass doors that opened to the pool derailed, took flight, and punched a huge hole into the lanai. The heavy doors rolled liked rectangular tractor wheels across the backyard and cut through the Yings' overgrown garden.

Traveling well beyond two hundred and fifty miles an hour, the driving rain soaked straight through the outside walls. Inside, the drywall turned to mush. Sheet after sheet became putty and released from their five-quarter-inch screws, sloughing to the floor, dissolving into curdled milk. Trusses lashed with hurricane straps buckled, bowed, and bravely fought a futile battle. And every time there was a loud crash, Robbie flinched, thinking the next one would do him in. With his heart pounding he held onto Charlie. His blood-soaked bandage stained the mattress.

Bradley cradled his laptop against his chest. Frightened, he nuzzled and shivered between his parents.

No one said a word. They closed their eyes and cringed, scared that injury and death would come any moment.

Chapter 40

With her head buried in the softness of the mattress Marci dreamed of her childhood, her father, mother, and first love.

Lev Krinov, Marci's biological father, mined coal. He'd emigrated from Russia with his beautiful young wife and her sickly sister. Lev found work in a soft coal mine in Thurmond, West Virginia, in the heart of Appalachia. His first two children were boys who died within weeks of their birth. Sad that he had no male heir, Lev innocently started calling the third child, Marci, by her middle name, Jodi. In fact, Marci became so comfortable with it, she didn't respond when called by her first name.

Situated on the eastern bank of the New River, tiny Thurmond was more a rail stop than a village. The town served as a riverside access point for coalminers eking a living hacking at narrow bituminous seams in folded hills behind the town. Thurmond's main street wasn't much of a thoroughfare, just a cart path that ran aside a layer of chunky railway ballast. A bank with a vault to hold miner payrolls stood two buildings down from the only intersection. Next to it was a hotel with a dining room aptly named the Banker's Club, where each year Marci celebrated a birthday.

The only drivable road into Thurmond crossed the New River from the west, sharing a one-lane bridge with the railroad tracks. The road split with the train tracks on the east side and missed the town by skirting uphill to the mines.

To escape isolated Thurmond and to attend church, Marci's family traversed an uphill switchback to the town of Oak Hill. But rarely did someone travel far away. The first time Marci left the county came two months before she turned sixteen, when her ailing aunt asked Marci's mother to come to Aripeka, Florida, and visit before she died.

Traveling by bus Marci saw flatlands, and the expanse of an ocean, for the first time. Unaccustomed to the summertime heat and confinement of her aunt's mobile home, tomboy Jodi went off each morning to explore this unfamiliar, tropical frontier with its icky gecko bugs, long-legged waterfowl, and unusual wildlife.

It wasn't long before Marci found a place to pass the sweltering afternoons. Walking a dirt road, she came beneath a massive stand of oaks with an unusual-looking octopus tree with tentacles. It had big fig leaves and massive suffocating vines that slithered through the oaks, dropping trunk-like roots that burrowed into the peat-like black soil.

At the peak of each day Marci meandered through the grove where it was cool, to a nook that opened at the base of an ancient oak. The enclave was lined with a comfortable mat of Spanish moss. It was where she spent her afternoons. And after falling asleep one day, she was awakened by a boy about her age and stature standing over her.

"Hello," Marci said.

The boy didn't answer.

"What's your name?" she immediately asked, hoping to make a friend.

"Buck," responded the boy, sharply. "They call me Buck after my dad."

"That's not your real name, is it?"

"It'll do," he said. "You got a name?" Buck asked.

"My dad calls me Jodi."

Though he seemed quiet, Jodi saw that his eyes carefully studied her.

"Would ya like to pick scallops?" Buck asked.

"Scallops?" She looked puzzled.

"Don't you know . . . a clam?" Buck said.

"I've never seen a scallop," Jodi responded.

"When ya shuck them they look like lumps of white turnips," Buck said.

"Where do you find them?" she asked.

"Yonder." Buck pointed west. "In the shallows off Horse Head Key. Wanna go?"

"Sure," she said.

They headed along a sandy path cut through the mangroves and climbed into a small flats boat lashed to a shabby dock.

"You got good balance," Buck said.

"Back home we have a johnboat. Dad takes me fishing on the river all the time."

Rowing from within a maze of mangroves they came to the open gulf. Buck watched as Jodi looked around at the abundant wildlife and found the beautiful, shorthaired blonde's unfamiliarity amusing. A pleasant, surprised expression jumped to her round face each time she saw something new. Like a flock of sunning seagulls pointing the sea breeze direction, or the oddball spoonbills sporting unusually shaped beaks.

"Look at that!" Jodi pointed to a rocky shoal. "A boat with a shack built on it."

Buck laughed. "That's Mr. Hoinky's home. It's a houseboat."

"Mr. Hoinky?" Jodi questioned the odd name.

"His real name is Bobby Mack," Buck said. "He got a fishbone stuck in this throat a long time ago and hasta blow real hard to make enough of a sound to make his words out. Kind of like a goose honk and pig oink that happens at the same time. Momma says it sounds like he has permanent strep throat.

"Wanna visit?" Buck asked. "He's got this big ol' sow with funny-looking legs that lives with him. Ya want to see it?"

"Sure!" Jodi said.

"Just don't laugh at Hoinky or his pig. It ain't nice."

Buck rowed closer and dropped a small anchor made from concrete poured into a coffee can. "Come on, Hoink's a real nice guy." Buck jumped into the warm saltwater and swam. Jodi followed, racing Buck to the anchored houseboat.

"Mister Mack," called Buck, standing chest-deep in swaying sea grass.

A leather-skinned man with frosted hair tied into a ponytail and a hefty handlebar mustache leaned over the gunwale and greeted Buck with a raspy honk-like voice. He reached for Buck's arm and lifted him onto the deck. Hoinky spotted Jodi. "This a friend of yours, Buck?"

"Yes, Mister Mack."

Jodi bobbed in the ocean. "This water is salty."

Each grabbed an arm and lifted her onboard.

Hoinky greeted her. "Welcome, young lady."

At first Jodi struggled to understand his words. It was odd to hear them come from his mouth. He took deep, chest-lifting breaths then exhaled, mouthing odd-sounding sentences. She tried to hold back her giggles.

"You come to show her Elnora, ain't ya, Buck?"

Buck nodded, then smiled.

"How's your momma doin'?" Hoink asked. "When's she's running another poker game at the Hacienda?"

"Mister Hoink . . . uh . . . I mean Mister Mack, Momma told me to tell you she's running a game Saturday. She said Judge Grady and Mister Cledus will be there.

"Tell your momma I'm in."

Hoinky spoke to Jodi. "Wanna see Elnora, young lady?"

"Yes!" she said, letting the sun dry her while examining the odd-looking boat. A cedar shack with square-framed windows, port, and starboard supported a pitched roof that directed rainwater into a cistern. Inside the shack was a small rope bed, a wooden table nailed to the deck, and a propane tank hooked to a tiny stove. Putting a home on a boat was a cool idea, she thought. However, there was this odd, five-inch pile of mashed oyster shells that snaked along the deck.

"What is that?" Jodi pointed, tracing the snaking shells that ran past her wet feet toward the bow, disappearing into a weathered doghouse.

Hoink's laugh was even more unusual than his strange sentences. "That's so Elnora can walk okay."

Climbing atop the doghouse, Buck reached down and batted the canvas flap draped over the rectangular entry. "Elnora's in here."

Several low-sounding grunts came from inside.

"My gal heard her name called," Hoinky said. "She thinks it's time to eat."

The grunts grew louder. Buck lifted the flap. Elnora's wet nose pocked out. Jodi watched as Elnora's floppy ears appeared. The pigs head punched and jutted, as if she were pulling herself forward using her snout and not her feet. Elnora's body emerged. Her right legs skipped and limped, laboring to step forward.

Hoinky and Buck watched Jodi's face ignite.

Deformed left-side limbs scratched at the shell mound that ran from the pen. Jodi's eyes bulged. Her mouth dropped. Buck leaped from his perch and jabbed her in the ribs reminding not to laugh.

"What's wrong with Elnora?" she asked.

"She's a pig with a human baby inside her," Hoinky said. "I usta work at a research lab on the Steinhatchee River where some bigwig university professors raised pigs to experiment on. I cared for the animals they used as guinea pigs.

"Some Ph.D. dude got the lamebrain, idiotic idea to inject human embryos into Elnora's mother. I guess you see what happened. She got half a set of legs as baby arms that poke straight from the shoulder and hip joint, sideways—not pointing to the ground like they should. They got fingers and knuckles, too."

Jodi wasn't sure if she should be amazed or grossed out. Tiny, nimble appendages gripped sharp shells and needled along. Elnora struggled with her balance, shifting each time she nudged ahead.

"She has a sad look," said Jodi, examining Elnora. "As if there's the soul of a child inside."

Hoinky watched Jodi's expression. "That's why I kidnapped her. Cuz they handed me a pistol and ordered to shoot Elnora before anyone got wind of the botched experiment."

Hoinky lowered his head and shook it. "I couldn't shoot. Elnora got those sad, crying baby eyes ya see there."

"Buck," Hoinky said. "Give her a carrot."

Buck went into the shack and retrieved a bundle of carrots.

"Go ahead, feed her."

Buck nudged a carrot to Elnora's snout. Quickly, the carrot disappeared.

"How'd your boat get stuck on these rocks?" Jodi asked.

"That's an odd story," said Hoinky with his peculiar voice.

"I lived next to the Steinhatchee animal pens on this here houseboat with my girlfriend, Samantha. The day I rescued Elnora, I floated down river and docked at Crabbie Jay's. After Samantha slammed a few drinks down her gullet, she got all hormonal and bitchy about living with a retarded pig and drove me friggin' nuts. After I got snookered and passed out cold, the pissed wench cut my gas hose and set me adrift. When I came too, Elnora and I had floated into the Gulf of Mexico. And I couldn't get to shore cuz I can't swim."

Jodi was fixated on Elnora's effort to move about using the ribbon of pasted shells to keep upright.

"The houseboat drifted for days until we landed here on these rocks. We's been here ever since," Hoinky said, nearly out of breath.

For Jodi, meeting Buck each day then rowing to feed Elnora became part of their routine. They explored the saltwater flats, drifting the inlets, teasing snakes suspended in the black and red mangroves. They chased clouds of mullets and startled clumsy red drums. Buck taught Jodi the secrets to living off the ocean. He hooked a red snapper, filleted it, squeezed lemons to improve the taste, then grilled the firm butterfish over a driftwood fire.

At the peak of day they ventured onshore into the coolness of the oak grove. Climbing the thick horizontal limbs of the lonely banyan, they pretended like squirrels, finding paths to the next tree without touching the ground. They snipped and gathered Spanish moss and baked it to rid the mites and chiggers, fashioning a spongy mattress by packing the gray leis between the lifted roots of their secret enclave.

They'd lie together and stare and point into the tree canopy, Buck telling Jodi the species of each bird that roosted, inventing clever names for the ones he didn't know.

Jodi watched him intently. Buck was contained, a thinker, skilled with his hands and confident with the ocean and weather. She felt safe. Each time he spoke, Jodi wondered in amazement at Buck's knowledge of nature—his resourcefulness. She'd touch him tenderly, with kindness and warmth. And each time she smiled, Buck noticed more of her womanly features—round, powder-blue Russian eyes, prominent cheekbones, and full lips.

On Horse Head Key they stumbled upon a moonshine still. Next to the cold copper kettle were mason jars of clear liquid.

"Momma buys the shine and brings it with her whenever she's running a poker game at the Hacienda," Buck told her. "Sometimes she comes home with a load of cash or owning a new piece of property. But Momma said stay clear of the stills, cuz it's operated by a young bootlegger named Deuce. Momma says he's from a bad lot."

Pilfering a mason jar, they headed to the enclave where, underneath the shade of the canopy, they sipped the tasteless mash and laughed and giggled and pawed and became intoxicated. They grew flush and warm and ignited. The cool, meandering sea breeze embraced them—its salty scent heightening their lustful intoxication.

Their lips touched . . . once . . . twice, then locked. Tongues meshed and tangled like slimy scallops.

When Buck cupped her naked breast, Jodi tingled. And when he pressed his bare chest against hers, his heart raced. It felt good and Jodi encouraged his exploration. Opening her thighs, she welcomed and shuddered when he inserted his firmness deep inside and arrived.

Jodi's mother waited on a metal milk crate that served as steps to the entrance of her sister's mobile home. When Jodi came closer she saw her crying—as if she witnessed Jodi's loss of virginity. Sadly, she looked at her daughter and said, "Marci, your dad died in a mine collapse."

By 8 am they were in New Port Richey on a bus to Thurmond, West Virginia.

A month later, a widow, Marci's mother moved to Ohio to live with relatives.

Marci found the Ohio countryside different—halfway between Florida's flatness and the Appalachian steepness. The towns were bigger with more people. Her mother, still beautiful with a thick, attractive Russian accent, remarried a conservative, God-fearing man who gave Marci a good home.

And to bury the past, her mother refused to call her Jodi anymore.

Chapter 41

The eye wall of Hurricane Kate arrived. An F-1 tornado leveled the eight-foot brick barrier that guarded Trinity Meadows. It raced along Leiram Avenue and veered into the cypress head and ripped the hurricane shutters from the backside of the Peltzes' house. Their patio doors sucked and spun away, leaving the family room exposed. The Peltz children squeezed their tiny eyelids tight. Their nimble knees bled as the buffeting twister ransacked their home. Their father screamed above the rage and fury, demanding they pray harder. "The Lord has come to take us."

Steel straps anchored to concrete lintels that secured the Lindums' roof twisted, strained, and snapped. Ragged slabs of stucco peeled from outside walls and took flight. Sand particles whipped within the driven rain undermined and dissolved the mortar that bound the cinderblocks that framed the house. The mortar joints failed as blocks tumbled to form a pointed pile. The garage crumbled and imprisoned Robbie Lindum's ski boat, crushing the many boxes of pain medication.

Next door, Jennifer Dink's home stood firm and stoic and fought the endless gale. Jennifer painted her nails, streaked her hair, and paced freely in black chinos and a close-fitting blouse. Her Internet went out—the transceiver ripped from the eaves. To push ahead the time, as she always busily did, she took her expensive collection of porcelain and crystal figurines and dusted them. She examined her treasures, sipped expensive Cabernet, and debated longer than needed on how to arrange, or perhaps move them to another spot.

For seventeen torturous hours Hurricane Kate pummeled Trinity Meadows. The flattened cypress clusters that lifted the value of the expensive community pointed the wind direction. The extended limbs of the toppled oaks that caught and sifted flying debris formed the base of a sand-packed linear mound, which broadened and heightened into a ridge packed with vinyl siding, furniture, stainless steel gas grills, splintered cedar gazebos, plastic playground equipment, terra-cotta, stucco, road signs, clothing, and dead pets and people. It swelled and grew and tightened like cement, and heightened and blocked more wind. A mountain formed, preventing the remains of the Lindums' home from being completely scrubbed away. All that remained of their home was the windward corner where Marci, Robbie, Bradley, and Charlie huddled, buried beneath a protecting clump of soggy mattresses.

Chapter 42

As the wind howled, the eye wall passed south and west of the
Flats. Sitting at his ornate, cherry rolltop with his spine
straight, his feet set flat, Dale Carter adjusted his reading glasses. He
sorted financial and bookkeeping records for the pawnshop and retail
stalls leased at Hoinky's. "Sit the position of a businessman," a
motherly voice preached within his memory. "Before you end the
day, or begin your liquoring, make sure your numbers are looked
over and thought about."

The pawnshop had had another great year. So good, he invested
five thousand dollars each month in tax-exempt bonds, and hid three
thousand in skimmed cash in a floor vault—cash to care for Cabbage
Ears tenants.

Shuffling his feet on the yellow pine flooring, Dale removed a
stack of deeds from a manila folder and flipped through them. Each
was titled to a trust so no one could track his fortune, which seemed
more an albatross than a blessing.

Outside, the carnage continued. Dale wasn't concerned because
years ago, when Florida construction was in another recession with
many Krackers' hard-luck stories, Florence offered Flats folk work.
She paid them to hurricane-proof her home. "Prepare it for the Big

Blow," she'd lament, often scolding sloppy Kracker workers when they cut corners. "Someday, you'll see . . . I'm warnin' ya . . . A nasty 'cane will come."

Florence had reconfigured and strengthened the Icehouse roof and poured concrete footers that ran extra deep. Bolted flexible straps with just enough give clutched concrete-encased rebar pillars. Buried within the sandy loam, oversize French drains diverted the soaking runoff away from the sturdy foundation.

Setting down the deeds, Dale allowed his thoughts to drift back to pleasant, youthful times. The days of visiting Hoinky and Elnora, and the agonizing question of why Jodi, his only love, had abandoned him.

Chapter 43

Holed in the cab of the dragline shovel, Critter stretched his hairy legs between levers and knobs. The drafty, uncomfortable cab dribbled rainwater onto the back of his neck. It took several tries to light a cigarette. Dale had ordered him to ride out the hurricane inside the dragline. And when he bitched, Dale explained the dragline was sturdy enough, saying he needed a lookout for when Fifty-Cal slept, to make sure jarhead Deuce didn't sneak into the Yard.

"Critter, if you do this task I'll exempt ya from having to barter for food after the storm smacks us. And give you the job of bossing the lazy Krackers, seeing they work for their keep," Dale told him.

With his grimy sock he smeared the moisture that collected on the spidery Plexiglas. A few feet away, Fifty-Cal, occupying the deuce-and-a-half, lifted her night-vision binoculars and panned the junkyard. She signaled Critter to look toward Dixie Highway. She'd spotted something.

A lone headlight worked its way toward the main gate. The light beam's forward progress slowed then halted. Seconds later, tiny shadows passed in front of the light. *Gotta be a vehicle comin'.* They must be clearing the roadway, thought Fifty-Cal.

Lacing her khaki army boots, she loaded a wad of tobacco and fired the deuce-and-a-half. She blasted the sour horn four times, a signal to Dale and Critter.

Shoving his smokes into his T-shirt pocket and pulling a poncho over his head, Critter walked the dragline's metal tread then leaped to the waterlogged ground. He fumbled with the clumsy raingear as it flapped in the buffeting wind.

"Sure is nasty," said Critter, ringing moisture from his beard after climbing into the rig.

"We got visitors," Fifty-Cal said.

"What kind of crazies are traveling in this weather?" he asked.

"I guess we're going to find out." Jamming the clutch and grinding gears she mashed the gas pedal. Knobby black tires chewed the chalky mud. "Let's see how this baby handles the shittin' weather."

The hurricane shutters didn't allow Dale to see Fifty-Cal pass; however, the diesel-knock was unmistakable. Gripping the latch he cracked the door. At the base of the grade where it flattened before it met Dixie Highway, the deuce-and-a-half's taillights glowed.

Snatching his truck keys Dale donned his raingear. "Wind's not too bad yet to see what's up."

Squinting, Critter tried to read the lettering on the side of the bus that arrived. He rolled the window to eye level. "Looks like the Sunshine Cruise casino bus with a busted headlight."

Lifting her knee Fifty-Cal mashed the emergency brake. "Go see what's going on."

"Hell no!" said Critter, puffing a cigarette. "Why don't you go?"

"I vote you," she said, working a chew and racing the engine to keep it from stalling.

"Damn dyke." He knew Fifty-Cal never caved when it came to a standoff.

Jerking the door handle, he shoved his shoulder and forced it. His cigarette glowed red then wisped from his lips. Leaning into the wind he took deliberate strides, his flapping poncho pulled tight against his round gut. He grabbed hold of the bus mirror and braced, then pounded on the bi-fold door.

Flipping a light switch and working a knob atop the dashboard, Fifty-Cal directed a bright searchlight beam at the bus driver.

"Huh?" The driver was elderly and wore a brilliant purple jacket, the kind they give to regulars at Scooter's.

The bi-fold door collapsed. Critter entered the brightly lit entry. And when he peered down the aisle his eyes grew big.

Blocking the glare with his hand he frantically gestured Fifty-Cal to come.

Hesitant, she didn't care to get soaked.

In the rearview mirror Dale arrived and stepped onto the running board.

"What's up?" he asked.

"Sunshine Cruise casino bus," Fifty-Cal said. "Crits' in there now."

This time Critter vigorously gestured her to come.

"Go ahead," Dale said. "I don't think he's goofing ya."

"There better be a damn good reason."

After leaving her comfortable cab she approached the bus. She heard singing. "Eighty-three bottles of beer on the wall, eighty-three bottles of bear, drink one down and . . ."

She stepped into the bus and stood next to Critter.

"Holy shit, we've struck gold!" she said.

Giddy, drunk waitresses from Scooter's Oceanside Grill bounced in seats and passed a rum bottle and toasted the driver. "Cheers for Cooterman Pat, our savior."

"They're from over on the Cottee River," said Critter, wearing a shit-eating grin. "Look at 'em all!"

He disappeared from the bright light as he went down the aisle. "Anyone need a smoke?"

Turning, Fifty-Cal shielded her eyes and singled thumbs-up to Dale.

Dale unlocked and dropped the gate cable.

Fifty-Cal spoke to the elderly driver. "What are you doing with a busload of snookered chickadees, old man?" Then she realized who he was. "I know you! You're that old bugger I see at Scooter's all the time."

"I'm Cooterman Pat," said the wiry driver.

"What do you think you're doing?" she asked.

"Our hurricane party got too dicey," Pat said. "We hadda skedaddle when the ocean busted into the restaurant."

Two seats away a chesty brunette shouted. "No one showed for the party except Cooterman. If it weren't for Pat hot-wiring the casino bus, we would have drowned."

A sweet-sounding voice called from the seat next to Fifty-Cal. "I love you, Cooterman!" A cheer erupted.

I gotta get in on some of this, thought Fifty-Cal. What a great way to ride out the hurricane.

"Cooterman, is this the nudist colony?" asked a shorthaired blond in flesh-colored thigh stockings.

Owning a wrinkled grin, Pat winked at Fifty-Cal. "I told them the only safe place was your nudist colony. The gals think we have to follow the rules and strip, otherwise you won't let us in." He winked again. "Isn't that right?" he said loudly.

Fifty-Cal thought for a moment. Why not go along with the old goat's ruse.

"Smell that perfume driftin' around the bus. I may be old but not stupid," Pat whispered. "They're drunk, and I can still make a boner. The hornies don't leave just because you got arthritis."

Fifty-Cal had to agree, the women smelt good.

"Listen up, young ladies. This here is a nudie camp and you gotta follow the rules, or I ain't letting y'all in," Fifty-Cal said.

From the back a bra flew past, followed by a pair of men's jeans and a man's shirt. "Take it all off," someone yelled.

Lifting the denim pants into the searchlight, Fifty-Cal said, "Critter ain't wearin' jeans."

Someone zinged a pair of underpants by the waistband, which landed on Cooterman's head.

"Thems ain't women's undies. And ain't Critter's cuz they're too small. Besides, he don't wear underwear."

"Must belong to the Greeks," said Pat, gripping the steering wheel and driving through the gate.

"Greeks?"

"We picked up two Greek fellows from Tarpon Springs before turning to come here. Says their names are Nick and Andres, waiters from Valaki's restaurant. They ain't complaining, if ya know what I mean."

Critter came down the aisle wearing a huge grin. He'd traded lipstick kisses planted on his forehead for cigarettes. "They're drunk and naked and think they're at a nudist colony. And got two naked Greeks in the last seat and taking turns fucking the lucky goddess bastards."

"Cooterguy, park this where I tell ya," ordered Fifty-Cal.

Dale hung the heavy cable and locked it after the bus passed through and stopped.

Fifty-Cal stepped off. "Waitresses from Scooter's, they need a place to ride out the storm. That okay with you, Dale?"

Dale nodded. "You better find a way to secure the bus."

"Not a problem. I'll pinch it next to dragline so it don't get blowed over."

"Let's get going, the weather's getting worse," Dale said. "The brunt of the hurricane is about to smack us."

Chapter 44

The surge crested the swampy shoals of the Anclote River, flooded grassy fields, overloaded retention ponds, lifted sewer covers, and slinked along the debris-littered streets of Trinity Meadows. Charlie's floppy ears swiveled; the random noises, the lingering scents differed. There were thumps, creaks, and knocks. Charlie buckled his snout as a foul, sour odor grew stronger. He'd smelt it before—on Robbie's pant leg mixed with his urine. The pungent, rotten aroma drifted toward the Peltzes' then faded.

When the wetness came Brad woke and heard Charlie's whimpers and splashing paws. He strained his eyes to see through the darkness. The mattress was a saturated sponge. "Mom . . . Dad . . . stuff's floating!"

"Brad, grab hold of my shirt," Marci said in a panic as the seawater lapped at her ankles.

Charlie barked and paddled. Suddenly, his nails scratched at a piece of furniture.

In complete darkness Marci reached toward Charlie and found the cherry bookcase floating. She shoved Charlie by his rump. "Get in there. Bradley," said Marci, trudging in the waist-deep saltwater. "Come toward my voice. I found something to hang onto."

Guiding Brad by his forearm she placed his hand on the floating bookcase. "Grab hold."

Holding his bandage Robbie spun in circles; he couldn't see in the darkness.

"Marci!"

"Robbie, over here; quickly, the water is rising."

The murk was chest-deep as he worked toward the sound of her voice. "Here, Rob, grab hold." The water quickly rose.

Suspended, they were unable to touch the ground and clung to the bookcase. Marci wanted to return to the dream she was having of her childhood. Was it this dark when the mine collapsed on her father? Was he scared like she was?

Frightened, no one spoke. There were seeps and trickles and clunks. Somewhere in the darkness, they heard soft murmurs. "Our father thou art in heaven . . . hallowed be thy name . . ."

Brad broke the silence. "Look at the Dinks' house, on the second floor, a flashlight!"

A tubular beam searched the watery blackness. It passed over their heads and illuminated a capsized boat.

"I wonder how miss goody two-shoes is making out? Bet you she's pretty freaked that her expensive furniture is ruined. Should've been her home that blew down, not ours," Marci said.

"He huffed and puffed and blew the house down," Bradley mocked.

"Not funny, Brad," Marci said. "The witch knows we're here and won't acknowledge we exist."

"Not good!"

Entwined in a tangle of palm branches, sneezing stinging saltwater that pooled in her nostrils, Piggy bobbed beneath the Anclote River

Bridge. When the surge arrived, an upstream eddy formed behind the bridge abutment. But the ocean swallowed the entire bridge and set Piggy adrift. The decrepit gator aimlessly drifted, crossing a pasture, traversing submerged fenceposts strung with barbwire, and into Trinity Meadows. Piggy pedaled her dangling claws and snapped her crooked croc tail and glided into the toppled cypress head, where every tree lay in the same direction. She rested her alligator head on the edge of a sunken refrigerator with its spilled contents bobbing about. The familiar scent of a rabbit grew strong. Her belly grumbled. Lazily, she maneuvered from her berth closer to the scent and rested, lying in stealth waiting for the prey.

When the surge hit, the Peltz girls crawled onto the dining room table, but the water continued to rise. Their caged animals chirped and squealed. Parakeets, hamsters, and lizards squeezed their tiny heads through the wire squares of their pens and gasped their last breath. Several rabbits escaped when a piece of driftwood nudged a latch.

Edward Peltz loaded his family into the canoe they owned. Using a flashlight, he made sure they didn't drift from inside the house.

They prayed. "Thy kingdom come. Thy will be done . . ."

And when the next dawn came the surge had receded, but not the driving rain.

The Peltz girls were told to start scrubbing the slime that coated the home, until Sahara, the oldest child, suddenly collapsed. Her father lifted the frail girl and said she showed weakness and must make amends. He sent her outside into the rain to the "penance mound" and told her to pray. "Show God you are worthy of his forgiveness," he demanded.

At first Sahara balked. "No, Daddy!"

But Edward Peltz pointed. "Sahara, go!"

Her sad, tired eyes pleaded. She looked at the torn-out section of their home and cried. "Daddy, please no. I don't want to go. I'm scared."

Edward Peltz cast his angry look and raised his hand to strike.

Sahara's wobbly legs picked their way through the muck to where stacked cinderblocks served as a prayer altar. "God, take me away from this sad place and my mean daddy."

Kneeling, she surveyed the flooded cypress head and saw Piggy's head poking from the water's edge.

"Hello, happy-looking alligator. Will you be my friend?"

Piggy raised her bulky head and pushed onto the embankment.

"Oh," Sahara said. "You understand. Alligator, what happened to your nose? Are you hurt?"

Suddenly, Piggy thrashed, knocking Sahara off the brick stoop. Tumbling, she landed next to Piggy and reached to stop from rolling into the water. She braced against Piggy's rough skin.

Instinctively, the gator snapped and caught Sahara's arm on the toothless side of her jaw. With a double head jerk Piggy adjusted her bite and caught Sahara by the shoulder.

"Mommy, Daddy," she called. "An alligator got me. Please come and get me unstuck."

With her powerful hind legs Piggy dragged Sahara into the flooded cypress head.

"The alligator is taking me. Come get me."

The gnarly bark of a submerged tree trunk scraped across Sahara's stomach.

"Ouch, Mommy, it hurts really bad!"

Opening her giant jaw, Piggy scooped the child headfirst, lifted, and slid Sahara into its wide-open mouth.

"Mommmy . . ." she cried as the fleshy throat suctioned her scalp.

There were muffled, bony snaps that sounded like twigs breaking as Piggy disappeared beneath the brown murk.

Chapter 45

Covered with filthy green-gray grime, the Lindums huddled atop their soggy mattresses. Occasionally, something solid whizzed in and knocked more blocks from the foundation. Daylight came. The wind direction shifted and blew from the east.

A mosquito sucked on Robbie's forearm. He smacked it and splattered blood.

Marci had stared at Robbie for some time and had seen nothing but a thin, balding, crumpled man who'd aged overnight. I can't depend on him anymore, she thought, his persona was to blame. He had dillydallied and ignored the urgency that left them trapped and in peril. If she was to survive, she must take charge—do things herself.

"Do you think this storm will ever go away?" Robbie asked in a weak voice.

"Seems the wind changed direction," Marci said.

"My face is throbbing. I need an antibiotic."

"Where's the first aid kit?" she asked.

"In the ski boat," he said.

"Dad, are we going to walk to the hurricane shelter to get some food? I'm hungry," Bradley asked.

"Yes, Brad, as soon as we can. But I may need to see a doctor first."

"Crawling from atop the mattress Marci stepped over the bookcase where Charlie lay. A slippery layer of muck coated everything. She tossed palm branches aside and picked her way. Finding a bag of Doritos, she wiped off the mud the best she could and tossed it to Brad.

"Thanks, Mom," said Brad, watching her gingerly move about.

"You know what we should do?" he said.

"What, Brad?"

"Make a clearing."

"Good idea . . ." But suddenly, her jaw dropped. Slowly she turned and gazed upwards.

Witnessing her dismay, Brad stopped munching.

"What is it?"

"My God," Marci said. "What is that?"

Brad crawled from the mattress hut and followed her gaze. "Look how high it is! How'd that car get up there?"

An unbelievably high debris mountain ran across Leiram Avenue. It buried several homes as it cut through the center of the cul-de-sac down the street and continued westward toward the Gulf of Mexico.

"Look at the top," Brad said. "The wind is blowing pretty hard."

"What's wrong?" called Robbie.

"Dad, come and look."

Holding the bandage Robbie peered upward. "How did it get here?"

"Careful, Brad, there's broken glass," Marci warned.

Bradley scurried onto a mound of rubble for a better look. "It squashed the houses across the street. I hope no one was in them."

"Brad, I told you to be careful," Marci scolded him.

"We're trapped!" Robbie said.

"Look!" Brad said. "The Dinks' home, it's still standing."

A hum emanated from beneath a pile of brush nearby. It was the Dinks' air-conditioner. "I can't believe it, the wench has electricity," Marci said.

Robbie pointed to a potted marijuana plant that stood intact among the rubble. "How'd that get there?"

Deny it, was Marci's immediate thought. *Make up something.*

"Uh, I have no idea," she said.

Brad pointed. "I know what that is . . . a pot plant!"

Marci pretended not to know what he meant. "I see that, Brad. It's in a pot."

"No, Mom, marijuana!"

"Why isn't it shredded like the trees?" Robbie noted. He pointed to the severely leaning cabbage palm. All the fronds were gone.

"Peculiar things often occur in a storm," Marci said. "Tornadoes can do the most unusual things."

"Look at those extension cords tangled in the trusses that blew into the swimming pool. There're lots of them," Brad said.

Marci bit her tongue. She sensed that they were narrowing in their minds that someone in the neighborhood operated a *grow house*.

"Regardless where they came from," Marci said, "we must focus our attention on other matters, like finding help."

Robbie joked. "We can get high to take us out of our misery."

"Robbie!" His statement shocked Marci. He was such a nerd.

"Brad, can you make a clearing so we can move around easier?"

"Sure, Mom." Brad finished the Doritos then went to work. He shoved what he could aside, tossing palm branches, splintered 2x4's, and drywall as far as he could away from what used to be the den. Using one hand, Robbie cleared a path to the kitchen and garage. Twisted trusses near the pool were too difficult to maneuver.

By midafternoon it started to rain heavily. Returning to the muck-covered mattress they drew a plastic tarp that Brad found to cover them. And when the rain slowed, they scrounged and found sodas and pretzels and sealed crackers and gobbled them.

Periodically, Marci looked over at Jennifer Dink's house. It amazed her how well the home had held up. Several fence pickets stuck in the walls like embedded arrows. How close did those projectiles come to our heads? she thought.

Marci questioned how the air-conditioner could be running. "It's ridiculous that she's got electricity!"

Frustrated, Marci set her hands on her hips and yelled. "She's in there nice and dry and clean. I bet you got plenty to eat."

Still not satisfied, she made her way to Jennifer's front door. "Jennifer!" Marci banged. "Let us in."

There was no answer. She yanked loose a picket and whacked at a hurricane shutter.

Bam, Bam! "Jennifer, you hoarder, help us out!"

Marci tried the doorknob. It was locked.

"Listen, you greedy son of a bitch, are you that big of an ass not to help a neighbor?"

To pass time Jennifer polished her granite countertops. She removed pots and baking pans and rearranged them to create more cabinet space. She counted the spoons, forks, knives, plates, and glasses and found one glass missing.

Debating where to store a wok, she noticed water seeping along the grouted kitchen tiles. She panicked and grabbed a mop. But the effort was futile; the surge had arrived and chased her upstairs, quickly swallowing the risers of her gorgeous balustrade staircase.

Jennifer prayed the rapidly rising water wouldn't reach the second floor.

By morning a black watermark lined the walls seven feet up. From her upstairs study she flipped a switch and raised the hurricane shutters six inches. Daylight came into the dark home.

She peeked out each window. The hurricane had devastated Trinity Meadows. It shredded and stripped every bush and tree. There were giant sinkholes with rills and gullies, and expansive bare spots that exposed the raw limestone bedrock.

The Lindums' home was flattened. Jennifer watched them string plastic and stack cinderblocks to reform the walls near where they slept. Brad moved a chair beneath the plastic and set Robbie in it. He appeared injured.

A large plant stood in a bucket where the living room once was. "That's a pot plant!"

All the secretive coming and going, thought Jennifer. Marci was a dealer.

"I was right," she said inside the empty home. "She isn't so clean-cut after all."

An hour later she heard Marci bang furiously on the hurricane shutters, cursing, calling her a greedy hoarder.

Chapter 46

After a brief nap Doctor Paola Estrada spent fifteen minutes remaking her face, applying a glossy layer of ruby lipstick. Entering the operation center she plunked into a cushioned chair, tilted back, and watched the overhead monitors. Kate had reentered the Gulf of Mexico directly over Cedar Key.

The latest satellite photos had arrived.

Estrada flipped her hair from her eyes, typed the computer keyboard, and pressed enter. The satellite images appeared on the biggest screen. There was considerable cloud cover.

Overlaying GIS data she pieced together the destruction caused by the eye wall and tidal surge, and prepared her presentation.

Governor Simon was present with a group of political leaders and emergency managers who waited eagerly for her damage assessment.

After making notes she moved to a podium and spoke with a slight Latino accent. "Clearwater Beach, along with all the Pinellas County barrier islands, is gone."

Using a laser pointer she described the destruction. "As far as infrastructure goes, Courtney Campbell Causeway, Bayside Bridge, and the Franklin and Skyline bridges are destroyed. The raised portion of the Lee Roy Selmon sank on its pillars."

"I told them that elevated highway was flawed," Levy County's Patrick Johnson said.

Paola's analytical eyes measured the group. The men were fidgeting. "I-4 west of Lakeland is impassable. In fact, it's gone. And it's the same with I-75 north of Tampa. A substantial portion of both interstates sank into the swamp. No doubt the roadbed gave way."

"How are we going to rescue everyone?" someone asked.

"We can't," the governor said. "They're on their own until we rebuild the roads, or find a way in from the north."

Doctor Estrada interrupted. "Not from the north. Kate's heaviest rain bands passed right over the Withlacoochee Swamp."

"Why is that significant?" asked the governor.

Patrick Johnson jumped up, approached the podium, and joined the conversation. "I can see you aren't a native Floridian."

Gnashing his teeth, the governor cast a hard, anchoring glare at Patrick. At times they were adversaries; the governor catered to greedy land developers who lined his political pockets with donations. Patrick was an environmentalist and sought any opportunity to expose Albert.

"Go ahead, get on with it," the governor demanded.

Doctor Estrada watched the tense exchange. Patrick was a hydrological engineer qualified to talk about Florida swamps and drainage arrays.

"Kate dumped the greatest amount of rain along the Withlacoochee River tract. For over thirty-six hours there was no letup," said Patrick, gripping the microphone.

"Doctor Estrada, can I borrow your pointer?"

A red laser dot appeared and circled on the overhead monitor. "See this giant swamp east of Zephyrhills? That's where much of the rain fell. We're guessing more than forty inches."

"And your point is?" the governor asked.

"Governor, you rubber-stamped the destruction of Florida's natural vegetation and the leveling of orange groves by okaying the construction of sprawling developments. You should've funded a project similar to the everglades restoration effort in this drainage basin," Patrick said rather bitterly.

He used the laser pointer. "The swamp's basin breached and overflowed. Forget using any roads to the north or east to bring heavy equipment," Patrick said. "Anyone west and south of the swamp is cut off. It will be a good while before you reach Port Richey, Odessa, Hudson, or any of those folks living along the Highway 19 coastal corridor. That's if anyone survived that forty-two-foot surge."

Firming his voice, Patrick carefully spoke the next sentence. "Add starvation to your list for the ones that survived."

The news was grim.

Sitting in their comfortable, air-conditioned situation room, there was nothing they could do.

"Let's continue," said Doctor Estrada, putting up the next satellite image.

"Patrick, I want you to take a close look. Is this one of those debris piles you mentioned?"

With his back to the audience, he stepped toward the overhead monitor, put on his glasses, and studied the color image. "Can you zoom in, Paola?"

"How about a 3D image?" she said.

"Sure!"

"How's that?" The image grew larger—more detailed—and lifted from the screen.

"Looks like . . ." Patrick studied the stereo photo. "Hmm . . . Yes, it is. Where's it located?" he asked.

Scrolling the mouse she boxed the snaking anomaly and overlaid it with the city and highway templates.

"That's better." Patrick flashed the laser dot at the image. He addressed the group.

"Folks, this is what you will deal with for the next few months. You must cut through these linear mountains packed with hurricane debris."

Patrick paused. *How could he explain so they understand?*

"The best way to understand is to think of a centrifuge with the center pin as Kate's rotating eye wall. A second vortex is in play here, which we've learned is unique to extreme Cat-5 cyclones. They develop this outer wind field that circulates independently at much greater speed. The outermost ring fills with soil, sand, and compact leaf matter, and dozers ahead of the arriving eye wall, sandblasting, scraping the earth surface. Once the cyclone loads, the released excess matter leaves these arcing, linear mounds, which trap, sift, and gather tumbling debris until it grows into a mountain like that."

The red laser dot traced the 3D image. "Leaving tightly packed ridge-like structures. The earth looks like God took a bush-hog mower and mowed across the west coast of Florida."

"Doctor Estrada, can you zoom a bit closer?"

The frame enlarged. The limp expressions of the onlookers grew pale.

"First, you must rebuild the highways that lead to Tampa," Patrick said. "And when you come across one of these anomalies you must tunnel through."

Governor Simon shook his head. "We ain't got equipment to do that."

No one answered. They all knew that.

"What about the gulf?" the Saint Petersburg mayor asked. "Can't we access Tampa Bay by ship?"

This time Doctor Estrada spoke. "If you're looking for your hometown, Tinky, try searching offshore. There's no way to bring a rescue ship close the mouth of Tampa Bay. There's too much sand from the barrier islands that's washed into the gulf. You'll need to resurvey and dredge new channels, which could take longer than a land-based rescue," Paola said. "The downed Skyway Bridge, who knows where all that bridge-cabling is. Not good for ship propellers."

"It's an impossible situation," the governor said.

Patrick pointed to the debris pile once again. "We must cut through them to rescue people."

"Where's that one located?"

"New Port Richey," Patrick said. "It starts in Odessa, cuts along Route 54, then slices through Trinity Meadows and continues, ending west of Lake Tarpon."

"Man, look at that," someone said. "Wasn't a new hospital just built there?"

"I think we snapped a shot of that area when the cloud cover broke," Doctor Estrada said.

There was silence as the next photo appeared.

"That debris pile sits right on top of the hospital."

A lump came to everyone's throat.

"Look, it missed the Trinity Meadows high school and the YMCA!"

"Let's hope most people stayed there."

"Not enough room at the inn," Patrick said. "They built too many homes in the Meadows. No way can that shelter support a population of ten thousand homes."

"Enough," the governor said. "Let's get moving and do something useful."

Chapter 47

What seemed to be an endless rain split their plastic tarp and drenched the Lindums. When it calmed they crawled from beneath the tattered plastic and went to the pool area. Marci stripped and washed in a section where the collapsed trusses didn't interfere. Bradley, uncomfortable witnessing his mother bathe, returned to the hut and rehung the tarp. He cleared more loose blocks and flipped the bookcase out of the way.

Marci returned slightly cleaner.

"You know, Mom, we should save the rainwater in case no one comes to help us."

"Good idea," said Robbie, overhearing him. "But I'm sure someone will be here before dark."

Marci was doubtful—all along Robbie had been wrong.

"What if no one comes tonight?" she said, resisting the urge to verbally assassinate him. It wasn't the time. Mosquitoes had gathered on his blood-soaked bandage and puss oozed from a cut that looked infected.

"Robbie, that slice on your face needs first-aid. Those mosquitoes are circling your noggin like buzzards."

Smack—"Damn mosquitoes." A red welt formed on her thigh.

"Where is the insect repellent?" she asked.

"In the garage, under the passenger seat of the ski boat, is bug spray," Robbie said.

"I'll go and get it," said Brad, volunteering. "I'm small enough to climb through the trusses."

Robbie and Marci looked at each other. "We need that repellent so we can last the night," she said. "Okay, but be safe, for God sakes," Marci said.

Brad made his way to the garage and crawled onto the tangle of rubble then slipped between several crisscrossed layers of twisted lumber.

"Are you all right?" called Marci, stretching, bobbing, trying to track him.

"I'm at Dad's boat."

Craning, she watched him roll over the gunwale. There were thumps. "Are you okay? I can't see you."

"Uh . . . ah . . . umps, it's a tight squeeze."

Sprawled along the centerline of the boat Brad lifted his rump. He backed into the narrow space next to the passenger seat, raised the seat cushion and reached for the first-aid kit, but jerked back. "Holy crap!"

"Brad, what's wrong?"

"There's a snake." Brad froze.

Because of his positioning he found himself unable to retreat.

"Ma . . . Mom," Brad stuttered. "It's coming toward me."

"Oh my goodness, Brad, don't move!" Marci crawled onto the rubble to where she could see him. She envisioned the deadly moccasin that clung to her nightgown a few days ago, fearing it took residence in the boat.

"Brad, are you okay?"

With his eyes locked on the legless creature emerging from under the seat cushion, Brad failed to answer. The snake slithered onto his bent knees, along his left arm to his shoulder and across the back of his neck. Brad closed his eyes, expecting it to bite any moment. He cowered in fear.

Marci climbed further. "Ouch!" A nail scraped her arm.

Sprawled on plywood sheathing she peered over. Directly below, Brad was a marble statue. The snake wrapped his neck. Grabbing a piece of wood, Marci jabbed towards the snake and startled the multipatterned reptile. It uncoiled and slinked into the stern.

"Brad!" Marci called. "The snake is gone. Get the first-aid kit and get out."

Frightened, he refused to move.

Marci called a second time, louder, in a commanding, directive tone. "Bradley Lindum, listen to me! Reach into that compartment and get the blue plastic box."

He followed her instruction and moments later wriggled free.

"Was that snake poisonous?" Bradley asked.

"It sure looked it."

"I'm scared, Mom."

Marci grabbed his shoulders and looked right at him. "I need you to be brave. Daddy needs you too, he's hurt."

"I'll, ah . . . I'll try, Mom."

Marci sat Robbie on a dining room chair they'd salvaged and inspected his bulky bandage. Using a glass shard she gingerly cut away the duct tape that held the dishcloth bandage in place.

"Ouch . . . Ooch," Robbie winced.

Mosquitoes swooned the gaping wound. It smelled like a decaying mango. Marci picked, removing mosquitoes that crawled around the edge.

"Did you find the repellent?" he asked.

She dug through the kit, thinking the repellent was inside. "It's not in the kit?"

"No," Robbie said. "It was on the floor next to it."

Marci cursed. "Damn!"

Brad wasn't ready to go back to get it.

Smack . . . Smack.

Marci swatted several mosquitoes that landed on her thigh.

"Robbie, the cut is all the way to the cheekbone."

Digging through the first-aid kit Marci found a roll of adhesive tape, a four-ounce bottle of peroxide, and a fisherman suture kit.

"What luck, something to stitch it closed."

Uncapping the peroxide she tilted the brown bottle. "I'm going to flush your cut."

"Wha . . . what? No, don't. It will sting." Robbie shoved her hand aside. "Don't touch it."

"It needs stitches. Plus, mosquitoes are crawling in it." Marci poured the peroxide onto his injured cheek.

"Ooh, ouch!" Robbie jerked away.

"You must let me do this!"

"Ah. . ." Robbie tried to get out his words. He stuttered. "Ya . . . you . . . mean with a needle . . . buh . . . but . . . that will hurt too much."

"Don't be a weenie," Marci said. "You have no choice."

For Robbie, it didn't sink in that a needle could be poked through his skin without feeling horrific pain. Never did he have stitches. He feared even a dentist drill, often selecting sedation therapy to have teeth cleaned.

He blocked Marci. "But . . . but, it's going to hurt too much. I won't be able to stand the pain." Robbie stalled as long as he could.

"If you don't stitch it, those mosquitoes are going to lay eggs in there and cause more pain than you could imagine. You better do something, soon."

"Cover my cut," Robbie said. "I can't do it."

Applying a gauze pad Marci decided not to fight him. "What a moron!"

She sat on the mattress and thought of a solution. Panning the rubble her eyes came upon a crushed liquor cabinet.

"That's it," she said. "Glenlivet. Robbie kept a full bottle for his father's annual visit. Scotch will do." Digging the Scotch bottle from the damaged cabinet she unscrewed the cap and took several gulps, then smacked her lips. They felt numb. She became warm and flush. "I needed this.

"Here, Rob, drink."

She forced the bottle into his hands. "Take a big gulp."

Setting her fingers under the bottle she forcibly guided it to his lips. The smooth liquor brushed his tongue and flushed his throat. Immediately, Robbie's pinched cheeks turned rosy. He felt the pain of the infection, then the smoothness of the aged Scotch. Again, Marci forced the bottle. This time he was less reluctant, his face scrunched and puckered. A rush arrived and momentarily stalled the throbbing. Soon the bottle was empty.

Brad came over with Charlie and squatted next to his father. He held his hand, saying, "You'll be okay, Dad."

Robbie's eyes were glassy; his head weaved and wobbled. "You know, honeybuns, you are a very pretty woman."

It was the comment that pissed her off the most. Inside, Marci wanted to slug his injured face. However, she saw Brad out of the corner of her eye watching, and wondered if he knew she was unhappy.

Weaving, Robbie fell from the chair and passed out.

"Rob . . . Rob?" Marci shook him.

"Good, you lightweight, you're a goner." Straddling him, she removed the gauze, unscrewed the peroxide, and poured half the bottle inside the wound. The clear liquid bubbled into a fizzing, Alka-Seltzer foam. Several dead mosquitoes flushed out.

"Brad, see if you can find me another bottle of liquor over there."

Brad retrieved a nearly full bottle of Vodka.

"It's been awhile since I used needle and thread," Marci said. "Not since I helped my mother make down pillows in West Virginia."

Marci took several swigs of the vodka. It relaxed her hands enough to thread the needle. She jabbed the pinpoint into Robbie's skin. With her thumb and forefinger she pinched the gaping wound closed, then forced the needle through the tissue. Brad watched as she drew the thread and tugged. The gash narrowed.

Gingerly, she flushed with more peroxide then looped another stitch, repeating until the gap sealed and the peroxide emptied.

"You'd make a good doctor," Brad said.

"I must say so," said Marci, admiring her work, feeling relaxed from the alcohol.

"Boy, Mom, Dad is out cold, isn't he?"

After dressing the wound Marci chugged more vodka.

"Brad," she said. "Sip this. It will help you shleep . . . uh, I mean sleep."

Bradley looked puzzled.

"It's okay, take some. It'll help you rest tonight."

Reluctant, he drank. It tasted awful. But Marci forced several more sips. His tongue numbed. He became melancholy and plopped his head on Charlie's stomach.

Marci guzzled the remaining vodka and passed out.

Chapter 48

The surge had completely destroyed Cabbage Ears trailer park. Dixie Highway flooded its entire length and then some. Gator Tales had floated from its Cracker House foundation and drifted across a grassy flat and nudged against the junkyard's barbwire fence. Several mutant piglets living inside the ruptured pontoon of Hoinky's houseboat survived inside an air pocket.

When daylight arrived, Dale flipped open a circular peephole cut into a hurricane shutter. His mother was wise, he thought, spying in the direction of Hoinky's. The best protection was beneath the seawater and close to the ocean, away from flying debris. That's why she wanted Hoinky's property. She'd often said the flea market would be there after the 'cane came, and easy to get up and running. It wasn't till now, looking at the intact buildings, that he understood how.

After Hurricane Kate moved onshore it seemed the rain had intensified and persisted for nearly thirty hours until Kate looped and exited back into the Gulf of Mexico. When the heavy winds subsided to buffeting tropical storm gusts, the cooped residents that occupied the metallic junkyard adobes crawled from their grubby fortresses and started clearing the nearby debris.

Dale Carter removed his hurricane shutters and set the two Adirondack rocking chairs he'd stowed back where they belonged— on the front porch facing the ocean. He lifted his binoculars and spied the boom of the dragline. The osprey nest was no longer there. "Wonder where the hell that rabid, pig-snatching fowl went?"

Wedged between the dragline and Fifty-Cal's deuce-and-a-half was the Sunshine Cruise casino shuttle bus. With fogged windows the bus seemed quiet. Fifty-Cal must've tuckered them out, thought Dale.

Walking to the corner of his porch Dale lifted his arm and signaled Critter inside the cab of the dragline. Critter had smoked nearly two cartons of cigarettes. His stomach grumbled because Flatch had left him containers of Spam, Vienna sausages, and a jar pickled eggs to eat. When Dale signaled, he grabbed a megaphone held in place with Velcro straps, climbed from the stinky cab, stood on the metal treads, and relieved himself before keying the sound.

"Listen up, cabbage heads." Critter paused and waited until his voice echoed back. "If you gotta take a dump, go to the edge of the mine and crap in the shitter pipes, like ya's been doin'. If I catchya cheatin', or if I step in one of your turd piles, Fifty-Cal will throw your sorry ass the hell out of here. Got it?"

As Critter continued to broadcast more directives, explaining the barter rules for when the flea market was set up, the Krackers crawled from their shelters. Fifteen minutes later he repeated the messages to make sure they heard.

Walking the entire perimeter of his wraparound porch while listening to Critter, Dale inspected the outlying property. In the distance, his favorite place, a stand of sturdy oaks, had lost only a few trees. A shallow dune lay where Gator Tales once stood—only the rectangular concrete posts that propped the popular hangout poked through the brown sugar sand. "That was a damn good barroom," said Dale, recalling the work it took to build it. "Too bad."

Lighting another cigarette, Dale stood stiff and stared at the vastness of the land he owned. Suddenly, he pounded his fist on the porch post and boldly said, "Okay, let's get our asses in gear, clean this mess like Momma said we should."

Tossing cabbage palm branches into a pile, Dale watched Critter walk down the grade toward him. "Critter, let's drag that wood chipper from behind Chadda's RV and fire it up. We got plenty of guys and tough gals that make a living trimming palms. Put them to work."

It took a half hour to free the chipper from the settled mud. Eager landscapers looking for barter arrived, and almost immediately the chipper zinged and crunched away. Woodchips flew into the air.

Flatch appeared with a shit-eating grin. Dale had no idea where he'd stayed during the storm until he came closer.

"Judging from your smile and those bloodsucker hickeys," Dale said, "you look like you got laid during the storm."

"It pays to be a bartender," Flatch said.

Standing nearby, Critter couldn't resist adding his two cents. "I saw you slip into the Cooter bus, you shit-ball. Explains that goddamn suck necklace tracking your Icabob gooseneck."

Flatch laughed. "Waitresses always take good care of the bartender. I gotta thank Fifty-Cal, though. She's the one that tipped me off about the busload of beavers."

"What's with that old goat bus driver?" Critter asked.

"Ya mean Cooterman Pat," Flatch said. "Fifty-Cal convinced several gals to ride the Irishman's boner. Said he won't be alive much longer and should give him a going-away gift. The geezer popped a Viagra and four of them humped the old man until he conked out. I think the poor bastard was trying to die with a hard-on," Flatch said.

Everyone chuckled.

"Shit, why can't that happen to me?" Critter was envious.

"Never you mind," said Dale, breaking up the chitchat. "We got lots to do and no time to get distracted. Go dig Fifty-Cal from that busload of thighs and tits."

Tossing his cigarette, Dale headed for his pickup. "Least when Cal's gotten her rocks off, she's good to go for a couple days."

"Flatch," said Dale as he dug his pocket for truck keys, "guess you know Gator's floated inland a ways." Dale allowed himself to laugh. "You see a barroom anywhere?"

Flatch spun in a circle; Gator Tales wasn't visible. He strained his eyes eastward. "You got an idea where it may be, Dale?"

"Yup, it's around the bend on the backside of the limestone pit." Dale chuckled. "I'm heading over to see if it's salvageable."

"Andy?" Dale abruptly changed his tone and called Flatch by his first name, which meant he needed his help. "When the wind subsides some more, and the tide's all gone, can you and Critter go see what it takes to get Hoinky's up and runnin'? If we don't get these here Krackers working, they'll get lazy and smoke dope all day. With all the alkies we got and miserable characters addicted to painkillers, the withdrawals are going to be a real bitch for anyone who ain't getting buzzed in time."

"Critter," Dale said, turning to give orders, "tell the Krackers to scrounge the useful shit in blowed-down buildings and bring it to Hoinky's. I'm sure the Walmart on Ridge Road got demolished. There's plenty of stuff buried that can be scrounged for barter. I told Fifty-Cal's to watch for freeloaders. Anyone who steals will dodge the smoking barrel of that dyke's machine gun."

261

With a stern and determined expression Dale spoke more orders.

"We got enough stuff in storage containers to last until I can organize fishermen to catch some grouper, shrimp, and stone crabs. For meat, folks can catch and kill only seagulls, cuz they's plenty. No one's to kill any other fowl. And feel free to roast any of those mutant pigs of Hoink's that you come across. Those who make themselves useful get free rent, food, and fresh water."

For the longest time, Dale had prepared for this day. His mother spent years collecting the right container trucks, military hardware, and water buffalos—even ice makers and refrigeration units. The Flats folk were set for a good while.

Chapter 49

Cooterman Pat lay in the aisle snoring with a frozen smile. Strewn throughout the Sunshine Cruise casino bus were pieces of fluorescent purple shorts and flesh-colored nylon stockings. A push-up bra hung from the bus mirror. The bus reeked of alcohol and stale womanly stench. Fifty-Cal gently shifted the shapely leg that clutched her waist and admired the young girl that clung to her.

Naked, with his arms and legs bound by knotted panty hose, the long-haired Greek waiter, Andres, meekly asked Fifty-Cal to cut him free. After admiring the olive skin Grecian, telling him how well-hung he was, she pulled her pocketknife and sliced the panty hose that tied his wrists. She buttoned her leather pants and adjusted her halter and emptied her silver jewelry from a beer mug. She inserted the silver posts into the multiple piercings, shoved a tobacco wad beneath her cheek, then headed for Hoinky's.

As the deuce-and-a-half entered the muddy lot of the flea market, juice dribbled Fifty-Cal's chin as the knobby black tires mashed fresh zigzag patterns. She noted the grime-covered red Mustang that belonged to that Trinity jailbait and wondered how Chadda made out with the cutie pie.

Driving alongside the flea market buildings she found Dale with a work crew unloading generators and pressure washers. "Dale, did you hear from Flatch that Deuce was let out of jail?"

Wearing rubber boots, Dale walked over and leapt onto the running board. He grabbed the door frame and mirror bracket to keep from falling.

"Yes," Dale said.

"Just checking to see if Flatch told you," mumbled Fifty-Cal while working the tobacco wad. "Flatch ain't right yet after scoring in that busload of drunken coochies. His nuts probably hurt him like a whorin' tomcat humping a dozen kitties in heat during a full moon."

Dale couldn't blame Flatch. He wasn't handsome; the man was a scrag. Getting laid by a group of young, tight-ass gals when you didn't deserve it would keep a man's mind wrong for a good long time.

"Cal, I need you to keep a keen eye out for Deuce. Even if it means you not doing all the work round here—more important that you track down Deuce and watch him."

"Can I put a slug in that bastard?" Fifty-Cal asked. "Got a special hollow-point set aside waiting the chance to splatter his gizzard."

Dale thought a moment . . . No doubt she'd been scheming— Fifty-Cal had good reason. Deuce molested her before she was nine years old. It would be a good time to rid that bastard.

"What'd ya thinks?" asked Fifty-Cal, egging for his blessing.

Dale didn't answer. His mother wasn't one for that form of revenge. If he nodded yes, Fifty-Cal would kill Deuce for sure and his blood would be on his hands.

"I know you got good reason to rid the earth of dirtball Deuce," Dale said. "The vagrant deserves to get tossed into the strippin' pit to sizzle like spilled muriatic acid. But it does no soul any good. You never know when that nasty deed will come to haunt us, Cal. Let nature take its course."

Fifty-Cal set a goofy, crazed face and whirled her dark brown eyes. She couldn't reason that deep. For her, enough was said. She would decide when the time came.

Sparks flew from a buzzing circular saw and sizzled holes in Critter's beard as he cut a fifty-five gallon drum lengthwise with a carbide blade. Flatch nailed together a wooden stand then set the half-barrels and covered them with rigid wire mesh. "That works fine," said Flatch, admiring the makeshift grill. Where's your charcoal-colored Haitian chef lady? I'm starved."

A dark Haitian woman living at the Flats had been hiding from Immigration. She'd been working at the Big Belly Deli in Hudson and arrived at the junkyard just before the hurricane hit. Critter had invited her to cook as a form of barter after hearing she made a mean-tasting marinade from mashed sour orange, lemons, and a secret spice that made any gamy bird taste like a Butterball.

"She's picking fruit from the ground and sharpening her gutting knives," Critter answered.

Satisfied that Hoinky's was becoming operable, Dale left to check on Chadda. Her trailer had several large dents from flying debris. He knocked before he let himself in. "How ya doing, Chadda?"

"Just fine now that Critter hooked up the electricity coming from the dragline's diesel." Chadda reclined in her La-Z Boy. A tiny air-conditioner set in the wood paneling blew cool air directly onto the back of her neck.

"Little missy Trinity saved my shittin' ass, Dale."

Kathleen Lindum was in the tiny bathroom washing soiled cloth diapers with her backside wedged in the narrow doorway.

The toilet flushed.

"One of my gals was breached," Chadda said. "Trinity over there reached inside my yammer and pulled the jammed bugger out."

Drying her hands and tossing several diapers across her shoulder, Kathleen came over and squatted in front of the air-conditioner. She'd bound her long black hair into a bowl-shaped wad on top of her head. Cool air passed across her neck. "Ah, that feels good."

"You like that?" Dale said.

"It helps," Kathleen responded.

He paid her a compliment. "Looks like there's at least one good gal from that snootyville who's worth any good." Dale patted her on the shoulder. "Thanks for helping my cousin. I appreciate it."

For the duration of the hurricane Kathleen had been incredibly busy. She didn't realize how much time elapsed. The three boys were continually antsy and the new infants needed constant care. Between feeding, cleaning, and occupying the boys Kathleen hadn't paid attention to her own self-interest.

"You doing okay?" Dale asked.

"I've been so busy," Kathleen said. "I didn't realize there was so much work."

"Looks like you're good at washing things." Dale gestured toward the diapers draping her shoulder. "Anything I can do to help?"

"Get Chadda's boys out of here. They're bored and sometimes fight and wake the babies."

"That's easy enough, I came for them anyways," Dale said. "Going to make them work with Critter, catching gulls and plucking feathers."

Samson's head bolted upright. He liked the hunting gulls part but didn't care that Critter's name was mentioned. He'd entered that defiant age and focused much of his anger on Critter.

"Let's go, doodlebugs," Dale called. "Put on your sneakers and long pants and jump in my pickup. Critter's going to teach you how to hunt gulls. And if you don't behave, you'll be clearin' prickly brush instead—especially you, Samson. And stay the hell away from any snakes you come across. I don't want you or Critter needing a hospital 'til I get it running." Dale looked directly at Samson. "After that, I don't give a shit what you two do to each other."

Dale was referring to an incident where Samson had captured a rat snake and slipped it into Critter's truck while it sat in Gator Tales parking lot. Driving drunk, Critter felt the snake crawl across his lap and veered off Dixie Highway into the head-high sawgrass. Stuck to the axles in muck, Critter climbed from the truck and headed in the wrong direction. A day later he emerged from the reedy coastal grass in Aripeka.

Dale gave the lads a hard look. "Critter knows where the pig gator is. And I gave him permission to tie you three lads to the pig gator's bent tail if you don't behave."

Samson, Buster, and Artie quickly scrambled from the trailer. But before they left, Kathleen made sure each carried a canteen and a snack.

For Dale, it was one of the few times he met a useful Inlander. She must got some Kracker blood in her, he thought.

Dale turned and spoke to Kathleen. "If you need a break, come to Hoinky's and git some grub and fresh air. If you're interested I got a job you'll be good at."

Chapter 50

Thrusting the pointed spade into the spongy sod, Edward Peltz grunted, lunged, and busted open the tough Floratam. Standing behind him was Cindy Peltz with her children whispering the Lord's Prayer. The clang and resonant thumps mingling with angelic murmurs drew Marci's curiosity. "Where is that noise coming from?" She crawled from under the plastic sheeting, straightened her wrinkled T-shirt, and listened. Her face, arms, and legs were dotted with mosquito bites. Her white tennis sneakers were dirt black.

Clank. . . humph.

"What's going on over there?"

There was a hardy northwest breeze. The humidity dropped a bit. The hurricane must be gone, she thought, jigging across the mushy lawn. Why are the Peltzes huddled like that? Then she realized. "Oh, that damn zoo they have. Betchya their pets died."

Beat red, Edward Peltz levered the shovel handle. Cindy Peltz, with dark circles surrounding her eye sockets, sent Marci a cold stare. Wearing long cotton dresses, the children turned their heads in unison; their faces were pale and drawn. They seemed stressed.

"Hello there," said Marci, struggling to sound cheerful.

The children's glum eyes rolled toward their mother, awaiting her nonverbal instructions.

Cindy Peltz walked her glaze up and down Marci's frame.

I know, thought Marci, I look a mess.

Often, Cindy Peltz began conversations with a distinct facial expression that told the direction the conversation would go. But this time, Cindy stared blankly, straight through Marci, as if she wasn't there.

"Hi, Cindy," Marci greeted her again. "How are you guys doing?"

Drenched in sweat, Edward Peltz paused. He dropped the shovel and lifted a two-liter water bottle and drank. He stiffened his stance and spoke rather sharply.

"Yes, Marci?"

The water made her thirsty.

"Did one of your pets die?" she asked, holding a distance.

"No!" His reaction was terse and bitter.

Marci glanced at the staring children. They turned away and looked at a black garbage bag. Chunks of black sod lay next to it.

Something's not kosher, she thought. Then it hit her; Sahara Peltz was missing!

"My God, it's Sahara!" She turned pale.

Cindy Peltz lowered her head. The children stood silent.

Ed Peltz, dropping to his knees, rolled the plastic bag into the shallow grave.

"It was an alligator." He pointed to the cypress head behind their home. "Over there!"

Marci's stomach knotted. What looked to be a large alligator lay within a tumble of twisted and snapped tree limbs.

"See that alligator," he said, angrily pointing. "It's the devil. It sits there and looks at us with the top half of my daughter in its stomach."

Marci wanted to vomit but nothing came out. She ran back to where her house once stood, buried her head into the mattress, and sobbed.

Chapter 51

Leaving Chadda's stuffy trailer, Kathleen Lindum hitched a ride to Hoinky's in the back of Fifty-Cal's deuce-and-a-half. Critter rode in the passenger side cursing, pissed he missed the all-night orgy inside the casino shuttle bus. "Dammit, Cal, everyone got laid including diddlyshit Flatch and that old fogey bus driver."

Sitting on a crab trap, Kathleen curled her finger through the wire grates and braced. Shovels, chainsaws, pressure washers, a crate of sponges, and four industrial washing machines rattled all around her. The truck splashed through giant mud puddles as it crossed the lot and parked next to an antique fire engine, where Dale and Flatch were busy rolling out lengths of fire hose.

"Go ahead, Dale, give it a shot," yelled Flatch after attaching the brass nozzle.

Dale revved the fire engine. The braided lengths of nylon hose that stretched into the mangroves became tubular and stiff. Flatch eased open the nozzle and pointed the pressurized stream at the pole building. Chocolate water ran down the patchwork of painted plywood siding. "Always wanted to be a fireman," yelled Flatch over the ear-numbing hiss of the spray and chugging throttle of the engine.

"Flatch, when you're done with the outside," Dale yelled back, "run that hose inside Hoinky's and wash the walkways. Plenty mud in there, too."

Fifty-Cal finally had enough of Critter's whining. "You're too damn ugly for any chickitty-chick to jump your hairy boogey boner, Critter. Get the hell outta my truck." She shoved him from the cab as the truck rolled to a stop. Critter hit the ground and tumbled.

"Screw you, lezbo!" Crawling to his feet Critter, limped away.

Fifty-Cal called over to Dale. "Where ya want the washing machines?"

Dale pointed. "Unloaded them on that concrete slab, where the produce stand usta to be. And leave me those generators too, Cal."

Approaching the tailgate, Dale greeted Kathleen. "Trinity, since you're good at scrubbing diapers, I have a job for ya. It's a tough one, but you'll be good at it cuz you're a toughie. Ya got some of Chadda and Fifty-Cal snot in you."

"I hope not," said Kathleen, chuckling, adjusting a bandana she now wore to hold her hair in place.

"Make you a deal," said Dale, clasping her around the waist so she could hop off the tailgate. "If you help me out, I'll take you back to your home as soon as the roads get cleared. Plus, I got a pal who'll get that Mustang running for ya. "

Kathleen smiled. She'd been distracted and hadn't thought much about her family.

"Do you think they're okay?" asked Kathleen, referring to her family.

"Depends," Dale said. "News is, things south of here are real bad. A big surge hit. Going to be a while before the roads get open." Dale hadn't much information yet and gathered from the storm track that it was pretty ugly further south.

"So what's the deal?" Kathleen asked.

"I need you to run my laundry."

"Laundry?" Kathleen seemed puzzled. "Aren't there more important things?"

"You got lots to learn, Trinity," Dale said. "Keeping clean is damn important. These crazy Krackers get pretty grubby. None of them have the brainpower to think of stayin' clean by washing their clothes and bedding."

After living with Chadda and her grubby boys she had to agree.

"Is all this your idea?" She was amazed with all the activity at Hoinky's.

"Yes . . ." Dale paused. Her surprised expression reminded him for a moment of Jodi. It'd been a long time since he'd seen anyone who resembled Jodi. Except for the black hair, Kathleen was the closest. Perhaps that was the underlying reason he hadn't turned her away after the storm.

"So, what ya say? Can you handle running the laundry?"

"Sure!" Kathleen said. "Might as well stay busy until I go home. It's a deal."

Dale smiled at her.

It was the first time Kathleen saw him smile at anyone.

Chapter 52

Mosquito larva hatching in the scummy green pool water prevented Marci from bathing anymore. Covered with welts and rashes, her skin was raw. Fearful help would not arrive, her anxiety deepened.

Lethargic, Robbie remained curled on the mattress and slept mostly. A thick, oozing scab had formed on his cheek. Marci found it increasingly difficult to motivate him.

Bradley, sensing her growing contempt, tried to motivate Robbie. "Come on, Dad, let's help Mom." He tugged his father from the mattress.

Reluctant, Robbie followed and started rummaging, combing for supplies where the pantry once stood. "Look what I found," said Robbie, showing some life. He'd found a Tupperware tub full of lollipops. "I wonder what flavor they are!"

He unwrapped the wax paper and started sucking. "Hmm . . . butterscotch!"

Resting on a ruined dining room chair and shaded by an eleven-foot patio umbrella held upright with stacked cinderblocks Marci eyes grew big. *Those treats are laced with a healthy dose of cannabis tincture.* But there was no way she was going say anything.

Watching Robbie's cheeks pucker and suck, she considered if he pieced any of this together—the intact pot plant, the tangle of orange extension cords, and now treats that got him stoned—how would he react? She wasn't ready to justify herself just yet. If she divorced him, there'd be an issue with the children; perhaps custody of Brad. The courts wouldn't tolerate a mother operating a grow-house in the attic.

For several days now Bradley cleared as much debris his small stature could muster. He freed sheets of plywood, pounded the nails flat then lugged them to the bathtub and toilet area. He made a room and covered the entry with thick vinyl that was once a lawyer's medical malpractice billboard. He filled the tub and toilet bowl with water buckets lugged from the pond behind Jennifer Dink's house. He wedged a broken mirror between bent nails and set out lipstick he'd found.

"There you go, Mom," said Brad proudly. "Take a bath, the water's not that cold."

Marci wanted to cry.

After sneaking one of her homemade lollipops, Marci hid the plastic box so Brad didn't get into them. She undressed and climbed into the tub and soaked while Brad wandered the neighborhood with Charlie scouring for useful items. But before he left, Marci asked him not to disturb the Peltzes. On rare occasions Brad and Sahara played together when her parents weren't home. Marci felt Brad didn't need to deal with Sahara's tragic death just yet.

After her bath Marci washed her clothes the best she could in the soapy tub water. It felt good to be clean and productive.

Returning from his scouting mission with an armload of dried fruit, Brad told Marci the only people left in the neighborhood were the Peltzes and the Yings. Though Marci had restricted him from approaching the Peltzes, Brad tried anyway and was rebuffed by a rude and angry Edward Peltz. But the Yings were kind; they offered food and mentioned to send Marci over for more.

"Why don't you go and get more fruit from the Yings?" Brad asked.

Marci went and found George and Olivia inside their mostly destroyed garage. They'd moved the shelving that lined the garage outside into the sunshine to dry the fruit they'd stored. Papayas and mangos were cut into eighths and arranged on shelves. George offered Marci dried jerky he'd made after snaring and skinning an egret.

Refusing the jerky, she did accept the fruit and thanked them and asked if they thought help would come soon.

"Not sure," said George, his hands busily slicing a mango. He told Marci they had lived in the Caribbean and at least once every five years experienced a direct hit from a hurricane, and left without food or water for many weeks—sometimes months.

"You guys are Caribbean; I would have never guessed."

George Ying looked as if he were considering telling her something.

"Marci," said George, setting down his slicing knife, "fresh water is critical to surviving. Did you know your sprinkler runs off a freshwater aquifer?"

"Yes, Robbie brags all the time how deep it is and that we don't pay to water our lawn."

"If there was a way you could get your lawn sprinkler working," George said, "you'd have plenty of potable water, Marci." That's when George Ying revealed a story she hadn't heard. "Did you know the eighty-foot hole for your well was supposed to be drilled on our property?"

"I didn't know that!" she said, surprised that he knew how deep their well went.

"Olivia and I love to garden, Marci, and paid our homebuilder handsomely to drill a well so we could use as much water as we pleased without worrying about Pasco County fining us during droughts. When we received the paperwork saying there was no rust and that the drill bit struck an aquifer, we were ecstatic. The driller said we should bottle and sell the water like they do in Zephyrhills. But after we moved in, we learned our well was hooked up to your home. By then our builder had gone bankrupt and there was nothing we could do."

"Oh?" Marci said. "I never knew this."

"Robbie knew. Didn't he tell you?" George asked.

"No," Marci said. "This is the first I heard."

On occasion, Robbie kept her in the dark when he thought she was unaware or not knowledgeable enough. And played her gullibility to keep the subtle dominance he believed he rightfully deserved—a behavior that wasn't helpful in preserving their marriage.

The whole time George talked he kept his hands busy. He picked a basket of slightly ripe grapes and separated them from their stems.

"What will you do with those grapes?" Marci asked, embarrassed about this new piece of information.

"Juice," George said. "It we can get your well running, I'll dilute the juice and share it with you."

Marci realized why the Yings didn't bother with them after the storm passed. They weren't fond of Robbie. It was Robbie who squealed on them about their steaming mulch pile and forced the deed restriction committee to prosecute, which cost the Yings several thousand dollars in litigation fees.

"Mr. Ying," Marci said, "I'm sorry about the well. What can I do rectify your hard feelings?"

"I've gotten over it," he said kindly.

Both Marci and George looked around. Not far off was the debris mountain that impeded them from venturing elsewhere.

When Marci returned Robbie was awake and chewing on dried fruit that Brad encouraged him to eat. Seething, she wanted to club him for not disclosing the mistakenly drilled well.

"Why didn't you tell me that our well belonged to the Yings?"

"Oh . . . um?" Robbie hadn't a good answer.

"You kept me in the dark because it saved hundreds of dollars a month in water bills." Marci was bitter.

"Please don't be mad at Dad, you're scaring me, Mom."

Angry, Marci folded her arms and abruptly spun away.

"Mom," said Brad with pleading eyes. "I don't think anyone is coming to help us."

Robbie worked the courage to speak. "Soon, Brad, I'm sure it will be any day now."

Again, the urge to bludgeon Robbie overcame Marci. All along, he insisted the road on the other side of the mountain of debris that kept them captive was open. And at any moment, someone would tunnel through to rescue them.

It's been a week and no help has arrived, thought Marci—not even a helicopter has been spotted. We're imprisoned.

She peered up at the towering tangle of debris that overshadowed them. How it got there mystified her. Did anyone on the other side care they existed?

"We should climb it and see what's on the other side," Brad said as a way to diffuse his mother's resentment.

"You're right, Brad. I'm tired of this squalor and my stingy neighbors." Across the street the Peltzes prayed and wouldn't give her the time of day. Jennifer Dink, with her backup generator and air-conditioner, was obviously comfortable. If it wasn't for the hurricane shutters opening and closing, a flashlight at night spying them, she would have considered storming the house.

But what compelled her to climb the debris mountain was Kathleen—her missing child—and an overwhelming need to go find her.

In the morning, she'd do just that.

Chapter 53

After another muggy, agonizing, mosquito-ridden sleepless night, Marci couldn't wait to start scaling the mountain that entrapped them. The pinching chiggers and stinging no-see-ems convinced her that better options existed on the other side.

"Come on, Brad," Marci said. "Let's climb before the day gets too hot."

Grabbing a small backpack that he carried when rummaging for supplies, Brad was ready. "This will come in handy." He stuffed it with the remaining water bottles and packets of Manchurian noodles they'd grown accustomed to nibbling on.

"Rob," Marci said, "Brad and I are going to climb that mountain."

Curled into a ball, lying in the shade, Robbie opened his eyes. His face was pale and drawn. His wound had stopped oozing puss. Stretching, he separated the plastic where it attached to the stacked cinderblock and peeked toward the debris mountain. It looked to be three times the height of the Dinks' house. "Do you think it's climbable?"

Marci took a deep breath. "We're about to try. Besides, Brad's more help than you are." She whispered the last part so Brad didn't hear.

"What do you think, Bradley Lindum? Can we do this?"

"I'm the Little Choo Choo who thinks he can," Brad said with pride.

"All right, Mister Chug-a-Lug Choo Choo, find us a way. I'll be the caboose." She zipped his pack and patted his butt. "Get going, son."

Befuddled by her parting comment, Robbie sent a stern look toward Marci, but didn't say a word.

Crawling over the rubble that was once their home Marci and Brad headed toward the debris mountain. At the base and directly in front was the exposed root ball of one of the fallen live oaks.

"Here we go."

Climbing onto the steeply angled tree trunk, Bradley took the lead. He shimmied upwards into the prickly tangle of the compressed canopy. "It's like monkey bars, you figure out the moves as you go."

Lodged within the tangle was a crushed car. They scaled it, making their way into another mass of fallen oaks.

"Follow where I go," Brad called down to Marci.

For a half-hour they climbed and soon found themselves at eye level with Jennifer Dink's second floor window. Her upstairs hurricane shutters were retracted. "You hoarding selfish bitch, I hope your husband left you. Do you want my useless husband? Go ahead, take him. Please!" Marci said under her breath.

Brad weaved his way, climbing uprooted trees stacked and laid like Pixy Sticks. Queen palms seemed the easiest to shimmy because the bark was rough enough to grip with sneakers, yet smooth enough that they didn't prick like the cabbage palms did. Calling to his mother he chanted, "I think I can, I think I can, I know we can."

"You're my little monkey, aren't you?" Marci encouraged him.

"Just like Donkey Kong. We're going to find the Princess," he said.

"Cute, Brad, you'll find her at the top." Marci studied her next move. She grabbed hold of a 2X4 then hoisted onto a piece of corrugated metal, then onto someone's emptied dresser. "Who does this belong to?"

Mixed within the tangle was plenty of shredded clothing. Brad tied pant legs, dresses, and shirtsleeves to fashion a rope, anchoring to whatever seemed solid. He pulled along the knotted garments to traverse spots where the footing wouldn't hold his weight. They climbed nearly two-thirds to the top when they came on a leafy layer of vegetation intertwined with pieces of downspouts, splintered studs, and more lanai screening. Bending one of the spouts, Brad formed a step. He yanked free one of the splintered studs and shoved it into the matted vegetation until it wedged, making a ladder-like step. "Careful, this stuff is sharp."

The sweltering heat arrived, making breathing more difficult.

"Ee . . . oooh. . . what stinks!" said Brad as a rotting odor overcame them. Pinching his nose he edged onto a billboard that pitched at a steep angle. Looking behind he said. "I bet if we get to the top of this sign we'll almost be there."

"Yuck!" Marci covered her nose. "What a foul smell!"

"Uh . . . Mom!" Brad pointed to the top of the billboard. A decaying human body hung over the jagged edge. A buzzard, with its claws dug into the ribcage, tugged and detached a strip of dangling muscle. Maggots swarmed the stomach cavity. The eye sockets were eaten and deep-green bile dribbled the slope of the billboard.

"Brad, I'm sorry you have to see that. There's probably going to be more. The sooner we get past, the better it will be. Let's go."

Bradley gingerly made his way past the decaying corpse. "Shoo, shoo buzzard." The ugly bird wouldn't move.

"Don't be afraid, just go around," whispered Marci, inching behind.

He held his breath.

"Move faster, Brad. Don't slip in that slime. Quickly."

After passing the corpse, they worked their way horizontally across a flimsy, six-inch pine tree that breached a chasm.

"Take your time and don't fall," Marci cautioned and questioned if the pine was strong enough to support her weight. With her legs wrapped around the sappy bark she set her palms and slid forward. A shifting breeze caused her to unbalance. She paused . . . I can do this, she thought.

Brad encouraged her. "A few more feet, Mom."

Keeping her composure, Marci made it across.

"There's not as much big stuff up here, mostly thin trees and broken-off limbs," Brad noted.

"Be careful where you stand," Marci warned as she transitioned onto a spongy layer of twisted palm branches.

Suddenly, it gave way. "Oh no!" she screamed as branches crackled and snapped. They fell several feet, landing somewhere inside the pile.

"Bradley!" Marci called. "Where are you?" It was dark and difficult to see.

"Right here." His voice was muffled. "You're squashing me."

"Sorry, Brad." She rolled off him.

"Looks like we're somewhere inside the mountain." She felt a breeze and smelled the ocean.

"Over there, Brad, I see sunlight and something solid! It's part of a roof."

They clawed through a tangle of vines and edged onto a nearly intact roof with most of its shingles missing. It jutted several feet from the top of the debris mountain.

"I hope that wasn't poison ivy we crawled through," Brad said, testing the roof's sturdiness.

"Careful, watch the nails," Marci warned.

They emerged near the crest the debris pile. The sun beamed down. A stiff, salty wind blew in from the Gulf of Mexico.

"Ouch, this wood is hot!" Marci said, scaling to the peak.

"How cool!" Brad said. "I can see the ocean."

Standing, Marci lifted her hair away from her neck. "Mmmm, feel that breeze." But her eyes grew wide. She set her hands to her face and gasped. "Oh my goodness, look at the devastation!"

Where Trinity Meadows once sprawled were barren patches of limestone bedrock. The few trees that had miraculously managed to stay rooted were leafless and leaning. Marci could barely make out where the Anclote River snaked through Tarpon Springs into the Gulf of Mexico. Nearly a hundred feet in the air, it took several minutes to take it all in. Every building was flattened or washed away.

"We are lucky to be alive."

Suddenly, Marci became overwhelmed and started sobbing. Kathleen must be dead, she thought.

"Come next to me, Brad." Marci hugged, kissed, and held him tight.

As the sea breeze cooled, they rested, sipped water, and contemplated how to descend. But before they did, Marci climbed higher to view her home on the other side, where only the Dinks' house stood intact.

"Lucky bitch," Marci muttered. "The snob doesn't deserve it."

Brad interrupted her. "Should we get going?"

She tried to map in her mind where Highway 19 ran.

"Look!" Grabbing Marci's belt loop, Bradley spun her northward and pointed. "I see people walking around."

Marci strained her eyes. "You're right. Good eyes, Brad. What do you think? Can we get there?"

"Look's about three miles, Mom."

"I'm guessing that's were Route 54 and Grand Boulevard intersect."

"Do you think they're the police?"

"I hope so. They're clearing the roadway."

"Let's go find out."

They found the windward side more compact, easier to scale, reaching the bottom with little difficulty. They crossed a pasture where the Bahiagrass was stripped, exposing the chalky bedrock. At the end of the field was a barrier of toppled cabbage palms mixed with fallen bald cypress.

"I think the Anclote River is on the other side, Brad, follow me." Marci made her way over the sharp bark of the cabbage palms and between the stacked cypress. "Keep your eyes open for snakes." The ground became mucky and sucked at their sneakers as they came to a barrier of cattails.

"This isn't going to work. I can't keep my sneakers on." Marci slipped them off.

"Mom, tie your shoes to your pant loop."

Separating the cattails, Brad pushed into the brown water. "Lie on your stomach and breaststroke to get across . . . Like this . . . It's faster." Brad swam though the crowded reeds into the shallows of the Anclote River. Marci pulled through using her arms. Though the water was lukewarm, it felt refreshing. Quickly, the river bottom disappeared from beneath. There was no retreat; the cattails had closed behind them.

"Brad, stop swimming, I don't think we should continue in this direction. We're heading toward another swamp."

Bradley stopped doggie paddling.

Tiny swirls spun around them.

"Let's drift with the current," Marci said.

The outgoing tide carried them around a bend. A bridge abutment appeared. "I know where we are," Brad said, stroking for the concrete pillar. "It's Perrine Ranch Road. I went skinny-dipping here once."

Marci quickly rolled and swam toward Brad. "Skinny-dipping!"

"Yeah, me and Sahara Peltz." Brad didn't realized what he just revealed.

Reaching a sandy shoal behind the abutment, they crawled onshore and rested on a ledge.

"You mean, you and Sahara took off your clothes and swam in the river?"

Brad finally realized he'd revealed something he shouldn't have. His mother had treated him like a young man, complimenting and listening to his advice. It slipped out. Now he had to lie his way out of this.

"But Mom, it was Sahara's idea."

"When did this happen?"

"A couple of weeks ago."

Marci couldn't fathom this. *Her son naked with a reclusive homeschooler?*

"How'd she get out of her house?"

Brad struggled to answer. "Sahara pretended she was sick and didn't go on a field trip, like they always do."

Marci realized that she hadn't paid much attention to her son lately. She thought he spent most of his time holed in his room on the computer.

"Come, Brad, let's get going. We'll discuss this later." She didn't want to consider the conversation any further. *Did they have sex? Nah, they're too young.*

The embankment leading to the roadway was thick with vines. Twice, they stopped and returned to the riverbank. Finally, Brad figured a way by tunneling beneath the vegetation. On their knees and elbows they crawled like rodents the last few yards and stood in the middle of Perrine Ranch Road.

"Huh, it's odd how lonely a highway feels when there's no traffic," Marci said.

Walking a short distance they reached an intersection. "This must be Grand Boulevard. The people we saw are somewhere up this road."

In their wet clothes with annoying horseflies hovering, they made their way. It was difficult; the twisted and torn-apart buildings that once lined the roadway blocked both lanes. In several spots fallen power lines with cast aluminum light poles obstructed them. For nearly two hours they maneuvered the obstacles until they reached a place where the road cleared. Debris was shoved to each side.

"Is that music?" Brad asked.

Marci listened.

Letting out an enormous sigh of relief, she smiled. "Yes . . . Yes, it's music! Everything's going to be okay, Brad."

Chapter 54

Freed from the Pasco County prison hours before Hurricane Kate struck, Johnny "The Deuce" Sledge made his way on foot to the only asset he owned, a five-acre fenced storage plot on the western bank of the Anclote River. Deuce used it as a drop-off for nighttime deliveries of illegal cargo shipped across the Gulf of Mexico from Nicaragua.

When Kate tore inland Deuce sought refuge at the north end of his property and huddled atop an Indian burial mound made of oyster shells. When the surge came it left the prison-hardened ex-marine clinging to the top of a canary palm. And when the water receded, Deuce crawled from the thorny perch and ventured into the ransacked neighborhood of Holiday to enlist like-kind indigents that also managed to survive.

Deuce gathered and organized the indigent men and provided for nearly every need, except their Oxycodone habit because he had none. They camped in strung hammocks and makeshift tents beneath a stand of soft-needle pines near the intersection of Grand Boulevard and Route 54. Across from the encampment, a building that housed a popular strip joint known as Moog's had escaped Kate's fury, because a man-made sand mound erected by the bordering Walmart to hide the pervert hangout from retail customers had deflected the hurricane-force winds. The Walmart was demolished but not Moog's.

While incarcerated, Deuce heard a rumor that Florence Carter planned to lease and reopen Hoinky's flea market immediately after the storm passed to capitalize on the despair. He surmised that desperate Trinity Meadows survivors searching for food would cross this way to get there. "Might as well make some bucks until the coppers arrive," he told his ragamuffin squad of hoodlums.

For years, there'd been an intense resentment by Deuce of Florence Carter, because she quiet-claimed a piece of land near the limestone mine left to him by his rum-running father. Deuce swore revenge. But shrewd Florence wasn't afraid. Using courthouse contacts and the gambling debts owed by a county judge named Grady, Florence set up Deuce. He was arrested in a staged drug deal that Florence orchestrated.

When Deuce heard Florence died he was elated and became more determined to return to Hudson to reclaim his birthright property. "I'll buy my way onto the Flats and eliminate Dale," he'd often lament to fellow cellmates. And once the storm abated, Deuce ordered his indigents to clear the intersection where the strip club stood. His crew worked south along Grand Boulevard toward Trinity Meadows and northward, up Highway 19 toward the Cottee River Bridge. And to control his band of scrawny rednecks, Deuce offered food and limited access to the moonshine he brewed, and promised that soon he'd have pole-dancing strippers.

Resourceful, Deuce salvaged goods from the demolished Walmart, where trailer loads of dry goods and bottled water had been delivered prior to the hurricane. He traded food, liquor, and porn for hard labor. Formed work crews to clear brush and shove aside debris. The job of burning rotting bodies was the nastiest work.

Corpses were heaped and torched using diesel fuel siphoned from the storage tanks of a nearby beer distributor. A tapped water company wellhead provided an endless supply of fresh water, which gave Deuce more power and control. He horse-traded with survivors in the town of Elfers by offering a gallon of drinking water for each hour of labor. . . . Work often started before sunrise. Deuce's ingrates toiled until the heavy heat of midday came. They returned on foot and by pickup, took slugs of moonshine, ate hearty bowls of heart-of-palm stew, and gnawed on beef jerky, then napped. For the most difficult work, and the men that cleared the greatest distance, Deuce let them rest inside the air-conditioned club.

Nearby was a cell tower with a backup electrical generator with a large fuel tank. He used the generator to cool his strip club. The only thing missing were good-looking women, to ease the anxious mood of workers and further fortify his control.

When Marci and Brad stepped onto the cleared roadway, Deuce was lounging on a white plastic patio chair. His cellmate, Phyler Pedi, napped on a leather couch that butted the strip club's longest wall. A boy holding hands with a lanky blond appeared from behind a Budweiser delivery truck flipped on its side.

"Hmmm," thought Deuce with his boots propped atop a ten-gallon chlorine bucket. "My first toll."

He scratched his prickly chin and squeezed a reluctant zit. "Phyler, what'd ya think?"

Phyler got up from the couch and spied the pair. His bulldog wrinkles rolled in a lumpy bunch away from his cheeks, backwards, toward his dirt-black ears. His decaying teeth became overexposed. "Looks like a dang woman and young lad."

Chapter 55

"**L**ook, people!" Marci said, thrilled and overjoyed.

"They're Krackers," Brad quickly observed. The tall man appeared beefy with tattooed Popeye forearms and a jug-neck that made the top half of his body seem stunted. His sun-baked skin looked like salted leather. The other guy was scrawny, shorter, with a long chicken neck. His rubbery oval face looked like a carved-out coconut—the kind sold at Orange Grove stores to Florida tourists.

Brad grabbed his mother's hand and asked to stop walking.

The men were fewer than twenty feet away and smelled awful. Marci noticed that the beefy guy had a yearning sailor look and gazed as if he were fondling her entire frame. Every womanly intuition said turn and run, but she wasn't sure if they could outrun the rough-looking men. . . . What to do? thought Marci. Perhaps talk her way through this?

"Can you tell us where to find help?"

"Ain't no help in these parts, tall lady," said Deuce, displaying an indulgent grin. "Ain't a cop in sight and don't expect none too soon."

Clutching his mother's hand, Bradley pulled her back. Coconut face gave him the heebie-jeebies.

"Have you heard anything about what might be happening?" Marci queried.

Scratching his chin, Deuce didn't speak right away. He stared, as if he were thinking it'd been a long time since he'd seen a woman.

"Yep," he finally said. "I got news for ya. But any information I got going to cost ya, good lookin'."

"What are you talking about?" said Marci, her heart racing.

"Thangs ain't free no more, sweet woman." Lifting a Mason jar, Deuce sipped his tasteless moonshine. He lowered the glass and burned a stare at Marci's waistline, then rolled his eyes down further and cocked his head, as if he was trying to scan her backside. "Phyler, leggy here must come from clean livin', she looks 'phisticated. I ain't never been laid by long wraparound legs like she got."

When Marci heard the "ain't never been laid" she became rigid.

"You know, lady, my guys cleared this road so you could walk easier. You must pay a toll."

"It . . . It's not . . . not your road." Marci fumbled her words.

"Who's going to say not?" Deuce said. "If it wasn't for me you'd still be on all fours crawling along."

Uneasy, Marci watched the other guy ogle Brad.

Brad tugged her arm. "Mom, we need to go."

Stepping sideways, Deuce moved to block them. "You and your lad look like yins need a good scrubbing and some grub."

"Yes, we do." Marci let out a nervous chuckle while panning her surroundings. There's nowhere to run, she thought. Any clearing that led off the roadway was blocked with downed trees further in. What looked to be open road to the west was impeded by the two men.

Deuce shoved his bear-paw hand into his jeans and adjusted his crotch. "What'd you going to pay your toll with?"

Marci hated to consider what he was implying, and prayed there was an alternative.

"Tell you what." Deuce removed his hand. "I'll throw in a shower. And the food is free, all you can eat."

"How much money do you want?" asked Marci even though she had none.

Brad nudged closer to his mother.

"Lady, you think money can buy you anything? What if this is the end of the world?" Deuce said. "Warden let me and Phyler out of jail then scrammed. Heard Al Qaeda had a few nukes and were using them. You may not see a cop for a good long time."

Marci's heart skipped a beat. *Was this true? Had he heard something?*

"So?" Deuce asked, becoming impatient. "How do you plan to pay your toll? Your lad looks mighty thirsty."

"Mom, let's go." Brad tried to turn his mother away.

Marci grabbed his shoulders and said, "No, Brad!" She hadn't worked it out yet—running would initiate whatever they planned to do with them. For their safety she must stall.

"Yo, kid, come sit next to me." Phyler stepped forward and snatched Brad's wrist. "Take a seat on my comfy sofa in the shade."

"No!" Brad ripped free and slid behind Marci.

Phyler didn't chase. Instead, he sat on a dingy couch beneath a canvas tarp strung from the strip club roof. He opened a small portable refrigerator next to the couch and produced a Mountain Dew. "Here ya go, sonny, nice and cold. Go ahead, take a swig and come get cozy."

Marci's head swam. *That Phyler guy looks exactly like the unshaven pedophiles displayed on the local news.* If she got violent and kicked and clawed, they'd rape her and no doubt abuse Bradley. She couldn't risk it and had to think quickly.

"Uh, I don't have money to pay your toll, but I got something else." Marci played a hunch that the Feldon stock buried under the garage trusses that was once part of her home might be of value to this guy.

"What ya got, longlegs?"

"Prescription medications," she replied.

Deuce became bugged-eyed. Phyler leaned from the couch.

"My husband is a drug rep and knows where a whole truckload is."

"You're bullshitting me," Deuce said.

"No, I'm not."

"Unless you tell me where it's stashed, ya ain't got nothing to trade yet. Besides, all I got to do is follow yins home and ask your old man. He ain't got nothing to lose except the both of you. It'll be a fair swap, I'm sure."

He had her. It was a mistake to mention the meds.

Phyler spoke. "Lady, I don't want to frighten you but there are other fellars napping in the woods over yonder. They thinks a lot like me and horn-dog Deuce, ya know. We can wake and ask them to join us in a gangbang, or you can pay your toll and move along."

Deuce moved closer to Marci. "Longlegs, are you good at anything?"

Marci trembled. His body odor grew stronger. How can I get Brad out of this? she thought.

"It's clear what your toll is," Marci said. "What guarantees do I have my son is safe and we can move on?"

"Depends how good you are at it." Deuce halted his advance and set a big smile. He lit a cigarette. "You's a sweet piece of white meat, honey. You look like one of them Trinity Meadows MILFs from over the bridge. Ain't never collected a toll from a softy gal like your type before."

Bradley saw coconut face approach and gesture it was time to join him.

"No, I don't want to go over there." He turned away and buried his face into the small of Marci's waist.

Phyler snatched Brad by the wrist. This time he twisted and yanked him away from Marci. His calloused hands burned his skin. "Come, lad, sit next to me."

"No!" He tried to jerk from his gnarly grip.

Marci dropped into a crouch and anchored to the ground and held Brad around his waist.

Deuce towered over her. "Suggest you let go of your young 'un," Deuce said. "Phyler's just 'musing himself. I won't let anything happen to the lad as long as you consent to pay my toll with those nice breeder hips and strap-around thighs you got."

Breeder hips! How can I avoid this?

"How do I know my son will be safe?" Marci said, stroking Brad, trying to comfort him.

"You don't. But if you're as good as I think you is, I'll figure a way to keep the lad untouched. Maybe you should work a deal with Phyler for sloppy seconds."

Phyler gave Deuce a mean look. "Don't you torture me, Deuce."

"You'll listen to me, Phyler." He winked without Marci seeing. "Don't touch that lad or you'll be burning dead bodies with the rest of the work crew. But if Blondie here don't pay her toll soon, you go at the kid all you like." Deuce upped the ante.

Marci released Brad and pushed him toward Phyler. "Go, Brad, sit and drink the soda. It'll be okay."

Brad didn't budge.

With Deuce standing guard, Marci walked her son to the couch and encouraged him to sit next to Phyler.

Bradley squirmed when Phyler came next to him. Marci saw the fear etched on his face. She had no other option.

Phyler set his hand on Brad's knee.

Brad shoved it away. "No! Mom . . . Please!" His eyes filled with tears.

Suddenly, Marci became defiant and boldly confronted Deuce. "Don't you let him touch my son!"

Deuce calmly smiled and said, "Using your kid is going to get me what I need, ain't it?"

Marci didn't answer.

"Phyler, now you listen." Deuce lifted his clenched fist and threatened. "Don't touch the lad unless I say so."

Deuce guided his thick forearm around Marci's waist and pulled her along. "Don't mess with the woman's kid. Or I'll shoot your narrow ass dead."

Forcibly, he escorted Marci toward the strip club entry. "Let's go inside, get you cleaned and get acquainted."

He had a firm grip. And when Marci resisted his grip drew tighter.

Quickly, he led her along a brick pathway, past the exhaust of a humming generator and into the seedy club. Before they entered Marci noticed several men sleeping across the street in suspended hammocks strung in pine trees.

"Wait a minute," Marci demanded. "I want to see my son at all times."

Deuce shoved her along. Her neck lurched back. "Get going," he grumbled.

Marci spun and glared at the crusty leatherneck. Anger burned in her face. "You might want to reconsider." She gambled and decided to be bold. "Otherwise, the person who'll enjoy himself will be your buddy."

"I doubt that. Don't' get all smartass, Blondie. Listen and your lad will stay safe."

"Prove it," Marci said.

"See that window? I'll leave it open so you can hear from inside. Not cooperate and I'll slam it shut, tie you to the stripper pole in the other room, and let you listen to your virgin-ass lad scream and call you while Phyler jams his willy where it ain't never been before."

Marci grimaced. Satisfying him was something she must do—a necessary sacrifice to keep Brad unharmed.

He escorted her through a dimly lit hallway. A grimy waterline left from the surge marked above their heads. Cool air from the air-conditioner circulated. She'd forgotten what it felt like.

Deuce pointed to the shabby dressing room on the right. "Go ahead. There's a shower. Get cleaned, cuz I want you smellin' sweet like yins Trinity woman do. I'll keep an eye on Phyler for ya."

Entering the cramped room, Marci left the door open . . . Sitting on a bench she unlaced and removed her grimy tennis sneakers. Her feet and ankles were charcoal. Off came her jeans, blouse, and soiled bra. She stood in front of a full-length mirror. How horrible she looked. Her hair was longer and out of shape, her face pitted and drawn. I've lost weight, she thought studying her thighs. My cellulite's completely disappeared. "I must've lost twenty pounds."

Turning on the shower faucet she thought about her predicament. Was her only escape to please him and move on?

Before she stepped into the stall Marci peeked out the open door and listened. Brad wasn't screaming.

A fizzy spray came from the showerhead. Finding a soap bar she went beneath and began to scrub.

Carrying a cigarette Deuce came into the tiny room and blocked Marci's exit from the narrow shower. "Nice," he said in a raspy voice. "I like small tits. And those eraser head nipples you got, must be the air-conditioning or what I'm packing in my pants that's makin' them pop like top hats."

Expecting him to lunge and maul her, Marci's heart pounded fiercely. Her stomach tumbled and seared with fright. What am I going to do? She bit her lip. The only way is through this guy's pecker. Perhaps if I tease him, he'll hold off and not attack.

Naked, the shower water spraying, she opened her stance to show the full length of her most prominent feature; well-proportioned, strapping legs. Softening her big blue eyes, she licked her lips and slowly soaped her chest. Inside, she agonized as she squished the soap bar in a sultry way. Using random, circular strokes she worked a pearly lather. Gliding her hands she cupped, squeezed, and teased her breasts, then went between her thighs with both hands, manipulating her disappearing fingers—all the time casting Deuce a seductive look, pretending to become aroused.

Deuces beady eyes locked on and followed her motion. Swallowing, his Adam's apple leaped and gulped as Marci leaned back and blocked the showerhead. Gurgling water bubbled within her blond hair until it flowed free over her face. She licked and collected the dribbling stream with her curled tongue. Cupping and lifting her small chest, she channeled the flow between her breasts, along the crevices of her stomach, washing away the suds.

The seduction's working, she thought. It's the way out of this predicament. She pretended getting bothersome, aggressively massaging and tweaking her rosy nipples. She dug and worked her fingers within her thighs and falsely moaned.

Bug-eyed, Deuce's crotch bulged. He was stiff and solid. But he'd spent many nights in brothels. "Nice try, lady. But you're not going to get me off that easy. You gotta dance for me."

Deuce wiped the beading sweat from his temple and cracked a nasty grin. "That was a nice show you gave. Looks like Trinity gals know how to get off in the shower."

Marci halted her eroticism.

Quickly, she jerked up her hands, closed her stance, covered her chest and turned sideways. The stiffening pose didn't help; it offered Deuce the opportunity to inspect her backside.

"Over there on the rack are stripper outfits," he told her. "Dry yourself and put one on." Chucking his cigarette into the shower he stepped aside and offered an exit. "Wear something red with lots of sequins. I want to see you work the pole." Deuce pointed down the short hallway that led to a small theater. There was a low stage with a brass pole in the center.

Marci reached for a dingy beach towel and wrapped her waist.

"I want to check on Brad," she said, passing. She went into the hallway and peeked out the small window. Brad sat on the sofa alone, drinking Mountain Dew. Close by, Phyler sat on a stool waiting patiently.

Deuce came behind her and slid his gritty palms around her waist. He cupped her bare breasts and held them firm. The stubble of his unshaved face scratched the side of her neck. There was the smell of booze within the stench of his breath. An electric, spidery chill ran along her spine.

"Are you happy, lady? I told Phyler not to sit next to your son unless I say so. Now, get going. Put on sometin nice."

Deuce released his grip and disappeared into the theater. "Better hurry, Phyler's getting mighty horny. Maybe if you jerk him off he'll stay away from your lad."

"Yuck," thought Marci as she walked the shack's dark hallway, quivering, with red handprints marking her chest.

She approached a clothing rack loaded with swank outfits. "This is humiliating." She selected a bright-red outfit with six-inch tassels and glittery sequins. The flimsy shoulder straps had lost their elasticity. The breast cups were entirely too large.

"And make sure you put on stockings to make your legs look nice. I don't care to see your mo-skeeter welts when you git on stage," said Deuce, lounging with his legs propped over the chair in front.

"I must do this," Marci murmured, mindful of her dilemma. "I must," she repeated, squirming into the gaudy outfit and fastening the guarder belt. "Let's get this over with."

"And wear some fucking nice and high stiletto heels," Deuce yelled. "I knowed you're a tall one, but I want to see those long legs git longer."

Selecting a pair of gloss-red stilettos, Marci fought to slip them onto her larger feet.

Clopping down the hallway she ducked under the low doorframe and entered the darkened theater.

Sucking a cigarette Deuce nodded with approval.

"You sure are a hot number. Your old man must love fucking you."

Deuce massaged his crotch. "Things are getting kinda tight." He unbuttoned, unzipped, and let out a giant sigh. "Gotta let my monster breathe before he gets busy. Nice job with that tease in the shower. Let's see if you can do that on stage."

She reluctantly stepped onto the lifted stage.

"The pole!" Deuce wagged his finger, signaling to move toward it. He reached behind and flipped a switch. A blinding bright light lit the shiny brass pole.

How do I do this? thought Marci.

Stepping into the cone of light, she grasped the shimmering brass. "Here goes nothing." Marci lifted her knee and slid it along. The metal was cold. Her leg muscle pulled tight and hurt. "Ouch!"

Suddenly, the heel of her stiletto snapped. Reacting to the imbalance she clutched the pole with both arms and spiraled, landing on her ass . . . *Oomph!*

"That ain't how you do it." Deuce bashed the seat with his boot. "I can tell you are going to be a clumsy one, rookie."

She heard his chair thump and flop. His muscular frame emerged from the darkness at the foot of the stage.

"Enough of this," he said.

He removed his sweaty T-shirt, unbuttoned his jeans, and dropped his pants to his ankles. He wasn't wearing underwear. What swung between his legs was firm and large. Marci stared at it. And before she could move away, Deuce reached and grabbed her ankles and removed the stilettos.

"No . . . No!" She rolled onto her stomach and clutched the pole tightly. She struggled to rid her mind that this was happening.

"Get over here, wench." He yanked and stripped the nylon stockings, tossing them across the stage. "It's time," he growled.

His big hands grasped her calves and flipped her onto her back. Her knees forcibly buckled. Marci squeezed her eyes closed and imagined her home on Leiram Avenue—its spacious great room with ornate molding running along the rim of the ceiling. She wanted to dream this nightmare away.

Deuce's massive frame cast an ominous shadow that made him appear large and dark, like Clarence Washington. He was tense and breathing heavy. His rough hands moved to separate her knees. His tattooed forearms rammed under the back of her thighs, lifted, locked, and yanked her bottom closer.

"No!" Marci screamed.

She closed her eyes, wanting to dream it all away.

He overpowered her. And no matter how much she fought, she wasn't able to free his viselike grip. His hardness slapped against the softness of her skin. He's about to enter, she thought.

Again, the thought of her Trinity Meadows home arrived. This time Clarence was there with that "look" in his eyes. He wanted her, and she wanted him. And it arrived and penetrated. The girth swelled and entered as Clarence slid deep within her womb, opening to a size she'd never known. She gulped. His fullness was endless. Her eyes rolled. Her lashes fluttered as his weight came on top, pinning her to the coldness of the stage. Slowly his penetration reversed, which seemed an eternity, as it withdrew—its width never relaxing until it exited.

There were spasms. There was the warmth of the light illuminating the stage. Then darkness, as it arrived again, with a long unending thrust inward, faster this time, firmer, smoother, gliding much easier from the lubrication she excreted. Once more, a long, taunting, quivering retraction happened. She now knew its entire length.

Marci watched from deep inside the horror of her soul, his clenched jaw, a fevered sweat draining from blackened pores. Jolting, thunderous thrusts shoved like a straining steam piston. She forced her mind to believe he was Clarence.

And then it came, the throbbing culmination, the pulsating arrival of a filling, acrid, warming cream from within a rigid stone. The ease at which it moved back and forth was seamless, as she slopped and sloshed inside, until her gummy womb quivered. Without her permission it pleaded for pleasure. Marci let out a satisfying moan that became louder, turning into a prolonged, pleasurable wail, calling Clarence's name.

Deuce released his hammerlock from behind her knees and mashed his hands onto her chest. Digging his bulky fingers he continued his pelvic thrusts. Marci found herself working him, accepting him, unleashing a tension she'd imprisoned for a lifetime. As a pleasant, commanding feeling overtook her, she whispered Clarence's name and didn't fight anymore. In her mind she was in her beautiful house with Clarence, making love. And for a second time, Deuce's face filled with tension and pleasure—his chest, shoulders, and forearms twitching. It arrived and exploded within her. Marci screamed and seized the ejaculation that filled her, allowing herself to cum once again.

"Mommy, Mommy," Bradley called from outside. "The man won't let me go."

"What . . . What?" Marci froze. Clarence vanished and Deuce reappeared.

But she couldn't move as Deuce tried for a third time.

"Mommy, Mommy . . . he's touching me!"

Chapter 56

Hearing Bradley's plea for help, Marci twisted, contorted, and flailed. Deuce was the weight of a granite slab that crushed her. His spine rolled in rhythmic waves and undulating thrusts. She fought to muster the strength to break free. But suddenly, dark red blood pulsed in prolonged spurts from Deuce's left temple. He collapsed on top of her. Blood flowed onto her chest, around her ribcage to form a puddle.

Thoowoocrack!

Marci heard the sound of the powerful gunshot then a resonant, echoing, metallic ricochet. A .50 caliber, copper-encased slug had burst the concrete wall block and exploded the wrought iron joint that secured the three-inch diameter brass pole to the low ceiling. A piece of shrapnel had sliced across Deuce's temple.

Rigid and still penetrated Deuce's dead weight pinned Marci to the dance floor. It was an odd, suffocating feeling. It would not come out of her. Reaching, Marci grabbed its hairy base and worked it side to side like a lodged wine bottle cork. After several tugs the frozen organ unglued and slopped free.

Outside, Phyler had removed Brad's T-shirt. But he too suddenly slumped. Again, the gunshot arrived a split second later.

Naked, Marci burst from the strip club and ran for Brad as more gunfire whizzed by. Slugs ripped into the grove of tall pines, exploded sappy tree trunks, kicked up the needley dirt, and startled the napping work crews. Like exposed and vulnerable cockroaches, they scurried and scattered until they disappeared deep into the woody cover.

"Bradley . . . Bradley, are you okay?"

Brad was weak; moments ago coconut face pawed him.

"Yes, Mom," said Brad, startled.

A hundred feet away, near the sand mound that had protected Moog's strip club from the hurricane, Fifty-Cal stood on the tailgate of her camouflage military truck. The nozzle of her machine gun oozed gray smoke. Her jet-black hair was pulled and tied into a tight braid. Her skin was golden brown, the color of stained leather. Taut, black leather shorts with silver pleats and shiny studs form-fit her Clydesdale buttocks. Beneath a studded leather vest, a black halter flattened her full chest.

Chewing her nicotine quid, a broad smirk arrived. "Little lad, are you okay?" Fifty-Cal leapt from the tailgate. A puff of chocolate dust burst from under her Vietnam-era jungle boots.

"Whoa!" Fifty-Cal saw Marci naked and covered in blood. "Where'd you come from, lady?"

Fifty-Cal studied her. "Woman, you're into some serious S&M shit, ain't ya?"

Concerned for Brad's safety, Marci hadn't stopped to cover herself.

Fifty-Cal spit out her soggy chew and spoke much clearer. "That blood all over you, miss hoochie?" She dragged her finger along Marci's triceps then licked.

"Sure as hell is!" Fifty-Cal tried to place Marci in her mind. "I know just about all the sadist sickos that are into the heavy shit and ain't come 'cross you yet, coochie pie."

Marci stood stiff while the tough-looking dyke examined her. What was she alluding to? How could this get any worse?

"She thinks you're a sadist." Brad's voice was shaky. He didn't like that she was naked. The blood and her moans; he didn't want to know what happened.

"A sadist?"

Marci did her best to cover herself with her arms.

"He your little Twinkie?"

"He's my son," she answered.

"Not a good idea leaving the lad alone with Phyler. He's a bad one. Runs with Deuce lots," Fifty-Cal said. "Would molest your Twink in a sec while you lap dance for wooden nickels."

Fifty-Cal eyeballed Marci's chest. "You got teensy weensy ones. You got gypped." She chuckled. "Moog's polers got big roly-poly knockers, jelly-filled ones."

"Oh, no, you have it wrong. There's a man dead inside. Tha . . . that Deuce guy." Unable to completely cover herself Marci kept switching arms.

"You killed that guy inside the club," said Marci as she struggled to free her mind from the rampant image of the dead man's alive organ stuck inside her. Then she thought of something extremely bothersome. She'd had several orgasms.

Fifty-Cal approached a slumped Phyler. "Didn't mean to kill this son of a bitch. Just wanted to scare him away from the Twink."

She turned her attention to Marci. "By the looks of you, I can imagine what's inside Moog's." Fifty-Cal didn't expect her to answer. Marci mentioned Deuce's name and Fifty-Cal surmised the blood was his. But she wanted to see dead Deuce for herself. And went into the club, finding him on the stage with his jeans at his ankles.

"Lucky bastard died with a hard-on. Better make sure you're dead, Deuce."

Fifty-Cal bent to one knee and turned him onto his back. The bleeding from his sliced temple had stopped. She felt for a pulse. "He's still alive." She grasped his throat and squeezed. "I should strangle you right now, you child-raping bastard."

However, as much as she tried, Fifty-Cal couldn't finish him off—Dale didn't see eye-to-eye with her on killing him yet.

Deuce coughed, batted his eyelids, and started to breathe after Fifty-Cal removed her hands.

"Take this, you fucker." She slugged Deuce and knocked him cold.

Outside, Marci rummaged for something to cover herself. "Bradley, don't look at me."

Fifty-Cal reappeared, rubbing her knuckles. She inspected the area. "Look at all this shit. Deuce's got quite a getup." For several minutes she walked the surrounding property. "Lookit here, a moonshine still." With a 2x4 Fifty-Cal smashed the still into a twisted pile of mangled tin.

"Well, I is done here, lady. You and the lad can ride with me if you want to leave this shithole. The fellas that skedaddled are just as bad-asses as Phyler." She tossed the 2X4 onto the low roof of the strip club.

Fifty-Cal came close and whispered to Marci. "You don't want to be hanging round here for long." She winked then pushed Marci a smooch. "That shittin' Deuce bastard had that big pecker inside me too when I was your Twinkie's age. He deserves to die. But I got bad news. He's knocked out. Bullet must've grazed him."

Marci wasn't sure what to think; the dyke saved their lives. The men sleeping in hammocks beneath the pine trees were a danger. There is no turning back, she thought. It might be best to go with the Amazonian rather than hang a U-turn and risk going home. Robbie would have to fend for himself.

"We'll go with you, but can I go inside and get something to cover myself?" Marci asked.

"Might as well," Fifty-Cal said. "Deuce ain't coming to anytime soon. Bring a wet towel for Twinkie here. Gotta scrub Deuce's blood off him, too."

Twinkie! Brad didn't like the nickname, but something internal said, "Be quiet." Even though the black leather lady was much like a video game character, thanks to her, they were better off than a few minutes ago.

Quickly, Marci jumped into the dribbling shower stall and rinsed Deuce's blood. The only clothing she found was a pleated, silver zebra miniskirt matched with a tassel top that tied in front. Reluctantly, she slipped on the snug outfit. Soaking a towel she came out and sponged Brad.

Fifty-Cal smiled. "I likes what you're wearin', lady. I take it you're ridin' with me?"

Marci nodded. "Get us out of here . . . Please!"

"Hop in the truck. I'll take you somewhere safe."

Marci felt she'd no choice but to go. The dyke saved her life and miraculously spared Brad from a horrific fate.

Fumbling with the uncomfortable outfit, she said, "Come on, Brad, let's leave this nightmare."

Chapter 57

With her deltoids flexing, Fifty-Cal cranked the hard-rubber steering wheel, popped the clutch, mashed the gas pedal, and headed north toward Hudson. A powdery swirl chased the camouflaged deuce-and-a-half. The machinegun turret bolted to the bed swiveled each time Fifty-Cal serpentined rubble piles.

There were no road signs to mark where they were. The best Marci could gather was somewhere near the coast. Mentally, she struggled to expunge the rape, rationalizing that it was a small price for Brad's safety. However, buried deeper was the overwhelming pleasure that arrived after imagining Deuce was actually Clarence.

Both Marci and Brad studied the tough-looking dyke. Running along her shoulders and neck was a labyrinth of colorful tattoos that told her life story and confused anger. Her jaw chomped and chewed until a syrupy dribble seeped from the corner of her pierced lip. Brad's face soured when she slurped the sap and swished like mouthwash, spitting an endless stream of putrid diarrhea out the driver's side window.

"What's your name, lady?" Fifty-Cal asked. "Hain't seen a skank the likes of you before. Least not at a strip joint swinging pasties in circles with nipple glue sucking them tight to your teats. What's ya doin whoring with Deuce's sad lot?"

Marci shook her head. This dyke was out in left field. "It—it's Marci. I live in Trinity Meadows."

There was a pause. The truck lurched as Fifty-Cal's foot slipped off the gas pedal.

"You're a Meadows MILF? Holy shittin' cabang!" Fifty-Cal took a long look.

"What the hell you doin' in that getup? Tryin' to make a few bucks to buy Twinkie here Christmas peanuts?"

Marci grew stiff. "No!" she said emphatically. "The hurricane destroyed our home. I had no idea those guys were criminals."

Glancing at Brad, Marci wondered if he'd heard her wails from inside the strip club. He seemed preoccupied with the passing wreckage and a bit consumed with how Fifty-Cal worked the clutch to maneuver so efficiently.

"That man Deuce forced me into an outfit like this." Marci jiggled a tassel. "I had no choice."

Fifty-Cal had already figured that out. Deuce was a problem for anyone that came across him. A Meadows MILF grinding the pole. Now that'd be interesting, she thought. *Can't blame the poor bastard Deuce for milking his oysters. Blondie's a cutie.*

"How many of you caged snoots survived the big 'cane?" Fifty-Cal asked.

"Caged snoots?" questioned a perplexed Marci.

"Ain't you got a big wall circling yins neighborhood with a swinging lock gate?" Fifty-Cal said while watching the roadway.

"Yes."

"Why didn't you evacuate?"

"We tried, but couldn't."

"None of us in the Flats 'vacuated, ya know," Fifty-Cal jammed the gearshift. "We stayed put."

"Flats?" Marci asked. "Is that were we are heading?"

"Yeperee," Fifty-Cal said. "Florence Carter's joint. Most of the Flats folks did just fine by stayin' in her junkyard."

"Junkyard?" Marci asked.

"You heard right, my little coochie zebra." Fifty-Cal spent as much time checking out Marci as she did watching the cluttered roadway. "Man, you look sweet. That stripper getup does you swell."

Brad perched his chin on the dash. His eyes rolled left then right, panning. Occasionally, he'd sit straight and mutter an awed comment about the devastation. "Wow, look at that boat, it crushed that house! How'd that get up there?"

"That there boat is the casino boat shuttle," Fifty-Cal said. "Them's white hairs living off Social Security and gambling Ford Motor pensions are going to get the DTs without their slot machines to drain their funds. That's if any of them left with their walkers and motor wheelchairs before the 'cane hit."

Suddenly the truck slowed, pitched forward, and gingerly rolled through a narrow, washed-out culvert. Fifty-Cal pumped the brake pedal. "We're at the Cottee River. Surge gullied the ground around the bridge."

Marci grabbed hold of Brad and pulled him next to her. The truck lurched. Its knobby treads mashed through the thick tidal muck and crept onto the concrete decking. Leaning her head out the window, Fifty-Cal slowed to a crawl and paid close attention to the rolling front tires. "Don't want any rebar puncturing my treads or shoving a hole in the oil pan."

She pulled her head back into the cab. "Betchya don't recognize any of this."

The military vehicle stopped atop the bridge.

Marci rarely traveled the coastal roads. But when she did, she used Little Road, east of New Port Richey because the surroundings felt newer, cleaner, less intimidating. From the bridge top she tried to picture what the area had looked like before the storm leveled it. "I have no idea where we are."

Gnawing like a cow chewing its cud, Fifty-Cal allowed Marci time to look around. The inlet contained a massive jumble of mixed debris, as if a tidal wave came and destroyed the docks and waterfront restaurants, sucking it all back into the Gulf.

The Cottee River channel was choked thick with floating plywood and splintered lumber, dock flotation, and wind-stripped vegetation. There were inverted and sunken boats. A briny dam of bleached rubble mixed with dried, flea-infested sea grass marked the highest tide. And higher up, where the surge went, were cars either upside down or flipped on their side with their trunks open.

"You can walk across and not even get wet," Fifty-Cal said.

The sea breeze blew through the truck cab.

"Twinkie, lookit there." She pointed westward. "There's where Scooter's wing joint usta to be. And guess what some old horn dog did during the hurricane? He rescued all the tight-ass chickadee waitresses and brought them to the junkyard." Fifty-Cal shook her head. "I'm going to miss that place."

Brad panned the seaward side of the bridge. Further out, a jam of drifting debris parted into vast floating rafts. "People are fishing out there."

"One's that survived gotta eat, Twink." Fifty-Cal revved the engine and rolled off the bridge.

Brad gave her a perplexed look. He wasn't fond of the nickname she'd given.

"From this here bridge and down your way, missy hoochie, looks to be the worst of it. Up the road we got clobbered but not as bad as y'all in the Meadows."

Fifty-Cal made no bones about checking her out. "I like that outfit you're wearin'. You look like one of those tall Russian gals I saw on the Internet."

"It was the only thing clean to wear." Marci tugged the short skirt, trying to cover her overexposed thighs.

"Where are the Flats?" Marci asked.

"Up in Hudson," Fifty-Cal said.

"Mom," Bradley interrupted. "Dad calls it Kracker Flats."

Marci lasered a hard glare at Brad. Set her finger to her lips and whispered, "Don't say that."

"Lookit here," Fifty-Cal said, lighting a cigarette.

"Where?" Marci asked.

"Over there, on the side of the road." Fifty-Cal pointed at two Sand Hill cranes grazing in a grassy plot.

But before Marci could focus on the cranes, she was distracted by a short Asian man pointing a shotgun. *Bang! Bang!* Feathers burst from the lumbering fowl and both birds flopped to their chest, frantically beating their wings against the ground.

"Oh my goodness!" Marci gasped. Instinctively, she placed her hands over Brad's eyes.

Brad removed them. "Come on, Mom, cut me a break."

Fifty-Cal yanked the steering wheel. "What a sorry-ass shot. Son of a bitch wounded them both. Chink gook fucker!"

She slammed the brake, and before the truck stopped rolling, she exited through the driver's side window onto the hood and unleashed her anger. "You sorry chinaman bastard, you ain't supposed to shoot them, you son of a bitch."

She spit.

"Mother fuckin' slitted slant-eye. I should rip your teeny wiener right off and stick your Vienna sausage up your punched-flat nose. You keep killin' all the birds they won't be any left to lay eggs."

Snatching both cranes she wrung their necks until each stopped flailing. Snarling at the short man she flogged him with the limp birds and told him to only shoot seagulls. "Cuz they breed like rats, ain't never going to wipe them out." Fifty-Call tossed the lifeless fowl into the truck bed.

She grabbed hold of the truck mirror and jumped onto the running board. "Tonight's dinner. No sense wastin' a good meal."

For nearly an hour they slowly rode, often passing scavengers pushing shopping carts. They picked through abandoned stores, tossing useful items into the wire basket. Marci noted an increasing number of buildings were intact. Trees that leaned north had the bark stripped only on the south side.

Finally, Fifty-Cal turned from the main road and headed toward the Gulf of Mexico. The deuce-and-a-half chugged and lurched. Thick steam hissed from beneath the hood. She checked the temperature gauge. "Ol' Pamela here is overheating. We ain't got far to go, but we better stop and give her a rest."

They rolled to a stop beneath a canopy of old oaks. Steaming radiator water sprayed the windshield. The diesel shuddered, puttered, hissed, and stalled. It became quiet. "This here shady place, we call Buzzards Banyan. These damn oaks are tough old bastards, came through the 'cane just fine. Mother Nature sure as shittin' is a neat gal, hain't she? Twinkie, you look like you're cooking. Ain't you usta no air-conditioning?"

Brad was nauseated. She was right, he missed air-conditioning—also his Internet.

Reaching under the worn seat cushion Fifty-Cal found a cloth-covered canteen. "Come-on, let's sit in the shade." With the canteen in one hand she snagged her cigarettes off the dashboard, lifted the door handle, then shoved her shoulder into the frame. "Oomph!" There was the scratching squeal of unlubricated metal. She smiled at Brad. "Now you know why it's easier to crawl through the truck window."

Fifty-Cal's boots thumped onto the soft earth. "When thangs go bad like this, you gotta be careful and care for your equipment and yourself, Twink. There's no hurry no more, every day belongs to you."

Marci forced open the passenger door and slid out. Unable to gauge the distance to the ground, she immediately stumbled and fell.

"Mom, are you all right?"

Her legs were rubber. The entire time she'd been internalizing the rape—how she couldn't, or perhaps didn't want to, fight back. And for a brief moment, enjoying an elevated sexual intensity she never knew possible. Was it rape if she acquiesced, selfishly seizing a moment of bliss? Or a necessary coping mechanism, to deal with the vileness of him forcibly in control, a psychosis that turned him into Clarence? Or was it that Robbie had never pleased her; therefore subliminally, allowing herself to lust the masculine, animal-like nature of such an aggressive alpha male?

Lying there on the moist ground, her thoughts turned to Kathleen's fate. Did she encounter Deuce? Or one in a hundred scumbags like him, and tossed into the Cottee River? Was her consent a self-inflicted punishment, a piling on of guilt, preparing for the realization Kathleen was dead—possibly one of those rotting bodies lying on the roadside?

Fighting her emotions Marci held back tears. She didn't want to frighten Brad. What happened at the strip club was disturbing. At some point this would affect him—resurfacing in other ways. At times Brad was like her; he internalized and didn't care to reveal

315

secret thoughts, especially his keen observations of her rift with Robbie.

"I need a good cry," Marci said to herself.

Brad arrived, helped her to her feet, brushed away the twigs and damp leaves. "There you go, Mom."

"Brad, let me be for a bit." Patting his head she straightened and wandered into the black shadows of the oak grove.

"Mom, where are you going?"

As she wandered aimlessly among the fresh chill of the darkening shadows, Marci's trickling tears turned into streaming rivers. Her pathetic marriage, she thought. This intolerable disaster. The grime. What next? Could she ever return to her comfortable, medicinal lifestyle? Would she, or her son, live beyond tomorrow?

Again her legs gave way. Collapsing to the spongy earth, curling into a ball on a mat of Spanish moss next to a lifted root, Marci bawled.

The echo of Marci's weeping wails drifted from the vastness of the oaks. Fifty-Cal brushed aside a solitary tear. She could relate. Beneath her rough, defensive exterior was the same deep sadness. "Come on, Bradley," she said. "Let's walk." She wanted him out of earshot.

"Is my mom okay?" asked Brad as they strolled in the opposite direction toward the Gulf.

"Yes, Brad," Fifty-Cal said. "She's letting the air out of her tires. Being a mom is a tough deal."

Brad did a double-take. *Did she just call me by my name? Was there a soft spot inside this tough, intimidating lady?*

"Why do they call this Buzzards Banyan?" Brad asked.

"I betcha you're an inquisitive little shit, aren't you?"

Brad smiled for the first time.

"Cuz the ugly bastard buzzard birds roost here at night. This here's the place they like to sleep," Fifty-Cal said. "Ain't you ever wonder where birds go at night?"

"No," Brad answered. "But I wonder which way a toilet flushes when it sits right over the equator."

Marci blinked . . . once . . . then twice; salted teardrops had gathered in the corners of her lips. Curled in a fetal position, as if the womb-like nook she huddled within suited her frame, she stared blankly into the constellation of crocked limbs. A black squirrel raced along the horizontal reaches of the snaking banyan. A blue heron gracefully stretched its long, stalking neck. It snapped forward and snipped a wiggly tree frog from its hideout. A flickering ray of sunlight broke through the broad figgy banyan leaves and warmed her face.

This all seems oddly familiar, thought Marci; the salt breeze, the clammy, decomposing aroma, the coastal wildlife. She sat upright and realized where she was. "I've been here before!"

She ran her hands along the walnut-hard bark of the oak root. There was a carved inscription. The scored surface had grown in and distorted the lettering. Marci took a deep breath. "No, this can't be? There's no way!" A rush of adrenaline came. Her hand pressed against the inscribed scar.

"Is it?"

Several times she traced the letters, as if she needed convincing. The aged words read: *Buck loves Jodi.*

"I can't believe it. All this time Buck was close by."

Fifty-Cal's voice called for her. "Honey, it's time to get a move on. Twink here needs to see if his mom's okay."

317

Standing, Marci brushed off the damp earth. She stared at the lettering and the exact spot she'd made love to Buck.

This time Marci heard Brad.

"Mom?"

Marci followed his voice and appeared from the shadows.

"Are you okay?"

"I'm all right, Brad. It's been a long day."

Brad held her hand and comforted her.

"We'll be okay, Mom." He looked up with his innocent eyes.

Marci cocked her head and studied Brad's expression. His childlike qualities had disappeared. His brow was bunched and seemed thicker. His hair was less flimsy. The cheerful lift of his choirboy cheeks were no longer. The masculine man that slept had awakened.

Chapter 58

A brisk wind raced across the jagged, complex face of the debris mountain. A cluster of buzzards stood guard over a corpse. In unison the fowls flinched and became unbalanced. The nap of their crimson black feathers broke rank and contested the sturdy wind. The vinegar stench of decaying death sank beneath the finishing breeze and crept low along the earth.

Robbie Lindum pinched his nostrils. "Man, that stinks!" He gazed at the mountain that imprisoned him. Within the pile a bright blue billboard with yellow lettering marked the spot he'd last seen Brad and Marci. The entire time they climbed, their voices carried. Until those sudden screams came. He considered if they'd fallen inside and died and wondered if the putrid odor that drifted his way was their rotting bodies. The bravado to search the wreckage wasn't within him. He'd never been that high off the ground—not even on a waterslide or Ferris wheel.

To go and search might trigger a panic attack and make him succumb to the same fate.

It was hot. Robbie hadn't a clue what time it was and couldn't wait for the afternoon cloud cover and cooling rains to arrive. Low on bottled water, he left his hut and rummaged for nourishment.

Finding a jar of Smuckers grape jelly he stuck in his fingers, scooped a purple glob, and sucked it off his fingertips.

"Mmmm, not bad, a sugar rush."

Charlie lumbered over and begged for a taste. "Have some, Charlie." Robbie scooped another glob and let Charlie lick his fingers.

"What do you think, Charlie? I shouldn't have allowed them to go up there?"

As he scratched Charlie's back, clumps of fur came off in his hands.

He watched Charlie go to the pool area and slurp the stagnant water, then seek a shaded spot next to the marijuana plant.

Something about that plant isn't right, Robbie thought. It's grown. The leaves aren't shredded. Where'd it come from? He batted the bushy leaves then crouched and inspected the bucket it grew in. The shipping label—his address was on it.

"What! That's the bait bucket I bought. It vanished months ago. Somebody must've stolen it . . . This plant belongs to someone in the neighborhood!"

Jennifer Dink's only access to the outside world was a radio. She kept the volume low and listened to hurricane reports. Kate had reentered the Gulf of Mexico, intensified, struck Pensacola, pushed inland, and flooded much of the Florida Panhandle, Alabama, and western Georgia. The country's military was embroiled in the Middle East. And there was a huge energy shortage.

Activating the outside cameras she scanned the neighborhood. Up the street on the other side of the Lindums' destroyed home, one of the Peltz daughters decorated a spot on the lawn. She zoomed. The frail girl set a small bouquet of garden flowers next to what looked like a memorial. "Aw, one of their pets must've died."

The debris mountain was across the street, directly in front of her house. It smothered several of her neighbors' homes. Jennifer spied a cluster of buzzards roosting next to a dead body. The ugly scavengers jabbed their sharp beaks at it. She feared venturing outside, not sure what the surviving neighbors would do if they discovered she had air-conditioning and plenty of food. They'd beg, perhaps demand to shelter in her house. It was bad enough the surge flooded her entire downstairs. She didn't want anyone traipsing mud upstairs, where it was clean.

That evening she spotted mold blotches on the wallpaper where the surge had soaked. Jennifer filled a bucket with pool water, mixed in lye, and soaked the black blotches. It was 2 am when she finished and went to sleep. And when she woke, the irritating mold had spread upstairs, spanning the vaulted ceiling. The bedrooms and hallway were covered with green-black speckles. Fuzzy fungus ran along the baseboards. The lye soak hadn't worked.

"God help me," Jennifer cried. "It's out of control."

Again, she filled the lye bucket and scrubbed all morning. By midday she'd saturated the walls and scraped the black gunk from the baseboards and door trim. But the mold worked faster; it crept onto the entertainment console and behind the glass frames of her expensive paintings. The plush carpets blackened and grew spongy.

With her chest tightening, her capacity to breathe was more difficult. Jennifer lowered the air temperature, thinking it would freeze out the fungus that triggered her asthma. Donning a fur coat she sat at her computer and waited. It became cooler—seventy, sixty, fifty-four degrees.

Nibbling dried fruit Robbie waited for Jennifer Dink's air-conditioner to click off. It'd been running entirely too long. Suddenly, a dot of light appeared and bounced around him. He tried to pinpoint the source of the reflection. It's got to be coming from the Dinks' roof, he thought.

He crawled over the cinderblocks that was once an outside wall and stood beneath Jennifer's eave. The white light darted frantically, as if it were searching for him. *It's coming from somewhere over my head.*

Rolling his head up and backwards Robbie studied the soffit. "Something's moving . . . Hmm, there's a black wire." Straining his eyes, he watched as a tiny glass bulb swiveled back and forth. The action matched the nervous movement of the reflection that zipped across the plastic blue tarp that covered his hut.

"It's a spy camera. That woman's watching me." He stepped from under the eave and waved at the camera.

The bulb froze and pointed at Robbie.

"Jennifer," called Robbie, waving his arms.

He waited. But nothing happened.

"I'll go and peek in her living room window."

He forced up a first-floor hurricane shutter and waited for his eyes to adjust to the darkness inside. Then he bent his knees and tried to look up the grand staircase. "Holy cow, she's got a mold problem."

He spotted Jennifer crouched on the top step with a fur coat pulled over her head and holding a handkerchief over her mouth.

Squeezing his thin hand through the shutter he banged the window.

"Jennifer, are you okay?"

Abruptly, Jennifer stood then disappeared upstairs. Moments later, she came down carrying a framed painting and headed through the kitchen and out the sliding doors.

Robbie rapped on the glass as she passed.

Wanting to talk, he raced to the back of her house. "Hey, Jen!"

Standing outside in the pool area behind the lanai screening, she finally answered. "What!"

"Is there something I can do?" Robbie asked.

"There's mold everywhere. Do you have any idea how I can get rid of it?"

Robbie scratched his head. He had no idea. Already, it looked like it was out of control.

"I haven't a clue," he said sheepishly. He fumbled for more words to engage her in conversation.

Frustrated that her expensive painting was destroyed, Jennifer blurted, "Neither do I!"

After setting the painting in the sun to dry, she cupped her mouth and nose with her hand and disappeared into the house.

There was a sharp clack of the patio door lock.

Chapter 59

A tattered American flag hung limp from the towering boom of the dragline shovel. Gray smoke plumes rose from burning mounds of brush into the evening sky. The deuce-and-a-half rolled through the open gate into Dale Carter's junkyard. Marci noticed a cluster of empty shopping carts haphazardly parked at the entrance and wondered what they were doing there.

A chocolate pit bull leashed to a car bumper tugged and pulled, trying to chase their rolling tires. Drying laundry hung from kinked electrical wire strung between cars that sat on blocks with tires removed. Rough, red-eyed, unshaved characters lounged in molded plastic lawn chairs. Some had bulging beer bellies. Others lay suspended in creatively strung hammocks with shade coverings. Lethargic teenagers sprawled on grungy mattresses strewn in trampled weeds. Children scurried about. Some playfully stoked and teased smoldering campfires that kept mosquitoes away.

It seemed to Marci that nearly every adult smoked. And the women held sunken, gaunt looks with knotted, frayed, sun-damaged hair.

"This here is where we live," Fifty-Cal said. "Least for now until thangs git normal again."

Marci couldn't fathom what normal meant for this lot of scraggy people.

Fifty-Cal rammed the clutch, shifted gears, and mashed the gas pedal to compensate for the shallow uphill grade. The speed picked up. "Coochie, in case you're wondering where we rode out the storm, it was in those junk cars and buses you see. They got a low profile and there ain't much big shit around to knock out windows.

"Clever," Marci mumbled. "Wish my home was here."

"I got lots of stuff to do," said Fifty-Cal, jerking the wheel, fighting elongated mud ruts. "Gotta pluck those cranes, gut and cook 'em for Critter, Chadda, and me."

"Critter? . . . Chadda?" Brad questioned.

Fifty-Cal winked at Brad. "Don't you have nicknames for your friends, Twink?"

"Uh . . . no!" he said.

She hit the brake pedal. "Going to drop you and little stink bomb at this here Chevy Blazer. Yins fend for yourself and figure what ya want to do. There's a duffel full of shit and some food to hold you a bit."

She pointed toward the top of the grade. "Over yonder are water buffalos for drinking and shitter pipes for poopin'. And if ya need anything else, just about everyone is going to ask what ya got to trade."

Fifty-Cal spied Marci's zebra stripper outfit. "You ain't got nothing to trade me, your tits are too flat. Ain't no fun pawing them busted balloons. Besides, I got a bunch of young, firm peaches waiting at the top of the hill." She flipped a glance toward the casino bus parked next to the dragline.

Marci covered her chest. *How crude.* She hoped Brad didn't hear. Fortunately, he seemed preoccupied with the spooky people that lingered about.

"Excuse me, Mom." Crawling over Marci, Brad shoved open the passenger door and ran around Fifty-Cal's truck. He tugged the driver's side door of the Chevy Blazer.

"Put some ass into it, Twink."

The stuck door opened.

Marci followed and inspected the rusted four-by-four. The back bench seat was removed and set against the rear bumper. A foam mattress filled the entire back of the Chevy. "I guess we sleep in there."

Fifty-Cal revved the engine and blasted the horn as she drove past Dale's house heading for her busload of Scooter waitresses.

"Mom," Brad said, "don't you think you should change?"

The tassels that hung from the hem of her bikini top stuck to her sweaty waist. She'd lost weight. No longer were there muffin-top hips. Her long legs had thinned.

Brad retrieved the duffel bag from inside and dragged it to the bench seat.

"Thanks, Brad." Marci unbuckled the duffel. "Let's see what's inside."

Unpacking, they found many useful items including hotel soap bars, tiny shampoo bottles, a hairbrush, toothpaste, an expandable water jug, clean beach towels, and a tiny bible.

"Every car must have one of these kits; who thought of all this?" Marci said.

There were several sets of hospital scrubs with the name Bippinotti stamped on the right sleeve. Desperate to change and cover herself, Marci crawled into the vehicle and wriggled into the pastel green scrubs. "Turn your head, Brad."

Carrying toothbrushes they hiked to the water buffalos. Several hard-looking characters watched them pass. Marci felt their cold stares.

"Look at that steam shovel!" said Brad as they approached the shitter pipes. He went behind a wooden fence and squatted. It made him nervous; the entire back opened to a cliff that dropped into a turquoise lagoon.

Darkness came fast. The only illumination came from smoldering fires and hissing lanterns. The no-see-ems pinched and bit. Mosquitoes buzzed all around them.

Lying close to his mother in the back of the truck, Brad made a wisecrack about the latrine. "It's hot and the toilets flush straight down. We're right over the equator."

"Funny, Brad." Marci tried to laugh but struggled find the emotion.

All night people roamed, tripped, and clunked about, spewing profanity. Marci listened to a nearby conversation about the flea market. They bitched they had nothing to trade and must clear brush to get anything to eat.

There was no chill to the dawn, just substantial humidity. Opening her eyes Marci craved air-conditioning and the background noise of the always-on television. For two weeks there had been no cool air, no music, and no television news. Only the sounds of the wind, the shuffle of her feet, and nearly routine afternoon rains. There were no interruptions, no cell phones or endless running to do things.

Nudging Brad, Marci whispered for him to sleep awhile. "I'm going for a walk, Bradley."

She stepped from the weedy grass that surrounded the Chevy Blazer onto the dirt road. Halfway to the quarry stood the only house in the treeless junkyard. "I wonder who lives there," she said. "It doesn't have much hurricane damage and has its own electricity." On the porch a man held binoculars. She felt him watching her.

Overhead, the royal blue dawn had dissolved into a peaceful, cloudless, powder-blue sky. It was hard to imagine the oak grove was a place she'd been many years ago. It must be a fluke, she thought. That inscription was perhaps a hallucination—her body tricking her—a reaction to what happened earlier that day. She wasn't sure and wanted to return. Because if it were true, a tender moment that was nearly true love, it happened there. And perhaps, he was close by.

As she walked beneath the oaks the dawn became day. A salty breeze softly swayed the loping forearms of the Spanish moss. Marci weaved her way, searching for the nook and the inscription. She found the spot, bent over, and traced her fingers along the bark. The inscription still read *Buck loves Jodi*.

What young, innocent fun they had. Playing in the ocean, sailing among the small island keys, pretending to be raiding pirates with the boy she only knew as Buck. Carefree feelings she'd abandoned. How'd my life get so complicated? she thought.

Slipping off her shoes she caressed the cool earth with her toes and stretched along the big root of the massive oak. Marci gazed into the canopy. The birds had left to feed. The glistening, lateral rays of the morning sun sparkled like shimmering star sapphires.

Chapter 60

Drifting along the Shine Island spoils, a sun-chalked, twenty-four-foot Kells relaxed its mainsail. A wiry, stubble-faced man with knobby knees, thin calves, and drumstick forearms leapt off the stern, plunged into the Gulf of Mexico, and disappeared. Fanning his arms, swimming above an undulating mat of sea grass, he reached and plucked scallops from the seabed. He surfaced and tossed them where the high tide hadn't reached.

Onshore, beyond the black mangroves, Critter scolded a gathering of lazy Krackers. They'd worked for only a few minutes. And when he turned his back, they slipped to the chow line set up on the north side of the flea market.

"You lazy son of a bitches don't get any food until . . . Ouch! What the fuck!" A large scallop, spinning like a Frisbee, clobbered the back of his neck. "Damn you, Samson," he accused Chadda's son, falsely, it turned out.

A wiry man emerged through the break in the mangroves carrying an armload of scallops,

"Mother of Jesus, it's Monkey Wrench!" Critter yelled. "Monk, you Okie, it's about time you got your skinny ass back to the Flats."

Monkey set the fluted clams on a tuft of grass.

"Dale's going to be glad to see you," Critter said.

Dale Carter wasn't far away when he heard Critter's scratchy voice call Monk's name. Immediately, he came from behind an industrial washing machine carrying a screwdriver and vise-grips. "Sure glad to see ya, Monk."

Dale spied the piled scallops. "Always thinking, aren't you?"

"Never miss an opportunity for a halfway decent meal," Monk said in a hoarse voice. "You still got that Jamaican voodoo gal who makes that mean-ass sour-orange marinade to cook these in?"

"Sure do," Dale said. "She's over there by the grills plucking gulls for tonight's food line."

"Nice to be back. I'da got here earlier if the wind hadn't died on me. How are thangs?" Monk asked.

"Not too bad," Dale answered. "Momma's plan worked as she always preached."

"Where's the old poker-faced bat?" Monkey asked.

Dale's face grew grim. He'd kept himself busy dealing with the hurricane and nearly forgotten about his mother until now.

Monk saw the sudden sadness in Dale's stiff expression. When he left for Iraq Florence hinted she may not be around when he got back.

"She's gone, hain't she?"

Nodding, Dale kicked at the hardpan ground.

"Sorry, Dale." Monkey half-hugged his longtime friend then patted his back. "Thangs will be fine. How's Chadda making along?"

"Good," Dale said. "Twins girls were born during the storm and are healthy."

Monkey smiled. "Guess I got my hands full, don't I?"

"You bet your ass," Critter interjected.

Monk noticed the bouncing generator and the heavy-duty hose spurting water.

"What's that contraption?" he asked.

"Makeshift Laundromat," Dale responded. "Folks work better when their clothes are clean. Ya'd think I got better things to do, but Momma says it's important to have a place for folks to clean their coverings. Monk, can I put you to work right away fixin' this washing machine?"

"Hand me your tools. I'll fix it lickety-split." He disappeared behind the washer. Moments later his voice bellowed. "Go ahead, shove a load in."

Kathleen Lindum flung sludge-covered towels and bedsheets scavenged from an abandoned Travelodge into a cage strung with chicken wire.

"Trinity, time to do laundry. Make sure you get paid in barter before you give their clean coverin's back. Otherwise you worked for free," Dale instructed.

"See that gal," Dale said as Monk came from between the washers. "She delivered your twins and been tendin' the doodlebugs, keeping them in line real well while Chadda's crotch heals up for ya."

Dale grinned. His teeth were perfect.

Monk handed Dale the tools then approached Kathleen. "Thanks, I appreciate you helping Chadda and those shittin' booger rats she got."

Kathleen had cut her kinky black hair because caring for it was a hassle. Around her neck she tied a confederate bandana to absorb her sweat.

"I heard about you," Kathleen said. "Everyone says you're handy."

"Sure is," Monk said.

"Do you think you can get my car running again?"

What an odd request, thought Monk.

Dale chimed in. "She's inland folk. Sometimes she ain't gotta a clue, but she's okay by me. Not like the rest of them *do-for-me's* over yonder."

"Sounds like I owe her."

"You owe her big time Monk, Chadda would've died if this tough young lady hadn't mustered the courage to yank the twins out," Dale said. "But I'm surprised to see her ask about her car. She ain't said much about going home. Been content here."

Dale led Monkey by the elbow further away. "Won't be surprised if her family didn't make it. Hurricane flattened everything below the Cottee River bridge. Big shit-ass surge pushed up the Anclote. Her parents are probably drowned."

"It looks like I should get her car running," Monk said. "Especially if she can keep my three doodlebugs in line, so Critter don't choke one of them."

"Ain't sure what she'll do with it. By the sound of it, roads won't be open anytime too soon."

Kathleen heaved two armloads of wash into the upright machine. She twisted the knob and pressed a button. Nearby, the chugging generator strained. A feeder hose flattened, gulped, then became firm. Lukewarm brine water gurgled into the drum.

"Going to take two days to get to the bottom of that pile," Dale said. "Plus, gotta find a way to run fresh water instead of filtering it from the gulf."

"Anything else goin' on before I head to see Chadda?" Monk asked.

"Yes," Dale answered. "It's Deuce. Fifty-Cal came across him south of here. That strip joint he usta hang at survived the storm intact. Deuce is holed there and gathering a gang. No doubt that ornery bastard will soon be up to trouble."

"He'll start brewing his liquor," Monkey said.

"Fifty-Cal says he's hurting a bit and won't be bothering us yet, cuz he's got a hole in his noggin to tend."

Both men walked to the separation in the mangroves and looked out at the Gulf. There was a light chop.

"Is that how you got here?" Dale asked, pointing to the listing sailboat.

"Yessireee!" Monk said. "It took four days to sail from Fort Walton Beach. After I landed in the States, I hitched a ride on a KC 135 to Eglin Air Force Base from Fort Dix. An Air Force general named Tanker flew in with me. He was coming from the Pentagon and told me Hillary was preparing to invade southern Iraq.

"Ya know there are blackouts all over the country," Monk told him. "Not enough petro around to last. The general said it's going to be a good long time before we're back to normal."

"Have you heard anything about what happened in Tampa before the hurricane hit?" Dale asked. "I heard everyone in the local government bailed."

"Sure did. Tanker told me most government folks in the know bugged out. Said the hurricane demolished Clearwater. Most folks that didn't skedaddle got drowned."

With the toe of his boot Dale kicked the sea grass deposited from the high tide. "Politicians weren't much help prior to the hurricane. Momma said they never were fond of us Flats folk."

Hobbling toward them, drenched in sweat and nearly out of breath was Flatch. "Monk, good to see ya."

"Where the hell you been, Flatch?" Monk asked.

"Down where Gators usta was." Flatch paused and caught his breath. "The surge lifted the whole damn jooke Kracker bar and floated it inland 'bout a mile."

"Holly shit!" Monk said. "A friggin' mile."

"Gotta cut a new road from Dixie Highway to where Gator now sets."

"If I don't get those taps flowing and start serving some homemade liquor, thangs going to be pretty rough round here. Most alky Krackers already got the nervous hibbitty jibbitty shakes from not getting stewed by noon."

"What's with the limp?" Monk asked.

"Tripped over one of Hoinky's mutant pigs back in the palmetto scrubs. Took a damn header. Didn't see the piglet scratchin' in the sand until it was too late."

"I thought Piggy ate 'em all," Monk said.

Flatch turned toward Critter. "Chewbacca over there is breeding and selling them to the carnies for their traveling freak shows. There all over the damn place, again."

Dale rubbed his chin. He hadn't heard that Critter was selling the pigs. "If we don't deal with the folks with the DTs someone's will get shot. Last night, I caught a kin of Hoinky's shooting at Critter's dog Dozer for pissing on his shoes. Good thing Hoink's kin had the shakes and missed."

"Don't ever wanna mess with Critter's pet," Flatch said. "He's a big baby when it comes to his friggin' fat old pup. It'd be like killing his mom."

Flatch patted his pants pockets looking for his cigarettes. "No doubt, he'd shoot a relative if need be."

"That's why I want to turn the Bippinotti into a makeshift medical clinic." Dale unrolled his Marlboros from his shirtsleeve and handed the pack to Flatch.

"The foreign docs didn't cut and run." Dale struck a match. "They're hangin' north of here. We've been cooking gulls and scallops and fish-head soup and runnin' it up to take care of the docs in exchange for medical help.

"Already, they tended a few nervous Krackers so far, but say they need more medication. Docs said most of the Flats folks are addicts. And what supplies are around are from raiding the abandoned Walgreen and CVS pharmacies and will soon dry up. Rumor has it there weren't any pharmacy deliveries a few days before the hurricane smacked us. Supplies were light."

"Wonder if there was a delivery on its way. Could be a marooned truck full of prescription drugs somewhere," Monk said.

"Could be," Dale answered. "Would love to stock the clinic and use it to manage some of the bad-asses having severe DTs."

Flatch handed Monk Dale's Marlboros. "Smoke?"

The men traversed the parking lot toward a row of picnic tables. Several people milled about waiting to eat.

"Nice to be home," Monkey Wrench remarked.

"Monk," Critter said, "you best better go and start wearing out that Okie noodle you got."

Monkey smirked. "Good to see your nasty sour mouth hasn't changed, you rotting hemorrhoid. Whatever happened to Piggy, Crits?" Monk asked. "You fuck up that moneymaking deal too?"

"That cattywompass gator is out there causing trouble for someone, I'm sure," Critter responded. "Last I saw her was at Deuce's storage lot."

Monkey was well aware how Critter could lead a conversation astray. He cut him off. "Dale, what else do you want to know about goings ons outsida here?"

Dale needed a time frame regarding when the outside world would arrive. If he could capitalize on anything, his mother would want him to seize the opportunity right now.

"My Air Force buddies at Eglin let me see satellite photos of Tampa Bay before I left for the Flats. Goddamn landscape is scratched clean off. Saint Petersburg is mostly gone. And it seems Ybor City is waterfront property. The Flats didn't get it as bad as a few miles south of here. My buddy says there are these big arcing mountains of debris shit packed tight like concrete all over the frigging place.

"How's things holding in the Flats?" Monk asked. "Cabbage Ears ain't no more, hain't it?"

"Most of those trailers in the Patch are sitting on the other side of Highway 19 in aluminum heaps," Dale said. "Everyone's been behaving and working for barter, least for now. Except a few lazy shits who sit in beach chairs and pretend they're fishing. They keep the lonely women plenty miserable too. Critter's got that under control so far."

"Critter ain't happy unless he's bossin' or bitchin' anyway," Monk said, looking at Critter from across the picnic table.

"You got that right." Critter finished his cigarette then flicked it away.

"You know, Monk," Dale said. "I got lots of fuel stored, thanks to you. And I tapped onto a wellhead and draw freshwater as good as the Zephyrhills aquifer."

"Nice," Monk said. "Told you those water buffalos you bought at the MacDill equipment auction would be worth it someday."

"How about my rug rats?" Monkey asked. "How much trouble they'd been in?"

"Samson, Artie, and Buddy are useful when they're not being kids blowing up shit all the time. Artie figured a way of rigging a mullet net using Polish cannons to snare gulls. Works like a charm." Dale chuckled. "Your lad ties spider crabs to a stake pounded into the beach to bait the gulls. Then that son of a bitch crouches as still as a frozen rabbit until enough birds gather. He triggers the cannons and launches the mullet net over the gulls that ain't fast enough to escape."

"Sounds like Artie got some craft in him. Must be my lad," Monk said.

"Samson loves to kill the gulls by wringing their necks," Dale said.

"That's cuz he's got Deuce's blood," Monk said. "How about Buddy?"

"Poor bastard is left plucking and guttin', cuz Samson told him that was his job."

"Ya know, Dale," Monkey noted, "your mother had set a damn good plan. Military couldn't do any better."

Fizz . . . swoosh . . . pop . . . bang! Several bottle rockets exploded over the Gulf. Critter grimaced; son of a bitch stinkers.

"Guess we talked long enough," Dale said. "Monk, your boys are up to mischief. Before you go see Chadda," Dale said, "I need to ask a favor from ya."

"Sure, Dale, what is it?"

"I need your help fixing the clinic. I hadn't done much with it yet. People will get sick soon. Got some hurtin' already. Can you take charge and get the Bippinotti ready?"

"Gotta earn my keep," Monk answered.

"Get those big generators they got stored on the roof running," Dale said. "With no cops or jail, the bad can come out of these Krackers at any time. And it won't be long before Deuce starts sending runners selling his shine and any Oxy he got his grubby hands on. Monk, one last thing you should know. Come over to my truck so I can get my binoculars."

Both men left the table and went to Dale's pickup.

"Take a look in the junkyard at the top, next to the dragline shovel."

Monk lifted the field glasses.

"See that bus."

"Sure, what's with it?"

"Fifty-Cal's heathen sin-bin. That's where you'll find her if ya need her. It's full of Scooter waitresses."

"Holy shit!" Monk said.

"And they got this old geezer in there named Cooterman Pat and two Greek waiters from Tarpon Springs keeping them occupied, if ya know what I mean. Fifty-Cal's been feeding and tendin' them; threatening anyone who comes near the bus."

Monk lowered the binoculars.

"We got creepy characters hanging around, sooner or later they're going to get up there and cause trouble. Fifty-Cal will shoot them dead if they move in on her booty," Dale said.

Chapter 61

Returning from her early morning walk Marci Lindum approached the junkyard entrance. The shopping carts were gone. On the other side of the road a tall, clean-cut man walked in the opposite direction. How odd to see a neatly kept person among this squalor of crass people . . . He passed. His eyes followed as if he'd seen her before. He's handsome, thought Marci. His hair was slicked into a wave. A healthy dose of cologne lingered. It's been a long time since she smelled a man's cologne. "How nice."

What a contrast this place is from Trinity Meadows, she thought, where neighbors were concerned about appearances, wealth, status, and possessions. It seemed these Krackers weren't troubled about anything; they simply existed. A lifetime of coping, hacking at each day, was their norm, in an odd, communal way. Surviving, continuing after the hurricane, was no different than before, for them.

Hearing his mother arrive, Brad pulled himself upright and grabbed hold of the dash. "Ouch, that's hot!"

He licked his hand then rubbed his eyes.

"Mom, do you think Kathleen is okay?"

"I can't be sure anymore, Brad. We may never see her."

Marci had thought about this for some time and felt she must express the reality he may never see his sister. Though Kathleen was often mean to her brother, the loss of his only sibling would be difficult. Fathoming her death was an uncomfortable notion for the both of them.

"Uh . . . !" Brad swallowed. He'd wished Kathleen dead many times and now worried it might be true.

The urge to vent her frustration and prepare Brad for the change that may lie ahead suddenly surfaced within Marci. A change she'd thought about for months.

"Your dad wasn't much help before or after the hurricane, Brad."

Marci couldn't believe she said that. *Brad admired Robbie.*

"I can't rely on him anymore and I am considering a divorce." A flood of guilt hot-flashed through her body. But she felt he must hear his father didn't amount to much and what she planned to do about it.

Brad's expression flattened; teardrops emerged and rolled down his tender cheeks. Marci saw that her blunt criticism had bruised. For some reason, she felt compelled to say it, and that it was necessary. She tried to soften the blow.

"You were a big help, you know. Without you, I don't think I or your dad would have survived." Marci wiped away his tears.

His somber face softened. "How, Mom?"

"You're smart and more mature than your age shows, and helped out when your dad or I couldn't think clearly. Like when the dining room window broke. You thought quickly and plugged the hole."

Proud-chested, Bradley straightened and smiled. "Thanks!" Her praise was soothing. "I'm hungry. Can we can go to the flea market and get something to eat?"

"Yes, we should. But I'm not sure how we do that, I have no money."

As they headed for Hoinky's, Fifty-Cal rumbled past with a mountain of wadded clothing piled in the back. Her trademark jet of sputum flew from the window, wisped backwards, and splattered the road.

Marci's legs were sore from the walking she'd done the past few days. Before Hurricane Kate they often drove, even if it was a few houses away. How spoiled we were, she thought.

At Hoinky's Flea Market several generators purred. Stiff hoses ran from the ocean through a pumping station into the corridors of the covered buildings. Muddy water ran out several entrances. A sun-baked crew of landscapers continuously fed a wood chipper. Standing on a ladder was a shirtless man with his entire torso tattooed. He nailed an overhead sign that advertised his tattoo shop. People unloaded heaped shopping carts onto unstable tables with goods scavenged from the demolished retail stores that once lined Highway 19.

Beneath the covered market, where'd it been washed and readied, were more formal booths loaded with sorted goods. There were lanterns, batteries, Sterno stoves, camping equipment, inflatable air mattresses, fishing supplies, bait, cigarettes, and even cold beer— anything people got their hands on that offered an opportunity to barter.

A chunky young woman with globular, cellulite saddlebags argued the value of her barter. The heavy woman refused a promise to barter in exchange for a supply of hard candy she'd confiscated from a Dollar Tree. "I ain't no Popeye, and you hain't going to be no Wimpy," she told the woman she argued with.

A bearded minister wielding a worn and swollen Bible traded prayers for anything tangible.

Brad and Marci stood in the middle of the once–parking lot taking it all in. Somehow, everyone continued with their lives; how industrious and capable they appeared, getting by just as before.

A sweet-sour scent of chicken floated past their noses. The aroma turned both their heads. A fifty-five-gallon drum cut in half and covered with a mesh grate grilled dozens of small bird parts laid over glowing charcoals. There was the sound of sizzling meat. A Jamaican woman smeared a tart, orange-smelling marinade. Their mouths watered.

The hefty Jamaican called to them. "You want to eat some jerk, mon?"

"Sure," Brad said as they approached the woman dressed in colorful calico garb. They spied the grill and the bucket where tiny bird parts floated in a creamsicle solution.

"What are they?" Marci asked.

"Don't ya know, tall lady? They're gulls. Look at those feathers."

Lined along a vertically strung windbreak were wicker baskets filled with gray feathers.

"Are you hungry?" the Jamaican asked.

"We are," Marci answered, licking her lips.

"Whatchya goinna trade, my lady." The Jamaican smiled. A broad bead of pearl teeth parted her plump Caribbean lips.

"What do you mean?" Marci asked.

"Ain't ya heard, mon, gotta trade something. Chadda's little fellers caught and plucked and gutted them gulls. For the lads, I mix up my orange jerk sour to yummy the taste. If you and squirrely boy want to eat, you offer a barter."

Marci was confused.

Give her something?

She assumed it was free and hadn't a clue what to barter for a meal.

Tugging his mother's arm Brad pulled her away. "I got an idea," he whispered in her ear.

Marci looked at the baskets of feathers then approached the cook, who was busy pricking and rotating the sizzling meat. "How about I turn those feathers into pillows for you?" Marci had recalled her West Virginia childhood, when her mother made down comforters from the geese her father shot during the fall migration.

The cook spied the feathers. She cricked her neck. Her smile became large. "A fluffy pillow." She blinked several times. "Yeah, mon. Tall lady, you got a deal. But ya don't eat 'til you make pillows."

Perplexed, Marci had hoped to eat first.

"Sorry, but that's the boss man's order."

Marci had heard grumblings of this man before. "Who's this boss?"

The cook lifted her head and pointed to the house that was visible from the flea market. "He lives in that shack with the porch, all by his lonesome. He's a good man. But if you be the devil and not follow the rules, you get chucked by the dyke lady. Two days ago, dyke lady sent a fellow packing for coming too close to the booby harem she got stashed at the top of the junkyard."

Using tongs the Jamaican reached into the marinade and lifted several breasts and set them over the hot grate. The burning aroma passed Marci's and Brad's noses. The cook gestured toward the basket of feathers. "There ya go. Bring back pillows and you'll eat for two days. But the wickers, they ain't yours unless ya got something else to trade."

They quickly emptied the feathers into a garbage bag the cook gave them.

"I need pillow fabric, Brad. Can you solve that problem while I'll search inside that building for thread to sew the ends closed?"

The smell of food lingered as Marci entered Hoinky's covered walkway. There were no fans circulating the dead air. How can these people stand the heat? she thought.

She wandered the drab corridors and gathered that there was no goodwill from these Krackers. She came across a stall where a haggard, elderly, arthritic woman sat at a sewing machine powered by a pedal.

I haven't seen one of those since I was a child, she thought. The Appalachian folk used them all the time.

The sewing machine operator was in conversation with another Kracker woman, telling how she worked underground at Disney World in Orlando repairing costumes. "Used to be a seamstress for Snow White," her voice crackled as the aged woman's foot levered the ornate wrought iron pedal. "Spoiled brats from Brooklyn gave me plenty of work. If Snow White didn't spend enough time with them, they'd tug at her costume and tear it."

"Uh, excuse me," Marci interrupted. "Do you have a needle and thread?"

"Do I have a needle and thread?" The old woman mocked Marci by wagging a finger with a marble-size knuckle joint. "Excuse me! Who the shittin' are you, some miss prissy polite?"

Marci yawed onto her heels. *What a vulgar woman.*

The seamstress looked at Marci. "What'd ya, stupid?" Spit flew from her wrinkled lips.

Marci spotted spools of thread and packages of needles on the table behind the vulgar hag.

The crotchety woman spied Marci's wedding ring. "That real gold. Give me that ring on your finger and ya can have an armload."

"But that's my wedding ring," she said.

"Take that up with your mister. No gold, then ya get nothin' from me."

Marci was stunned—her wedding band was worth much more. All she wanted was a spool of thread and a sewing needle. But her stomach ached, and maternal need to feed her son was stronger.

Slowly, she twisted and removed the reluctant band. Lifting the solid gold circle to eye level, Marci rolled it between her thumb and index finger. It was as if she were divorcing Robbie right now. Her hand felt naked, with a translucent circle where the ring was.

The seamstress swiped the wedding band and tapped it against the cast iron throat of the sewing machine. "Hmm, got some gold in it. Your mister hain't a cheapskate. Go ahead, fetch some rolls of thread and a pack of needles and a bolt of fabric if ya want."

At first Marci hesitated; the hag had snapped it away too quickly. She wasn't sure she wanted to do this.

Reluctantly, she went into the cluttered stall and selected the needed items.

Outside, Bradley spotted three boys flinging oyster shells using a slingshot. They argued who winged it the furthest. To Brad they looked like a gang of hoodlums. The one nearest his size bore an unfinished tattoo.

"Do you know where I can find pillowcases?" Brad asked.

The one with the tattoo lowered his slingshot. "You from here?"

"No," Brad answered.

Samson immediately recognized the opportunity to be mischievous. "My brother Buddy knows where you can get lots of pillowcases.

"Hey, Bud," Samson said. "Show this dude where the free pillowcases are."

Buddy gave Samson a long look.

Samson went over and whispered to Buddy.

"That's right, at the Laundromat. Follow me," Buddy said.

Chadda's boys led Brad to the laundry area and approached the rear of a cage stuffed with smelly clothes.

Kathleen Lindum had finished hanging a load of wet towels, pillowcases, and sheets that Critter confiscated from a wrecked hotel. She sat on a bench smoking a cigarette.

"See that clothesline," Buddy said. "Take what you need off the line."

Bradley started unpinning the dripping pillowcases. Mom's going to be proud of me, thought Brad.

Samson snuck around the cage and sat next to Kathleen. He tried to bum a smoke but Kathleen would have none of it. "No, Samson, scram." She smacked the top of his shaved head.

"How come you can smoke and I can't?" Samson challenged her.

"Smart ass." Kathleen swatted him again.

"Not as smart as that kid stealing your pillowcases." He pointed at Brad.

"Hey, shit ball," Kathleen yelled. "Put those back or I'll stuff your head into the lagoon shitter pipe." Tossing her cigarette she ran to slug the thief. Samson picked the cigarette off the ground.

Brad froze. "That can't be Kathleen's voice? Sure sounds like her, though!"

"Asshole, didn't you hear? Put those fucking pillowcases back."

After hearing the volley of curse words, it was obvious. The voice was Kathleen.

Brad saw her coming in baggy jeans and unlaced hiking boots, with a bandana around her head. It can't be, he thought. Maybe a lookalike.

Wheeling a clenched fist Kathleen charged him.

"Kathleen, is that you?"

She swung. But before her fist struck, it lowered and weakly tapped Brad's shoulder.

"Brad!"

Her eyes grew big.

"Where's Mom?"

"She's inside that building."

Kathleen had consumed herself with work to pitch off that her family was likely dead. Krackers whispered behind her back that anyone south of the Flats did not survive the surge.

Standing there, Kathleen stared at her brother. "You look older."

When Brad saw his mother coming from inside the building, he darted ahead calling for her. "Mom. . . Mom, Kathleen's here! She's alive!"

At first, it didn't sink with Marci. She was rubbing her naked ring finger, mulling a multitude of emotions. Regretting the deal she made.

Brad grabbed and pushed her forward, toward Kathleen. "She's over there!"

"Who!"

"It's Kathleen!"

Kathleen stood there dressed as a Kracker in baggy jeans, an oversize T-shirt, and confederate bandana.

"Kathleen, it's really you?"

"Yes, Mom."

Instantly, Marci dropped the armload of goods and fainted.

"Mom!" Brad knelt and shook her.

Marci opened her eyelids and stared at Kathleen. Lifting to her knees, she set her face into her hands and wept. "It's a miracle."

Helping her mother to her feet, Kathleen told the story of Fifty-Cal and riding out the storm with Chadda, delivering her twins. "Plenty of people owe me around here; get whatever you want."

To Marci, it was clear Kathleen had changed. Overnight she'd matured.

They went to the grilling area where Kathleen called the Jamaican on her barter. Brad devoured several gamy gulls and washed it down with warm soda and got a stomachache.

For the rest of the afternoon Marci and Brad helped Kathleen do laundry. They talked, something Marci thoroughly enjoyed. And when the topic turned to Robbie, each had little to say.

Chapter 62

L ast night was too quiet, which wasn't normal for the Flats, thought Dale. Someone will find a way to stir up trouble. Two days ago he'd set an example by evicting a nasty drunk who laid punches on his girlfriend. Fifty-Cal hog-tied and dumped the drunk at Itchy Fingers. She pinned a note to him that said, "If I see your woman-beating mug near the Flats, your sorry Kracker ass will be riddled with bullet holes like the shot-up school bus you woke in."

Hoarded items like cigarettes, liquor, and narcotics brought the best barter. This made Dale nervous because eventually a trembling alcoholic or delirious addict with the jitterbugs would resort to robbery—or worse yet, pull a gun. He wanted to prevent this at all costs.

It seemed the Scooter's girls finally realized the junkyard wasn't a nudist camp. Critter found a way to be useful by working a deal with Kathleen to clean their delicate, formfitting purple outfits. And happily shuttled the girls to Hoinky's, where they applied their trade of serving food. Their presence, in scant outfits, running hot meals between the grills, kept some of the hardcore characters calm and distracted.

The two Greek waiters from Lavaki's arrived at Hoinky's to eat, and argued with the Jamaican cook that her food wasn't as good as Greek food. The next day, two voodoo dolls that looked eerily like the two Greeks swung from shoelaces above the Jamaican's slicing bench.

Cooterman Pat spent much of his time wandering the junkyard, bending the ear of anyone who'd listen. Telling of the perfect job he'd had for the past twenty years as the gate guard at Tropical Harbors Beach Club on the Gulf of Mexico.

Since his mother's plan was moving along as best it could, Dale figured he'd steal a few hours at the grove. He needed to get a grip on his emotions—the oak grove was where he went to gather and center himself.

A brilliant double rainbow with vivid indigo and violet layers arced along the inland sky. A thunderhead boiled with mixtures of irregular dark gray and bubbling white cotton ball clouds. The arriving rain will force the wildlife into the trees, thought Dale, lifting from his rocking chair, making his way off the porch and down the grade toward Dixie Highway.

When he passed through the junkyard gate and crossed the road, in the opposite direction walked a tall blond. Dale watched as she passed. Must be a straggler, someone who'd wandered in. As he continued walking the image of the tall woman stuck with him. That drawn, hardened Kracker woman look wasn't present. She looked familiar, a look that opened Dale's memory of Jodi. A memory he'd carried all the time because it was a good thought, a place of comfort when he needed to occupy his emptiness.

Yesterday, Flatch mentioned it was time to take on a woman to keep things right around the Flats. He told Dale that folks were questioning his want of a woman, because he ain't been with one in some time. "They thinks you might be gay, Dale."

Dale didn't let it bother him, because Kracker women were too darn alley cat nasty. Most either had a bad case of the angries, or were too damn husky fat. And bringing someone in from outside wasn't a choice either. Who'd ever live in an oceanside junkyard?

Carting the contents from the sloshing washer, Marci unknotted and handed dripping laundry to Brad, who strung it on the clothesline. She never fathomed that a makeshift Laundromat would have any relevance after a disaster. And wondered who had the foresight to think of such a need.

They ate well, thanks to Kathleen's knack for tough bartering. And Marci noticed that her daughter had thrived and thoroughly enjoyed the oddball community that accepted her. She questioned if Kathleen would return home, and considered if her righteous temperament was more the product of the self-loathing Trinity Meadows lifestyle they'd lived.

Returning to the nasty seamstress that bartered her ring, Marci tried to barter it back. The old woman rebuffed her, saying, "A deal's a deal." Not even Kathleen could get her to return the solid gold wedding band.

With the midafternoon heat building and the threat of rain, the Krackers shut down Hoinky's and headed to their dwellings to nap. Kathleen and Brad tossed a tarp over the dirty clothes, leaving the freshly washed garments to rinse in the rain.

With his stomach comfortably full Bradley crawled into the Chevy Blazer and zonked out, dreaming of a day when he would return home, game on the Internet, and be with his dad.

Continually rubbing her ring finger, Marci couldn't stop thinking how surreal discovering her middle name carved into the tree was. Did her first love live nearby? Or was he long gone? Her way of life had drastically changed, so did her children's. How would she rebuild her life and cope with the trauma of the rape? This last question she endlessly debated.

It was too humid to lie around all afternoon, so Marci decided to head for the oak grove—a place that reminded her of her innocence, a time when she was naïve and carefree.

Heading down Dixie Highway, Marci watched the inland lightning leap from the towering thunderheads. Looks like the rain-line is hovering over Trinity Meadows, she thought. How clever and in tune with nature these Krackers are. They knew it rained less near the coast; that's why they lived here . . . As a child she loved the outdoors, but somehow had unwittingly swapped it for the relentless taunt of television, interrupting cell phones, and unending email demanding an immediate response. She'd lost the simple joy of sitting beneath the sky, watching the clouds mold into cartoon characters. But now her thoughts were different, focused on basics, like staying clean, finding food, keeping hydrated, and remaining cool.

A refreshing breeze tossed the floppy elephant-ear leaves of the reaching banyan that invaded the oak grove. Marci allowed the coolness drifting from the shade to caress her. "Just like air-conditioning but for free." Large random raindrops fell from the sky and blasted the chalky roadway, chasing Marci beneath the trees. A flock of snow-white egrets glided overhead and gracefully disappeared into the leafy canopy with her. She weaved through the banyan's root-drops. Tailing an unsuspecting raccoon working the sparse grasses, rummaging for grubs, she arrived at the nook. But suddenly the raccoon alerted, sniffed the air in the opposite direction, and disappeared into the grayness.

"Someone's here!" Marci became concerned. "Likely vagrants seeking to stay cool."

She got scared.

Relaxing, watching a flock of egrets arrive and roost within the upper limbs, Dale Carter reconsidered what Flatch had said. "Krackers gossiped if he liked women at all." They'd accepted him as a loner, but Kracker men were compulsive when it came to a feminine scent. They expected Dale to mirror that same lack of control. And when the egrets twitched nervously and rotated their beaks in the same direction, Dale quietly left the nook. And sure enough, the egrets were right; a wandering shadow cut through the shafts of sunlight. The damp crunch of footsteps drew closer. The stride, the pace, was difficult to fix. The gait seemed manly, but the lighter footsteps were distinctly a woman's.

Nervous and debating if this was a bad idea, Marci inspected the inscription one last time. Suddenly, the egrets alerted in a massive, squawking, evacuating flurry, disturbing the tranquil layer of cooler air. There was the heavy odor of a man's cologne. Someone is behind the big oak. Her heart raced. It's that Deuce guy!

"Is. . . Is someone there?" she called.

A tattooed forearm appeared. Oh my God, not again!

"It's safe," said the male voice. "You interrupted my nap."

Marci was a ghost. She expected him to lunge any second. But the tall man sporting a dark tan took several steps backwards to suggest he was nonthreatening. His eyes studied her and gave a puzzled, cautious look.

I must look familiar, Marci thought, then realized it was the guy she'd passed earlier today, the man on the porch, the man with the cologne.

"Jodi?"

The words shocked her. To hear him call her middle name, her memory raced insanely. *Where did he know her?* I never sold my pot to men. Perhaps Patti Washington knew him.

Again, he called her. "Jodi, it's me, Buck." His tattooed forearm directed toward the inscription on the lifted root. "We did that."

"Buck?" Marci's legs turned jelly. She sat on the mat of Spanish moss.

Dale approached.

"How can it be?"

She studied his face, searching for his youth.

"Buck, it's really you!" It was hard to imagine the young boy who owned her virginity now stood in front of her. This guy seemed raw, distant, weathered.

There was silence. ". . . Buck, you're all grown up. In my mind you never aged."

Dale remained quiet and considered if his mother sent Jodi back into his life to answer the question he feared he'd never learn.

Struggling to ask the question, Dale leaned against the tree and folded his arms. "What happened? Where'd you go the next day?"

It took a moment for Marci to gather what he meant. Then she realized the question. "Buck . . . Oh Buck, I'm so sorry! I never told you. You never knew."

Marci's expression became sympathetic. "After . . . ah . . . well, you know." She flicked her wrist back and forth, pointing at him, then her, then the moss mat. She wanted to say "made love" but couldn't.

She continued. "I went back to my aunt's and learned my dad died in a mine collapse. We left right away. I'm so sorry, Buck. But we were so young, you know."

Dale began to relax. "After all these years I have the answer to why you disappeared."

He's grown into such a handsome, rugged man, observed Marci.

She leaned toward him and softened her voice. "So, how are you?"

"Can I sit?" asked Dale.

"Sure!"

"What's your real name?" Marci asked. "Not knowing always puzzled me."

"It's Dale . . . Dale Carter."

"I heard about you at the flea market. They say you run the place."

"Yes," said Dale, perched on a root raised the height of a stool.

They talked for hours. Dale shared with Marci his life, the recent loss of his mother, the junkyard and his mother's mission to care for the Krackers. He explained Florence's obsession with a doomsday hurricane. How she planned and prepared. Dale told Marci he'd always thought of her and that his heart had been heavy for a long time.

Marci saw the adventurous adolescent boy she once knew was sad. She shared her life journey, the hurricane and how unprepared her family was. What a goof Robbie was. She told him of the mess south of here, the impenetrable debris mountain, but did not mention the strip club incident. She went into detail about her daughter and shared a hard laugh about what a coincidence it was, and how well Kathleen fit in at the Flats.

They talked until the sun hinted the day had aged.

"Where do I go from here?" Marci said.

"We better go; the rain line is coming this way." Dale pointed to the darkening sky. Clasping her hand he lifted Marci to her feet, grasped her waist, and guided her amongst the trees toward the road.

Dales grip was firm. His hands were well-worked. And when he touched her, it sent a chilling shiver through her and felt good.

There was a snap of lightning and clap of thunder. "Oh!" Marci flinched.

"Come on, Jodi" Dale said. "Move fast, otherwise we'll get drenched."

But it was too late. The rain arrived in soaking sheets.

"Do you remember when we played pirates and got caught in the rain like this many times? We never minded," Dale said.

Throwing up her arms, Marci cried out, "Where'd my youth go? Why can't I feel this way all the time, as if it were springtime each day of my life?"

Dale looked at her and smiled. "There's the spirited Jodi I usta know."

They slowed their pace, and so did the drenching rain. Marci's thin hair hung straight. The buttons on an oversize blouse, which obviously came from the Salvation Army, were undone nearly halfway down. The pale pink cotton fabric clung and showed her womanly form.

She caught Dale watching. It felt good to feel his gaze wander her body. It'd been a while since a man looked at her like a teenager.

Holding hands, arriving at the yard in the dark, Dale invited Marci to his house. "I bet you're hungry and could use a hot shower?"

"I am, but should see if Brad is okay."

Trudging the wet sandy grade, they stopped at the Chevy Blazer where Brad slept. "Looks like he's out cold," Marci said. "He's been through a lot, you know."

Chapter 63

At each corner of the Icehouse, tiny gullies had gouged the soil at the end of each waterspout. "So this is your place," Marci said, walking up the squeaky porch steps.

"Yes," Dale said, following.

For a fleeting moment she debated if she should go. Dale's house looked inviting, cool, homey, country-like. "You got hot water?" Marci asked.

"What do you think?" he answered.

"Should I check on Kathleen?" she asked, feeling a tinge of guilt that she should remain with her children.

"She knows her way around pretty well," Dale said. "More than likely she's with Chadda and Monk and the doodlebugs playing cards."

Marci decided it was okay. Dale wasn't as Krackerish as the others she'd seen. His diction was clear. And he made her feel comfortable. As the time passed and the more they talked, she saw the young Buck she enjoyed. And it felt good to be thrown back in time, to her carefree youthful days. It suppressed all that she'd been through.

Opening the screen door, Dale escorted her down the narrow dog-run hallway. "Welcome," he whispered.

The walls were covered in Victorian-era wallpaper. The furniture pieces in the sitting room were dark, ornate, and thick. "I can see this home is still your mother's. What is this?" Marci touched a picture frame with five playing cards fanned beneath the glass. "It looks like a poker hand."

"A full house, aces, and jacks. The hand Momma held that won her this here property."

Sopping wet, she became chilled.

Dale turned on the lights.

"There's no difference in you," Dale said. He gazed at her. "You are as I imagined, except for the mosquito welts."

Marci blushed; she knew that look. It was of a man who'd not been with a woman in a very long time. He was tense and tried to be polite. Obviously, he wanted her.

"Dale?" Marci asked. "Is there a place I can change, perhaps remove these wet clothes?"

His gaze fixed upon her. "How about Momma's room?"

He walked Marci halfway down the hallway and led her into Florence's bedroom. In the center was a double-stack, king-size bed neatly kept and strewn with embroidered pillows. A lit Tiffany lamp on the dresser added its own feel.

"How do you have electricity?" she asked, entering and looking around.

"The dark colors, it feels cozy." She couldn't believe how well-kept the bedroom was with its expensive furniture. *How'd it fit through the narrow hallway?*

Dale lifted the window. The breeze that traveled the hallway diverted and rushed around them. The hemmed tassels on the bedspread danced. The flowing linen curtains that framed the window fled through the opening to the porch.

Again, Marci became chilled.

"Did you see that old dragline shovel at the top of the crest?" Dale asked.

"When I was a child in West Virginia, my dad often took me to the one at his mine."

"It's got a reliable diesel generator. Runs all the time, sending electricity to the things that are important. Shhh!" Dale put his fingers to Marci's lips. "Listen."

Their eyes locked. "Can you hear the diesel running?"

For some reason when Dale touched her, Marci felt compelled to kiss his fingertips, softly, with tenderness. Drawn to his warmth, she came close. There was a tension within him. She'd felt it the whole time. And there was this urge within her to tend it. As if she solely possessed the ability to release him.

Gently, his hand drifted and caressed her neck.

She ran her hands along both his arms. He was a strong man.

Drawing closer, their lips touched. Marci was unable to pull away. She wanted to acquiesce. To be owned.

Joining in a deep, probing, tangled kiss, Marci became warm and pressed against him. He lifted her to the comfortable bed. It engulfed her. There was nothing Marci could do to rescue herself. He unbuttoned her blouse; quickly the rest of her garments disappeared. She lay naked and vulnerable within his muscular arms. His heart raced, his tension pleading her permission.

Wanting him, she pushed off his damp jeans. Her hands skated the thick hair that lined his strong thighs and measured the firmness of his buttocks. A delirium arrived as Dale guided his knee along her inner thigh, gesturing.

And it happened; he went inside with a swollen force, Marci easily accepting all of him, feeling blissfully omnipresent. She melted—her body mashed beneath with every point of contact aroused and sensitive. For a moment she lost consciousness, her orgasm arriving.

The sunlight that reflected off the Pulaski mirror touched Marci's face. She lay curled and wrapped within Dale's arm, his bronzed torso warming her entire backside. She felt his shallow breath against her neck and that familiar smell of masculinity and allowed herself this moment.

"Do you remember Mr. Hoinky?" Dale asked with a softness that held a coarseness.

Marci chuckled. "How could I forget? That pig was ugly. Whatever happened to him and Elnora?"

"Hoinky drowned trying to save Elnora after she fell off the houseboat. They say it was the saltwater that did him in, after it got stuck in his messed-up throat. Coroner said he had a fishbone stuck in his vocal cords all them years."

"That's sad," Marci said.

"He wanted to marry Momma awful bad. Pursued her all the time. Told her the only way she'd own the flea market was by sharing his last name. Mom told Hoinky it ain't worth it. Sometimes I think he drowned to piss her off and leave us with all those mutant pigs."

Marci uncoiled, rolled to face Dale, and brushed back the tuft of hair that drooped. Tenderly, she outlined the deep stress lines of his face. "Mr. Hoinky was odd but I remember he was kind."

Lying on her back, letting the morning sun warm her, Marci saw it in Dale's eyes again. He loved to look at every part her. There was no scrutiny, just lust.

"You know what makes me feel good, Dale? The way you look at me. You smile and study all of me and like what you see."

Until now, Marci had put the thought of Robbie and Deuce out of her head, and wouldn't permit it to arrive until she'd left.

Dale was quiet.

"Can I take a shower?" she asked.

"Sure, but first…" Dale pulled Marci on top. He was ready.

Marci smiled, kissed him, and they made love once more.

Wrapped in a bathrobe Marci pushed the screen door forward, stepped onto the porch, and sat in Florence's rocker. The wicker complained and stretched. The well-worn lattice became comfortable. "What a neat chair!"

Reaching for the coffee Dale had set on the banister, she looked across the horizon to the flea market where people were beginning their day. It's a haggard place, she thought—not even remotely as nice as Trinity Meadows.

A pickup rumbled down the road from the top of the mine. It slowed. It's that Critter guy, Marci observed. He eyed her, smiled, tossed a cigarette butt, and drove away.

Marci called into the house. "You know that Critter guy drove by a moment ago. I think he wanted to stop."

Dale came outside and smiled. The screen door smacked shut.

"Nice to see you're putting Momma's chair to good use. That was her favorite spot."

"Oh." Marci set her feet flat on the porch boards and stopped halfway through her rock.

"No, don't stop," Dale said. "Momma would've been pissed if I made that damn chair her gravestone. Critter passed?"

"Yes," Marci said. "He drove slowly."

"He was checking you out. He ain't ever seen another woman at the Icehouse before. They're all worried about me being a celibate."

Rocking back in the Adirondack Marci flipped her hair to air it out. "You're all man," she said.

Dale set his hand on the back of the rocker. Her feet lifted from the deck, leaned and kissed her.

"Folks around her are simple-minded," Dale said. "That's the stuff they think of all the time. It's why I don't feel like I'm one of them."

Chapter 64

Bradley Lindum shook the sand from his sneakers then guzzled a refilled water bottle that Kathleen left and headed for Hoinky's to search for his missing mother.

Kathleen was already working at the laundry. Chadda's boys helped but weren't too happy about it. Each had to fold five baskets before she allowed them to go eat.

"Kathleen, have you seen Mom?"

"No," she answered.

Busy, Kathleen seemed unconcerned.

"Is that your brother?" Samson said. "He looks like a weenie." The boys started laughing.

Accustomed to their obnoxious behavior, Kathleen ignored them.

Lifting a peashooter hidden in the pocket of his baggy shorts, Samson slipped a ball bearing into his mouth and shot Brad.

"Ouch!" It hit him in the throat and stung. "What the fuck!"

"A sissy that curses," Samson said.

What did I do to get his kid to hate me, he thought? He rubbed the stinging welt. Another ball bearing struck; this time it lacerated his cheek.

"Cut it out." It hurt worse.

Brad feared if he punched one of them they'd all attack. It was clear the kid with the tattoo wanted to scrap. And if he lost, they'd torment him all the time.

Kathleen cut them a stare. "Stop picking on Brad."

Samson tucked his peashooter into his waistband. "Do we have to fold all these towels?"

"Your mom wants them cleaned, so when people come to the market she can trade them. And if you brats don't stop causing trouble, I'll have Critter put you to work scrubbing Port-O-Potties toilet seats."

The boys had reached the limits of their attention span. Wetting the corner of their towels, they spun and snapped them at each other. Kathleen decided to chase them off; otherwise, they'd work over Brad even more. "Why don't you boys scram?"

Artie, Buddy, and Samson bolted for the mangroves and launched a rowboat they'd stashed.

"Where do you think Mom is?" Brad asked, holding a washcloth to his bloodied cheek.

"I have no idea but Critter might know," Kathleen said. "He's over by Hoinky's houseboat."

Secured by a forty-foot chain, Hoinky's houseboat had miraculously survived the hurricane surge. Several mutant piglets had also survived and lived inside the ruptured pontoon. Crouching, whacking the tubular aluminum with a baseball bat, Critter tried to flush the piglets from inside.

"Come on, little piggies," Critter called.

Bang. . . Bang! The aluminum pontoon let out a hollow echo.

"Shit, they ain't going to budge."

Tossing the bat he went to his pickup, retrieved a jug containing a green-brown puree, and unscrewed the cap. "Phew, this pig slop stinks." He poured the soupy solution into a large dog bowl and shoved the slop under the hull, near the pontoon slit.

"Little piggy, where are you?"

Kathleen and Brad walked up behind him.

"Critter, whatchya doing?" Kathleen asked.

"Tryin' to capture Hoinky's pigs. If Dale finds out they're still alive I'm screwed."

Bradley watched the burly guy lying on his stomach trying to shove the bowl closer without spilling it.

"I give up," Critter said, sliding from under and pulling to his feet using the side of the houseboat. He lit a cigarette and offered one to Kathleen.

She accepted.

Brad was appalled. "Since when did you start smoking?"

Sucking the cigarette, Kathleen blew the smoke away from Brad. "Uh, I don't know, most people smoke around here. Guess I started because everyone else did."

Though he appreciated that she was much calmer these days, she may have turned into a Kracker. "Kathleen, we gotta find Mom."

"Is that your brother?" Critter asked.

"Yes."

"He's a runt. I can use him."

Brad didn't care for the runt comment.

"Kid, crawl under and drag out my pet pig?" Critter pointed beneath Hoinky's grounded houseboat. "See that clump of weeds where the pontoon is wrinkled? There's a split in the aluminum."

Critter nabbed Brad by his shoulder. "Kneel with me and look under. . . . where I shoved the slop bowl."

Brad wanted to break away but Critter had a firm grip and shoved him further under.

"See that dribbling pig snout," Critter said. "It's sniffing the slop."

Brad wasn't inclined to help the man that called him runt.

"Go ahead, Brad, help him," Kathleen said. "But before you do, tell him you want to barter."

"Shut up, wench. I gave you a smoke."

"Going to cost you a whole pack for Brad to help you capture that pig," Kathleen said.

Critter thought for a moment. "That's a bit much. What ya going to trade me for tellin' ya where your mom is?"

He had her.

"You know where she is?" Brad asked.

"Sure do, runt. And ain't going to say unless you shove that slop closer to that hole."

Suddenly, Brad felt a stinging pain on his right ass cheek. "Ouch!" He grabbed his thigh. It hurt so hard he started to whimper.

Laughter erupted across the lot. This time it was Buddy who'd hit Brad using a homemade slingshot.

"Look, the weenie kid is crying," Artie said.

"Toughen up, kid," Critter said. "Otherwise, they'll work you over bad. Ain't you bigger than them?"

Kathleen yelled at her brother. "Brad, cut it out. You're whimpering like Dad does. If you don't go over and slug one of them and grind their snotty faces into the dirt you'll be looking over your shoulder all the time."

"But there are three of them," said Brad with tears flowing.

Critter wanted to capture the piglets before Dale arrived. Chadda's boys were a distraction. He crawled from under and ran them off. "Scram!"

Brad wanted to leave Krackerland and go back home to his dad.

"It's a deal," he said, wiping his tears. "Where is my mom?"

"I saw her this morning but I ain't telling until you drag that piggy out."

"You dumb shit," Kathleen said. "You could've got him for more. Samson knows you're a weenie and won't stop harassing until you slug him. And that's not going to be easy. Critter could've protected you. "

Critter smiled. "Your sister's right. Listen, all ya gotta do is snatch the hind leg and nowhere else. Or that son of a bitch will gnaw off your knuckle."

With his ass smarting Bradley crawled further beneath the houseboat.

On all fours Critter watched. "Shove that slop bowl closer so he can smell it."

Scraping along his stomach Brad reached with his fingertips, gripped the rim, and slid the bowl ahead, nearly into the split. "I see a wet nose. It's sniffing."

"Cool, kid. Keep that bowl in front and don't startle him, or he won't come all the way out. Remember, snag the hind leg and swing him away from the hole."

Sprawled, Brad waited.

"Lad, a pig can't resist swine slop. Don't let him grab the bowl and drag it in. They're smart bastards."

"I see him. He's coming out," Brad whispered.

The hesitant piglet poked its tiny head and awkwardly jutted its portly body in a lurching, forward motion.

"Shhh . . . here he comes," Critter whispered. "Move to the side so I can see, and so you can get a better angle when you snatch him."

Bradley shifted to his left. "There's something wrong with it. It can't walk right."

"Be quiet, kid. Don't scare it. He's skittish."

"What's wrong with its legs?"

"Ugly, ain't it. Them's are baby arms. Don't chicken out and I'll tell ya where you can find your mommy. All ya got to do is grab his hind quarter and fling real hard toward me."

Brad inched his arm ahead. "I don't think it knows how to walk right."

"He can't move very fast, so don't worry," Critter said. "When he sticks his snout into the bowl go for it."

The tiny animal scratched its way, lowered its snout, and slurped.

Critter whispered, "Grab it. Toss the little shit my way."

Bradley guided his opened palm behind the hoof and flung the piglet like a wet rag. The sow let out a squeal, snapping its jaw, its baby arms twirling in tiny circular spirals. The piglet tumbled then rolled like a log, around and around, finally stopping in front of Critter.

"Eeooh!" Brad said. "It has hands with moving fingers. It's creepy."

"Good job." Critter snatched the piglet by its hind leg and tossed it further, toward his pickup truck. The tumbling piglet squealed and struggled to right itself.

"You ain't going anywhere," Critter said. "Ain't got enough legs."

Brad crawled from under and watched the mutant scratch in circles. It could not lift its portly stomach off the ground.

"Thanks, kid, now I gotta find a way of getting that little piggy into my pickup."

"Ouch!" Brad saw a flash of bright light. Something struck his head and cut a gash. It bled. He heard laughter behind the mangroves. Suddenly, a barrage of saucer-shaped scallops clobbered him.

Critter couldn't care less what was happening to Brad. That was the runt's problem. Besides, it kept Chadda's boys occupied.

Wiping his shirt against his forehead to clear the blood, Brad yelled, "Tell me where my mom is!"

"Just a moment, kid." Critter circled the pig looking for the right angle to flip it into the truck bed. "Here goes nothing."

The pig screeched as Critter grabbed its hind leg and flung it into the air. At the apex of the arc a dark shadow raced toward the piglet. The claws of an osprey dug into the piglet's spine and halted its descent.

"What the heck?" Critter had a surprised look.

Clutching the squealing animal, the osprey swooped to gather speed, tightened its turn, and flapped hard to gain altitude.

"It's got the pig," laughed Kathleen.

"No shit, Sherlock," said Critter, watching the osprey with the dangling piglet squealing so loud everyone at the flea market stopped to watch the airborne commotion.

Flapping hard, the large bird of prey lifted higher, over the mangroves toward the open ocean. Critter prayed the wriggling pig would work free and drop into the Gulf. "If Dale catches wind of this!"

Critter cursed. "Oh shit, that crazy fowl is coming overland again. Shit . . . Shit, Dale's going to have my ass."

The osprey headed for the quarry. Several of the Scooter waitresses standing near the casino bus pointed into the sky.

"Why don't you drop the motherfucker into the lagoon for me," Critter yelled.

But the osprey didn't fly in that direction; instead, it banked and soared past the dragline's boom towards the Icehouse.

Critter nervously watched. "Crap, my ass is grass."

Brad had never seen anything like this. The black and white bird dipped its wingtip and darted toward the house with the big porch, gaining momentum, launching the piglet like a torpedo. The flight path of the noisy sow chased for nearly a hundred feet—swooshing in—barely missing the woman sitting in the chair.

"Mom!" Brad said. "That's Mom on the porch." He started to run.

"Gotta skedaddle," Critter said. He hopped in his pickup and sped away.

Chapter 65

After sipping her coffee Marci set the mug on the porch. "What a magnificent view, Dale. I can see all the way to the ocean."

Dale passed her his binoculars. "Take a look at that crazy osprey, she's back. I thought she left for good after the hurricane took out her nest."

Soaring, circling the dragline boom, was the osprey. It tipped its wing, carved into the firm onshore wind, and dove for the mangroves. "It must be time for breakfast," Dale said.

Pressing the binoculars to her brow Marci followed the majestic bird. It flew low, gliding, careful not to let her slipstream disturb the tall grasses that wisped inches below her tucked talons. The osprey disappeared just as Hoinky's pole buildings came into sight. "Oh, I lost her."

Marci panned the flea market and spotted Brad with his sister. She was pleased they were getting along, fending for themselves. But she felt guilty for leaving Brad alone last night. However, it was necessary he become more independent.

"I see Brad and Kathleen," Marci said. "Can we go?"

"Let me get my truck keys." Dale went inside.

Marci focused the binoculars. Several Krackers pointed in her direction. She heard squealing. It grew louder. A wobbling mass swooshed past her head, smacked the cedar shacks and splattered blood across the porch. Marci screamed. The ugly pig lay next to her feet choking, convulsing, its baby hands squiggling.

Panicked, she raced down the porch steps and into the sandy lot.

The screen door burst open. Dale nearly tripped over the dying pig. He cursed. "Fucking crazy bird. Are you okay, Jodi?" Dale lifted her into his arms and comforted her.

Marci buried her head into his chest. "Can I go see my children?"

As they rode along in the pickup toward Hoinky's, Dale told Marci about the osprey. That it was old and its behavior was unstable and strange.

"The deformed piglet must be Elnora's offspring," Marci said. "How'd she get pregnant?"

"When ol' Hoink played poker with Momma at the Hacienda Hotel, he didn't like leaving Elnora on the houseboat alone. So Hoink tied her in the oak grove where it was cool. Seems Elnora went into heat and got herself knocked up by a wild boar. The whole dang litter was mutant. And Hoink hadda let them fend on their own. And it don't help that Critter sometimes breeds Elnora's descendants and sells them to the carny freak shows wintering in Gibsonton."

The pickup lurched to a stop. Brad ran toward them.

"Mom!" Brad yelled, huffing, arriving at the passenger side window. "Where were you?"

"Brad, this is Dale Carter. He owns this place." Marci purposely evaded the question.

Brad looked at Dale. He was much bigger than his father.

"Hi, Brad." Dale tried to be polite.

"Mr. Carter," Brad said cautiously after catching his breath. He looked back and forth at both of them. He'd seen him lift his mother into his arms and kiss her after the pig landed on the porch.

Marci saw it in his eyes. Brad knew. In the middle of the night she'd considered returning to the Blazer, but something selfishly compelled her to stay and deal with the result.

"Mom, when can we go home and see if Dad's all right?"

The question caught her off guard.

"Soon, I guess," she said. "When it is safe." Marci flashed Dale an awkward look.

Dale was comfortable around kids and dealt with all kinds of mixed-up Kracker families. It was a fact of life around the Flats that children fended for themselves.

"Brad, we can take you home," Dale said. "But not right now."

Dale wasn't ready to lose Marci. Their lovemaking was incredible. She quenched a longing that dogged him and wanted to pursue her further, hoping Marci would move to the Flats. Also, her daughter was fine here. He considered if Marci's husband was still alive. Confirming he was a goner might move things along.

"Mom, can we leave today?" Brad begged.

"Brad," Dale said, "it will take some preparation to go inland. I have work to do to keep this place running. Can you give me a few days?"

"Brad, be patient and hold off a few more days?" Marci said. She stroked his face. "You know how difficult it was to get here. Plus, you need to consider other people's needs."

Brad was tense. A few more days didn't sit well.

"Come on, Brad, get in." Marci swung open the door.

Reaching for the handle, he slammed the door shut and stormed off.

After arriving at Hoinky's Dale found himself tending to numerous problems. The most serious was an addict Kracker who lapsed into a seizure. There was nothing he could do except watch him shiver and shake on the ground. I've got to get that medical clinic open, he thought.

Monkey Wrench arrived with Chadda and the new twins.

"Dale," Monk said, "we got a problem."

"What's that?"

"I've been to the Bippinotti. It's in rough shape. I got the generator on the roof running and the air-conditioning flowing, but it's going to take some time to close off the windows. Most are smashed to smithereens. And the docs tell me people are pointing guns at them demanding Oxy and Vicodin. Accusing the docs are hoarding it."

"Tell me about it," Dale said. "See that guy on the ground surrounded by his buddies . . . Look! Flats folks are going through withdrawals and before long we're going to have shootings." Dale shook his head in disgust.

"Dale," Marci said, interrupting them. "I know where there's a shipment of medication. We can solve two problems at once."

Dale looked at her warmly and waited for the explanation.

"My husband's a pharmaceutical rep—or was. His distributor had dropped an entire tractor trailer of painkillers prior to the hurricane for safekeeping at my house."

"Jackpot," Monkey said. "When can we go and get it?"

Chapter 66

For several days Robbie paced the proximity of the rubble that surrounded him. He listened to Jennifer Dink's air-conditioner endlessly spin its cooling fan. Overhead, buzzards swooned and picked at dead bodies trapped within the towering knot of wreckage that trapped him. Though he held out hope, Robbie had started to believe Marci and Brad were those decaying corpses and couldn't yet fathom losing his son.

Yesterday, the Yings, wearing identical blue backpacks, left and didn't bother to say where they were heading. He guessed the Petlzes had departed because the tiny heads of their daughters no longer bobbed when they passed the shattered dining room window. And their monotone prayers that drifted within the nighttime quiet had ended.

Fire ants swarmed a torn fig newton package that Charlie chewed apart. After flicking away the ants Robbie ate the gooey treat. The snack made him thirsty. He recalled that he'd stored a case of bottled water somewhere inside the garage, and went and found the buried bottles, tossing them one by one into a divot where a planted Brazilian palm once stood.

"Man, it's humid," said Robbie, resting while squatting on a box of Oxycodone Clarence had delivered. "There's a crap load of painkillers here. Feldon owes me rent for this stuff." He considered the street value—perhaps several hundred thousand dollars.

After collecting the bottled water he returned to the hut. But something seemed different. It was quieter. The Dinks' air-conditioner no longer ran.

He thought it odd that Jennifer Dink remained caged in her home alone, comfortable, refusing to come outside. No one should be that stingy. "It's about time she helped me out. I'll give it another shot. Marci said she was kind of a pack rat. Betcha she's got plenty to eat," he said, mustering courage.

Approaching the front entry, Robbie noticed a black, gummy substance that ringed the doorframe. He studied it. "Looks like mold?"

As he twisted the knob, the heavy oak door unstuck and swung inward. Clumps of mold dropped and splattered like mush onto his sneaker. Shaking his foot Robbie poked his head inside. "Jennifer? . . . Jenny?"

There was no answer. The walls were mold infested. So were the paintings and light fixtures. The slimy carpet squished beneath his feet.

"What a shame," he said, moving toward the grand staircase.

"Jennifer?"

Still no answer.

His sinuses became irritated and itchy. He lifted his shirt collar to cover his nose and mouth, then grabbed hold of the stairwell railing and started up the steps to search upstairs where it was brighter. "Oh my gosh!" Jennifer Dink was curled into a fetal position halfway up.

"Jennifer, are you okay?" Gingerly, he worked his way up the slippery steps to the first landing. What could be wrong? he thought.

When he tried to move her an empty prescription bottle rolled and clinked down several steps. "She's tried to kill herself."

He dragged her by the armpits down the stairs and out the front door and laid her outside on the grass.

As a pharmaceutical representative Robbie was familiar with overdosing. Turning Jennifer's head to the side, he stuck his finger down her throat to activate a gag reflex. Jennifer gulped, coughed, and vomited stomach contents. Wetting a washcloth, he used it to cool and comfort her. Tipping a water bottle he dribbled it across her lips.

For several hours she drifted in state of semi-consciousness, until finally, her eyelids fluttered, batted, then opened. "You're Robbie, aren't you?" she said weakly.

"Yes," he said, surprised, expecting a different response. "You and I don't ever talk much."

Shutting her eyes Jennifer spoke in a soft voice. "My home has mold. Everything I own is ruined." Tears leaked and traced the fine hairs of her temple onto Robby's cradling forearm.

"Why did you try to kill yourself?"

"Because I have nothing to live for. My husband left me more than a month ago for a twenty-three-year-old. And now my gorgeous home, what I wanted most in life, is destroyed. I have no family, no children. Everyone will look at me and just see a . . . spinster lady."

Robbie wasn't sure what to say; his nature was not to be consoling. He struggled to offer encouragement. "Jennifer, it can't get any worse. And besides, you are a stunning woman."

"Thank you for the compliment," she responded.

"Jennifer, it's about to rain. Can you stand?"

Helping her to her feet, he escorted her into his clumsy shelter. She smiled again and thanked him, then fell into a deep sleep atop the grimy mattress.

Lying next to Jennifer, Robbie pulled a cover to ward off mosquitoes. She's stunning, he thought.

During the night Robbie was disturbed. At first he thought it was Charlie, who tended to paw his arm when a nocturnal animal wandering in the darkness came close. But it wasn't; it was Jennifer. She'd rolled and thrown her arm around him and pulled him close. Her full chest squashed against his bony frame. It felt good and he didn't want to move away.

When daylight came, low-hanging rainclouds let loose a deluge that battered the plastic tarpaulin that sheltered them. Jennifer continued to hold onto him. And each time Robbie wriggled away, she grabbed and pulled him back.

What should I do about this? he thought. Does she want me?

Finally, Jennifer Dink stirred.

"Good morning," Robbie said, expecting her to jump away because their bodies were touching.

Jennifer squirmed, lifted her long lashes, and smiled. She was comfortable, cozy—contemplative.

Why isn't she pulling away? he thought.

Finally she spoke. "It's raining," she noted. "Thanks for taking me out of the house. I'd tried everything to kill the mold. Then I took those pills because I was so depressed."

"You said your husband left you." Robbie nudged away. But when he tried to increase the distance between them, Jennifer pulled him close. As if it was a reflex she wasn't aware of.

Finally Robbie had to ask. "Why do you keeping pulling me close?"

"Because I can't stand to be alone," she answered. "Even when my husband was cheating, he still slept in our bed. It's because my parents were never around when I was a child. I was lonely all the time and desperately wanted company and to eventually marry so I could have someone in my life every day. It was nice of you to lay with me all night. It felt good. Thank you," she said.

"Glad to oblige."

Wow! he thought. Marci never talked like this, or slept so close. It was quite the opposite when they lay together—a canyon separated them.

"I hope you don't mind," Jennifer said.

Robbie thought for a moment. *Now, what do I do with this?* She was so beautiful, her lips full, her face unblemished, her waist so narrow.

Robbie chuckled. "I know it's kind of depressing that your home is full of mold, but mine's gone."

Jennifer offered him a tender smile.

Robbie continued. "If we strip the drywall and wash inside your home with freshwater from the pond out back, at the very least, you'll have a roof over your head."

"You can get rid of the mold?"

Suddenly, Robbie found he had a purpose.

Jennifer smiled. "Do that for me!"

"Sure, why not?" he replied.

Softly, she touched his shoulder and stroked it. "You know, it's going to be a while before any help arrives."

"Why do you say that?" Robbie asked.

"I heard on my radio the government left us stranded."

Robbie was silent.

"That explains all those vehicles heading east before the hurricane struck."

Then Robbie asked her something that'd plagued him. "What's with the cameras?"

"Oh, sorry about that," Jennifer said. "That's was my husband's idea. He didn't trust anyone and liked to keep track of people strolling by, particularly those Kracker landscapers. For me, it passed the time. As long as I knew you were out there, I wasn't so alone."

Why are you suddenly so candid with me?"

"I guess because I have nothing," Jennifer said. "It's sad. You're the first person I've talked openly to in a long time. And it's sure nice to talk," she added. "You're so kind."

Robbie blushed.

"Look at the scar! You look like a villain in a spaghetti western." She touched just below it.

It was a comforting feeling having a beautiful woman accept, compliment, and touch him, saying he looked tough.

The driven rain that battered the hut kept them trapped inside. Rainwater, funneled by a bow in the tarp, poured into an overflowing bucket. To pass the time they talked. Robbie confessed his marriage wasn't all that good and he feared his entire family was dead.

Jennifer revealed Marci was lucky to have someone around all the time. "It's not as bad as being husbandless, like I was most of the time."

Finally, when the rain paused and the sunshine warmed and dried, they stood and stretched. Jennifer walked over to the potted pot plant and brushed the dripping leaves. That's when she told him what she'd seen in his driveway late in the night the past months. And when she explained, it all made sense to Robbie—the power failures, the incredibly high electric bills. His wife grew marijuana in the attic. That's why she was defensive when it came to discussions about the attic. If she was arrested, Marci would go to jail; maybe the both of them. It explained many things, including her anxious, angry behavior that he'd written off as hormonal.

It was late afternoon when Robbie went inside Jennifer's home. He retrieved a jug of apple juice, pretzels, canned tuna, and several citronella candles. Together, they dined on a makeshift table. And after the meal, after the heat of the day subsided, Robbie took a hammer and cat's paw and started tearing away the drywall in Jennifer's home.

Jennifer did what she did best, neaten and clean Robbie's hut. She rinsed his clothing in soapy water and hung them to dry. She covered the mattress with sheets and scrubbed Charlie, rinsing him with freshwater from the pond out back.

Exhausted, they fell asleep, comfortably wrapped in each other's arms.

Chapter 67

At sunrise Robbie was back at it. The drywall peeled away with ease—so easily that he used his hands, progressing much faster. Jennifer saw to it Robbie was hydrated, making him take a break at noon because the heavy humidity made it difficult to continue.

"Work like the Latinos," she said. "Siesta, then in the evening, work until dark."

After stripping three rooms he lugged the mold-ridden drywall and piled it into a heap in the debris-filled street. He flung smaller pieces the size of Frisbees onto the top of the growing pile. By noon the entire downstairs was done, including the removal of the carpeting.

Regularly, Jennifer arrived to see if he was okay, offering plenty of water, making sure he'd didn't overexert.

It amazed Robbie that this person living next door was so friendly. He'd taken quite an ego hit from Marci over the years, and wondered how much of his daughter's disdain was encouraged by Marci. But now, there was someone who liked him. His communication with Jennifer was fluid and good. And when he revealed his unemployment, Jennifer offered a soothing hug. "I'm sure you'll do fine."

She was more than two steps above Marci, with her good looks and supportive nature. If Marci was alive and returned, he'd have none of her attitude. And if the grow house was real, he'd demand she turn herself in to the authorities.

Jennifer handed him a wet towel and asked him to remove his shirt.

She sponged him.

"That feels so good," Robbie said.

"It's time to take a break," she said.

"Two more days and I think you can move in," Robbie said.

"You mean, *we* can move in." She offered a comforting smile.

Taken, his heart raced. Not since college days with Marci had a woman showed such deep interest.

Reclining on the mattress he noticed the fresh sheets. "You're so industrious."

"That's the one thing I do well," Jenny said. "I love to clean. It's an obsession of mine."

"You've made me feel much better," Robbie told her. "I'm more confident because of you." He kissed her on the lips. In his mind he was saying, *Wow, I'm making an advance on her, as if I'm good enough. Where's this coming from?*

Jennifer grasped his shoulder and pulled him on top. And as they kissed, it started to rain.

Their heavy petting lasted over an hour. Unsnapping her bra, Jennifer revealed her most valuable asset—customized, voluptuous breasts. She encouraged him to remove the rest of her clothes.

For Robbie lovemaking never lasted this long, like she'd known him for his entire life. And could trust her to manage and deliver him.

Finally, with the drumbeat of the driving rain engulfing them, she allowed him, wrapping her arms tightly around his shoulders, locking him firmly in a hot and bothersome tangle. She pressed against him. Her eyes were closed and comfortable and he was confident that he pleased her.

Chapter 68

Facedown, with his head comfortably buried in the warmth of Jennifer's bosom, Robbie listened to rhythm of her heartbeat. There was a soft tap on his ankle. At first he thought it was Jenny's foot, but when he looked at her sweet face, he realized she was asleep. Again a soft tap, this time on his big toe. A child stood there looking at him.

Immediately, he pulled the sheets to cover them.

"Mr. Lindum, I'm hungry," the child said, her face smudged with mud, her dirty blond hair knotted. She appeared emaciated.

"Who are you?" Robbie asked.

Tears filled her sad eyes. "I'm hungry."

Jenny woke and instantly recognized the child. "You're a Peltz girl, aren't you?"

"I'm Lilly." Her voice was broken and weak.

The sad-eyed child pleaded. "Please feed me and my sisters." Lilly knelt on the mattress edge, folded her hands, and whispered a prayer.

Jennifer gently offered a drink. "Sip this, sweetheart, slowly."

"Jenny," Robbie cautioned, "be careful and not let her drink too fast."

After a few sips the tiny girl offered a polite thank-you.

"Can I have food to take to my sisters?"

Jennifer wanted to cry. "Where are your parents?"

"My mom isn't with us," she said. "She climbed the mountain and never came back."

"Did your daddy go with her?"

Lilly grew stiff. A sickness returned to her expression. She asked for more water then shook her head. "No!"

"Rob, something's wrong. Let's go over and see."

Lilly nodded her head vigorously.

Jennifer hugged the child. "It's okay, honey. We'll go and get your sisters." She gave her a pack of peanut butter crackers.

"They must be alive," she said to Robbie.

"I thought it odd," Robbie said. "I hadn't heard praying the past few days. Do you want to come with me?"

"Yes," Jenny answered. "You may need a hand. Lilly, rest, sweetie."

They went to the Peltzes' house and circled to the backyard where it was easier to enter.

The other children were nowhere in sight.

"There should be three of them," Jennifer said.

"No," Robbie said. "Two. Marci mentioned that an alligator ate Sahara."

Suddenly, Robbie became stiff and pale. Quickly, he covered Jennifer's eyes.

"Don't look toward the fireplace. Turn away."

"What's that smell?" she asked.

"Please don't look," Robbie said. "Ed Peltz hung himself."

Hanging from a noose strung from a ceiling rafter was Edward Peltz, dangling. His bloated corpse dribbled bile. Feasting white maggots filled his eye sockets. Rats scurried along the mantle and chewed his organs. A swarm of fire ants migrated along intestines that dangled to the ground.

"You'll never get over the sight of him," Robbie warned.

Removing his hands, she gasped. "My goodness, where are Lilly's sisters?"

"They must be alive," Robbie said. "Lilly asked for food to feed them."

"Let's look."

Cupping their noses it didn't take long to find the girls underneath the dining room table, huddling.

"Robbie, they're traumatized," Jennifer said, reaching for the youngest child. Their knees were raw and infected.

"It's okay, darlings. We're here to help you." She coaxed them from under the table.

Returning to the hut she whispered in Robbie's ears. "Bury the body."

"I should . . . shouldn't I?" Robbie said. "I can't imagine how horrific this is for them. The least I can do to is rid them of the thought."

"You better wear a mask."

Jenny dug into a box of clothing she'd gathered and pulled a scarf she never wore and tied it around Robbie's nose and mouth. "This should help." She looked into his eyes and smiled. "Go ahead, Lone Ranger." She patted his tush.

"Wait." She dug into a Tupperware utensil container and handed him a knife. "You're going to need this to cut him down."

Crossing the cluttered street, Robbie wanted to do this task quickly. Finding a barstool, he climbed on the mantle, held his breath, and sliced the noose. Ed Peltz's decaying body dropped. The rats scrambled. The flung maggots peppered him.

"Eee. . .ooh!"

Wrapping the rope around his fist he dragged the wasted body to the corner of the property near the toppled cypresses. Stepping away briefly and taking several deep breaths of fresh air, he tried not to stare. Ed Peltz's face was eaten off.

Quickly, he dug a grave that filled with groundwater and rolled the mess into the wet trench, burying what remained. Robbie stomped the spongy soil. No one will believe I had the courage to do this, he thought. He recalled Ed Peltz's rudeness. "For what you did to your daughters I should roll you into that swamp and let the turtles eat you."

Sweating profusely from the adrenaline rush, Robbie sat on a nearby cinderblock to catch his breath. Batting busy mosquitoes he didn't see the ripples in the water that flooded the cypress head and the red pomegranate that broke the surface. And before he could react, Piggy lunged from the murk. All Robbie saw was the wide-open white mouth of the gator. And again, Piggy caught his leg on the toothless side and held it firm.

Robbie screamed. "Jennifer, Jennifer, help me, an alligator."

Piggy tugged and pulled. Robbie reacted and reached for the cinderblock. He rolled it and dug the corner into the grassy muck. The brick carved a groove across Ed Peltz's grave. He struggled and jammed his free foot against a submerged tree trunk. But his knee buckled.

"Jenny, Jenny!" He flailed and splashed, trying to hold his head above the surface.

Robbie heard Jennifer calling. "Robbie, what's the matter?" She came running along the side of the Peltzes' home and stopped at the water's edge and saw him clinging to a limb. The gator's bent tail swung back and forth, splashing, trying to roll over.

"Hold on," Jennifer said. "I'll be right back."

"Get something! Use that shovel!"

Jennifer ran out of sight.

"Where are you going?" His calf hurt but he couldn't feel any penetration, just a vise-grip pressure that didn't let up. Behind, the gator struggled to drag him under. Clinging, he felt the limb bow and then snap.

Returning, carrying a plastic container, Jennifer raced into the waist-deep pond choked with fallen timber and forged toward Robbie. She held the container over her head and bravely approached the alligator, reached out, and poured the powdery white contents onto Piggy's open sore. On contact the powder bubbled and sizzled. The giant alligator immediately released Robbie. It thrashed and snapped violently, flinging water everywhere.

"Duck!" yelled Robbie. Piggy's giant broken tale nearly struck them. Robbie grabbed Jennifer and quickly opened the distance between them and the mayhem. As their hearts pounded, Piggy thrashed, breaking limbs, flinging mud clumps. It went on for some time.

They held each other close, Robbie thankful she rescued him, Jennifer thankful she was not alone once again.

After several minutes, they gathered themselves.

"What did you pour on that alligator?"

She put her arms around him, wiped a lump of dirt from his face, and said,

"Lye; it doesn't go well with water."

Batting her thick lashes she smiled and kissed him.

Chapter 69

The hurricane damage to the reflective glass shell of the Bippinotti Pain Clinic was extensive. The plywood Monkey Wrench needed to enclose the exterior had blown too far inland. Nearby strip malls, an alternate source for repair materials, had been constructed using metal sheathing. But much of it was bent and unsuitable to reuse. It was a snafu neither Dale nor his mother considered.

The Kracker crew Monkey Wrench assembled wasn't in a hurry either. They bitched and quickly lapsed into their lazy contractor ways, finding excuses, leaving the job for hours, bailing when no one was around to supervise.

Bradley Lindum wasn't pleased with his mother's behavior. She showed Dale Carter more than enough affection. It was a distinct change, and a kindness she never afforded his father.

And the message Brad got from Dale, Critter, and even his sister about Chadda's aggressive boys was that he better fend for himself by fighting Samson. His mother, who often supported him, stood idle and noticeably silent. As a socially accepted kid who'd never been bullied, the fear and lack of support was demoralizing.

Several weeks had passed and the promised trip back to Trinity Meadows never materialized. Dale kept delaying, telling Brad he needed more time to complete the repair work on the clinic. Marci supported the delay, telling Brad that "more important tasks prevailed."

Brad moved into roomier living quarters with Kathleen and Marci—an Airstream next to Chadda's trailer. For electricity they tapped onto the dragline generator. However, air-conditioning wasn't available because it was too much of a power draw.

It was Artie, supposedly Monk's kid, who displayed ingenuity when it came to stalking and harassing Brad. Artie had stolen a roll of surgical tubing from the Bippinotti and made what the Krackers called a potato cannon—a lethal slingshot that worked by anchoring to stationary objects with roughly six feet of space between. Junkyard car bumpers worked best. And before long, Chadda's boys shattered several windows on the casino bus, killed a pelican in flight, and bombarded Hoinky's with burlap stink bombs. Buddy captured several mutant piglets and launched them into the quarry. The boys giggled and threw rocks from the cliff as the tiny pigs swam in circles until their legs melted away.

The rusted bucket of the dragline was the ideal spot to intimidate Brad. It offered a direct, horizontal shot with the potato cannon the moment he stepped from the Airstream. Whenever Brad heard the snap of the rubber tubing and the screeching squeal of one of the flying pigs, he'd drop to the ground. The pork mortar whizzed in, barely missing, making a disgusting bloody mess. Sometimes, the fingers of the dismembered baby arms continued to wiggle and scratch at the dirt for several more seconds.

Confined in a steaming hot trailer and always on the lookout, Brad had little to do. Kathleen left early for Hoinky's, where she'd developed an extensive network of friends—just like high school.

The only difference was that she was Top Dog here. And Marci made excuses to why she left to help Dale each day. But Brad couldn't shake the feeling that this man occupied his mother's thoughts. More depressing was the sight of her treating him so warmly.

Chadda's trailer bounced and rocked when Monk arrived after a long day at the Bippinotti. Barely two feet away Brad heard everything, including Chadda's disgusting grunts and foul, in-heat language; which got louder as she reached a climax.

Late one night several gunshots rang out. Someone screamed. There was cursing, arguing, and a scuffle. Brad bolted to where his mother slept in the Airstream. She wasn't there. He raced from the trailer and found a small crowd formed into a circle.

"Hog-tie and ship him to the clinic," Fifty-Cal said. "Goddamn DTs. Too bad the poor bastard's hand shook so much he shot himself and not his girlfriend or kids."

In the darkness, Brad trudged to the Icehouse searching for his mother. The screen door was propped open to allow the breeze to flow freely through the hallway. Grains of sand crackled beneath his sandals as he snuck passed the twin Adirondacks. He heard laughs and giggles coming from an open bedroom window. Soft, flowing linen curtains gracefully flapped in the breeze.

It was his mother's laugh. And though he never heard Dale giggle, it sure sounded like him.

The laughter stopped. He heard them smooch . . . kiss . . . then his mother's groans. The bedsprings squeaked and the headboard smacked the wall many times.

Unable to bear the thought, Brad sprinted back to his trailer.

He had had enough. He loaded his small backpack with supplies and headed home to Trinity Meadows.

Chapter 70

At daybreak, Dale asked Marci if she'd join him at the clinic. He needed her help.

"It's going to disappoint Brad," she said. "He wants to go home."

For several days Brad had nagged her, threatening to return on his own. Marci couldn't bear to tell him the trip was delayed once more. Quietly, before she left with Dale to the clinic, she had snuck back to the Airstream and wedged a note in the door saying she was sorry and promised they'd leave tomorrow.

Pushing a horsehair broom down the glossy central corridor of the Bippinotti Clinic, Marci felt the air-conditioning kick on overhead. She paused under the vent, letting the cool air circulate around her. It'd been a long time, she thought. How she'd taken for granted the comforts of electricity.

Dale entered from a side door where the work crew had gone for a cigarette break. He carried a glass jug.

Stepping over the broom and standing under the vent with Marci, Dale lifted the jug. "See this, it's a problem. Explains why they're so sluggish and sloppy with their work."

The liquid in the jug was crystal clear. Marci immediately recognized the moonshine.

Dale nodded. "Caught the crew nipping. Frigging Kracker contractors, nothing ever changes."

"Where'd it come from?" Marci asked.

"Seems Deuces gotta snitch drumming up business here. He's brewing moonshine."

Dale unscrewed the cap. "Take a whiff."

Marci set her nose to the jug. "There's no odor."

"Exactly," Dale said. "It's pure. If this shit makes its way around the Flats, it's trouble. Worse than you could know."

Marci saw the concern. Dale was a deep thinker, endlessly mulling what to do next . . . Waiting for his expression to change, she let several minutes elapse. She slipped her arms around his waist and leaned her head against his chest. His heart raced. "It's that Deuce guy, isn't it?"

"Yes," he said. "He must be dealt with."

"You know, Dale, it's not good to keep your feelings bottled inside."

"True, but it's who I am . . . It's time we head south."

The sudden realization of heading back to what was left of Trinity Meadows made Marci's head swim. She'd allowed herself the opportunity to explore outside her marriage, and enjoyed every moment. By now, her children were aware of Dale. Brad disapproved. Kathleen was ambivalent. Soon Marci must decide; leave Robbie to start a new life, with or without Dale.

"You've gotten quiet," Dale said as they rode in the pickup back to the junkyard.

"I'm sorry," Marci said. "I was thinking."

"Let me guess, where from here?" Dale said.

Marci rolled her eyes toward him and set her hand on his forearm. "Tomorrow, I'll be back in Trinity Meadows to confront a choice."

As tears filled her eyes she set her head onto his shoulder. "I don't know if I have the courage or willpower to decide. Lot's changed."

With her index finder she traced the design of his tattoo. "It hinges on Brad, how he'll cope with all this. Will my life ever get back to normal?" Marci wiped away her tears.

"Yes," Dale said. "Eventually, all this gets rebuilt, perhaps better. It happened in New Orleans after Katrina."

Her watery eyes gazed at Dale. He wasn't much with words but when he spoke, openly expressed himself.

"You know, Marci." Dale tapped her knee. "You and I . . . I want it to happen."

Nuzzling closer, Marci stroked his arm again. "I am at a crossroad. Do I return and make amends with Robbie, or leave to live with you?"

"I don't want to pressure you." Dale grew a bit edgy over the fact she clung to her marriage. "You know you are the only person for me. I'd leave the Flats, but I'm not sure I could cope, living as an inlander. This is my home."

"You shouldn't move," Marci said. "You'd miss being close to the ocean and the property your mother left you. It's unfortunate we met later in our lives, when change is difficult."

Dale laced his fingers through her hair and admired Marci's beauty.

"Let's give it some time. Who knows what's ahead," Dale said as the pickup reached the junkyard entrance. "It may change by the end of tomorrow."

"Agreed," Marci said, sitting close, fixing her hair. "For the children's sake, they should know what happened to their father."

"Fair enough," Dale said. "Let's leave in the morning. Make Brad happy and see if your husband is all right. Also, I should get hold of that medication stored in your garage. Word's spreading like wildfire amongst the Flats folks about a mother lode of Oxy, thanks to flapping lips Critter."

Dale shut off the engine and sat silent. He did this often. And Marci had learned not interrupt, using it as an opportunity to show him affection while he was deep in thought.

Finally he spoke. "I must put a stop to Deuce."

Chapter 71

Dale entered Monkey Wrench's trailer. "Monk, I need your help. We must head south and deal with Deuce."

"Sure, Dale, let's get going!" Monkey Wrench rattled his cigarette pack, making sure he had ample supply, then followed Dale out the narrow doorway to his running pickup.

"I got a funny feeling if we don't neutralize Deuce, we'll be in for a load of bad-ass trouble."

Dale flipped on the high beam, drove to the top of the quarry, and parked next to a cluster of storage containers.

"This darkness reminds me of the night I almost drove my swamp buggy into the quarry with my boys," Monk said.

"Don't think anyone's taken a header into the lagoon in a good long time." Dale fumbled with a ring of keys that opened the padlocked storage units.

"Me and the boys pert near did when a clan of those mutants laid in the middle the road. Had no choice but to run over the ugly mongrels; otherwise, me and the doodlebugs woulda been sizzling in that acrid lagoon lime juice. Found the guts of one inside my engine a couple of days later."

"I hear ya," Dale said. "If it ain't for Critter breeding the sow for his goddamn freak show we'd been rid of them. Now I hear Critter sold them to the Gibsonton carnies. Before long, those crippled pigs will be all over Florida."

Leaving the headlights on so he could see the edge of the quarry, Dale unlocked the storage container and swung open the metal doors. "Can't be too sure where the edge of the pit is at night."

The containers blocked the steady nighttime ocean breeze that arrived after sunset. Monkey and Dale lit cigarettes.

"Deuce is sending moonshine this way." Dale entered the container.

"Yeah, Fifty-Cal filled me in. In fact, she's got several jugs herself. And using it to keep the Cooter gals snookered most the time."

Dale shoved plastic storage tubs aside, working his way further. "That's what I'm talking about. Fifty-Cal on the shine ain't no good." His voiced echoed from inside the steel container. "The last time she got hold of some white lightning Fifty-Cal spent eleven months in the pokey for squeezing the buds of a fifteen-year-old. No telling what she'll do when she's guzzling the shine."

The metal door blew shut. Dale pushed it open.

Kicking several irregular stones from the hard ground, he wedged one at the base of the door. "Monk, you ever hear what they did to Deuce's dad back before we's were born?" Picking one of the loosened stones, Dale tossed it. Several seconds elapsed. There was a kerplop. "He was machine-gunned right on Dixie Highway and thrown into this pit for selling his mash up in Levy County."

"Huh? I never know'd that one." Monk stared into the blackness that opened below. "Deuce's dad's bones are down there with your old man's?"

Dale didn't bother to confirm. Unsnapping a flashlight clipped to his belt, he shined it inside the storage unit. "Ah huh, there it is." He hauled out two dust-covered wooden crates. "I think we'll need these boxes of dynamite for when we head out in the morning.

"Monk, I ain't got no plan for Deuce except maybe destroy the still, flatten his strip club, and put the fear of God into his scraggy crew so they don't mess with us up here."

"You going to take your married girlfriend back home?" Monk asked.

"Yes, I'm returning her to her husband. And she won't be coming back."

"Are you sure? You guys seem darn chummy."

Dale set the dynamite on the tailgate and dusted the lid. He sucked hard on his cigarette then flicked it away. The ember brightened as it disappeared over the edge of the quarry.

"As many times as I run it in my head, I come up with this idea. For Jodi, I mean Marci, I'm just the dude of the moment—a feller who provides for her now that times are tough. It's no fault of her own, she's doing what she's biologically geared for."

"What's that?' Monk asked.

"Screwing to improve her family's chances of surviving the shitty situation she's stuck with." Dale fumbled for another cigarette. "When she gets back to her place, even if her neighborhood is destroyed, she'll stay, cuz they's more 'fisticated. She'll realize moving to the Flats is a backward step, particularly if she's got good options for staying at her place."

"I had this conversation once before," Monk said. "With my first sergeant while I was in Iraq. Poor bastard got a Dear John letter. His old lady, who was a real babe, left him for a pudgy banker back in the States during the building boom. Only when times are bad does a woman want a man who can swing a hammer and put food on the table to feed the pumpkin heads she's been breeding."

"It's getting late." Dale shoved the crated dynamite forward and shut the tailgate. "Based on what Marci says about the debris pile near her home, we'll need chainsaws and a piece of machinery like a Kubota to move downed trees and sections of collapsed buildings."

"Gotta cross the Anclote too," Monk said. "The bridge might be a goner. That crik's plenty deep. I should know from all the noodling I done did in it."

"Any suggestion?" Dale asked.

"You'll need a flattop barge to get the pickups and Kubota across," Monkey said. "A floating dock won't be hard to find. There should be plenty Styrofoam blocks around. Look where the surge stopped and you'll find what you need. All we got to do is bring a trailer axle, a hitch, and working boat motor."

"Monk, what would I do without you?"

"I'm obligated," Monk said. "Gotta square thangs with your woman's daughter for saving Chadda's life and caring for my boys."

Chapter 72

Each time the three-quarter moon became obscured by the drifting cloud cover Brad paused and waited for the moonlight to return. A deliberate, westerly sea breeze allowed him to ascertain his southerly direction. On the roadway much of the muck from the surge had washed away to expose chunks of black macadam with random bits of reflective yellow and white highway markings. By sunrise, Brad had walked nearly three miles.

Along the way he encountered survivors and upped his pace, jogging to avoid them before they got any ideas. The familiar hump of the Cottee River Bridge loomed ahead . . . Minutes later he stood on the bridge deck, observing. The waterway was free of debris but not the shoreline. The repeating tide had gathered and deposited much of it ashore in a twisted, matted mass. The gulch that Fifty-Cal had driven through was filled and graded. That's odd, he thought. The road south was cleared the width of one lane. The downed streetlamps and tangle of telephone poles and electrical wires were moved to the roadside.

"Maybe help arrived," Brad said loudly. "Dad, I betcha they've already rescued him!" He lifted his pace and broke into a jog until he got winded. Suddenly, a primer gray pickup with two men on the roof and several huddled in back sped by. All heads turned and looked. Brad recognized the man driving. The brake lights became bright red. The men on the roof tumbled onto the hood, cursing, then smacked the roadway. The driver yelled, "Grab that kid."

"Crap," Brad said. "It's that Deuce guy." He darted behind a brush pile then raced into a collapsed Mexican restaurant and hid near the walk-in freezer.

"Hey, you son of a bitch, where the hell you think you're going? You still owe me a goddamn toll. There's the kid I'd been telling ya about," Deuce said to his companions. "His old lady knows where a load of Oxy is. Betcha it's that missing shipment that was supposed to be delivered to the pharmacies before the hurricane hit." The truck engine revved. Tires spun and raced toward Brad, smashing into the collapse.

Scurrying from the pickup Deuce's scrags surrounded the destroyed restaurant. Brad was trapped. One of the men approached and poked with a long pole, jabbing. The man's face was severely pitted from a nasty case of acne, and he grinned like he enjoyed the hunt.

Out of choices, Brad made his way from inside the rubble. Crater Face snatched his right arm and passed him off to Deuce.

"Get in the truck cab, kid," Deuce demanded.

Someone yanked off his backpack, pilfered through it, and tossed the pack to the road.

The cramped cab smelled of sweaty men odor. "So, kid, the last time I saw your mom, she said your daddy knows where a truckload of medication is."

Brad knew what he was talking about but didn't answer.

"Kid, where do you live?"

Again, Brad didn't answer. Though he was frightened, he realized from watching Kathleen barter that he had something they needed—

an address. As long as he didn't tell, he had something of value to keep him safe.

"Ain't you going to say, you little shit?" Deuce swatted Brad atop his head.

"Ouch!" Brad worked up his courage. "I got something you need. What will you trade?"

Deuce did a double-take. "The kid learns fast. I'll give you time to think about it," he answered. "That's what I'll trade."

Brad made a smart remark. "You don't have my mom to threaten anymore."

Crater Face rubbed Brad's shoulder and said, "Way to go, little weasel; thinking like a Kracker already. You'll do just fine as long as you tell us where that stash is."

It took only fifteen minutes to reach Moog's strip club. When they arrived music blasted from inside the building. Huts and lean-tos had replaced the strung hammocks and random cots. A hand-operated cement mixer churned while teams of shirtless men scooped mortar and set used cinderblocks. Another crew was shingling a nearby roof. A cluster of men had formed a semi-circle. But Brad couldn't see what had their attention.

"Look at 'em," Deuce said. "They can't wait 'til the next batch of moonshine is done dripping into the jug. Wait 'til they find that his lad here has something better, and lots of it. So you know, kid, moonshine is the only thing they got to knock themselves unconscious, for now. The Oxy you got is much better, and will hold them from going stir-crazy. You might think twice about escaping because I can't stop these drug-crazed bastards should they get hold of you. They might chop off your ears to get you to tell them where you live."

"How would they know I gave them the right address?"

"Listen, don't be a smartass. I may be a bastard for boinking your mom, but I ain't stupid like those crazed son of a bitches that work for me. They're dumbass stupid, too dumb to realize that you'd fooled them by telling the wrong address. Meanwhile, you'd lost an ear or two and perhaps your little popper."

Boinking my mom! Brad had suspected that's what happened. It explained her odd behavior of using Dale as a protector. He'd never thought of it that way.

Poor Mom, thought Brad. She's traumatized and was looking out for me. Guilt-ridden, he wanted to forgive her.

Crater Face spoke. "Yeah, you don't want to lose your popper. You're going to need it for poking women when you get growed."

"I know what I need it for." Brad was defiant.

"You are some arrogant shit, ain't you?" Deuce said. "In the morning we're heading to your place. And by dark, if we ain't in possession of the mother lode, you won't have a pecker to piss out of." Deuce grabbed his own crotch and jiggled.

"Son," he said, snatching Brad by his shirt collar. "I ain't letting you out of my sight. You're valuable in ways beyond what you know. I'm going to tie your feet to where you can't run. You can make tiny midget steps. No way in hell am I letting you get away." Deuce's voice was stern.

He tied a short rope to Brad's ankles and duct taped a rebar spike around his waist. "Learned this while I was in boot camp," Deuce said, shoving the spike down Brad's shorts and securing it. "You ain't bending over to untie that rope. The spike will puncture both your stomach and bladder."

Deuce handcuffed him and led him into the strip club, where it was cool and dark. Scratchy music from inside the theatre came to an abrupt stop. Deuce told Crater Face to guard Brad while he got ready for the morning trip.

"Sit there," he demanded. "On that couch."

Brad sank into the musty velvet cushions. "Ouch!" The spike jabbed his stomach.

The ugly-faced man drew a barstool and positioned so he could see both Brad and the dance stage down the hall. "Deuce said he'd kill me if you escape. So be a good boy and enjoy the show. Ya might learn sometin'. We got a hottie MILF from your neck of woods working the pole."

Outside, a backup generator confiscated from a toppled cell tower site hummed loudly. An air-conditioner shoved through a tiny window dribbled water onto a section of the couch. Several of Deuce's gang arrived through a side door, passed Brad without seeing him, and took seats in the small theater. Someone worked a knob that controlled the spotlight that illuminated the stage.

"Every see a titty show, lad?" Crater Face didn't wait for an answer. "Son, you're about to."

The spotlight brightened the seedy stage. A wrinkled curtain opened and out strutted a fair-skinned woman in a slinky lace outfit. The striptease music blared. The dancer shook her chest, lifted her leg, and hooked the brass pole. She inverted, snapped into an upside-down cheerleader split, and spun. The men cheered and whistled. "I ain't never seen that move before."

"I know her." Brad leaned to his left for a better look. "That's Mrs. Peltz, Sahara's mom." He was stunned. *She's too religious.*

When her top flew off and disclosed her bobbing chest the men cheered. The music continued and Cindy Peltz danced and lewdly stroked and adored the shimmering brass. Erotically, she slid from the stage and performed lap dances on the men in the front row. And when one got too rough, a brawny bouncer pulled her from his clutches. However, Cindy immediately jumped back onto him and started grinding, again and again.

Brad reasoned Mrs. Peltz must've gone bonkers. She'd always seemed stressed and unhappy . . . She'd finally lost it.

Suddenly, Brad realized something important. He shouldn't let her see him. If Mrs. Peltz recognized him, they'd know where he lived. He tucked into the dark corner where the air-conditioner dripped and became barely visible.

Chapter 73

The note Marci had left Brad remained wedged in the door handle. She entered. But there was no Brad. He might be at Hoinky's with his sister, she thought. But that didn't make sense. *How'd he leave without dislodging her note?*

Immediately, Marci panicked. She fled the cramped trailer and raced to the quarry.

"Dale, Brad ran away," she said. "Can we leave right now?"

Dale saw the anguish on her face. "It ain't safe to travel at night. We have to pick our way around the sheet metal and glass that's out there."

Marci pleaded. "I'm afraid he'll run into that Deuce guy." She dropped her arms. Her face was twitchy, anguished.

If something happened it would devastate Marci, thought Dale. Perhaps end their relationship. Though he doubted she'd return to the Flats, Dale held a glimmer of hope his assessment might be wrong.

"We'll go as soon as we get everything together. It's almost a full moon, which might help some."

Before midnight they headed south in a caravan of three vehicles. Marci, Kathleen, and Dale rode in his pickup. Critter and Monkey

Wrench towed the Kubota. The two pickups were equipped with everything from extra fuel, food, spare tires, boat motor, chainsaws, and blasting caps for the dynamite. Fifty-Cal drove the deuce-and-a-half with Flatch. Her machine gun was mounted on its tripod and bolted down. But before she left, Fifty-Cal went to the casino bus and told the Greek waiters to come with her.

Nicholas and Andres objected; so did the Scooter girls. "But they keep us happy," a gorgeous waitress said, pouting.

Gnawing her chew, Fifty-Cal said, "Yeah, too happy, cutie. I heard some of ya upchucking breakfast. Three of ya have the morning barfs, cuz your fertilized baby-makers are simmerin' youngins. Before long, the whole busload will spit out grape-wrap gyro babies."

"Can Cooterman Pat stay?" asked one of the girls.

Fifty-Cal looked at Pat. He hadn't shaved in days. "How many of thems babies do you think are yours, old man?"

Cooterman smiled. "I'm sure plenty."

She decided to let him stay. He was entertaining and reminded her of her horny grandfather who taught her how to shoot straight.

"Put on your clothes and come with me, Hercules and Ulysses. You're going back to Tarpon Springs."

The girls let out a sad sigh. "We're going to miss you guys."

"Come visit us at Lavaki's," Andres said, pulling his shirt over his head and buckling his jeans.

As Dale indicated, nighttime traveling was slow going. Each time they encountered an obstacle, Monkey Wrench unloaded the Kubota and dragged whatever it was out of the way. It got so bad they didn't bother reloading the Kubota anymore. By sunrise they'd reached the Cottee River Bridge. The small caravan stopped, took a break, and shared cigarettes. On the south side of the bridge Highway 19 was cleared the width of one lane.

"What do you make of the opened road?" Dale asked.

Monk answered first. "It's Deuce's work."

"I have to agree," Critter said.

Fifty-Cal spit over the bridge railing. "We got to deal with that son of a bitch sooner or later. I got plenty of ammunition for that."

Everyone looked at Fifty-Cal's truck. The freshly oiled machine gun glistened. Box loads of ammunition were secured with bungee cords.

"Only if you have to," Dale cautioned.

"Dale," Fifty-Cal said. "The cops done skedaddled and let Deuce run free. It's time we become the law."

"Cal, I know you got a hankering to shove a slug in him. Just don't let me see it happen."

Dale didn't want to argue. She was too gung-ho. However, killing someone was serious. If the cops returned to the Flats they'd sling her ass into prison—even if the killing was justified. The pawnshop she ran for him was profitable. Though Fifty-Cal was a wild card, she freed him to operate his mother's other moneymaking enterprises. And she was extremely useful in difficult situations.

Anxiously waiting, Marci paced the width of the bridge. The two Greeks remained in the back of Fifty-Cal's truck.

"Let's stow the Kubota," Monk said.

Critter backed the trailer into the washout on the north side and Monk drove the loader onto the flatbed trailer. The caravan rolled ahead. But they didn't travel far before Marci beat on Dale's shoulder and frantically screamed to stop. She flung from the truck and snatched Brad's backpack from the ground and held it in the air.

"This belongs to Brad. Why would he lose this?" she asked, hysterical.

Jumping from the vehicle, Dale inspected the ground. "Either someone stole it or he got nabbed."

Monk inspected the roadway and nearby footprints. "The guys who cleared this road got him. Look at the tire tracks. They're pretty fresh. Your lad's footprints go no further."

"Oh my God, Deuce's crew!" Marci's stomach knotted. Her mind filled with everything bad that could possibly happen. Her only hope was that Brad used his wits.

Dale tried to calm Marci. "Come on, let's find him."

Moments later they were off.

It didn't take long to reach the intersection of Highway 19 and Route 54. That's where Fifty-Cal booted the Greeks from her truck. She grabbed Andres by the ass. "Nice and firm, too bad you and I didn't rumpus in the sack."

The caravan traveled eastward a short distance. The vehicles stopped in front of the man-made mound that had protected Moog's from the hurricane-force winds. They were a hundred yards from the strip club compound. There wasn't much activity.

"You've been to Moog's lots, ain't you, Crits?" Dale asked.

Through his thick beard, Critter grinned. "Got fond memories. Moog's gals had humongous boobies and no jelly bellies, and hadda pass a limbering test to make sure they spread nice and wide like football cheerleaders."

"What'd ya think, Monk?" Dale asked.

"Deuce must have a pretty big gang to clear that length of road and rebuild those new buildings over there," Monkey said. "But it looks like most are gone somewhere."

"Critter, you know those guys. Why don't you stroll over and asked a few questions?"

Worried, biting her nails, twisting knots in her hair, Marci waited inside the pickup. She was on the verge of a nervous breakdown.

Kathleen was much calmer and left to bum a cigarette from Monkey Wrench. When she returned Marci snatched the cigarette and took several puffs.

Cough, cough!

"We've changed," Kathleen said. "Haven't we?"

Holding the cigarette, Marci pondered her question. Finally, she nodded . . . *Yes.*

"Mom, is our house really gone?" Kathleen asked.

"Yes, Kathleen." Marci struggled with her words. "There's nothing left but rubble."

"Our neighborhood was so pristine," Kathleen reminisced.

Marci stared at Kathleen. Her daughter was dressed like a Kracker, her hair wrapped in a confederate bandana. *Is she missing her home? She must have mixed emotions.*

"Mom, where do we go from here?" Kathleen asked.

"I don't know," Marci answered.

"Do you love Dale?"

Again, Marci was taken. *Kathleen wasn't stupid. She knew what was going on.*

"We aren't at that point yet, Kathleen."

Then Kathleen said something befuddling.

"Hudson is okay but we belong in Trinity Meadows."

"What? I thought you had adapted." Marci's expression was one of shock.

"I've been thinking differently now that we're heading home," Kathleen said.

"The Krackers are good people but not educated. They're slobs and don't want to further their lives. Kind of like a small town where no one ever leaves. You've always said we should go to college and do something with our lives."

Kathleen had pointed out to Marci the obvious difference with Dale. It gave her reason to reconsider. Sleeping with him had filled a gaping hole in her heart—a knee-jerk response to a failed marriage. Or was it that she just didn't fit in at her phony Trinity Meadows neighborhood, and sought to return to the country girl she once was?

She and Robbie had created a family. But was the family salvageable? She wasn't sure. Had she changed into such a harsh person that the failure of her marriage was partly her fault?

Was it she who must change?

Critter strolled from behind the grassy knoll, past the dripping moonshine still, and into Deuce's compound.

"Hey, Disco Jack, where's Deuce?" Critter asked of a wiry-haired man sporting a stringy goatee who seemed to be looking after the place.

"Gone," Jack said as he cautiously eyed Critter. "I've seen you here before, hain't I."

"I come here lots when I'm down this way," Critter said. "Where'd Deuce go?" He acted casual.

"Deuce took the entire crew across the Anclote looking for a stash. The good stuff, Oxy and Vics. Says he'll be back tonight."

"Wuz a kid with him?"

"What's it to you?"

Pulling a pack of Marlboros from his jean pocket Critter tossed the entire pack.

"Marlboros . . . Sweet! All we got is salvaged generic shit that Deuce trades for hard labor."

"Ever hear of Dale Carter?" Critter asked.

"The Carters . . . Deuce hates their guts. Bitches all the time that Florence stole his birthright property. Drives us like slaves to open the road all the way to Hudson. And rations the shine so he can sell the rest to influence the Krackers up that a ways."

Disco Jack lit the Marlboro and savored the aroma. "Real tobacco." He smacked his lips.

"Keep the pack if you tell me more about the kid."

"Deuce got the lad handcuffed with his ankles tied so he don't run. Kid knows where the stash is but hain't tellin'. Says he'll lead them there but they have to cut through a mountain of hurricane debris to get there. That's why no one's around. Cuz Deuce took everyone with him."

"Thanks for the info." Critter walked away.

Critter reappeared from behind the dune and signaled Fifty-Cal to relax. She was squatting behind her machine gun hoping Deuce would charge over the mound.

"Ain't no one to slam a slug into, you dribbling Amazonian jizz queen."

He went to Marci first, telling what he learned from Disco Jack and assuring her nothing bad happened to Brad.

"At least we know he's alive," she said, a bit relieved.

Dale turned to Monkey Wrench. "Monk, what do you think?"

"Figures like Deuce will beat us there," Monk said. "From the sounds of it, we won't need all this equipment. Let Deuce do the heavy lifting by tunneling through the debris mountain."

Dale deliberated. He spied Fifty-Cal eagerly waiting her chance. Then he said, "We travel light?"

Monkey's grin grew big. "Like the Taliban, in pickups."

"Unbolt your gun, Cal, and bring it along," Dale said. "That's plenty of firepower."

It wasn't long before they were traveling along Grand Boulevard with Fifty-Cal perched atop the truck cab . . . They reached the Anclote River. On the opposite shore, lashed to a pine tree, was a beached pontoon boat modified to carry a vehicle. Tire tracks entered the river and exited on the other side.

"Who's going for a swim?" Dale asked.

"Okie, why don't you go?" Critter volunteered Monkey Wrench. "Didn't you noodle for catfish here?"

Monk blasted Critter a nasty look. "Lazy bastard, ain't you afraid to get your tootsies wet?" Monk shed his shirt and walked into the brown water with his sneakers still on.

"Why don't you noodle me a catfish while you're at it?" Critter asked. "And why the hell do all you Okies wear jeans when you swim in criks?"

"Leaches," Fifty-Cal said, standing next to Dale rolling a wad of chew with her tongue. "He don't want leaches sucking on his ball-sack."

"Oh!" Critter said. "That'd suck."

There were several chuckles.

Flipping to his backside Monk swam at an angle against the outgoing tide and ferried across. He arrived at the boat and climbed aboard.

"No keys in ignition," he called out. But that didn't stop him. Lifting the motor cowling Monkey hot-wired the ignition coil and revved the smoking outboard. Moments later both pickups were loaded and floated to the east bank of the Anclote.

"Can you fix it that only we use this boat?" Dale asked.

"Already on it." Monk dug in his toolbox and pulled a large wrench and lifted it into the air. "They named this baby after me." Wading into the muck, he removed the propeller. "Deuce won't know what to do without this." Monk tossed it into Dale's truck.

"Critter, turn around," Monk said with concern. "I think one of those leaches found you. Hold still." Monk came behind and slipped his knuckle through the belt loop of Critter's jeans. He tugged and slipped an eel into Critter's ass-crack and smacked his rear. "Here, have a water moccasin, smartass."

Feeling the wiggling eel in his crotch, Critter unleashed a torrid of curse words as he stripped and leapt into the river, naked.

There wasn't a dry eye. Even Dale and Fifty-Cal laughed hysterically.

"Everyone, pipe down," Monk said. "I hear something."

In the distance the pitchy whirl of angry chainsaws sounded.

"I need to find higher ground." Monkey shimmied a nearby cabbage palm to see if he could locate Deuce's work crew. "Ouch, prickly friggin' tree!"

He crawled into the center of the fronds and positioned like a sailor in a crow's nest. "Holy shit," he called down. "I ain't never seen anything like it!"

"See what?" Dale asked.

There's a mountain of shit that runs east. Must be a hundred feet high and runs clear out of sight."

"Marci, you weren't kidding, were you?" Dale said.

She shook her head. "I wasn't. Brad and I climbed over it."

"Let's wait until the chainsaws stop before we go any further," Dale said. "Let them get tuckered. Once they cut through, Deuce will be busy packing the load. I betchya his guys won't listen. They'll rip open and pop painkillers right away."

"Count on it," Fifty-Cal added.

"But what about Brad?" Marci asked.

"We'll hit them before anything happens. I promise."

They waited several hours. Fifty-Cal polished her gun. Critter and Monkey debated if there were any fish in the Anclote and shared stories of Piggy—guessing where she might be living these days. Kathleen was quiet and unusually reserved. Marci and Dale found a shady spot near the river. They were anxious and agreed to wait until Brad was safe before they discussed their future.

When the whirls of the distant chainsaws ended, Monk snuck ahead to spy on Deuce.

It wasn't long before he returned. "Saddle up folks, it's time. They cut a hole wide enough to run a pickup through. Oh, by the way Marci, I saw your munchkin in the cab of Deuce's truck. He seemed okay."

Chapter 74

The moment they emerged from the tiny tunnel Brad's eyes scanned the destroyed homes, searching for his father. He hoped his dad wouldn't recognize him until there were assurances that they'd both be safe.

"Looks like you got the worst of it, kid." Deuce inched the truck into a clearing. Several men had to walk through the tunnel because the dilapidated van they drove didn't fit through.

"Which house is it?" Deuce asked.

Bradley was reluctant to point where his home once stood, which ironically was a short distance away.

"What happens once I tell you?" He waited for the answer.

"You're a tough rascal." Deuce rubbed Brad's head. "You go free as soon as we get the goods."

"Tell your guys leave me alone, too."

Within minutes a small Honda Civic towing a confiscated lawn trailer arrived and parked near a mound of piled drywall about eight feet high. Next to it was a heap of trashed furniture and mold-covered framed paintings.

Gathering his crew Deuce said, "If anyone touches the kid, they'll be banned from the MILF that's boinking them for free at the strip club."

"Over there!" Brad pointed towards his demolished home. "You'll find what you are looking for where my dad's garage was."

Jennifer Dink had gathered the Peltz girls into a circle and handed each a hairbrush and made a game of brushing the other sister's hair. The children laughed and responded to the tenderness Jennifer displayed, and seemed to shed a portion of their shyness.

Imagining herself a mother, building a family, was something Jennifer Dink realized she wanted desperately. She despised her last name. And during her peaceful moments, with Robbie asleep next to her, she mouthed *Jennifer Lindum*. It was a small improvement and didn't rhyme with stink.

Operating the pressure washer, Robby sprayed inside Jennifer's house, ridding the last of the mold that clung to the wiring and plumbing. He'd grown accustomed to the heat, working more than eight hours each day. Marci and Kathleen were a fading memory. And the likely loss of Brad he had suppressed, not wanting to consider any of it.

The sound of the generator that pumped the pressurized spray had drowned the drone of chainsaws chewing through the debris mountain. Dunking a bath towel and draping it around his shoulders, Robbie let the water run the length of his thin frame. Suddenly, he heard what sounded like Brad calling from near the debris mountain.

"Dad, it's me, Brad."

Robbie thought he was hallucinating. Brad was handcuffed, his legs tied.

Brad hobbled closer.

For Robbie, this came as an incredible surprise. He'd left him for dead, but hadn't yet mourned. It took a moment for him to reboot the absent emotions.

"Brad, it's really you!"

Brad tried to hug him but the handcuffs prevented it.

"Where's your mother? Is she okay?"

"Yes, Dad. But Mom's not with me."

"What's wrong? Are you in trouble?" Robbie asked, seeing his son bound.

"See those men?" With hands clasped Brad pointed towards the parked vehicles.

Robbie was startled. Until now, Jennifer and the Peltz girls had occupied him. He'd grown accustomed to them being the only people he'd seen in a while. Suddenly men milled all around them. They unloaded equipment and carried it to where his garage once stood. And before he continued his conversation with Brad, Deuce appeared with several of his men.

"Here you go, lad." He tossed the handcuff key.

"Dad, they said they'd let us be if we let them take the medications."

"From the looks of it, we have no choice."

Sensing trouble, Jennifer had quickly gathered the girls and hid in a plastic bin where she stored pool supplies.

Within minutes chainsaws rumbled. Deuce's crew made short work of the trusses and removed the valuable stock. Several boxes were immediately opened to verify they got what they came for. Immediately, the men stuffed their pockets with blister packets.

"We've struck the mother lode," someone said when one of the boxes was ripped opened.

Just then, as Deuce was about to scold them for pilfering and popping pills, a stick of dynamite exploded. Tiny paper particles floated and drifted to the ground. Deuce's crew scrambled for cover.

Dale Carter appeared and stood at the tunnel opening.

"Deuce, it is Dale Carter." His bold voice echoed.

Fearlessly carrying a stack of boxes, Deuce set them in the truck bed. "I guess it's time to settle the score, Dale." He wasn't going down without a fight.

Dale lifted his arm.

Hiding somewhere in the debris pile Monkey Wrench lit another stick of dynamite. There was a traveling sizzle. The stick landed, rolled close to Deuce's truck. But before it exploded Deuce leapt for cover.

Kaboom!

One of the pickups flipped onto its side.

"If you want to leave, there's the tunnel," Dale said loudly. He positioned himself to allow Deuce's crew to escape. As a safeguard, Critter was on the other side in case they tried to regroup for an ambush.

About half the crew left.

For Dale this meant only the meanest, most drug dependent remained.

"Dale, why don't we make a deal? I'll split the goods with you."

"This is the end of the road," Dale said.

Again, he waved and two sticks of dynamite came from different directions. There was a horrific explosion and the Honda Civic with attached trailer flew into the air.

Deuce ran behind the Lindums' damaged air-conditioner and used it as partial cover.

Suddenly there were hollow thumps as bullets pierced the copper coils in front of Deuce. Freon sprayed from the unit. The lethal sound of Fifty-Cal's gun arrived a full second later.

"Jesus, gotta ditch this cover," Deuce said. "Someone's shooting."

It was the delay, followed by the deafening blast of exploding rounds, that intimidated the men that remained. There was no cover as Fifty-Cal let loose another volley, strafing the men, running a string of bullet-strikes that backed them toward the tunnel.

Dale stepped aside and allowed them to retreat.

With her hands gripping the gunstock, Fifty-Cal stepped from her hiding place. "Scat, before these slugs catch you up your narrow Kracker asses." She jumped from her bunker and fired into the tunnel, over their heads, to the left and right and behind them. The men ran and didn't stop until they swam across the Anclote.

Vulnerable, Deuce darted toward the Peltzes' property and disappeared behind the house.

Dale chased him and kicked in the front door.

Next to the fireplace, where Edward Peltz hung himself, stood Deuce.

"What is it, Deuce? Do you want to settle things?"

The tough ex-Marine wasn't afraid of a good scrap. He'd heard through his snitch that Marci had hooked up with him.

Deuce tried to provoke Dale. "You know, your long-leg Trinity wench was a good screw."

Though Dale didn't show, it got to him. Fifty-Cal had told him about discovering Deuce with his pants down and a hard-on.

Angered, Dale lunged. Deuce stepped to the side.

Dale tripped and rolled along the ground. Before he could get up Deuce kicked him in the ribs with his well-worn military boots. Dale's ribs snapped. But Deuce wasn't quick to pull away. Snagging his ankle, Dale lifted and launched Deuce backwards. Both men flung fists and landed punches. Wrestling, they tried to pin each other. They broke, came to their feet, faced, and circled. This time Deuce lunged.

Using Deuce's momentum, Dale grabbed him by the shoulders and spun them both into the flooded cypress head. There was a big splash as fists flew, each man trying to drown the other. Finding a firm footing Dale reeled and landed his fist firmly into Deuce's face. Stunned, Deuce flung his arms back. He wobbled and stumbled backwards, trying to keep his feet underneath him. He lost balance and fell onto what he thought was a submerged tree trunk.

"Had enough?" Dale said.

Deuce didn't answer. He was distracted. Whatever he straddled wasn't stable. It moved.

A confounded look ignited his bloodied face.

"Shit!" Deuce cried.

Piggy emerged and lifted him from the water. Snapping her head back and forth she tossed off Deuce.

Instinctively Deuce reached for what he thought was the knob of a log. It was Piggy's pomegranate nose.

Blinded from the lye, Piggy reacted to the sharp pain and flailed wildly. She rolled and caught the top of Deuce's shoulder with the teeth-filled side of her gator jaw. Her grip was firm. She snapped her enormous gator head, opened her massive mouth and swallowed the entire top part of Deuce's torso.

Dale stood on the shore and watched Piggy death roll several times. Deuce's muscular frame crackled and snapped and became mush. Piggy submerged. Air bubbles trickled to the surface for several seconds.

Winded, guarding his ribs, Dale watched the water for several more minutes, making sure Deuce was a goner.

Chapter 75

Hearing the muffled bursts of machine gun fire, Marci and Kathleen took cover. They flinched each time the dynamite blasted. Minutes later Monkey Wrench came through the tunnel and said the coast was clear.

Exiting the tunnel into her destroyed neighborhood, Kathleen asked, "Mom, is this really Trinity Meadows?"

"Yes, Kathleen."

"Where's our house?"

"It's gone," Marci said. "It was over here."

"Look, the Dinks' house is standing!"

"I know, don't remind me."

Marci wanted to locate Brad and also find out how bad off Robbie might be.

Dale arrived. He was bloody, limping, and held his side. His clothes were torn, his left eye swollen shut.

"Dale, are you okay?"

He nodded. "I'm hurt, but fine. You won't be seeing Deuce anymore."

Marci didn't need to ask what happened; the explosions told the story. "Is there anyone else around?"

Dale pointed to Jennifer Dink's home. "Your son's in there."

"Bradley!" Marci raced toward the front steps.

Robbie appeared in the doorway.

"Marci . . . Kathleen . . . Is that you?" he asked.

Stepping onto the stoop, Marci halted.

Jennifer Dink appeared at Robbie's side and put her arms around his waist.

"Who is it, dear?" Jennifer asked.

"It's Marci and Kathleen. They're okay."

"Oh!" said Jennifer, acting surprised. She stood there and held Robbie close, not letting go of his waist.

It took a moment for Marci to realize who the woman was with her arms around Robbie. "Oh, it's you, Jennifer."

Jilted, seeing another woman with Robbie was a shocker. *Am I reading this right—Jennifer Dink hooked up with my husband?*

Hobbling, Dale came and stood behind Marci.

"This is Dale Carter." Marci stepped aside to introduce him.

Dale reached forward and shook Robbie's hand.

Marci studied the obviously at ease couple. They'd bonded. Jennifer showed no discomfort. She stuck close to Robbie in an ownership kind of way—much like the treasures she'd kept inside her home.

"Robbie." Marci was awestricken. "I must ask. Are you two an item?"

"Ah . . ." Robbie hesitated. He was never good at lying when Marci asked a direct question. He fidgeted, then blurted, "I thought you died."

Marci looked at Dale. He wasn't offering any help. It was her decision. She knew that.

The Peltz girls appeared and clung to Jennifer. Brad emerged from inside the Dinks' house with Charlie, who had licked and slobbered all over him.

Bradley gave his mother a big hug.

"I love you, son . . ." Crying, Marci smothered him with kisses. She broke down and bawled.

"Mom," Brad said. "I'm okay."

"I couldn't have survived without you, Brad." She held him a long time, sobbing into his soft hair.

Kathleen greeted her father.

"Hi, Dad," she said, giving him a hug. "I'm glad to see you survived the hurricane." She wasn't as stunned as her mother.

Right away Robbie saw Kathleen had changed. Her face was relaxed. "It's a relief to see you're okay."

As everyone struggled for words, Jennifer abruptly said, "Robbie, I have great news. I'm pregnant."

Dumbfounded, Robbie twisted his head, first at Jennifer, then at Marci.

Nudging closer, Jennifer lifted her chest, raised the arm she held around his waist, and wrapped Robbie's shoulder as if to say *he's mine now*.

It left Marci shocked and fumbling for words. Before and after the storm she hadn't been nice to Robbie. She'd treated him poorly. How could she say he was hers anymore?

Approaching, Marci touched Robbie's face. "Your scar heeled." His muscles were slightly larger. That befuddling buffoon slouch was no longer present. He stood straight.

"Where from here?" Marci said as tears emerged from each eye.

"Marci, ah . . . I . . . ah." Robbie couldn't express himself.

"Go ahead, honey, you two talk." Jennifer gathered the Peltz girls and disappeared into the house.

"There's no compulsion for you to want me back, is there, Robbie?"

Marci studied Robbie's expression as he searched for his answer.

"No . . . No, you put our family at risk. I figured out who the pot plant belonged to," Robbie said firmly.

There was silence.

Finally, Marci looked right at Robbie and said, "I'm so sorry, I let you down."

Robbie reached and traced her chin. "We let each other and our children down," he responded.

Marci placed her hand over his and held it against her heart. Her saddened eyes lowered. Her hand slid from his and dropped to her side. Sadly, she turned and walked away.

At a distance Dale Carter waited. Marci came to him and collapsed into his waiting arms.

Dale lifted Marci and carried her away.

The End!